ORIGINS

ORIGINS

THE TOWERS SERIES: BOOK ONE

ORIGINS

THE TOWER SERIES: BOOK ONE

Lee R. Hadley

www.LeeHadleyBooks.com

BookWise Publishing
Riverton, Utah
www.bookwisepublishing.com

Library of Congress Control Number: 2015919561

Cover and interior book design: Eden Graphics, Inc. www.edengraphics.net
Cover illustration: Brian Hailes, hailesart.com

ISBN: 978-1-60645-139-7 eBook
ISBN: 978-1-60645-140-3 Amazon Create Space
10 9 8 7 6 5 4 3 2 1
First Printing

Dedicated to the King of self-existence
and the intelligence of the great I AM;
and in appreciation to my parents,
J. Leroy Hadley and Jennette Shirley Hadley,
who taught me the truths of courage, charity, and grace.

And as always, to Sandra Quinn Hadley,
who, after 43 years of marriage,
continues to be my dearest companion
and greatest human influence.

TABLE OF CONTENTS

PROLOGUE

▶▶▶ Monsters – 2001, Tehran, Iran

"Will there be monsters? A smile spread across Haleema's face as the game began. FarZan, her seven-year-old son, feared monsters but loved to be scared by bedtime monster stories.

Tucking the bedding around him, she answered, "That depends. What is a monster?"

"Monsters are big and strong, stronger than men, and they have sharp teeth and eyes that are red as coals—and they roar at you, rrrraaahh."

FarZan's hands sprang into the air, fingers curled like the claws of an Iranian Cheetah. The look in his eyes projected courage which Haleema knew would slink away after the lights went out. At the same time FarZan nervously watched the shifting projections of shadow and light on the plain wall behind her, which were cast and transfigured by the blowing and billowing window curtains. A playful growl escaped Haleema's throat, and her eyes opened widely to express the potential incarnation of bedroom monsters. She envisioned the workings of FarZan's mind, thinking he might conjure evil shades of grey and black pierced by shards of occasional light; the combination translating into both his thrill and fear—monsters.

Haleema was born in 1985, six years after the Islamic Revolution of Iran. She was sixteen years old and married with three children. Satisfied with the comfort and repose of her daughters she continued to lavish her attention on her only son, FarZan.

It was just after sunset and the family had completed the evening Salaat, known in Islam as Maghrib, the final prayer of the day for Shia Muslims. Merchants in the Grand Bazaar were closing their shops and securing their outdoor displays, the activity sourcing the erratic light displays.

"No my son, the story has no scary red-eyed monsters, but there are monsters of another sort."

"Another sort, what does that mean?"

It means that they are monstrous in what they do but they don't have sharp teeth and scary red eyes."

"What do they look like?"

"They aren't animals like Cheetahs or lions. They don't walk on four legs."

With large feigning eyes he asked, "Are they snakes?"

"Oh no, not snakes my dear, our monsters don't slither across the ground, but they are cunning and devious."

The monster game had become a nightly ritual which Haleema often used to teach new principles to FarZan.

"How will I know if I see one?"

Haleema added a new facet, "You can't always tell them at first. Some monsters look scary. Other monsters may look beautiful or handsome, but if you could see inside, they would be scary."

"You mean their tummies are scary?"

Chuckling she responded, "No, that's not what I mean by inside."

"I don't understand," FarZan said in a more serious tone.

Haleema moved closer to FarZan, and in a quiet voice continued, "We don't have real monsters in our world, but there are those who act like monsters. Some people call the monsters man, but I don't like to use the word man because I think mankind, as a whole, is good. I believe that the worst monsters are simply inside some men."

Not quite catching the change from childhood games to real life, FarZan playfully asked, "Men, you say the monsters are men?"

"Some men are monstrous, but not all. Most men are good. Women can also be monstrous, but that is more unusual."

FarZan finally caught the shift from fantasy to reality, and more thoughtfully asked, "How can I tell if a man is a monster?"

FarZan was very intuitive and Haleema confidently believed, that over time, he would understand.

"You have to watch very carefully. We all have monsters inside of us. Most of the time, our monsters are controlled and hidden away.

Sometimes the monsters in men act like monsters in caves. They come out in their fierceness to attack their prey then slink back into their cave for its protection. A man's monstrous nature may show in his face then slink back into the shadows of pretense. We see the evidence of a man's monster in his actions."

As Haleema spoke, her mind flicked to an image of her husband, and her self-applied label of "monster". She wanted FarZan to grow into something more benevolent than her husband.

"Some men purposely let their monsters out to feed them, making them more powerful. To know which men have fed their internal monsters you must observe them, watching carefully, examining their actions. If they do many bad things, their monster has become strong and powerful, and that man may have grown into a monster. If they do good things, they have likely learned to control their monsters. The great majority of mankind has monsters that they have learned to control."

Lovingly brushing a wisp of hair from FarZan's eyes, she uttered her inner prayer, that he would become a man who controls his monsters.

"If there are monstrous men around, will you protect me from them until I can tell who they are?"

"I will as long as I am with you. But if I should ever leave, Allah will help you recognize the monsters and keep you safe."

"I hope you are always with me, Mother."

"So do I, my dearest son."

"Since there are no real monsters, will this be a true story?"

"It is a story with both fiction and truth. It is for you to recognize the truths in the story. Just remember that most of the story is fiction but you may gather truths and use them for your good."

"How did you learn the story?"

"I learned it through life."

Haleema watched FarZan as he turned to look at the window with skittering light along the edges. She saw him look back across his small bedroom to the phantoms playing on a wall void of everything but a poster of the Persian Tree of Life. She loved the evening moments when she told FarZan her invented stories. Haleema leaned over and kissed FarZan on the forehead, at the same time anticipating his quiet tip toe over the wooden floor of their urban apartment seeking her reassurance that there were in fact no monsters. That solace was often brief or unattained, his father's stern and scolding voice too often sending him hurt, and scurrying back to bed. Even worse was his monstrous unwillingness to let her go to FarZan's bed to comfort him.

"Okay mother, you can start now." FarZan looked at her seriously, revealing both his fears, and a growing understanding. He added, "But help me know who the monsters are."

"I will, my son, I will. As long as I have breath, I will."

As FarZan nestled close to his mother, she told him a story that included far too much reality. It came from her heart, experiences, hopes, and from deeply held fears. But most notably it came from her dreams; dreams that tormented her troubled mind over and over in the dark hours of the night. The substance of her dreams was unfathomable. It ebbed and flowed, in and out of her midnight sleep like the unrelenting waves along a shoreline; and they made no sense. From her point of view, everything should make sense.

The focus of her dreams was an ethereal view of her world hurtling through the cosmos. She saw the planet coursing through the silence of space, and began to understand that the ever-present activity of Mother Earth is rarely sensed by human intellect. Plunged into daytime thought by her unrelenting dreams, Haleema became fixated on the planet where darkness reigns through half of every rotation, while the other half enjoys the light. Clearly, the light that crept around the Earth, driving the darkness before it, was life evoking, animating and illuminating. She wished that her dreams could be illuminated like objects in the light of day.

Haleema was not a believer in the chance or "somehow" of life. Only an Alpha/Omega planning session by the great Allah could have created the annual orbit as a life-giving cycle for the teeming, living inhabits. To her it was impossible that a hyper-lucky throw of the dice, trimmed in coincidence, could locate life in such a system, in a perfect orbit where life was conceived, and progression continually striving to better itself. How could it be a matter of chance?

Haleema believed that life on Earth was glorious. It was a superb realm for the living. However, along with the celebrated moments of life, she was all too aware that beauty was required to coexist with the ghastly; both states simultaneously existing within the Earth's perfectly established orbital trek.

Looking toward the Earth from the vantage of her dream-point, she saw the ferocity of the Earth's core. It was heart stopping. Constantly in motion, she saw that the Earth is not the semi-tranquil home that surface life enjoys. From her cosmic, x-ray view, she knew more assuredly that the roiling center of molten iron and an ever shifting rocky crust belies the seeming passivity of the planet. Many and notable have been the geological events of time but her dreams suggested the beginning of something beyond the most notable episodes.

Inside Haleema's dream-scape, in the earthen depths of her spinning globe, an unimaginable event was unfolding. Molten magma was forcing itself to the surface in plying fingers of diverse liquid elements. Each thrust and reach was tendril-like—a probing and exploratory penetration of suitable cracks and fissures. It seemed a purposeful search for the most direct paths of outward travel, coupled with an unwillingness to follow previous volcanic channels through the Earth's mantle. She began to understand that the sentient surface dwellers, in her midnight visions, were oblivious to the rising calamity. Then, all at once, in a lucid moment, Haleema realized that each molten shoot had a specific terminus on the Earth's surface. It was as though they had chosen their individual destinations, and she feared that her beloved city was a targeted objective, providing the dreams were a true portent of the future.

Pushing through the mantle and into the crust, she saw fiery molten shoots which took on a form previously unknown, and undefined by men. None could have hypothesized the phenomenon. Almost as swirling tornadoes, elements within the fiery tendrils mixed and cooked under great pressure. A concoction beyond human imagination was forming in the deeply hidden cauldrons of the Earth. The blend became a fabrication that Haleema, in her dream-state, watched again and again as it breached the surface of the Earth in multiple world-wide locations, shooting up like great pinnacles of rock, including her beloved city of Tehran.

The thrusting pinnacles of peculiar rock were not the only amazing elements in Haleema's world of dreams. She also saw great traces of light, lifting from the ground, and arcing through the sky. Blinding energy exploded from the pinnacles of stone colliding with the arcing lights in brilliant bursts that seared her mind and ended the moment of the dream; but not the return of the dream. It came to her, again and again, all too often and with too much anxiety.

Haleema could not have known the myriad forces of thought and action; the precursors to the dream. After all, they had started at the beginning, at a time and moment that may be unseeable and unknowable when looking back. Unaware of the beginnings, all she could do was wonder at the meaning. Are my dreams a portent? Are they a warning? Or are they just dreams?

As Haleema walked the course of her life, she would, in the end, gain an understanding. Its message is one that she could not have guessed. In the suddenness of a moment she would learn the meaning of the arcs and the nature of what would become known as the Towers: both as destroyers and saviors. She would come to know her place in the dream and in the ongoing story. The retelling of that story is a step by step discovery of the clashing forces. One must always go back to the beginning to understand the end, if for nothing less than the assurance that monsters do not fill the Earth.

BOOK ONE >>> ORIGINS

CHAPTER 1
A FOUNDATIONAL MIX OF MINDS

1:0 ⫸ 1940 – A Simple Rice Farmer

The muddy water swirled about his feet as Soung Dae-Ho hefted the dense earth from the silted bottom to the top of the life-giving bank. A loud sucking noise filled his ears as he pulled his foot from the thick mud of his rice paddy. It was the unusual volume of the sucking sound that caught his attention. It stopped his mind and body, freezing them both into a sudden awareness. As the swirling water came to rest he realized the Earth had become deathly silent. The air was perfectly still. There was neither bird song nor beat of an insect wing to disturb the quiet. There was no whistling reed or shuddering leaf. The water moved in his rice paddy without the sound of a ripple. It was as though Mother Nature had suddenly stopped in her tracks. It was the collective holding of a breath before the strike of some unknown but impending terror.

Soung Dae-Ho scanned the valley of rice paddies and the ring of hills around it, in awe of the tranquility. He looked to the clear blue sky, now an open invitation for the burning rays of the sun. The blistering heat upon his skin was his only tactile sensation. As strange as the world felt around him, it was not his first experience with such a moment. He had experienced it before.

Dae-Ho grunted as he hurriedly turned from the quiet and focused on the task of repairing a weakened ditch bank. It must be made strong enough to hold the water in his rice paddy. A broken ditch would release the water and jeopardize his crop. He rarely thought of the risks to his farm and livelihood, but he was now acutely aware of the approaching menace lurking beyond the horizon. Just as the breath of nature was released, he noted a sudden buzzing of flies around a shed, just twenty feet away, near the head of the paddy. The flies were beginning to gather in untold numbers; numbers higher than he had ever seen before, a portent of a coming storm. As the breath of nature released, the air, earth, and all living things seemed alive once more; all creatures were at once preparing for a change.

Dae-Ho thought of past storms, remembering some that blew hard enough to bend the rice plants into the water. The battered and beaten plants weren't destroyed, but after the brutal assault, they struggled to regain their upright and productive stature. Such damage diminished the yield of his fields.

He continued to shovel water sodden earth onto the bank. He worked quickly, knowing his time was limited. Though slight in form, his sinew was tough and powerful. Both water and earth gave way to the strength of his seasoned muscles. There were also other areas that needed his attention. Assured that this bank was repaired, he tracked through the mud, attentive to every inch of his prized farm hoping to secure it from the bruising forces of a storm that he knew would soon strike.

The fury of the storm strike was greater than he could have imagined. Soung Dae-Ho battled the wind, rain, and flooding torrents of water attacking his small farm. He moved from one weakening bank to another trying to shore them up in the hope of saving his life-giving farm.

It didn't matter that he gave all the energy of his being, nature was, on this day, too fierce. Water flooded down the Han River, washing over its banks and up into his system of ditches and paddies. Surface water raged down the hills above his farm in gushing sheets. His battle continued to the point of exhaustion, but his purpose had not been achieved. Nearly collapsing under the strain of exertion, he stumbled toward his home, a home built on small knoll, barely safe from the rampaging waters.

Having retreated, he stood weakly at his front door, looking over his wind and water swept domain. He saw countless breaks in his dykes and ditches. Bending his knees and slumping to a hunching position on his bare feet, Dae-Ho could see no standing rice plants. They had either been washed away or buried in a tomb of mud. Using the door sill as a hand-hold, he lifted his exhausted body into a bent form and stumbled through the door of his simple home, falling onto his minimal bed.

Dae-Ho's eyes caught the vision of his only son, Soung Man-Shik, clinging to his mother's clothing. He closed his eyes against his son's wide-eyed stare, who was too young to help but clearly understood that a terror was upon them. Driven by pride, Dae-Ho turned away from his wife and son. He could not bear to see the self-invented, piercing look of their eyes. He folded into a fetal position, his back towards those he had failed. Their future was at risk and he was responsible. For many moments he lay still, but for his heaving shoulders. Unseen by his family, his grimacing and muddy face was washed clean by his tears as they flowed into the camouflaging weave of his blanket. He lay in place until his tears were exhausted and much of the mud had been washed from his cheeks.

Suddenly he sat up. Shouting to no one he asked, "Why would our ancestors allow this terrible affront?"

He turned his head, his eyes imploringly upon his wife, but he expected no answer. He knew she would never question the actions of their revered predecessors. In the calm of her verbal silence, Dae-Hoe continued in his verbal rampage.

"Our land is ruined, our crops are gone. This winter will be hard; the most difficult we have ever faced."

As Soung Dae-Ho wallowed in his mixed world of anger and morass, he thought of endless days in muddy water, under the hot sun, amid the torment of mosquitoes, and other biting things. *I have worked so hard.* Lying back into his bed of despair, surrounded by his decimated farm, he felt smothered by the cumulative years of hardship. His nearly depleted mind cried out in its anguish: *How long can I go on?*

Near the point of giving up the fight, from some unknown place of power, a glimmer cautiously sparked in the mind of Soung Dae-Ho, slowly becoming a flicker of possibilities. The wavering prospects sputtered into a glowing ember of belief in his evolving mind. The ember at last burst into a hope that tomorrow would be a better day.

Soung Dae-Ho sat up and looked out the window. The tear tracks were gone and the grimace had departed. He saw blue skies and heard birds singing. The air was fresh, calm, and invigorating, all tantalizing evidence that there was hope. His eyes darted back to his wife and son. They were the substance of his life. He felt a stir of determination, a resolve to be their savior. This was his home, his farm, and they depended upon him. As with so many in the flow of humanity before him, the fortitude of the depth of his being amassed the power to rise again, to look once more into the fields of his world, dredging up the courage to try, one more time.

Soung Dae-Ho left his bed of despair to once again challenge the elements of nature. In time, the dykes were re-formed, the paddies were re-flooded, and new crops of rice were both planted and harvested. The farm became as it had been before: productive. Though not achieving wealth, Soung Dae-Ho proudly watched his son learn to work beside him. Moved by the intoxication of his success, Soung Dae-Ho was sure that Soung Man-Shik would revere him, just as he revered his father. That respect was the wealth he hoped for.

Soung Dae-Ho had lived his entire life near the small village of Daeseong-dong, Korea without traveling more than thirty-five miles in any direction. Though poor, he was swollen with pride over the small rice farm he called his own. He had grown up on those rice fields. He had worked hard for his claimed piece of Earth. It was a treasured, yet tenuous possession where he hoped to enjoy a prosperous and happy future. On this small patch of land that he called his home; he performed the life-giving work that supported both his country and his family. He was an entrepreneur in its truest sense, in the most risky of all enterprises: agriculture.

1:1 ⫸ 1941 — The Japanese Rule of Korea

Soung Dae-Ho's mouth was dry, and his nerves were stressed to the point of bodily shaking. Dae-Ho had learned to spit in the eye of storms but the thought of conscription into the occupying Japanese military terrified him. As he sweated and trembled in the long, hot line outside the door of a low government building, he saw a neighbor ahead of him. They exchanged glances as their place in line moved into the building. Dae-Ho intently watched as his friend pleaded with the officer. He felt the man's grief and disappointment as he heard the officer's command to report for duty. He saw a drooping body with sagging shoulders, laden with dejection, shuffle toward the door; his eyes too disheartened to look up into the furtive stares of the men of his community.

When his turn arrived, Dai-Ho cautiously looked into the officer's eyes. They appeared stern and void of kindness. *Can I avoid fighting in this war?*

Soung Dae-Ho saw himself as the master of his home, yet he had discussed the call to involuntary military duty with his wife. He needed the wisdom of his ancestors and his wife if he were to remain on their rice farm. As Dae-Ho silently pleaded his cause and his plan with his ancestors, he wished for the presence of his father. He wished his father was still alive so he could attend to his family and provide them with food.

They had formulated a plan based upon rampant rumors circulated by his peers that some would stay to grow rice.

The officer looked up and spoke to him, "Soung Dae-Ho, you have a reputation as a productive rice farmer."

Soung Dae-Ho's chest rose slightly and replied, "Our farm has the highest production in the valley."

Dae-Ho was to say more than that, to recount his memorized plea, but his words would not form, and he could not utter the planned defense.

The eyes of the Japanese soldier knowingly pierced the being of Soung Dae-Ho, successful rice farmer. As though the officer knew the question of Dae-Ho's heart he spoke out, "You shall serve your Emperor in another way. You are to stay on your farm, raising rice for the armies of Japan."

Completely overwhelmed, Dae-Ho remained silent. He wanted to shout in jubilance, in gratitude of being spared from military service. He wished to show joy to the officer. Instead, Dae-Ho calmly and serenely bowed his head, thanked the officer and said, "I will be a productive servant of the Emperor."

Through the years of the war, Soung Dae-Ho served on his rice farm. His farm was productive, but much of his rice was taken without compensation. More hungry than satiated, the family endured their homebound sentence.

1:2 ⟫⟫ 1945 — The Loss of Winning

Soung Dae-Ho poked his head through the doorway of his humble home, "It has happened," he shouted. "The Japanese have been defeated!"

The news had spread like fire before the wind and people began gathering to celebrate the imminent freedom from the Japanese. But as the days passed, they began to realize that freedom might not fill their future.

More news seeped into their reality. On one particular day, a group of men had gathered together, looking north across the Han River. Dae-Ho stared wistfully across the new dividing line between North and South Korea. One of the older, wiser farmers had made a disturbing statement, "They say we are not capable of governing ourselves."

Dae-Ho turned to him asking, "Who has said this?"

The old man looked down at the ground, "Our new masters, the conquering governments."

"What is to be?" Soung Dae-Ho respectfully asked.

"The Americans will be our 'trustee' as they call it, here in the south. The Russians will control the new North Korea."

Dai-Ho shifted uneasily, "What will become of our friends and families in the North?"

"We may never see them again. A very wide zone has been contrived to separate us. We will not be able to cross."

1:3 ⟫⟫ 1945 — The Division of Korea

In successive months, more changes could be seen across the river to the north. Soung Dae-Ho stopped momentarily to lean on his crude but common shovel. He gazed at the new buildings that were appearing. The changes gave the impression of a better life for his Northern countrymen. He shifted in the mud, the movement of his foot making the water swirl.

"I wonder if life could be better in the North?" Dae-Ho muttered out loud.

Rumors had been spreading that the North wanted South Koreans to defect. They were being lured with promises of better living condition. Some of his countrymen had already left. Dae-Ho thought back to his discussion with his wife.

"They say there will be free medical services," she had said.

Dae-Ho had replied suspiciously, "Yes, free, but for what price. They are also told what to do and when to do it. Some are no longer allowed to be rice farmers."

"But they will also be educated. My dear husband, our young son is uneducated. Will you not consider the benefits offered in the North?

"I may and I may not. I will choose."

After much thought, and over the course of many days, Soung Dae-Ho made his choice. He continued to work on his farm with his son, Soung Man-Shik. He loved his son. He was growing in strength and ability. His efforts were becoming helpful, benefitting Dae-Ho and his crops. While father, mother, and son continued to work the rice paddies, planting and harvesting the rice in their personal domain, their new political trustee fostered their independence.

1:4 ⟫⟫ 1950 — Perils in the Night

It was early morning when Soung Dae-Ho swung his feet out of bed. A strange noise had awakened him. He walked inquiringly over his unfinished floor and looked out into the small valley. He watched in horror as infantry troops marched up to, over, and past his farm in the early light of day. They held mostly to the roads but were reckless in their haste. He recoiled at the damages being inflicted upon his small holdings, while his mind foresaw a new, bloody, and vicious war. It was the beginning of the Korean War. His village was soon overrun, forever changing the life of this humble South Korean family.

It was difficult to obtain trusted information. Most of what the Soung family learned was from rumor and half-truths. The North Koreans said one thing and community rumors frequently painted a different picture, but after a few days they were assured that the North Koreans had captured Seoul, the capital of South Korea.

In early September, Dae-Ho burst through the door with exhilarating news. He had been preparing for the October rice harvest when friends shared the fantastic rumor, which was soon confirmed by North Korean troop movements.

"The Americans have joined us," he said. They have re-taken Seoul. The North Koreans are retreating and the Americans are only a few miles south of us."

Fearing the wrath of the fleeing North Korean Army, Soung Dae-Ho gathered his small family, what foods they could carry, along with blankets and started walking towards the hills above their village. Dae-Ho hesitated as they left their home, looking back at two grave markers. His parents slept side by side.

I give honor to you and promise to return.

Hidden within the trees of the hills, the Soung family watched as the harried North Korean Army tromped pitilessly over their farm. The Americans followed and even more destruction was heaped upon the means of their livelihood. The soft and muddy earth gave up its checker board form to ruts, and tracks of disarray.

Dae-Ho watched the devastation of his rice crop. Harvest time would yield very little. Though he felt like tears would flow once more, he held his head in stoic pride.

"We will have very little to eat this winter," he confided to his wife.

She closed her hand around his arm, "What will we do?"

Still staring at his farm he replied, "Perhaps the Americans will help us."

After the Americans pursued the retreating North Koreans, Dae-Ho moved his family back into their farmhouse. It did not take long before their small store of provisions had been eaten. They began to look for assistance. There was little for anyone to eat and he obtained only modest assistance. He occasionally resorted to begging from the Americans just to keep his family from starving, a humiliating experience for this once proud farmer. Wood from the hills provided warmth but there was very little rice to be cooked and meat was rarely available. It was November of 1950 and a cold winter was fast approaching.

For the third time, Soung Dae-Ho was roused from his bed, this time in the middle of the night. The American and South Korean Armies had retreated from the north and were amassing in the valley around Daeseong-dong, in the valley of his nearly ruined farm. Troops and equipment were pouring in like flies to carrion. It became clear that the Americans had been in retreat, but it looked like they might be making a stand on the south side of the Han River, their men and equipment now spread across his farm.

Soung Dae-Ho looked into the face of his clearly pensive wife. The lines of toil and sun were pinched together in fear. His vision swept to his still sleeping son. Taking in all the changes in the world around him, the safety of his family outweighed his love for the farm.

"We must move again," he whispered in a tone of despair.

Armored equipment already covered his farm, and it was clear that it had become part of the American staging area. Dae-Ho feared that they would soon be bombarded by North Korean/Chinese artillery shells in what looked like a new offensive. The Americans were not running away so it appeared that they would have some time to make better preparation. This time their lives were in absolute danger. In front of a simple sanctuary in his home, Soung Dae-Ho knelt amid wisps of incense, petitioning his ancestors.

"Please, have compassion on us. Protect us from the certain approach of cold and disease. Provide us with food that we may not starve. Protect our family farm, the legacy of our labor, that we may soon be restored to the home of our fathers."

Soung Dae-Ho rose and began packing their belongings. They took everything they could gather and carry, using blankets turned up at the corners for bags with food being the most important consideration. Dae-Ho's wife stood limply by an empty shelf. Dae-Ho joined her, putting his hand on her shoulder. The shelf was covered in dust. Where bags of rice and other foods had once covered the unpainted wood, it now bore a layer of dust and dead flies.

Mrs. Soung started sobbing. She was a strong and brave woman, but this last insult had broken her patient demeanor. Dae-Ho pulled her in tight and they took a moment to cry together. Their son, who had been standing apart, joined in the embrace. His mother reached down and drew him in ever so much more tightly. Though tears flowed freely, it was a moment of galvanization. The future would be harsh. They had no shelter to flee to and very little to sustain them through the quickly approaching winter, but they would press forward as a family.

Soung Dae-Ho guided his two most precious possessions through the door and out into the rapidly cooling weather, carrying their partially filled bags over their shoulders. Dae-Ho had been thinking about his little cart and thought to use it to carry more of their belongings.

No, where we are going, it cannot come. The terrain is too rough and we will tire through the work of moving the cart.

Carrying their few belongings, he led his family first toward the two grave markers. He simply could not leave without paying his respects to his parents. Through several moments of silence he offered his heartfelt honor and pleaded for their support. His spouse leaned into him, grasping his arm, almost as a crutch. Man-Shik wrapped his arms around his mother and pulled at her clothing, wanting to be lifted into her arms. She bent down, picked up their son, and as a family, said their goodbyes. When at last it had all been spoken, by mouth and in his heart, Dae-Ho turned to face his wife, "It is time."

His wife put Man-Shik on the ground and, while holding his hand, they began their escape. It was several hundred yards to the base of the small hill. They walked slowly, dreading their loss. Dae-Ho felt little hope that life could become as they once knew it. At the base of the hill, he turned back, gazed over his farm, and attempted to indelibly absorb the valley that had been their home. He thought of the peace and in some ways the plenty they had enjoyed, but cursed the years of bloody battles and brutal bloodshed. He cursed the Communists who had taken so much. The Korea he had loved had become a country split and depleted of food and shelter.

The Soung family moved far away from the valley of their ancestors. Although frequently within earshot of the battle, they were far enough from the war to feel a measure of safety. The battles had grown into a stalemate with their farm in the midst of it, in what later became known as the Demilitarized Zone, or DMZ.

In the first days, they worked hard to create a makeshift shelter. It was nothing more than logs and branches staked and tied together to keep the approaching snow from falling upon them. Their one iron pot was infrequently the center of meager meals. Dae-Ho had returned to their home several times to remove small items that they used to improve their surroundings. Logs became their table and chairs. Their blankets, laid over beds of leaves, barely protected them from the cold ground. Only the passage of time would tell the story of their safety or demise.

1:5 ⟫⟫ 1950 — Flight Through the Snow

The winter of 1950 to 1951 was bitter. There was never enough food to ease the painful pangs of hunger. Despite a supply of forest wood to burn, they were always cold. Each day was a desperate search for bits of food to eat. The normally close Korean community had dispersed.

Time, hunger, and cold began to take its toll. Dae-Ho peered over to his son, Man-Shik, who had become lethargic and feverish. Concerned about his son's condition, he'd gone to the Americans and was given a little food and another blanket, but was told there was no medicine for Korean nationals.

The fever continued into the third day. Dae-Ho had given up his own blanket in an attempt to warm his son. He heated rocks near the fire, then using branches and sticks as tools, he slid them across the icy earth and into the shelter, near their son. The fever raged on, Man-Shik's breathing became labored and his lungs began to rattle.

It was the beginning of the fourth night. The rattling in Man-Shik's chest had become gurgling and the boy looked deathly ill. *If I can get him through the night, I will carry him to the American camp.* The thought ruminated over and over in Dae-Ho's mind.

Dae-Ho and his wife watched over their son into the early hours. They kept the fire hot and continued to place warm rocks near their son. An hour before dawn, when the Earth was at its coldest, Dae-Ho saw his son's eyes open, but his eyes were dull with the look of death. Man-Shik struggled to breathe, his lungs gurgling with fluids. He burst into a coughing spell, blood-speckled mucus saturating the soiled cloth they had been using to wipe his face.

In a labored effort, he spoke, "Father?"

Dae-Ho answered, "Yes, my son."

There was no audible answer, just a gurgle. Dae-Ho at first regarded the feeble attempt to raise his hand as a hopeful sign, but experienced new dismay as his son had not the strength to continue. The hand dropped back to the boy's side.

Dae-Ho watched as his wife stroked their son's hair. It was dirty, stringy, and black as night. Sweat beads formed on his forehead. Another grubby rag was used to wipe them away. His wife bent over Man-Shik. She placed a loving kiss on her son's forehead, and then she placed her check over the same spot as if to gauge the level of the fever.

"I can wait no longer," cried Dae-Ho.

Now desperate, Dae-Ho lifted the boy into his emaciated arms, struggled to his feet, and set off towards the army camp. He trudged through the woods in a black starless night. Branches tore at his face. Roots grabbed at his feet. Slick snow and ice pulled at his tiring frame. The boy was emaciated, light, and would have been easy for Dae-Ho to have carried just months before, but Dae-Ho was himself weakened from malnutrition and cold. He labored under the load and over the rough landscape. Despite his weakness, he never faltered in his mind while staggering over every lift of the terrain, and floundering out of every depression. At last the sun rose and he could better see the whipping branches and grasping roots, but the cold was just as bitter.

In the distance he saw smoke rising from the fires in the American MASH unit. Searching for physical strength, he reached back in his mind to the day of the savage storm and to the moment in which he had wanted to give up. He pictured his own beaten and discouraged body on the bed of despair and sought to remember the flicker that had awakened his strength. His search was weak and erratic, but he continued to force his mind to re-discover that same glimmer, in the hope of fanning it into a flame of strength. Soung Dae-Ho called upon his ancestors. He called on the being that must be God and asked for help. He sought the very core of nature to ease his burden and make his footsteps light.

It was imperceptible at first. Dae-Ho didn't even notice its beginning, but somehow it had been awakened. It started in his center. It breathed strength into his limbs. His body was reinforced by the power of heightened determination. His footsteps become surer, his strides longer, and his breathing easier. Though it was still a struggle, he found the strength to continue.

At last the struggling miles were covered. Dae-Ho stumbled towards the tent with the big red cross on it. Suddenly two soldiers stepped out, barring his way, unwilling to let him pass. He pleaded for help in Korean and broken English. The sentries, feeling compassion but respecting orders, held their ground. North Koreans had tried to smuggle explosives into some American camps. There were also highly infectious diseases from which they must protect their wounded patients. And most assuredly, the unit simply did not have the resources to treat every sick Korean that came to their camp. They ashamedly pushed him away and told him to go home.

Dae-Ho dropped to his knees. He held out the boy who was unspeakably close to death and pleaded for their help. To his fortune, a kindlier nature came across the scene. The older officer commanded the sentries to take the boy inside the medical tent. They removed the precious burden from Dae-Ho and carried the small limp body into a warm mobile hospital room. Dae-Ho followed them into the facility and for the first time in two months, he felt complete warmth. He was directed to a chair which he gratefully accepted. He moved it close to the flaps serving as doors to the treatment room, parting them frequently to observe the doctors. He gave thanks to his ancestors for their strength and support. In moments a cup of hot broth was slipped into his hands. Though delicious and warm, it could not appease his concern for Man-Shik.

Soung Dae-Ho watched through wisps of hope, trying to believe that they could save his son. The doctors seemed sure of themselves. They worked quickly, shining a light in his eyes, checking his pulse and listening to his lungs with the stethoscope. A mask went over his nose and mouth, and people were squeezing a big black ball on the end. Dae-Ho noticed a furtive glance toward him while the doctors continued to labor over his son. One doctor started kneading his chest with the balls of his hands. He pushed weakly at first, but the pressure became greater and more furious. A tube was rammed down his throat. *Is it going into his lungs?*

There was considerable discussion among the doctors which he didn't understand. Then one doctor closed his fist and in a mighty blow struck his son on the chest. Hearing bone snap, Dae-Ho jumped to his feet, shocked at the vicious blow to his son's chest. Orderlies grabbed and restrained him. Dae-Ho fought back but he was too weak to break free. The men kept pushing on his son's chest and hitting Man-Shik repeatedly. It was a scene of wanton abuse. *Why are they hitting my son?* Still restrained, Dae-Ho could not control the tears flowing freely down his cheeks.

The madness seemed to go on and on, but then, in the midst of all the fury, a hand reached out to the doctor who had been pounding on the boy's chest. The hand stayed the arm. *Good, they will stop hurting him.*

The kindly man who had stopped the pummeling turned to Dae-Ho. He wasn't smiling. His face was ashen and sad. *What has happened? My son was alive and now they look at me as if he is—dead.*

The man walked toward Dae-Ho, who was breaking free of the orderlies to rush to his son's side. The benevolent doctor stood in front of Dae-Ho, blocking his path. In a sudden burst of understanding, Dae-Ho fell into the arms of the doctor. Sobs erupted from his chest and tears rushed from his eyes. The last of his strength had been given and he fell to the ground in exhaustion.

Soung Dae-Ho collapsed into a world where pain, hunger, and cold were locked away from consciousness. The orderlies lifted him onto a bed and covered him with warm blankets. They knew he would all too soon awaken, and they shrank from the devastating reality that this father would be forced to face, as would so many fathers and mothers around the world.

1:6 ⟫⟫ 1951 — Bitter Fruit

Late that same day, Soung Dae-Ho started the long walk back to their crude camp. Had he not known the landscape, he might not have found their scant refuge. Using sight more downcast than usual, he spotted his wife loyally watching for his return. He could see that she recognized him from afar, as she stumbled more than ran toward him. He grieved at the message he would have to deliver.

As she came closer he read the concern on her face. She fell into his arms, her body nearly limp, exhausted from worry, hunger, and cold. His throat constricted from emotion and sobs welled up from is heart. She could not ask the question welling up in her breast.

Dae-Ho's words were weak and faltering but he finally spoke them aloud.

"Our son . . . is dead."

His wife slipped heavily from his grasp. He had not the strength to support her. He lost his will and crumpled to the ground with her. Dae-Ho's weeping joined hers in a bitter, impromptu dirge of a death requiem with movements of both passion and pain.

It seemed an hour before he could wrestle his wife off the ground, only to stagger across the cold forest floor whose icy fingers pulled at them in a clamp-like grasp. They lurched into the camp with fingers and toes nearly frozen. The fire was sputtering and virtually out as if to express their near state of death. Soung Dae-Ho clumsily placed fresh wood on the fire. They held each other, covered themselves in their blankets and sat up against a large cold rock. They closed their eyes and both, within the unity of honest love, sought release from the mortal pains of their labor. In this cold, it should come quickly.

1:7 »»» 1951 – Stalemate

Life stubbornly clutched at the now childless Soung couple, refusing to let go. Giving in to life more than fighting death, Dae-Ho managed to hang on with his wife committedly by his side. After days of mourning, fighting the cold of his existence and the ice in his heart, Soung Dae-Ho rose once more from his ashen and cold-laced despair. He conjured up another ripple of hope, believing that if he just stood up, he might live through the war.

And he was right. The short cold days and long frigid nights grew into longer spans of sun and warmth. As spring approached, Dae-Ho made more foraging trips towards Daeseong-dong. At first the excursions were measured, cut short by fear, but as the fighting abated he became more confident. His walks around the countryside revealed that South Korean, American and United Nation troops were holding their position at the 38th parallel. The many months turned into more than two years; the war officially labeled a stalemate. Dae-Ho and his wife began to exist rather than subsist. The truce between the warring parties made it possible to obtain food and to create better shelter.

Dae-Ho kept track of the peace talks. His friends began to congregate again to share the news that each had overheard. At last, the stalemating treaty of 1953 was signed. This was great news for Dae-Ho. It meant that he and the still living, but displaced, farmers on the DMZ could return to the ghost fields of their shattered lives.

But Dae-Ho's hope was nearly crushed when he analyzed the ruins. The rice paddies lay in shambles; canals and ditches were torn and broken. His farm was little more than a collection of craters and tracks. It would be impossible to flood the rice paddies with water until repairs were made. It was late in the season, July 1953. Even if repairs were made quickly, an almost impossible task for men with little more than shovels as their tools, it was too late to plant rice. It would not mature in the remaining days of summer. No matter how many times Dae-Ho went through the actions in his mind, there was not enough time to plant and harvest a rice crop. It was a bitter comprehension for Soung Dae-Ho, but it did give him the remaining summer and fall to repair the fields. The work was not limited to waterways but also to leveling the fields, which were pockmarked by craters, foxholes, and equipment tracks. The worry of land mines also weighed on his mind as he toiled once more towards productivity.

Magnifying the acrimony, Soung Dae-Ho suffered from the absence of his son, Soung Man-Shik. The loss was devastating. He missed his son, but he was also concerned with the future. There would be no one to work the fields with him. There would be no one to take over in his late years. They would not enjoy the presence of a family, unless there was another birth.

1:8 ⟫⟫ 1955 – Hope Through Life

It was the middle of the night. Dae-Ho thought, *It seems always to be this way; a most inconvenient time.*

Soung Dae-Ho paced the floor through endless hours. It had been a little over seven months since his wife had come to him in glowing exuberance. She had announced a miracle. She was pregnant! Dae-Ho had burned incense to his ancestors as an offering of gratitude.

A midwife attended the mother of his soon-to-be delivered child. For hours, little more than muted voices penetrated the thin wall of separation. Then just after 3 a.m. a change in intensity hinted to a more rapid progression of delivery. The groans rose in frequency and pitch, gradually becoming shrieks of pain. Dae-Ho hoped the baby would be a male who would grow to work with him in the fields, strengthening their financial opportunities. After a cyclical barrage of screaming, the quiet dawn was punctuated with the cry of a babe; the shrieking supplemented by whimpers of relief and happiness. Final tasks completed, the midwife opened the door to the husband and new father.

Soung Dae-Ho stepped quickly through the simple door frame, smiling at mother and his new—*what is it?*

His wife beamed with joy as she raised the infant to her husband and whispered, "It's a boy!"

Dae-Ho could not hide his ecstasy. Once more he would give thanks. He had received a son. His future took on a brightened hope. After inspection he was relieved to see ten fingers, ten toes, and a perfectly normal-looking baby son. His mind shot into the future when his son would work by his side. He experienced great joy as he projected their future life. Dae-Ho had a new son, born on August 5th, 1955—two years after the treaty announcing the stalemate of the Korean War.

1:9 ⟫⟫ 1955 – Moving North

Soung Dae-Ho worked hard in the fields, throwing strength and focus into his farm. However, in too many introspective moments, the hope of his personal legacy loomed as a legacy of defeat. As he worked the rice patties, he was often filled with brooding. Bile would rise from his gut and creep like poison into his heart. Despite this new young son, he was angry over the loss of his eldest. He was angry over the destruction of his farm and the avalanche of time and work it had taken to repair it. His anger spawned malice towards the Russians and North Koreans for starting the war, and to the Chinese who backed the destruction. From that malice grew a plan. As the plan blossomed in his mind, he grasped the idea of using the North Koreans as unwitting and unknowing assistants in its execution, which was to plant and harvest the seeds of the re-unification of the Koreas.

It was both easy and difficult to move his wife and son into North Korea. It was difficult to be labeled by his friends as a traitor. It was also difficult to leave his ancestral farmland. It was, however, easy to get the North Koreans to accept his defection. He joined a North Korean Collective Farm just over the Han River in a village known as Kijong-dong. The collective promised all that life could offer: a hospital, a school system from kindergarten to secondary schools, even childcare facilities. The collective, with all its amenities, had a grand purpose secretly set by the northern government: to attract defectors with the appearance of greater fairness.

At first Soung Dae-Ho worked harder than he ever had, if that is possible, to prepare a place for his son. As he traveled each day from his home to work in the fields, Dae-Ho noted changes in Kijong-dong. It began to evolve into something very different from the original farm collective. New homes were being built, made of cement. They were brightly-colored on the south sides, but plain and unpainted on the north sides. He noted that everything looked good from the southern view but quite plain when seen from the north. His life had not been made easier, and even worse it bore less incentive. Each day he labored for the state, and the benefit of all. He had lost control of his life and his farm. The hypocritical, two-faced cement homes and pride-less farm work continued to eat at his soul and fester in his mind.

Soung Dae-Ho's bitterness was carefully covered, and in keeping with Kijong-dong's air of appearances, he put on his own air. Outwardly he exhibited devotion to Communism and the Party, but Dae-Ho also carried an intense desire to see the downfall of Communism and the reuniting of the Koreas. It was that desire that gave him purpose beyond the state farm and the ability to ignore his fears. Despite the danger, he worked most strenuously to plant his own desires into the heart of his son.

To accomplish his purpose, Dae-Ho asked for and was given permission to plant two saplings in pots near his common building. He committed to care for them and transplant them so all could enjoy their fruit. Dae-Ho took great care in planting and nurturing the two trees, making sure his son understood each step in the process. Dae-Ho was preparing a special experience for his son.

1:10 »»» 1962 – Conjunction

Havaa Mstislav looked over the rolling hills of Karachay-Cherkess, admiring the verdant green terrain and galloping horses with their flowing manes and tails unfurled in the wind. The view was breathtaking. Havaa was a descendant of the great Genghis Kahn. His ancestry not only included royal Mongols but also Russian rulers and devout Muslims. He had grown up near the small town of Karachayevsk in the Russian Republic known as Karachay-Cherkess, called by some the Territory of Enchanted Horses. Havaa was a fine horseman, as would be expected of a descendant of Genghis Kahn. He became familiar with the Basayev family who raised some in the finest horses of the Caucasus Mountains.

Havaa loved the hills, the horses and the Basayev family. His eye was not only on their horses, but also upon a daughter named Lamaara. In Lamaara he saw not only the beauty of a woman, but also recognized horsemanship honed sharp by preceding generations of horsemen in the shadows of the Caucasus Mountains. In Lamaara, Havaa didn't just see the beauty of their world but he also felt it in his heart. Her sensuous long hair was the archetype of the flowing mane on a galloping mare; her genetically unusual green eyes were as deep and green as the grass of the hills in springtime. Her mind was quick, her wit sharp, and her heart was big. She had mastered not only the skills of a horseman but possessed the knowledge of an educated woman. She was the perfect product of her family, the land, and all its beauty. Havaa loved the land of his youth and the woman who had become the love of his life.

The days away from the work of wrangling horses were easy and romance filled. Their time together was spent on horseback, riding through green foothills of long, swaying grass punctuated by gurgling streams and pastoral valleys. They would ride for hours at a time, sometimes at a gallop and at other times in meandering walks. They stopped by small brooks to water the horses and often ate picnic lunches on the banks of pristine lakes. The blanket tied to Havaa's horse would be unwound and laid upon the soft grass where their supine bodies would watch white clouds in deep blue skies as they floated over their heads, whispering tales of fantasy and romance. It was the romance so many dream of, but few experience.

Havaa learned much from Lamaara. She exposed him to Eastern Orthodox Christianity, being of Persian Ossetian descent. Lamaara was very familiar with Islam, and as the two became closer, the differing points of Christianity and Islam faded into a marriage that spanned religious divides. It was a marriage conceived out of respect and admiration rather than religious tenets.

Havaa had been intrigued by Lamaara's heritage from the first days of their meeting. In addition to the traditions of her Persian Ossetian ancestors, the traits famous in the Cossack/Russian cavalry were present in the genes and character of his mountain girl. It magnified her love for the equestrian business of her father.

Along with this mixture of genes came other perspectives. For generations Lamaara's family had provided horses for the Cossack cavalry. As a result she was steeped in the view that the Cossacks had been used and maltreated by the Russians who conscripted them into their wars and persecuted them in their culture. Lamaara disdained the Russian attitude that painted Cossacks as a lower class of people, considering their Slavic heritage to be unfit for inclusion by the Muscovites. The place of the Cossacks was in the dirty work, from the infantry of waged wars to garbage removal. Havaa's feelings were not divergent from Lamaara's attitudes.

One of the children of Havaa Mstislav and Lamaara Basayev was known to most as Aayan Nikita Mstislav. Havaa had chosen his name with particular care, not with premonition but with a hope that greatness was in his veins. In its fullness, Aayan meant a "gift from god, unconquered and unconquerable in vengeance and glory." Aayan, like most children, had been dubbed with a nickname by his parents. It was a name of affection: the Russian name, Geni. Geni portrayed a similar but kindlier tag: "well-born."

1:11 ⫸ 1964 – Heritage

Aayan Nikita Mstislav adored his mother. He treasured the time she spent with him. She was more than a mother, she was also his teacher. They spent hours together discussing the broad history of the world behind them and of the current and future world before them. He was a voracious student, absorbing every word spoken by his mother. On one particular day, Lamaara taught Aayan Nikita about the great Genghis Kahn and the revelations were staggering: *I am a descendent of Genghis Kahn!*

Aayan Nikita had been born in Chechnya on March 21, 1964. As he grew, the significance of his birth date, in many ways, became the basis of his identity. He had learned about many cultures, and religions, as well as astrology. He was fascinated with astrology and pleased that he was born under the Chinese Zodiac sign of the dragon. The dragon is considered a highly intelligent creature, and intelligence was one of Aayan Nikita's great assets.

Understanding his place as a dragon at the age of nine was evidence of his mental acuity. He was also filled with certain traits of the dragon: energy and enthusiasm, and he had already cultivated the idea that he was not a common boy. Aayan Nikita had also noted another aspect to his birth. In western astrology, he was Aries the Ram with attributes of leadership, courage, and aggression. Aayan Nikita did his best to formulate his life around the character traits of both the dragon and the ram.

From the teachings of his mother, Aayan Nikita understood that his native country, Karachay–Cherkess Republic, had never been more than a footstool to the Bolshevists, the Stalinists, and the Soviet Union. The land surrounding the Caucuses Mountains was merely a land between the

Caspian Sea and the Black Sea; a land to be trodden and crossed to get to the trading empires of the Persian and Ottoman Empires of the past.

Aayan Nikita learned that his heritage flowed from *the* Genghis Kahn through his son, Jochi Kahn, who ruled the lands of Eastern Europe. Jochi's son, Batu Kahn, had a daughter who married a Russian prince. It was through that Russian prince that Ivan the Terrible descended. Aayan Nikita's father, Havaa Mstislav, though not a direct male descendent, was of the lineage of Ivan the Terrible. He grew to believe that ancestral identity was an important part of a person's life.

Aayan Nikita marveled at the idea of descendancy from the leader of the largest contiguous empire of all time, the Mongolian Empire. His mind expanded as he took in the details of the kingdom of Genghis Kahn, through Ivan the Terrible, and to his father. In a very self-absorbed moment he came to believe that he was in fact of royal heritage.

With his mother's words ruminating through his mind he asked the question, *Could I ever become as great as Genghis Kahn. No, I will be greater.*

1:12 »»» 1966 – The Lesson of the Sapling

Rising from the breakfast table in their bi-colored common building, Soung Dae-Ho turned to his son, Soung Jun-Sun. Jun-Sun was now eleven years old.

"Jun-Sun, come outside with me. Today we shall discuss the opportunity to grow in fertile ground, and we will talk about freedom."

The lesson had been long in development, beginning years before, when Dae-Ho planted one fruit tree in a large fertile pot and another in a smaller pot with poor soil. After a time of training and observation, Dae-Ho asked Jun-Sun to assume the duty of caring for the trees. Dae-Ho hoped that Jun-Sun would begin to question the growth of the two trees. One became vigorous and healthy. It gave every sign of becoming a productive fruit tree which would provide delicious refreshment to its master. The other tree was dissimilar. It was shorter, the branches were ill-formed, and the leaves seldom showed the healthy synthesis of sun, water, and minerals into green and robust foliage.

On this day, Dae-Ho told Jun-Sun that he wanted to discuss the trees. As father and son approached the two trees, the differences were evident.

"Jun-Sun, you have been tending these trees. By your comments, you have noticed that this second tree does not have the vitality of the first?"

"Yes, father."

"Have you concluded why this is so?"

Jun-Sun changed his focus from his father to the saplings.

"Yes, it is in a smaller pot and the soil seems rockier. It dries out more quickly and the leaves shrivel up. I've given it extra water, but it doesn't help."

Dae-Ho stepped over to the small tree and picked it up by the trunk and pot. In one quick motion he slammed the pot against the ground. Shattered shards revealed the roots.

"Jun-Sun, what do you see?"

After a moment of silence, he responded, "Father I see the roots of the tree."

"How are they formed?"

Jun-Sun reached out and fingered the roots.

"They are all tangled up in a ball."

"What can you tell me about the soil?"

Jun-Sun poked at the earthy contents of the former pot and pinched the soil with his fingers.

"It is mostly rock with little dirt."

"Now that you've seen the roots and the rocky soil, can you tell me why this tree has done poorly, despite your great care?"

Dae-Ho watched as Jun-Sun picked up the tree to hold the root ball in his hands. He pulled at the tightly packed roots and picked at the interwoven rocks. He pinched at roots that appeared to be rotted.

"Father, the roots are bound up and some have rotted. There is very little soil."

"Good observations, Jun-Sun. Have you ever wondered why this tree was in a smaller pot?"

"I thought, in the day it was planted, we had very little and this was the only pot available."

"That is a good supposition, but I'll tell you the true story."

Dae-Ho pointed to the buildings on their collective.

"Look at the buildings around us. They are bright on the south sides and unpainted on the north sides. Inside they are dreary. They have been built close together. Our quarters are small and we have little room."

Jun-Sun's head pivoted as he looked at the small yard between the cement buildings.

Dae-Ho continued, "We are told when to go to work in the fields and what to do. People are given jobs that are not of their own choosing. We pool our work and our goods together for all to enjoy, but there is rarely enough for all."

Dae-Ho took the sapling from Jun-Sun and placed it next to the remains of the broken pot.

"In many ways, we are constrained like this tree. We have been placed in a small and unfertile pot. Do you see the similitude of our lives with the life of the small tree?"

Dae-Ho was pleased that Jun-Sun looked once more at the buildings around them before answering. He was glad that his son was taking a thoughtful approach. Dae-Ho had often watched him observe and ponder, a trait he had taught Jun-Sun. He had discouraged him from making hasty, ill-founded conclusions. He then noticed that Jun-Sun looked beyond the brightly painted southern exposures with their dreary northern sides, to the valley south and across the river. Dae-Ho's eyes focused on the same view. He could see his old rice farm. *It looks productive. Will Jun-Sun understand the principles that made the difference?*

"Father, I think that this little tree has been confined in a pot too small for its needs. I believe that its roots couldn't find nourishment. Like the tree, I believe that we too are restricted in our growth and do not always have enough food to eat."

Dae-Ho nearly burst at the response, feeling great joy that Jun-Sun's understanding had developed to such a high level. *What more might he comprehend?*

Finally Jun-Sun spoke again, "Is it Communism that restricts us, limiting our opportunities?"

"Know this my son; all living things need nutrients to grow, but they need even more than nutrients. They need freedom to use those nutrients for their growth and progression. I purposely planted the seedling in a small pot with poor soil. I wanted to demonstrate that only the best of soils and the best of environments can produce a prosperous tree. This pitifully small pot could never have provided the freedom to grow strong and productive. The poor soil, so full of rocks, could never have supplied prospering nutrients.

"You have learned the lesson of the sapling and have understood that it also applies to us. We will now plant both trees into their permanent places. Soon the larger tree will bear abundant fruit, but this little tree will struggle. However, do not despair and do not give up on it. Be dedicated in your efforts to nourish this little tree. One day, with proper care, it may also become a proud and fruitful tree."

Considering Dae-Ho's words, Jun-Sun asked, "Father, will we ever have the freedom to choose for ourselves?"

"A very important question, my son, and I do not have the answer. This answer is one of many that you will seek in your lifetime. Today is an important day. I had hoped you would see and understand. You have made me very proud. Not only have you listened to my words, but you have heard with your heart and understood with your being. I believe you will make a future that is bright and prosperous and I ask that you now consider very carefully what I say."

Dae-Ho squatted to the level of Jun-Sun's face, looking directly into his eyes. He wanted to make the impression of a lifetime upon his one son.

"Your greatest duty is not to create for yourself a bright and prosperous future. Your greatest duty is to help others have the same bright future that you have achieved. As you bless this poor sapling with love and sustenance, you must also learn to bless those around you to become strong and healthy. You must, however, with each breath, remember the principles that make this so."

Dae-Ho knew that Jun-Sun was truly a gifted student. He found a lesson in every act he observed and those he experienced. The conclusion of this one long-planned lesson marked the beginning of many new lessons and subsequent understanding. Dae-Ho made every effort to see that his son's thoughts were well-groomed and his perceptions clearly focused.

Dae-Ho had raised his son under the strictest of covers: show devotion to the state but also harbor a desire to change a system that runs rough-shod over house, home, and personal goals. He hoped Soung Jun-Sun would grow up with the look and actions of a devoted Communist but with a heart that sought freedom. Soung Jun-Sun was intelligent and hard-working. As he grew, his skills singled him out, distinguishing him from his peers, gaining him training that most peasant citizens would never receive.

1:13 ⟫⟫ 1968 – The Brass Lamp

U.S. Navy Lieutenant James Anderson squealed the tires of the borrowed Air Force sedan as he pulled out of the base at Mountain Home, Idaho. His disdain for being stuck on an Air Force base effused his need to mash the accelerator to the floor in an attitude of "get me outa here!"

Anderson represented the perfect All-American male, blond-haired, 6' 2" with a strong physique, and blue-grey eyes. He carried a confident and knowing look, possessing the vocabulary and presence to support it. People saw him as knowledgeable and capable. He was both.

Lieutenant Andrew Jameson, seated in the passenger seat, was quick to add concurrence to the violent acceleration. "I'm so damn glad to get away from the base. Those flyboys are way too anxious to dust our ships with their anti-submarine crap. Once we're done, I never wanna see that desert slab again."

Jameson was an inch shorter, dark-haired and with a heavier beard than Anderson. He was just as smart and capable as Jim, but didn't exude the air of assertion Anderson exhibited. His skills were occasionally underrated, but his talent was equal to Anderson's. They were a formidable pair, each with extraordinary character strengths. Both were highly regarded officers.

Rather than taking the paved road to Mountain Home, Lieutenant Anderson suddenly veered onto a dirt road that wound through the high Idahoan desert.

Once on the dirt road, Jim said, "Andy, it's not so bad. Look at what's in front of us—beer and pizza. What a great way to relax, unwind, and enjoy our escape. The only thing missing is the sea air and the girls back home."

Lieutenant Anderson gunned the car, spinning a tire and throwing gravel into the air.

Jameson shouted, "With you driving, we'll be lucky to get to the pizza! And what are we doing on this dirt road?"

"I'm taking a short cut today," said Anderson, as he made a power-slide through a turn. "One of the flyboys told me about it."

"What could be shorter than the Interstate?"

With a broad smile Anderson replied, "They say it's thirty miles of desert road with the perfect combination of straights and curves to work out the kinks and adjust the attitude."

Jameson cringed as sagebrush whipped by, scratching at his door. "Great!"

Clearly enjoying the challenge, Anderson shouted, "They said we'd love it and compared it to the sirens of the sea, begging the captains of cars to push the limits and their nerve. Of course, they offered to follow behind us to pick up the pieces after we roll over into the sagebrush."

The words had barely escaped Jim's lips when, in the middle of a sweeping corner, the rear of the car drifted into a sand trap in the road. Lieutenant Anderson's higher than normal speed and aggression nearly confirmed the need for Air Force assistance. The right side tires caught on the surface and the car teetered on two wheels. From the corner of his eye, Anderson saw Jameson grab a handhold as the sandy berm of the roadside menacingly reached out for the car. If they hit the berm, the car would most certainly roll over into the desert. At the last moment the rear tire hit a slick spot and slid outward, changing the center of gravity and saving them from a sure rollover. The car fishtailed across the road's surface, Anderson barely managing to maintain control as the car slid across the dusty road.

Ah, perfect! A better sailor than racecar driver, and driven by an ego as dominant as the noon-day sun, Anderson reveled in the moment.

Excited by the challenge, and watching Andy continue to grasp the handhold, Anderson shouted out, "Yeah, this is a great drive and there you are, hanging on like a sissy. Relax and enjoy. What a great day!"

Not letting go, Andy responded, "Ha, you hypocrite! I saw you reach down to clean your pants. You're the one who ought'a be scared. You ought'a be damned scared because you're the driver and you know how bad your driving is. They'll never let you drive anything more than an inner tube with an oar."

With a big cheesy smile Anderson looked at Jameson, "As long as it's nuclear, I don't care!"

With his eyes on the road, Jameson responded, "You'd better buy stock in a rubber band factory. That'll be your engine power."

Jim noticed Andy had released his grip on the handhold, probably due to a straightening of the road, but he was surprised by Andy's next statement and wondered where it came from.

"Jim, have you ever wished our names weren't so close to the same?"

"That's an odd question. No, I've never had that thought. Our names singled us out at the academy and brought us together, and here we are both Anti-Submarine Warfare (ASW) experts. Look, here we are today, at the top of our game and headed for the open sea. No, the upperclassmen had no clue that they were actually making us better men. They didn't know what a remarkable pair we'd become when they had their fun with our names."

Jameson looked squarely at Anderson and said, "Well, I didn't know that either, but it sure put us through a lot of grief."

Jim was aware of Andy's sometimes second-place feelings and always thought it odd. He had a boundless respect for Andy. Jim thought back on those similarities and on past events: James Anderson and Andrew Jameson. They endured the endless hazing dished out from upper classmen, including the handle "Twin Pukes." *No, I don't regret it; I savored it. It made us better. It made us stronger.*

The Naval Academy and the Air Force were long gone from their minds as Jim pulled off the street in Boise and into the parking lot of the Brass Lamp Pizza Parlor, considered by locals to be the best pizza on Earth.

Lieutenant Anderson was first to walk through the door where his senses were wonderfully assaulted. The first battering was the aroma —a sensuous mixture of specialty meats, garlic, and hickory smoke, which he absorbed with great satisfaction. Barely recovering from the olfactory incursion, the next strike was to the eyes. Along the walls were quaint-looking brass lamps with small, glowing, life-like flames. The lamps created the sense of a hideaway, highlighted with soft lighting, and Jim loved it.

Still hostage to the moment, Jim was met by the effusive and friendly smiles of Angelo, the owner. After the smiles and greetings, Jim and Andy were seated in the back of the restaurant, their favorite place of repose.

Looking up at the rotund Italian, Jim said, "Angelo, we've eaten here before but tell us why your pizza is so good, because it's fantastic!"

Angelo puffed his chest and said, "It is our tomatoes. The tomatoes have descended from the gods, ripe and rich, and created just for you."

They joined in Angelo's loud laugh, which was part of his performance, and all enjoyed the act.

Always the analyst, Jim asked, "Where do you get ripe tomatoes in the winter time?"

"They are grown here in the Idaho desert, in nurseries heated by geo-thermal springs."

Pointing to Andy, Jim said, "My friend loves the sauce."

Andy spoke up on cue, "The best."

"Thank you," said Angelo. "The recipe comes from the old country. I am a third-generation American-Italian and keeper of a very secret recipe, enhanced with herbs and spices that my family sends to us."

"I'm going to enjoy one of your micro-brewed beers," Jim said.

"Me, too. Bring us your best," Andy seconded.

Puffing out his chest even more, Angelo replied, "We only serve the best and it's here just for you."

And with that, Angelo scurried off.

"What a pleasant guy," said Andy.

Settling into their booth, the two navel Lieutenants enjoyed the delightful sensory overload and pure, loving welcome, but the best was yet to come: the taste of the pizza. Jim considered this pizza parlor as the ultimate gratification and a near perfect house of pizza pleasure.

Their pizza soon arrived. Jim sucked in the aroma .through flared nostrils. His eyes took in the fresh vegetables that topped their combination pizza, also grown in local nurseries where possible. He knew the meats were of the finest grade. He remembered the taste of the crust, which was coated with a light touch of extra virgin olive oil, a trace of garlic, and a smidgen of sea salt. And it was accompanied with the slightest hint of hickory smoke from custom-built ovens. The brick ovens had a particular functionality: to add a minimal suggestion of sweet apple-wood smoke.

Jim looked around at the décor and the clientele. He considered it to be a gourmet pizza house but without the gourmet ambiance. He noted the absence of families with young children. Most nights the tables were filled with college students, young couples, and local or traveling businessmen.

The two officers relaxed in the dim, life-like, but pseudo-gas flames that filled old-style, wall-mounted brass lamps, creating a sedating and mind-easing ambiance. The thick smell of baking pizza with its hint of garlic and apple-wood smoke, and the inevitable brewery buzz, drew people to this not-so-cheap pizza parlor. The ambiance and the privacy of the back tables made it the perfect place for them to consider the world and their role in it.

"You seem pretty pensive today, Andy."

Andy placed his pizza slice back onto his plate, reflecting a very serious look.

"I've been thinking about the war and how it's being run. And I wonder where the politicians keep their heads. Whose side are they on anyway? By the way they limit bombing, you'd think they have relatives in Hanoi."

After washing down a bite of pizza with a sip of beer, Jim added, "Yep, 500,000 troops in Vietnam, and no one can sneeze without White House approval. We've got potheads running free in the streets of San Francisco, and good men returning home to protesters."

Holding his glass in his hand, Andy spoke out.

"It makes me wonder who'll lead this nation in thirty years. Can you imagine this bunch of pot-smoking, LSD-popping hippies walking the halls of Congress and filling the White House?"

Shaking his head, Jim added, "May God protect us from ourselves."

"Jim, who's gonna do the heavy lifting? Who's gonna' keep this country from going down the toilet?"

"You and me brother. You and me."

"And what are we going to do about it, Jim?"

"I know what I want. I want the power to make a difference." Then Jim's face twisted into a fiendish Captain Nemo look. "Yes, the power of the atom. I want it and you want it, and there's only one place to truly control it."

Andy's dour look transformed into a devious smile, "Yes, in a nuclear submarine with nuclear missiles."

"See, Andy, without all that hazing we wouldn't be sitting her eating the best of the best and jointly seeking one of the most powerful positions in the entire world."

Andy raised his glass, "To the nuclear missile submarine captains of the future—you and me."

Jim and Andy talked over their ideas and made a commitment. They would acquire the power to protect the free world.

"Andy, no matter the cost, if the day comes when it's up to us to protect the world, I won't hesitate."

Andy raised his glass one more time.

"I'm with you Jim. The world had better not mess with us."

1:14 ⟫⟫ 1974 – The Perfect Storm

Aayan Nikita Mstislav sat in his parents' home reading. He was alone but enthralled by stories of brave Cossack cavalrymen. Suddenly, the staccato of gunfire jarred Aayan from his reading. Hesitant at first, he rose to his feet, curiously walking to the window. Parting the curtains, he saw nothing unusual, but heard the distant noise of battle. It wasn't the first time he had heard the sound of armed clashes.

Spurred by curiosity, Aayan moved toward the door, guardedly opening it. The day was young. His parents had left the home much earlier, not specifying where they were going. The air was crisp and clean, carrying ear-assaulting booms, mixed with machine gun and rifle fire. Tell-tail plumes of smoke were rising several miles away, their origins blocked by undulating terrain and irregular stands of trees. Concern filled Aayan Nikita's mind. Quickly slipping on his shoes and a jacket, he set out to investigate; his parent's hushed, but recent discussions of Soviet troops ruminating through his mind.

Aayan Nikita's walk turned into a jog. As he quickly moved forward, he saw people driving and running towards him, away from the battle sounds. Many were shouting and some were crying. All seemed filled with a mix of terror and rage. Ignoring the danger, Aayan kept jogging toward the evident base of the billowing smoke columns. He dodged a number of his friends' parents who told him to turn back. He resisted their words and their grasping hands as he quickened his pace. Watching for his own parents, he was determined to learn the source of the conflict with its increasing intensity.

Out of breath, he rounded a growth of heavy brush and spotted the cause of the commotion. He saw a number of town's people with a variety of weapons firing on Soviet troops who were advancing toward them. Hopelessly unable to withstand the assault, he saw the people fire their guns, scramble backward to a new place of security, only to fire again. Just 160 miles from Grozny, Chechnya, the people of the Karachay–Cherkess Republic were often caught up in the same rebellion against the Soviets.

On the far left side of the battle, Aayan noticed a familiar coat. It was the bright red coat that his father had always worn. He was kneeling behind a truck. On the ground next to his father was an unmoving form. Spikes of horror pierced his mind. *Could that be my mother?*

As the troops advanced toward the broken truck that protected his father, other townspeople moved back. Soon Havaa Mstislav was the last rifle facing the Soviets. Just then the air was split by a thundering explosion. Close to the action, Aayan was thrown to the ground by the surprising power of the concussive blast and burning heat mixed with the ear-bursting thunder. Lifting his head from his prone position, he saw a burning hulk in the place of his father and the truck. There was no red coat; there were no visible bodies, only the confluence of flames. In a rage driven by understanding, Aayan dashed toward the inferno. People from his town began screaming at him, some saying, "Run!" some "Stop," and some shouting, "No"! His ears heard the words, but his body and mind ignored them. He quickly found himself at the edge of the roiling flames.

Tears streamed down his face as he slumped to the ground, peering into the conflagration. Fire leapt into the air, intertwined with smoke and the smell of burning flesh. As the flames swirled, he could make out lumps that looked like two bodies. One wore the last and darkening bits of a red coat, the other was unidentifiable. With his hands above his head, grasping and pulling at his jet black hair, he wailed at the scene before him. He was certain his father was dead, and nearly as certain that his mother had been killed with him. In the blinding tears of his wretchedness, unknown but strong arms scooped him up. He fought and twisted to break free from his captor, but it was no use. The man was too strong and Aayan Nikita's struggle too undisciplined to affect a release.

As Aayan succumbed to the jolting rush from the scene, he closed his eyes and blocked out the sounds and smells. Despite his recoil, he understood that he was being carried through brush and thick foliage by someone other than the Soviets. At last the jostling stopped and Aayan was dropped to the ground. Opening his eyes, he saw the unidentified back of a man's head. Aayan instinctively kicked at the man, his right foot catching him squarely in the back as if the violence would bring back his parents.

The black-haired man winced and spun around, "Aayan, it's me, your uncle."

It was seconds before Aayan Nikita's unfocused eyes and fragmented thoughts put the picture together. In that moment, he jumped to his uncle, throwing his arms around him. He squeezed with all his might, trying to fight off the horrifying images of fire and death.

In an urgent voice, his uncle broke the moment, "We have to leave. They could be searching the woods and I don't want to be found here."

Aayan Nikita's uncle scooped him up once more and ran into a deep grove of trees, not stopping until they were both safe on his uncle's small farm.

Often without warning, without regard for the peaceful and serene, a perfect storm has sometimes vented its fury upon unsuspecting voyagers. Aayan Nikita Mstislav, shaped by the events of his life, was on his way to becoming that perfect storm. His driving passion, ill-defined at first, began to coalesce as life's events unfolded around him. Sustained by the people of that small farm, the conjugation of Aayan Nikita's future was born of rage and reprisal.

1:15 »»» 1975 – The Network

"I'll trade you three of my "cloud-ies" for two of your "flints.""

Aayan Nikita would have made an excellent horse trader had he been older, but as a ten-year-old, his initial stock and trade were marbles. There is always someone willing to trade marbles, he would mentally remind himself as he started each day. He had amassed a collection far greater and worth more than any of his friends.

Aayan Nikita absorbed many lessons early in life. The traumatic loss of his parents indelibly imprinted a lesson into his character that he would never forget. He learned in the skirmish that killed his parents that guns and bullets were powerful multipliers of strength. Though cared for by his uncle, he considered himself an orphan, harboring a festering anger deep inside. He determined that he needed to shed the boy to become a powerful man—a man who could exact revenge. He decided he was not of the class of people who could legally earn large sums of money. Persuasion and theft became his trade.

"I'll give you ten of my "flints" in trade for your father's pistol."

The exchange seemed an easy conversion. Trading marbles had turned into a quest for more valuable items. Once acquired, a prized commodity could be traded for even more valuable goods. He learned that many people would pay handsomely for items that they couldn't personally obtain. Aayan also found that he could acquire most valu-ables at no cost. He was young, but had an innate talent for locating and obtaining merchandise prized by others.

Still a very young boy, Aayan was forced into the guise of anonymity. No one would buy guns from a youth, so he secretly recruited older boys, even men, to work for him. He managed this trade from the shadows, never allowing anyone to learn his true identity. They perceived him as an older, unmet mentor. His mature minions would procure saleable goods and make deliveries. He also developed a "special request" service, which became legendary in the black markets of Chechnya. As he aged, he became tall and stocky and could mask himself to look much older. Concealing his age and identity, he approached a soldier who was said to have serious gambling debts.

Without even an introduction Aayan said, "I will help you pay your debts."

The soldier looked at him in astonishment.

"How do you know this, that I have debts?"

"I know more than that. You have a habit that is expensive. I know that if you don't satisfy your daily habit, your life will become intolerably miserable; but which is worse my friend, the misery of your habit or the pain of broken fingers? Or worse yet, the absence of your fingers, which you may lose if you don't pay your debts. I can help you."

The Chechen soldier nearly fell to the ground as the truth rang in his ears. Aayan saw his face flush and observed the soldier trying to moisten his dry mouth.

"How can you do this thing?"

Aayan showed no emotion. He was all business.

"You have access to automatic weapons. I have customers who want to buy them. Some of my profits will become your profits. You can pay your debts and satisfy your needs."

"How can I trust you?"

"I will provide partial payment in advance."

Aayan let that statement sink in.

"But know this, if you do not honor our agreement, I will break more than your fingers. Your neck will become precious to you and the target of my wrath if you fail me."

1:16 ▷▷▷ 1979 – How and Why

Michael Benson was only five years old. He was engrossed in a book too advanced for other children his age. His mental skills were astounding. He intently studied and questioned everything.

Michael opened a book entitled *How and Why*. It was from a set of latter-edition books that had been published in 1950, twenty-five years before Michael was born. He had opened the books without prompting and sat cross-legged on the hardwood floor next to the family's easy chair. Light streamed through the window, illuminating him and the book. It was as though the rays of heaven were enlightening his mind. Michael's face was awash with fascination. He looked up as his mother sat down in the easy chair beside him.

"These are interesting books!" Michael commented as he turned the pages.

"What are you reading about?" his mother inquired while peering over his shoulder.

"I'm looking at the index again. It says, "Little Questions That Lead to Great Discoveries" by Eleanor Atkinson. There's a whole bunch of dates here. She wrote it a long time ago, in 1912."

With a smile, his mother confirmed his statement. "These are very old books. I bought the set years ago. I treasure them very much. I never thought to show them to you."

Taking in every detail of the book, Michael added, "This first page shows a painting of a mother in a chair with her son on the floor. He is reading a book. It's just like we are right now."

"Isn't that something?" A smile of amazement swept her face.

Peering at the book and already knowing the answer, she asked, "Is there a caption under the painting?"

"Yes."

"What does it say?"

"'You expect great things of him.'" Michael rattled it off without hesitation.

Twisting down to look into Michael's face, she asked, "Is she talking about her son?"

"I think so."

"Do you think I feel that way about yourself?"

Michael's face lit up with a dawning awareness. "I guess so."

"Michael, I do expect very great things from you. You are a very special boy."

Continuing to flip through the pages, he said, "Mom, who was Hans Gutt—en—berg?"

"He invented the printing press. He pioneered the idea of printing books. His invention makes it possible for you to have many books just like the one you are reading."

"Wow! That is cool! And Galileo? Who's he?"

Looking back toward the book, she asked, "Are those names in the book?"

"Yes."

"What does it say about him?"

"It says that he was a great Italian teacher, and because of his teachings he was put on trial in Rome."

In a voice of empathy, she said, "He was a great man, Michael, and in many ways a pioneer. We have much to thank him for. He helped people recognize truths that their leaders had selfishly hidden."

With his eyes widening, he asked, "Did they put him in jail?"

"You know, I'm not sure. I think he was in jail for a while, but I think they let him out."

Looking back to the book, Michael's intrigue grew. "It says that he developed the telescope."

"Yes, and in that telescope the stars looked thirty-two times larger than they really were."

"Wow, that's big!"

He continued scanning the "General Index" of the *How and Why* set. At last he said, "At the top of the page it says, 'Our Debt to Scientists.' What did she mean by that?"

"It means that scientists have done many things for us that have made our lives better, and that we should appreciate them. You know that calculator that you like to play with?"

"Yes."

"It is a recent invention. We didn't have calculators when I was a girl. Many of the wonderful things we enjoy have been developed because someone asked a question like, 'How does it work and why is it so'? Or how can we do this better?"

Michael looked up in amazement, "Hey, that's just like the book! *How and Why.*"

His mother put her hand on his head, tenderly brushing his hair with her fingers, happiness in her heart. After a moment she said, "If you look at the world and ask those two questions—how and why—you'll gain great understanding, maybe more than most people. You might become a master teacher one day."

Michael paused for several minutes before answering. He looked up at his mother and said excitedly, "I want to be like one of these scientists."

CHAPTER 2
RIPPLES IN THE WATER

2:0 »»» 1985 – A Leap of Faith

It had been thirty-six years since Kinza had been smuggled into Iran. It was the point of no return for Kinza Bagâbigna, known as Pearl to his Mossad handlers in the Israeli Intelligence Service. His Iranian friends believed him to be a naturally-born citizen of Iran. But he had lived a double life and today was the first true test of a lifetime of preparation.

The stress of this day contributed to abnormal sleep cycles. His sleep had often been disturbed by abstract dreams. Falling into a black hole with no destination but darkness was one. Running through festering marshes of thick ooze became another frequent nightmare. The goo sucked and pulled at his mud-caked and water-filled boots, making it impossible to run from the unknown terror behind him. The most chilling dream included a harrowing scene of rifles pointed his way; the countdown of death inexorably approaching the command to "fire," but at a pace that matched the process of petrifaction. The eventual command to "fire" was punctuated by a hail of projectiles flying through time and space as though in slow motion. Watching in horror, his mind's eye saw each bullet fly straight and true, each a harbinger of the death that must surely befall him. In a bed of sweat he would awaken in terror, just before the barrage of bullets hit their mark. The recurrent dreams always ended in a brilliant flash of light and a sudden jolt to wakefulness. As he grappled with reality, his mind tried to cast off the pall of terror.

Kinza hoped for success where there had been little; though many had tried. Most had suffered discovery and a firing squad. As a covert plant of the Mossad, he had been tasked with flaunting the odds of successfully infiltrating the Islamic Republic of Iran Army.

Kinza presented his papers to the officer charged with the conscription of soldiers into the Iranian army. His forehead damp, his underarms perspiring, and the back of his shirt sweat-stained, he stood before the officer behind the counter. *Is it hot enough to justify the sweat on my clothing and the wiping of my brow?* He took a chance and with an embarrassing grin commented on the heat.

"It is very hot today in our beautiful Iran."

The officer in charge grunted but continued to scrutinize his papers. As the officer studied each sheet, Kinza thought about his future. *Will I become a soldier or a prisoner facing a firing squad? Will the torrent of bullets become my reality?* His recurring dream flooded his mind.

Kinza steeled his mind against the piercing eyes of the officer. He assumed the officer was good at his job. *Does he have a sixth sense? Will he see through my façade? There is something in his expression. Does he believe I am hiding something?* Kinza called upon his training to keep his heart from racing, his breathing in check, and his sweating pores from releasing an even greater cascade of perspiration.

"Tell me about your parents," the officer asked.

"My birth parents were killed in an accident in 1964. Their names were never revealed to me. I was adopted by EsamAeel Bagâbigna. He and his wife raised me as their own child. Blessed be Allah," said Kinza, quoting a sacred Islamic phrase. It was the phrase that Allah used to praise himself for revealing his 'Noble Qur'an to his Noble Messenger.' Muhammad was the Noble Messenger and, by using that phrase, Kinza gave credit to both Allah and to Muhammad.

It was important to Kinza that a connection be made. He followed the blessing with an explanation. "My adoptive parents took me in as an orphan boy, caring for me as the teachings of Muhammad prescribe. My adoptive father is an artisan. He creates many beautiful art pieces. He was also an activist in the overthrow of the Shah."

Kinza had a purpose in telling the officer of his adoption by the Bagâbigna couple.

"Blessed be He," the officer said in a late response to Kinza's mention of Allah. His eyes had been fixed on Kinza's, and he nearly missed the speaking of the name of Allah.

"Blessed be He," repeated Kinza, hoping his expression of deep gratitude masked his reason for restating the words that he hoped would protect him. He then added, "Blessed be Muhammad for teaching compassion for orphans. My parents are true followers of Muhammad." *Have I gone too far, been too obvious?*

The officer stood as though transfixed. All Kinza could see was a stoic face and the fixed and piercing eyes. It took steel-like nerves to avoid melting before the penetrating stare. After a long moment the eyes softened. Perhaps it was Muhammad's love of orphans that had touched the officer's heart.

Kinza witnessed the loud stamping of his papers and silently praised Allah as the officer motioned him to move along. Kinza had successfully become a member of the Islamic Republic of Iran Army as his first official task in a lifetime of subterfuge.

As he walked away, Kinza mused in his mind. *I just thanked Allah and not Jehovah.*

2:1 ⟫⟫⟫ 1989 – Break Up of the Soviet Union

Aayan Nikita Mstislav reveled in the Soviet/Chechen skirmishes, though they had been at their lowest point in fifty years. He tracked the episodes of contention as they fomented into more serious clashes. His republic, Karachay-Cherkess, and Chechnya were both under the control of the Soviet Union. Many rebellious citizens of Chechnya and the nations bordering Chechnya wanted guns from untraceable sources to be used against the iron fist of the Soviet Union. Aayan was now twenty-five years old and had become clever beyond his years in providing such weapons, amassing a near fortune in his fifteen years of black market dealing.

The breakup of the Soviet Union gave Aayan unexpected opportunities. Authority was lax; organization became non-existent. Even the chaos was in disarray. He took advantage of every presented opportunity.

The targets of his teen years, highly lethal service pistols, and poorly guarded small, but valuable military devices, had become overshadowed by automatic weapons, namely AK47s and other assault rifles. He added RPGs and explosives to the quickly increasing sale of small arms. Never content, he watched for larger, more destructive, and profitable weapons.

It became rumored that the Chechen rebels had been armed by a man said to be a descendent of Genghis Kahn through the bloodlines of both the Russians and the Cossacks; and a man friendly to the people of Islam. As his reputation and power grew, he began looking toward Ukraine, a repository of many nuclear devices. He began to develop plans to access those poorly cared for armaments.

Aayan continued in anonymity, but by reputation he was known as Kahn to his network agents. Far older in his capabilities than his age, he used a time-tested method to protect his identity: death to anyone who broke their oath of secrecy. Using this tool, he protected the truth of his age, his identity, and his growing network.

Aayan understood early on that disaffected people often yearn for luxury and ease. The Soviet breakup, along with the turmoil in Chechnya, provided a supply of the disaffected that he drew upon to enlarge his network. As in any culture, there were also people in the Ukraine who lusted after wealth. His first contacts with such people were tendril-like, cautious and exploratory. He developed lists of candidates who might be tempted by quick money. He profiled the names on the list to discover those who had direct access to the most valuable weapons, especially nuclear weapons, including nuclear materials. The list was refined to expose people who not only had access, but were also likely to sell nuclear devices for a handsome payment. Nuclear material and weapons offered a much greater promise of wealth than small arms.

People who possessed specifically unique qualities, proving themselves with patterns of success, became his leaders. Their reward was riches. In time the riches became lavish and unbreakable addictions. Kahn chose his generals and prime ministers from his motivated and addicted leadership, to whom he delegated the management of his network of agents. Two network members had stood out as Aayan Nikita studied their successes: Neg and Khoyer. They became his prime ministers.

On this day, Neg and Khoyer were seated before him; his number one and number two. No real names were used, just Neg and Khoyer, literally "one" and "two" in Mongolian. They were both Muslim Chechens. A measureable difference between them and other network members was their congruent purpose with Kahn. Both had been mistreated by the Soviets and both sought Chechen independence. These two men had become his prime ministers and the only people who had direct contact with the faceless head of the network entitled: *Kahn.*

"Let's review our recent work," said Kahn. "We have amassed a sizeable fortune. Our resources are growing, and our client list continues to expand. We have reached a level of maturity which I believe will provide an opportunity to plan and enact a project that has been in my mind for many years."

Neg and Khoyer sat forward in their chairs with intense interest.

"You have been dedicated and loyal to our cause which we will now expand. As usual, you will be the only people who know the entirety of the plan. Our network of agents will only know their individual parts."

Neg was the first to respond. "You have my continued commitment."

Khoyer added, "And my commitment as well."

"Good, the plan includes the acquisition of nuclear materials and weapons. We will develop certain fanatical parties as our pawns and take our fight to the Russians, the United States, and the Europeans."

Kahn saw eagerness in the eyes of his prime ministers.

"We shall provide dirty bombs for deployment by terrorists in America. I would like to provide technology and certain nuclear tools to the one country that might actually launch a nuclear attack on Israel. I have a plan which will coordinate the detonation of one or more nuclear devices in America. Europe will be torn open by terrorist activities and the life blood of Russian oil will be spilled in the destruction of their petroleum infrastructure. In every country where motivated jihadists exist, we will arrange for support and armaments. There is plenty of money in the oil coffers of the Middle East, enough to finance our efforts."

Kahn paused to evaluate his prime ministers. His eyes asked the question: *What do you think?*

Neg spoke first. "It is an ambitious plan."

Khoyer followed. "But an enticing one."

"You are both in favor?"

Kahn's question was answered with nods of approval. He then sat back in his chair. "Good, we will work out the details and methods to influence the world into our control. We will speak with thunder on that day."

2:2 ▶▶▶ 1989 – Confidences

It was a highly secret gathering. The President of Iran, Abbas Rashad and the Supreme Leader of Iran, the Ayatollah Alborz were both present. They had traveled to a private retreat in the country. The drivers were told to wait in the cars. The security detail formed a large circle around the isolated compound. The interior was air-conditioned and the furnishings were lavish. The complex was not connected to any form of communications or power grid. Electricity was provided by a diesel generator. The President of Iran had called for the meeting, and he wanted to be absolutely sure no one could infiltrate their secrecy. After the pleasantries of the obligatory greetings and physical refreshment, the meeting began.

The Supreme Leader of Iran opened the discussion, "Why are we here, President Rashad? You said you had a most important matter to discuss."

President Rashad was glad the Ayatollah had spoken first.

"It is about our place in the world, my leader."

The Ayatollah scoffed and declared, "We've learned that we cannot trust the world. They wish no place for us."

President Rashad was pleased with the Ayatollah's passion.

"My leader, you are correct. They feign assistance, then remove it. They now work to systematically control us and our place in the world. They fear our goals."

Rashad had to tread carefully. As the highest ranking cleric in Iran, the Supreme Leader, the Ayatollah Alborz, held the greatest power in the newly formed Islamic theocracy of the Republic of Iran. He gave the Ayatollah plenty of time to respond—and he did.

"This is true. Our people suffer and our position in the world is constrained."

The President sat back, hoping to appear level-headed.

"Yes, my dear leader, and there are dangers. We lack the strength to protect ourselves against the nations of power. In particular, we are convinced that Israel has nuclear weapons."

"Yes the Jewish stain has much power over us. We cannot let that stand."

"No my leader, we cannot. I have been thinking of something that could be beneficial to our Islamic paradise."

"What are you thinking?"

Rashad thought he detected a knowing look in the Ayatollah's eyes. *He may already suspect my proposal.* But Iran was facing a problem. The Ayatollah had recently proclaimed that the development of nuclear weapons was contrary to Islam's tenets. Rashad had watched the Ayatollah carefully however, and it appeared that his determination had been diminishing. Nonetheless, Rashad's thoughts would be a refutation of that position.

"I feel that we need to continue with our development of nuclear power, and in the end, the ability to manufacture our own nuclear weapons."

Silence hung in the room. The Ayatollah, at first, made no response, but finally asked, "How could this be done given our official position?"

"Our need for industrial power can be justified. The development of nuclear weapons must be secret. We must hide our actions from prying satellites and spies. We must keep our development secure from the inspectors who watch everything that we do."

"How can this be done? What will it cost? Where will the necessary resources come from?"

Rashad sat forward in his chair.

"We must work underground. That is the only way we can hide from the eyes of the world. We must also acquire the technology to finish our reactors and to enrich nuclear materials. This requires very expensive and sophisticated equipment. It will also require technically advanced centrifuges, which we do not possess."

The Ayatollah asked another difficult question, "What will it cost? What are the necessary resources? Our resources are meager."

"Yes, it is true," replied the President, "but sacrifice is necessary if we want to develop the strength to protect our place and promote our cause."

The Ayatollah rose from his chair and turned toward a draped window.

"It is clear that we need help. Who might assist us?"

Watching the Ayatollah finger the drapes, he gave his prepared response, "I have been in contact with an arms dealer who has offered to sell us nuclear materials, possibly even dirty bombs. We have dealt with him in the past. He has always kept his agreements. He has no love for the West. He is a Muslim and he likes our money."

The Ayatollah looked hard into the face of Rashad and simply stated, "Nuclear materials and weapons?"

"Yes, and there is another potential source. Ideas have been exchanged in veiled words with Argentina. They appear to be willing, and I believe it is time we worked more closely with them and buy their reactor technology."

"Is there any reason not to openly approach Argentina?"

"No, and, in fact, I now recommend it."

A smile crept across the face of the Ayatollah as he turned and stepped closer to Rashad saying, "Let us go forward with Argentina. We shall hold the discussion of nuclear weapons until another day."

The president smiled in compliance, "Yes, my leader."

2:3 ⫸ 1989 – Nuclear Development

Welby was a senior analyst for the National Security Agency (NSA). His boss had been invited to a briefing of the president, and Welby was included for the purpose of providing technical support, should it be necessary. Welby's job was to attend, observe, keep his mouth shut, but speak up when asked to personally comment. He had strict instructions to answer questions but to say little more.

Welby looked around the Oval Office. President Reagan, newly elected, leaned back in his chair listening to the Secretary of State report on the state of current geo-political changes, which included little new information. Welby scanned the faces of the Secretary of Defense, the Chairman of the Joint Chiefs of Staff, and the Director of the CIA. It was a pensive gathering of power lords. Each spoke in his own turn, often using reported Intel to promote their personal agendas.

President Reagan turned to the Director of the NSA. "I can see you brought some support with you today, and we haven't heard from him."

"Yes, Mr. President. Mr. Welby is our chief analyst. I can honestly say he has a better grasp of world nuclear development than anyone else in the NSA, at least with regard to U.S. security."

"I'd like to hear from him," said the President, his eyes resting upon Welby.

The NSA Director gave Welby a nod, which included a slight pursing of the lips and furrowing of the brow. Welby interpreted the message: be careful.

"Mr. President, I'd like to specifically speak about Iran. It's no secret that we've tried to stall Iranian reactor development. We've pressured the French and Germans to support our position. We now know that Iran has signed an agreement with Argentina to make their reactors operational using low-enriched uranium. They have been installing that technology, and I believe that Argentina will start delivering low-enriched uranium within three years."

President Reagan remained impassive in his reclined position.

Welby continued, "The development of Iranian nuclear reactors will continue. They believe they cannot depend on the world to assist them. Over the years, many agreements and contracts have been offered, only to be withdrawn or broken. Their two Bushehr reactors were damaged by Iraqi bombing raids during the war but they are repairing them.

"The Ayatollah has written a declaration that Iranian nuclear weapons development is evil but I am certain the reactor development will continue, and I don't think the Ayatollah's public statement represents his true convictions.

"Should Iran decide to develop nuclear weapons, there are several countries looking for cash or destabilization that will assist them. India and Pakistan are after the money. The Soviet Union would love to blunt U.S. influence."

President Reagan sat forward in his chair. Welby sneaked a look at his boss. His face was serious.

"Mr. President, despite the Ayatollah's declaration, I believe that

Iran will not only complete their reactor development, but they will also secretly work toward nuclear weapons. They believe that they stand alone in the pursuit of their own security. We believe that Israel has nuclear weapons, as do most of the middle-eastern states. Iran feels an honest need to possess such weapons for their own protection. I believe the time frame will depend on outside help." Welby glanced once more at his boss, but continued.

"I project that Iran will have nuclear weapons within thirty years."

Welby noted there were no gasps in the room. His opinion seemed to concur with most of those present. He knew he had walked a tight-rope but felt like he'd stayed within his given boundaries.

"Thirty years," the President said. "I can't help but believe that you are right."

Welby watched carefully as the President looked around the room. It had remained quiet. The President leaned back in his chair once more. His eyes focused on the ceiling for a moment, then scanned the council members one more time, before looking back at Welby.

Welby held his ground.

The President sat back up to his desk, appearing to have made a decision. "Gentlemen, we need to look more closely at the situation. I want to see increased inspections by the International Atomic Energy Agency. I want our intelligence services working overtime to keep track of Iranian developments."

2:4 ⫸ 1990 – A Major Break

Kahn lived in modest housing, partly because he moved often. He also felt it foolish to spend money on personal comforts. Sacrifice is necessary in the pursuit of purpose. He would gladly sacrifice his personal wealth and comfort to accomplish his purpose, or Al-Qadar. His Al-Qadar had become a very ambitious and clearly delineated plan that he had shared with his two prime ministers. He hoped it would be far-reaching.

Kahn preferred people with a dogmatic grasp of Islamic jihad to work in his network. Some were driven by a desire to seek the conversion, but more often they sought the destruction of the heathens. Many of the newly independent Eastern European countries included significant populations containing poor young Muslim men, who would gladly sacrifice their lives for riches, or, if not riches, to fall into the arms of Allah in paradise. In addition to fanatic Islamists, there were also passionate Communists who hadn't given up the idea that all comrades are equal in a classless society. There were also modern socialists, motivated by idealism, but very often lovers of riches. In most cases, ideology was a key factor; but never far away were the secondary keys: money, prestige, and power. Just as in his well-born status, Kahn believed that money should be well-spent.

His profilers had passed along a name to Neg, his number one prime minister. Neg knocked quietly on the plain door to the office of Kahn.

"Come," was the reply.

Kahn sat calmly behind his desk reviewing something that looked like network personnel files. His countenance exposed his Mongolian heritage. His state of being was revealed in his aura of royalty and dedication of purpose.

His dark eyes, framed by high Mongol cheekbones and surrounded by jet-black hair, focused on Neg. Neg confidently crossed the space from door to desk, but in a spirit of respect, just as Kahn expected.

"What do you have for me?" asked Kahn.

"We have located a possible source of nuclear weapons and material."

"маш сайн," said Kahn, meaning, "Very good."

Kahn liked peppering his conversation with Mongolian phrases as a reminder to his subordinates that his heritage originated with Genghis Kahn.

"Proceed."

"The man's name is Anton Pipenko. He has access to nuclear material and tactical nuclear artillery shells in Ukraine. He may even be able to supply one or more nuclear bombs. Anton has taken small bribes in the past for small favors. I believe we can convince him to take much larger payments for much larger prizes."

"So you recommend this choice?"

"Yes, master, I do. He is capable and greedy, both dependable traits."

"Good, I want you to deal directly with him. This opportunity is too important to trust to subordinates. Go to him. Offer our resources. Let us see if he will sell his soul for money. But remember, your identity is worth protecting. Take precautions."

"Yes, master, I will make the arrangement immediately. What shall I offer as payment?"

"That is of no concern. I will pay the amount that you feel is required. Start low, but if he shows determined interest, I am willing to pay handsomely for nuclear materials and warheads. I will pay even more for nuclear bombs."

Kahn demanded strict loyalty from his network and was convinced of Neg's loyalty and skill. As his network grew, the over-arching principle of management consisted of two elements: money and ideology. The under-girding foundation was loyalty. Each member swore on his life that he would never reveal information about the activities or identities in the network. All members agreed they would both take a life or give their own life to protect the network. Through this system of oaths and covenants Kahn established a network of secretive, dedicated, and loyal agents. The laws of management were immutable and followed to the smallest detail. Leadership, generals and agents alike, were protected by the principle. Kahn had complete confidence that Neg would keep his identity hidden.

2:5 ⫸ 1991 – The First Nuclear Materials

Chechen rebels had been some of the first pawns to be manipulated by Kahn but he turned quickly to other sources. Ukraine became fertile soil for weapons acquisitions and bold network members who would steal for wealth or ideology.

A year after approaching the Ukrainian, Anton Pipenko, the man known as Kahn was waiting for news about a mission for which Pipenko had been preparing. He was working at his desk in the anticipation of success; success was the only acceptable outcome.

Neg had worked with Anton in the development of a plan to steal enriched uranium. It had not been difficult to steal. The greater concern was how to hide the theft. The concealment of the theft was accomplished through Anton's manipulation of the paperwork. Kahn's network included a number of forging experts. They had provided replacement forms that documented lower amounts of enriched uranium which would hide the stolen material. Once the false certifications were in place, the theft was a simple matter of managing people and logistics.

Kahn did not plan to hold the materials. They would be quickly sold and delivered to a developing client: North Korea. The next task was to parlay the sizeable payment into greater sums of money and more powerful armaments.

2:6 ⟫⟫ 1991 – Network of The Kahn

Kahn had long since dropped his given name: Aayan Nikita Mstislav. As his success continued and his network grew, he began to be regarded as an all-powerful mystical entity rumored only to be a Russian Cossack and descendant of Genghis Kahn. Although network members knew the name, they did not know his face and place of operation, thus the mystery.

As time passed Kahn gained a reputation as one who relentlessly kept his promises to his clients. Promises made to his network were just as solemn in terms of rewards and punishments. His meticulous management of the network kept it secret and safe. Each agent was known by a code name. Only Kahn, his prime ministers, and his generals knew the real names of the agents. His network was organized into multiple branches. No cross-branch information was ever revealed. The generals knew nothing of their counterparts.

Kahn became a man who was both feared and revered by network members, and he took on a god-like persona. Over time, the nameless, headless, mystery man known as Kahn was given a new name. It became more of a title, since he had no identity. He became known as *The* Kahn. For this time and place and forever forward, Aayan Nikita Mstislav was The Kahn.

The Kahn met once more with Neg and Khoyer. He reviewed the steps of the mission accomplished by Anton Pipenko. Even though the mission was successful, there had been a near disaster. It was the first time they had delivered merchandise to North Korea. He listened to Neg as he described the transfer of the materials. The shipment had nearly been detected when it was transferred from a small boat to an ocean freighter.

After listening to Neg's report he asked for Khoyer's perspective. The Kahn made careful notes. After Khoyer had finished, The Kahn drummed his pencil against his wooden desk. Both Neg and Khoyer waited patiently.

"I believe our mistake was making a transfer in the waters of the Mediterranean. As we plan future missions, I'd like to make our transfer in ports controlled by members of our network, working in conjunction with Muslim fanatics. The transfer will appear more common and there will be many friendly eyes to assure success."

Neg and Khoyer had been through the exercise many times. Called *Intelligent Practice*, it was The Kahn's method of action. He personally reviewed the successes, failures, and difficulties of major missions. Using the results of those missions, he developed new theories of operation. The theories were applied in subsequent missions. The new results were again reviewed and, if successful, they became his new practices. It was a refining process. As The Kahn continued to apply *Intelligent Practice*, his methods became more polished, and he became more successful. The Kahn was a pure pragmatist, filled with the intelligence and fire of the dragon and the undeterred and blunt-force power of the ram.

2:7 ⟫⟫⟫ 1991 – A Supplier Named Dean

Names were important to The Kahn. It was one of his quirks. As he expanded his network he began to feel a need to separate his procurement network from his fulfillment network. He called his two prime ministers into his office to discuss the matter. Once more Neg and Khoyer were seated in front of The Kahn.

"Neg, as we work on the larger worldwide stage, I want to take a different name among our clients. I want to restrict my title, The Kahn, to our network."

"Do you have something in mind, master?"

"I have some ideas, but I'm not sold on them. I'd like some suggestions? Khoyer, I pose the same question to you. I want a name that is common to all, particularly Muslims, but not to exclude the West, the Russians, and the Chinese."

"A tall order," Neg replied.

"Master, I have a thought."

It was Khoyer who spoke up. The Kahn required candor and a fearless willingness to speak up, to offer ideas, and to actively participate in their "what if" sessions.

Khoyer offered his thoughts. "The name 'Dean' has roots in Islam. It is not a common Islamic name but it is known and respected. Among the Americans and the Europeans it is used daily. The Russians and Chinese would think nothing unusual about the name, suspecting it to be English. You could use it as a first name, a last name, or just a name."

"Маш сайн, Khoyer," said The Kahn, slipping into Mongolian vernacular. "I like it. I will be known simply as 'Dean' to our ever growing world of clients. Khoyer, for you there is a bonus today. You have offered a very important suggestion."

Scribbling a message on a piece of paper, he handed it to Khoyer. "Here are my instructions to the banking branch. Present it and have them draw $10,000 American dollars for yourself."

Such a reward was not common, but it was also not a rarity. Khoyer bowed his head in gratitude. The Kahn had maintained awareness of Neg from the corner of his eyes. He was pleased with Neg's reaction. The Kahn fully expected Neg to feel no jealousy or disappointment, and it appeared that he was not jealous. The integrity of The Kahn's leadership was as fair and considerate as it was ruthless.

2:8 ⟫⟫ 1992 – Jihad: A Teacher's Definition

Aadil Rouhani was in awe of his mentor, Naveed Khonsari. As he seated himself in Naveed's humble office, his mind quickly sketched a memory of the impact of Naveed's training, while he waited for Naveed to finish making notes on a legal case. He so loved the man. He was kind, gentle, and willing to teach. His experiences were rich with an understanding of the Law and its impact on Iranian citizens. Through many moments of amazement, Aadil had sat in the presence of Naveed, absorbing his wisdom and knowledge.

Aadil was an Iranian cleric and a newly appointed jurist. He had worked hard to prepare himself to adjudicate legal cases in the courts of Iran under the Law of Sharia. Aadil had entered Naveed's office with the hope of receiving additional wisdom from the man who had already given him so much. He owed his position as a jurist to Naveed, and he trusted his opinion. A recent matter weighed heavily upon Aadil's mind. Passing judgments on civil cases had cast a shadow over his idealism and he sought to reconcile his inner dichotomies. One of his decisions had been almost impossible to justify as the principles of moral character dramatically clashed with precepts of the Law.

At last Naveed looked up from his work. Aadil found the courage to ask a tough question in the warmth of Naveed's smile, but he was cautious as he began.

"Naveed, will you explain once more the lesser and greater jihads as spoken of by the Prophet? I want to make sure I clearly understand the finer points of the law."

Aadil felt more than saw an inquiring speculation in the mind of Naveed. *It is as though he can read my thoughts.* It was difficult not to shrink from the knowing eyes.

"Aadil, there is much misunderstanding of jihad. There are those who claim jihad to disguise their murderous hearts. There are also those who use jihad to cleanse their hearts. In its purest sense, it means to struggle with one's self. It is the struggle to personally submit to Allah and, as such, it is a process of purification."

"Thank you Naveed, I am very concerned about distinguishing between the two."

Aadil noted that Naveed's face transitioned into a more somber look.

Naveed added, "Do you not remember the part of the hadith describing Muhammad's return from a battle with the Meccans?"

"Yes," answered Aadil, "they were victorious in battle and exultant in their triumph, but Muhammad cautioned them, explaining that the jihad they had won was merely the lesser jihad. He went on to say that they now had the duty to fight the battles of the greater jihad, the battle within. Many murmured over those two statements."

Aadil hesitated for just a moment but continued, "And that, Naveed, is the reason I have come to you. I have been thinking about the adjudication of cases of violence in our courts which appear immoral or brutal. The accused have often claimed that the acts were committed under jihad, and therefore justified by jihad."

"So you clearly understand that fighting with swords and guns for Islam and our nation is the lesser jihad?"

"I do," said Aadil.

Naveed challenged him. "You also patently accept that the greater jihad is the struggle within."

Aadil cringed slightly. "Yes, just as you have spoken."

Naveed leaned closer to Aadil and spoke in quiet tones. "The concept of jihad is very much abused. Fanatics claim jihad for violence. The peaceful people of Islam accept the greater jihad as the struggle to put off hatred and violence, to treat others kindly, and to be peaceable in their journey to paradise."

Considering Naveed's statement, Aadil asked, "Then how do I approach this subject in my court?"

Aadil focused deeply on the eyes of his mentor. *I must understand the lesson that I am about to receive.* His focus was met with something just short of a look of warning. The moment was drawn out by Naveed, and Aadil felt the weight of the warning.

"With infinite care, my dear Aadil. You must apply all the wisdom of your life to judge these cases. There are those who claim jihad to excuse their violence, and there are powerful people who support violent jihad, no matter the consequence. You must analyze and identify the violent parties and from whence they receive their power. You must remember that the law of Sharia exists to support peaceful justice, but also consider that the interpretation of jihad is an important deliberation in adjudicating the Law. There will be guilty parties, worthy of conviction that you should not convict. Watch, learn, and discern the political landscape surrounding those before you. Your personal sense of well-being will depend, in some cases, upon adjudicating strictly by the law. In other cases, you're safety may require a more lenient position."

Aadil's mind spoke, but his lips remained silent. *It is as I thought, some who should be convicted will not be convicted. The order of power is not always with the jurists but with those who rule.* Aadil's quiet thoughts hadn't interrupted his focus on Naveed, but they appeared to have been sensed by Naveed, whose countenance became even sterner.

Aadil held his tongue, encouraging Naveed to continue. The tactic worked.

"It is important that you infallibly learn the background relationships before rendering judgments. The powerful, yet lesser, jihadists are too often intolerant of those who oppose them. Tread carefully when adjudicating jihad. There will be times when your very life may be at risk."

Aadil treasured up the words of Naveed. He had begun a new journey, and he wanted to serve Allah most faithfully; but he also wanted to survive.

2:9 ⟫⟫ 1993 – Risk and Reward

Anton Pipenko's feet rested on the edge of his old metal desk as he leaned back in his chair. A feeling of satisfaction swept through his heart. He closed his eyes and thought about his old position in the Rocket Troops and Artillery Branch of the Soviet Ground Forces. After the Soviet breakup, his Ukrainian superiors had given him even more important responsibilities: to safeguard the entire Ukrainian nuclear arsenal. He had a tremendous number of nuclear artillery shells in his care, along with bombs and missiles. They were very safe; safe from everyone but Anton's personal access and greed. His steadily increasing foreign bank account was evidence of his new opportunities.

Anton knew he had a flaw, but he didn't care. The former Soviets, and now the Ukrainians, had failed to identify his flaw, but The Kahn's network had discovered his penchant for riches. His sense of national duty and his moral compass were overcome by the promise of wealth.

Anton also felt great trepidation as he delineated the details of his last two missions. The current and final missions were considered so dangerous that The Kahn suggested Anton retire from his acquisition duties. Anton salivated over the promised payment.

But that is only fair, don't you think?

Anton was taking a monumental risk in exchange for a nearly unthinkable sum of money. His life would be put in deadly peril, but the lure of a lifetime of ease was too compelling to resist. Of course, after retirement, Anton knew he would be watched. The task of the network mercenaries was not limited to mayhem and death. They were also used to protect information. In this case it was the information in Anton's mind. He would never be allowed to share that information. At the slightest hint of treasonous activity, he would be terminated without consultation. He knew the ultimate risks.

Anton's carefully plied incentives worked miracles in the movement of information and misplaced armaments. Using his access to personnel, logistical records, and armament locations, he offered significant bribes to complicit subordinates.

Anton partitioned his personal activities in the execution of his last two thefts. Both were important but the dangers were very different. He decided to participate in the less perilous of the two. He delegated the more dangerous task to other trusted associates. They would manage the theft of two nuclear warheads, a theft so secretively planned that it was never written down. It was highly compartmentalized and never openly discussed.

For his own mission, Anton used, as his pawn, a trusted subordinate who had constant and legitimate access to tactical nuclear weapons. The weapons of interest in Anton's mission were nuclear artillery shells. The artillery shells, with small nuclear yields, had been planned for use in battlefield scenarios with the Soviet version of the American self-propelled Howitzer, the 2S7 Pion.

The Pion carried four 203 mm ZBV2 projectiles in its belly with a supply of additional shells in an accompanying transporter. Each shell was capable of a one Kiloton nuclear blast. The nuclear projectiles were ideal for the purposes of The Kahn. They could be easily dismantled, hidden, and transported. The nuclear contents could be used to make multiple dirty bombs.

The eight-inch wide tactical artillery shells were stored in crates of four on large pallets. Anton calculated that during the inspection process, the pallets could be restacked in a way that hid the absence of the stolen crates. Several stacks of pallets were arranged with fork-lifts to conceal two missing crates of four nuclear artillery shells. Each shell was nearly three feet long, eight inches in diameter and weighed 260 pounds. Anton, using the guise of management duties, kept other people away from the projectiles while his now wealthy subordinate kept an eye on the re-arranged pallets, at the same time hiding the now "misplaced" shells.

There were several aspects of the plan where there was a danger of discovery. One was the transfer of the nuclear shells into two heavy duty containers. The containers had been sitting in the facility for over six months. They were stenciled with simple words that described non-nuclear shells for the Ukrainian 2S7 Pion. They appeared to have been misplaced and sat waiting for relocation to their proper armory. Chaos and bribes allowed for such errors and delays.

The relocation priority of the two containers labeled "Conventional Artillery Warheads" was low. They became a familiar fixture, both wearing layers of the dust of unimportance. Under their wooden skin, each container included a layer of specially woven lead and fiberglass material. Once the nuclear projectiles were placed into the containers and covered with the woven lead material, the emitted radiation was no longer sensed by outdated and ailing radiation detectors.

One day the layer of dust was disturbed and the crates became important enough to be moved. Loading the two large containers into the specially selected transportation was another point of danger. At any time security could ask to see the contents, since non-nuclear shells were an unlikely stock at a nuclear facility. But Anton's bribes helped to reduce the risk.

A medium-sized truck, driven by Anton, left the facility in the evening just as darkness fell. The final transfer would take place in the cloaking secrecy of the black of night. Anton mused: the darkness seems a fitting backdrop for the passing of stolen goods, hidden payoffs, and ominous secrets.

Anton drove the truck to the prearranged transfer location. Of all of the arrangements, this was the most dangerous. Even though he had already received great sums of money intended as bribes for his accomplices, he now faced the moment when he would exchange the artillery shells for his final payoff. Sweat beaded on his forehead from an acute awareness that the enterprise could be a sting sponsored by the American CIA.

Anton arrived at the address of a nondescript block building. He had been issued a numerical code necessary to unlock and enter the secure structure. It had no windows and only one heavy steel door. He climbed out of the truck and entered the code. Large industrial electric motors opened the great door, pushing it laterally along the outside of the building. The code worked. He looked inside. It was very dark. Nervously, he returned to the truck and drove inside the building. Motion-activated lights came on. After he and the truck had cleared the doorway, it slowly closed behind him. There was no turning back.

He had been directed to drive the truck over what looked like a lube pit designed for large vehicles. Without a spotter, he did so with extreme care. At the same time, he searched the building corners and ceiling for signs of danger. The building appeared to be unoccupied, but Anton was not unintelligent. He knew that by some means he was being observed, if not directly, then by some type of electronic surveillance. His hands trembled and sweat tracked down this face, neck, and back as he turned off the key. While he worked, he surveyed the building. As promised, there was another truck in the building, an exact duplicate of the one which Anton had driven in.

Anton opened the cab door, carefully exiting the truck. His knees wobbled as the weight of his trembling body settled onto them. Despite his sweating flesh, his mouth was dry, his breathing rapid and shallow.

The sensors buried in the walls and ceiling recorded much about Anton. Infrared images displayed readings, highlighting his state of mind and body. His sweat-soaked shirt appeared cooler on the monitor screen. Had he been carrying a weapon, it would have been detected.

Unknown to Anton, the building was equipped with a defensive weapon. The propane heater concealed canisters of noxious gas that would quickly disable and kill, should the need arise. Blissfully unaware of the noxious gas, Anton worried that the second truck might be hiding security personnel intent on eliminating smuggling rings. He kept his senses sharp, unaware of two entities watching his every action on closed circuit monitors.

After hobbling to the other truck on weak knees, Anton fumbled with the combination lock on the truck's rear door. His fingers could barely operate the mechanism. He started over more than once, his hand/eye coordination faltering. At last the lock opened. This was the moment of truth in which two possibilities existed. He could be stopped cold by the intimidating and deadly barrels of AK47s, or he could be invited into the truck by millions of American dollars, along with gold, in the form of South African Krugerrand coins. His heart pounded in his chest, not knowing which of the two scenarios to expect.

Anton eased the door open. Every sense searched for sounds or smells that might divulge the unseen contents. He turned on his flashlight to illuminate every corner of the truck. When he saw no danger, a breath of relief escaped his lungs so loudly it registered on the acoustic monitors. The adrenalin coursing through his body began to abate, but not willingly.

In the center of the truck, secured to the floor, was a very large roller bag. Once more Anton fumbled with the lock using the supplied combination. Opening the case was another act of bravery. There could be deadly traps set to disable him—or worse, take his life.

His eyes looked upon a scene that caught his breath. There were bundles of money wrapped in plastic—hundreds and fifties and twenties. His heart continued to race as he handled his new found fortune: $15,000,000. It was more than he could imagine and had been the motivation for his last two sales. He would add the sum to his previously banked payments.

There was another bag in the truck; he turned to look at it. The bag, also a roller, had a plastic shell and another combination lock. A little more confidently, he released the lock, but still cringed as he raised the lid. All that glitters is not always gold. The slightly modified axiom ran through his mind, spawned by glinting forms that looked like coins and jewels. In this case, the statement was true, but in a good way; there was more than glittering gold in the case. Accompanying the gold were boxes of both cut and uncut gems along with finished jewelry. He could see diamonds and rubies and emeralds.

The sound was sudden and pierced his being. He dropped to the floor as though shot. Assuaging his horror, he realized it was just a metallic voice.

"Are you satisfied with your payment?" queried the voice.

His thoughts came quickly, but his speech faltered as he squawked an awkward, "Yes," over dry and constricted vocal cords.

"Then per our agreement, you are free to leave. The weight of your delivery truck is exactly as it should be, and we consider your promise fulfilled."

Anton hadn't considered how his very illegal load would be confirmed as authentic. They had done their homework. The confirmation was comforting, but he was well aware that additional certainties would be established within minutes of his departure. His mind raced forward, screaming that he was still not safe, demanding that he leave the building immediately. He politely asked, "Then I may leave now?"

"Yes, you're free to go. Remember you are to secure your proceeds then take the truck to the specified location."

Anton wasted no time climbing into the cab of the truck. The building door that had slid closed after entry was opening again. Gratefully, the truck started at the first turn of the key. The clutch worked and the transmission slipped into low gear. His body stiffened as thoughts of an explosion raced through his mind, but none came. With only a small lurch the truck was moving toward the door, which he cleared in seconds. As he looked into the mirrors, he saw the door close behind him. He felt an additional wave of relief when it reached its fully closed position.

Anton opened the window. He felt stifled and his body was overheated. The fresh air and his sweat soaked clothing cooled his flesh and began to settle his nerves. The longer he drove the more his nerves calmed. The fight or flight chemicals began to break down in his muscles and organs. His breathing became regular and he felt the pall of fear dissipate.

At length he arrived at his destination. No location was completely secure, but he had rented a storage facility to which he backed up the truck. He had reconnoitered the complex facility and knew where the security cameras were. He maneuvered the truck into a position that obscured the unloading. With some struggle he wrestled the two bags of cash, gold, and jewels into the storage facility. He opened the bag with the cash and began to fill his pockets with twenty and hundred dollar American bills. In the process, he was surprised to find cash from his native Ukraine. He returned the American cash and loaded up various denominations of Hryvnia, realizing that he would need Ukrainian money long before he completed the movement of his new fortune to more secure investment houses.

He hadn't thought of asking for Ukrainian currency for immediate expenses. It was a nice touch and a wave of appreciation mixed with relief swept through his body as he closed the storage door and climbed back into the truck. Anton considered the reputation of The Kahn and became even more convinced that despite the darkness of his operations, customer service was a valued principle. Every detail had been considered and acted upon.

Once more the truck started and moved with efficiency as he drove out of the access road and onto the main highway. Anton watched his mirrors as he drove down the road. Pricking his interest, two cars came up quickly behind him. His senses heightened as he nervously watched them. The minutes seemed like hours as they followed closely behind and sweat began to flow again. Suddenly the lead car shot into the oncoming lane, passed him and quickly pulled into his lane. The second car quickly followed the first but slowed down as it pulled alongside his truck. Anton watched nervously, feeling hemmed in, and his mouth became dry once more. The window of the second car began to roll down. Having seen many gangster movies, he nearly drove off the road, expecting violent flashes from a machine gun barrel.

At first he didn't understand what he was looking at. What was this danger he faced? It didn't compute. His mind finally interpreted the unexpected scene. With great relief he saw two full moons projecting through the rear side glass of the car. A blond face appeared in the front window. She thrust of a bottle of vodka out of the window and yelled, "Гарного дня!" Before he could react, the car accelerated away, matching the speed of the first car. He watched both cars speed down the road, yielding tears and laughter as a response.

Have a nice day. He repeated the woman's directive in his mind. His final relief came when the unbridled thrill-seekers made a turn in another direction. With a broad smile, he now shouted the young woman's wish, "Have a nice day!"

As the excitement melted away, Anton became a solitary figure in a lone truck on a dark highway involved in a dark plot that appeared to have been successful. In the realm of darkness, he strained his mind to imagine a beautiful sunlit beach in the tropics. He preferred the South Pacific. His vision called up a place of peace and rest, an abode of comfort, luxury, and security. *Security,* he thought. *I wonder if I will ever feel secure. Stealing and selling nuclear weapons is among the most dangerous endeavors in life. Will I ever feel safe, or will I live a life burdened with fear, continually looking over my shoulder?* All at once he had the feeling that security would never again be his companion.

Anton had been given a final task by The Kahn. He was to submit a report detailing his activities after the delivery. Anton questioned the request, wondering why it was so important. As he considered the events, forming a report in his mind, he began to believe that The Kahn was in the end verifying Anton's state of mind. Anton made a personal commitment to accurately and clearly report each detail in a way that would demonstrate his personal confidence in the promises made by The Kahn, and to communicate his determination to keep the theft secret until he drew his final breath. Anton believed that his security was held in the resolve of his everlasting loyalty.

Independent of the report, Anton's mind considered the matter more intently. *What is The Kahn going to do with these artillery shells? And what is he going to do with nuclear bombs? The Kahn has spent a lot of money and we all have taken huge risks.* Over and over he pondered and spoke aloud, "What are the purposes of The Kahn?" After one too many questionings, he remembered his personal commitment and determined to let the questions rest, to be forever unanswered.

2:10 ⟫⟫ 1993 – A Moment of Terror

After the truck cleared the building and the giant door was locked, an air of safety prevailed. The whir of an electric motor initiated a system that lowered the truck to the floor of the so-called lube pit. The back wall started moving and declined away from the rear of the truck. Within moments a fork lift reached into the truck extracting the containers on their pallets. The fork lift, maneuvering in the small space, rested the pallets on the floor.

There were only two team members—Malkan and Deshi. Disassembly began immediately. Malkan was the lead man. The materials were dangerous, and the triggers could be fickle. Deshi, doing most of the work, but supervised by Malkan, tried to control a trickle of sweat that began to run into his eyes. He desperately needed to wipe his forehead but his hands stubbornly continued to grip the mechanism. The oozing sweat was stinging his eyes, and he was losing focus. He looked up at Malkan who could see his predicament. Malkan pulled a handkerchief from his pocket and began to wipe Deshi's forehead. That helped, but Deshi's eyes were still burning.

"Malkan, I cannot see. The sweat is blinding me. You must take hold of the nuclear materials while I wipe my eyes. If I proceed, I may kill us both."

Changing positions was tricky since the trigger was still connected to the nuclear materials. Both were Muslims and neither wanted to meet Allah that day. Deshi watched patiently as Malkan steadied himself, carefully wrapping his hands around the devise so Deshi could release his grasp.

Deshi wasted no time wiping his eyes, but the stinging was intense and it was taking time to relieve the burning.

"Hurry up," pressed Malkan.

"I am," cried Deshi. "It hurts and I can't see."

While Deshi was nursing his own burning eyes, he didn't notice the trickle of sweat forming on Malkan, but Malkan became vocal about his own predicament, "Come on, hurry up. I'm sweating, too."

Deshi was finally able to comfortably see again and turned back to Malkan. Unexpectedly Malkan's fingers slipped and the device fell with a thud. It was resting awkwardly, partially in its cradle. Deshi flinched, expecting to feel the fire and concussion of a nuclear detonation—none came.

Malkan swore a Chechen oath. He couldn't let the device rest in the artillery case for even a moment. The triggering mechanism was out of place, and the wrong jostle would send them both to paradise. Deshi reached in to lend a hand. The sweat began to seep into Malkan's eyes.

He cursed again, deriding himself for his folly.

Malkan commanded, "You put your hands under both ends of the device to support it. I will reposition my hands to get a better grip, and we will, together, lift it back up."

After Deshi gained control of the ends of the device Malkan let go and wiped his sleeve across his forehead and eyes. After clearing his vision, Malkan reached out, once again, to help Deshi remove the nuclear material. Long seconds passed as they carefully pulled the material away from the case and trigger. In near unison, they sighed with relief as the material cleared the casing. While Deshi held the material, Malkan released the triggering mechanism, and disconnected the wire leads. Deshi turned around to a work bench and set the device on top of it. He turned back to Malkan who was showing the birth of a wan smile. Deshi's face broke into a big smile and the two men hugged, kissing each other's cheeks, grateful to be alive.

The moment of celebration was short lived, however. There were seven more shells to disarm and separate. Without incident, the nuclear material in the other shells was removed and secured, both men sporting cotton bands around their foreheads to protect their eyes. The radioactive materials, each rated at one kiloton, were loaded onto a specially built self-propelled cart. There were eight devices all together; and there would be hell to pay at the armory when the missing shells were eventually noticed. Malkan hoped he would be long gone before the discovery and an investigation, which would surely be quickly initiated.

Malkan commanded Deshi to move the cart. He maneuvered it around the small space and into a tunnel. The loaded cart began creeping down a long tunnel. Deshi was the driver, and Malkan watched the edges of the cart, keeping it away from the earthen sides. The large pneumatic tires moved easily over the musty earth. After moving down a slight grade of 150 yards, they reached another door. The secure door was unlocked and the cart drove inside.

This second building was positioned just over the brow of a small hill and set into the hillside, out of sight from the first. This became the escape point, just in case authorities were watching the first building. A second forklift moved the pallet from the cart to the bed of a light duty van. Within minutes the load was secured. Malkan climbed into the passenger seat. Deshi, sitting behind the wheel, started the van and drove it away from the building. He steered the van down a gravel road to the base of the hill. Finally, Deshi pulled onto a highway and the van was quickly on its way. All appeared to have gone well.

2:11 »»» 1993 – Safe Keeping

The Kahn felt confident that he had out-witted the great intelligence services of the West, including the Mossad, and the Russians. He believed that they knew nothing of his priceless acquisition of the two nukes. The two buildings where they had transitioned the eight nuclear artillery shells would be temporarily abandoned but also watched from afar. Should they remain secure they could be used again. If not, they would be completely abandoned and considered to be the cost of doing business.

The worth of the nuclear warheads was far greater than the value of the eight artillery shells, even considering the large payment to Anton. They were next transported to a location near Odessa, Ukraine to a facility where they would be stored.

The production of the sixteen dirty bombs, two per artillery shell, was an entirely different matter. His plan included holding them until a time when they would satisfy his specific needs. The holding place was a secure room deep in the bowels of a storage facility filled with rare and collectible cars owned by a very wealthy but uninformed Muslim benefactor in the port city of Varna, Bulgaria. The facility was perfect. Temperature and humidity were both meticulously controlled to preserve his multi-million dollar collection of automotive rarities. Though innocently owned, an employee and network member controlled the clandestine use of the facility. The chamber was lined with lead to prevent exposure or discovery. The pallets labeled "Car Parts" were positioned next to another labeled "Transmissions." The two containers would rest in this protected and unsuspicious place until their time of need. The Kahn felt that his treasure would be safe from prying minds.

The banking arm of the network paid out over thirty million dollars for the acquisition of the bombs. In addition to the $15 million paid

to Anton, there was also the cost of bribes, transportation, and concealment. The Kahn had been in business for more than fifteen years.
His cash flow was immense, his investment holdings vast, and his cash
stockpile was substantial; but despite his resources, stealing and holding
the bombs would make quite a dent in his cache of cash.

CHAPTER 3
STEPS IN THE SAND

3:0 ⟫⟫ 1993 – A Long Sought Promotion

Captain James Anderson had been serving as an Executive Officer (XO) on an attack submarine known as a Hunter-Killer. They acquired this name due to their mission—to hunt and track enemy ballistic missile submarines. Should the need arise, the hunter becomes the killer and the enemy submarine destroyed.

Anderson's performance had been noted as exemplary by the top brass. After three tours of sea duty, he was promoted to captain of a Hunter-Killer where he once again excelled in his duties. His skills were so well-developed that he was eventually assigned as an XO on a ballistic missile submarine, the very type on which he had been trained to hunt and kill. Recently returned from a tour of duty, Anderson had received orders to report to Admiral Holloway.

James Anderson calmly entered the office of Admiral Holloway. Anderson was not easily intimidated. Standing in front of a commanding admiral was just part of the job.

"Captain Anderson, you've served long and well."

"Thank you, sir."

"You've been an exemplary XO on one of the most valued ships in our fleet."

"Thank you, sir."

Anderson appreciated the compliment. *Where is this leading?*

"You've long sought to be captain of our most highly valued ships, true?"

A tingle swept up and down Anderson's spine. *Could it be?* The thinnest form of a smile, almost imperceptible, began to form on his face.

The Admiral smiled broadly and simply said, "That day has come."

The synapses of Anderson's brain flashed a message that only he could hear. It was the culmination of a lifetime of work.

"Your ship is the USS Concord. She is one of our best. I expect you to make her *the* best."

Captain Anderson's mind salivated at the thought. "I am honored to be chosen, sir."

"Who do you want as your XO?"

"There is only one officer for me, Admiral. Andrew Jameson."

"I will make it so."

Leaving the admiral's office, Anderson felt as high and exhilarated as the fly boys who had just launched from a carrier deck, shedding the bonds of Earth and shrieking into the heavens, and he wondered: *how is it possible to be high on the idea of skulking under the surface of oceans, avoiding every chance of detection with the goal of hiding from a sea battle?*

He could hardly wait to tell Jameson. The dreams they had envisioned in the Brass Lamp so many years ago were coming to fruition. He and Jameson would make the USS Concord the lynch pin of MAD: Mutual Assured Destruction.

His mind dwelt on Jameson, his longtime friend. They had shared so many life experiences. Now they could share them in the same sub. In his mind, he proposed that there had never been, nor would there ever be again, a team like Anderson and Jameson. In that moment he coined their nickname: MAD MEN. The future would be protected through Mutual Assured Destruction by Mutually Engaged Numskulls—MAD MEN.

His could not contain his grin, and he nearly danced as he made his way back to his car.

3:1 ⟫⟫ 1994 – Michael's First Publication

Dr. Michael Benson, driven by his childhood mantra of "How and Why," received his first PhD at the age of nineteen. Though easy for him, he understood that for many students, physics was beyond their understanding. So he felt compelled to develop a better method of teaching physics. In particular, he hoped to help the world gain a better understanding of space-time and Einstein's famous equation: $E = MC^2$.

Michael seriously considered a troubling situation. There were few people who understood the ramification of space-time. Most people equated Einstein's famous energy/mass equation with nuclear bombs, rarely surmising the real genius in the equation. He also knew they seldom questioned the phenomenon called gravity. Quantum mechanics was like voodoo to the greater population. It was also unusual to find individuals in the general population who pondered the differences and similarities between large bodies of mass, like planets and suns, and the fundamental particles that make up atoms. His awareness of the great scientific voids in the minds of most people became the basis of his concept and creation of a book designed for non-scientists. His goal was to help these non-scientists understand complex scientific principles.

He had scheduled a meeting with the Dean of the California Institute of Technology. In the quiet office of the Dean, Michael felt intimidated. Though a genius, Michael was only nineteen years old and in awe of the esteemed professor of science.

"So how can I help you, Dr. Benson?"

"Sir."

The Dean stopped Michael before he could say more.

"Knock off the 'sir,' just call me Ed."

Despite his nomenclature, the Dean's office simply did not convey the trappings of an "Ed." The massive oak desk, a score of certificates and wall plaques, photographs with important politicians and celebrities, and shelves filled with scientific publications all inhibited Michael's willingness to simply call the man, "Ed."

"Sir, ah—ah—I mean, Ed, I have an idea that I believe will help younger students grasp scientific concepts that they struggle to understand. I believe it could help us bring more young minds into the sciences."

"Okay, let's hear it."

"Sir," Michael felt his face flush. It took him a few seconds to begin.

"I'm sorry, Ed, I'm proposing a different way to teach some of the more advanced scientific principles. I'm proposing a text book filled with 3D holographic images."

Puzzled, the Dean asked, "How will that help?"

"As you know, for many years we presented illustrations of atoms and electrons as if electrons were planets orbiting the sun. We've tried to adapt better methods of teaching but haven't found the sweet spot."

Michael hoped that Ed, whom he noted from the photos on his walls was an avid golfer, would understand his reference. Apparently Ed had understood.

"Go on," he said.

"What if we used holographic 3D images to convey three-dimensional probabilities of electron movements within an atom as students peer through 3D glasses while moving the book into various positions?"

The Dean's face took on a look of intrigue.

Michael continued, "That principle could be used to present a great variety of movements and events at the sub-atomic level. And I'd like to add another detail. The Internet is a wonderful invention, but it is still embryonic. Oh, it's great for universities and government institutions but is of little use to the public. What if we designed animated graphic presentations that complimented the text and 3D illustrations in our books? Students could log onto the Internet, enter special URL addresses, and hear audio explanations, or see audio/visual presentations."

Michael held for a moment. He wanted the idea to penetrate the obviously interested mind behind the massive desk.

"Do we have the technology?" the Dean asked with a furrowed brow.

"No sir, not really."

Sitting up with both elbows on his desk, the Dean asked, "Can we develop it?"

With just a slight hesitation, Michael answered. "Yes, I think so."

Michael watched the Dean's face transform into a smile. His own face began to flush.

"Relax Dr. Benson. You know, you may have a good idea here. Even though our department or even the university may not have the money necessary to fund the project, it's possible we could bring a consortium of universities together. We could also seek private donations."

With a look of hope, Michael could only manage, "That would be great, sir."

"Dr. Benson, you may live up to your genius billing yet. Not only are you smart, you have the sense of an educator. That's an uncommon trait among your colleagues. Work it up. Let's see what happens."

The genius of Michael's book was his youthful perspective. Though a literal genius, he could still view life from the eyes of an older teen. He understood the *cool* factors that young college students often latched onto and was confident in the success of this new educational tool.

The project and book became a success beyond his imagination.

3:2 ⫸ 1994 – OPLAN 5027-94

It was a tense day. The President of the United States was seated in the Oval Office. The Secretary of Defense, Secretary of State, Director of the CIA, and all the Joint Chiefs sat solemnly as the President agonized over a new variant of OPLAN 5027. The new Operations Plan stipulated strategies between the United States and South Korea to prevent or stop an invasion by North Korea.

The 1994 variant of the plan called for flights of cruise missiles and F-117 stealth fighters to destroy a small nuclear reactor at Yongbyon, North Korea. The United States hoped to stop North Korea from developing nuclear technology.

President Bill Clinton surveyed the faces of his vitally important administration members. At last he asked the question critical to the purpose of their meeting, "What will North Korea do if we take this action?"

The Secretary of State spoke first, "We believe it will almost certainly bring war. The North Koreans will not acquiesce to such an attack. Our interests in South Korea will certainly be jeopardized."

President Clinton sought the eyes of the Secretary of Defense, "What do you think?"

"I am not as certain as State that we'll have war, but there certainly is a risk. I am not concerned about North Korea attacking anything more than the South Koreans and our assets there, but China is another matter. There could be all kinds of repercussions from the Chinese, and they could hurt us."

"Okay, CIA. I know your Korean sources are not aware of this plan, but can you give us a feeling for the political terrain in North Korea?"

"Sir, you are correct. I can't provide a response to an unstudied plan, but I can say that Mr. Sung, the North Korean Premier, is as intransigent as ever. I believe that he would find some way to respond and an attack on South Korea is most likely."

The President turned to the Chairman of the Joint Chiefs of Staff, giving him a nod.

"Mr. President, we cannot say for certain what the response of the North Koreans will be, although my bet is that they will not lay down. However, we certainly have the means to thwart anything they can throw at us. Our plan includes the pre-positioning of additional troops in South Korea. They will be at an acceptable level of risk. We will also have long range bombers in South Korea, plus we'll have positioned another carrier group nearby. We estimate that the loss to both sides could top a million and a half people if North Korea were to respond militarily. It is very likely, if this breaks into a ground war, that they'll have Chinese advisors at the least, and Chinese troop support at the worst. But Mr. President, whatever their response, we can counter it."

"Would that be the worst of it?" queried Clinton to no one in particular.

The Chairman of the Joint Chiefs added, "One possibility is that as we are building up our ground troops and putting an additional carrier group on station in preparation for the strike, North Korea might see the action as inflammatory, which it will be, and they could launch a first strike, citing the need for self-preservation."

President Clinton nodded his head. "And if I were them, I'd feel the same way."

Considering the possibilities, the President seemed to come to a mental conclusion. Then he asked, "State, what is former President Carter up to over there?"

"As you know, he's gone to North Korea as a citizen, not as a representative. He hopes to improve relations with North Korea."

"I wish he'd stay out of it," retorted the President.

The President fidgeted uncomfortably in his chair while taking another look around the room. Let's table this for an hour or two. Be prepared to meet with me again on short notice."

Before the two hours were up, the President received a call from Jimmy Carter.

"President Clinton, I have some good news."

Clinton doubted it but asked Carter to proceed with his good news.

"Kim Il Sung is willing to negotiate. I think we can work out a plan to freeze their nuclear development. In return they'll want some concessions. They'll need some way to meet their growing energy needs."

After the call, President Clinton asked the Secretary of State to immediately begin negotiations with North Korea. He was pleased with the end results of the negotiations. It included a halt to the construction of a nuclear reactor that could produce weapons-grade plutonium. In return the United States would allow new oil imports. The United States didn't reveal OPLAN 5027 to Kim Il Sung. It would likely have changed the tenor of the negotiations.

Former President Carter was also pleased with the results and issued a public statement, "I look upon this, this commitment by Kim Il Sung, as being very important."

3:3 ⟫⟫ 1995 – White House Briefing

It was one year after the agreement with North Korea. President Bill Clinton had two items on his agenda. The first was North Korea and their promise to stop construction of the reactor at Yongbyon. The second was the development of Iran's nuclear program. Clinton had asked members of his administration to review the history of Iran's nuclear development. His Chief of Staff had taken the reports and compiled them into one brief. Those who had written the reports were in the room, should there be questions, but the Chief of Staff, Darren Stevens, was to present a combined report.

The briefing was given in the Oval Office. An invitation to the Oval Office was a two-edged sword. It was exhilarating to be with the President in a room rich in historical significance. Most of the critical decisions had been made in the Oval Office. Many a president had paced the floor, knelt in prayer, or leaned back in the chair of Presidents to contemplate the decisions before them. The trappings of the room were intimidating and intoxicating. Every person in attendance had hoped to find recognition in the eyes of the President, but there was also great pressure to get it right.

"Mr. Stevens, I don't want to put you on the spot, but before we cover Iran, let's talk about North Korea."

Rolling with the punch of a different topic, Chief of Staff Stevens began with North Korea.

"Mr. President, we continue to monitor North Korea. Our satellite monitors have given us the best look. It appears that construction has come to a halt. However, the consensus of the reports indicates that the stoppage is only temporary. Our people believe that North Korea will begin construction again."

The President responded with, "I don't think we can trust them. State, I specifically want your opinion."

The Secretary of State quickly spoke up, "The attitude of Kim Il Sung has not changed. I can't see him giving up that reactor permanently. I think it is just a matter of time and we'll see new progress on the reactor."

The President asked a general question to the rest of the administration heads, "Does anyone else want to add anything?"

It was the Chairman of the Joint Chiefs who spoke up, "My bet is a renewed effort to finish the reactor, Mr. President."

"As for North Korea, thank you all for your candor, and I'll say that I concur with you all. Just one year ago, we gave them concessions, and it looks like they will not abide by their promises. Okay Darren, let's have your Iranian history recap."

Chief of Staff Stevens began again. "There were, and are still, many complicit beliefs and actions that have brought Iran to its current state of development. It took the actions of multiple nations to spin the world into this condition. 'Atoms for Peace,' first uttered by President Dwight D. Eisenhower in 1953, was the initial effort made by the United States to assist other nations in the development of peaceful nuclear programs. Nuclear power generation was the goal. The results were not as expected."

"I knew we could find a way to blame the other party if we looked hard enough," quipped the President.

The statement was made in jest but taken seriously by some in the room.

Stevens continued, "The atomic era of Iran began with the coup deposing the Prime Minister and installing the Shah of Iran. Knowing that oil supplies were finite, the Shah became determined to establish a network of nuclear electrical power-generating plants. He believed that oil was too valuable to burn and should be used as a raw product for manufacturing plastics and other petroleum-based products. Electrical power should come from a practically infinite source— nuclear power. All of that changed when the Shah was deposed."

"Actually that's not a bad idea. Let's keep that in mind as we consider future policies," said President Clinton.

Clearing his throat, Stevens continued, "The Iranian program went through many ups and downs. Varied nations assisted Iran from time to time. A partial list includes the United States, England, France, Germany, Argentina, India, Pakistan, and Russia."

"An impressive list," stated the President with a smile. "The Who's Who of the atomic age."

"Yes, Mr. President. That list of nations includes all that had successful nuclear programs at that time, except Israel."

After a brief hesitation to see if the President had more to offer, Stevens resumed, "After the revolution of 1979, the world looked more carefully at an Iran, now ruled by what some considered a fanatic clergy. Trust became an issue on both sides. Iran felt rebuffed by the breach of previously held agreements. Money, a form of aid, was given at times, and withheld on other occasions. Distrust followed distrust; Iran didn't trust the world to abide by their agreements, and the world didn't trust Iran's promise to limit their nuclear development to peaceful purposes."

The President interjected, "And who would trust them, given their public position toward the destruction of Israel?"

In response, most of the heads in the room nodded in agreement, supporting the view of their Chief.

Stevens continued once again, "Iran began to experience the loss of world support for their nuclear program, not just in money, but also

technical support. The program suffered through many disappoint-
ments, both for Iran and for the world. Iran found the means to carry
on with help from Argentina, the former Soviets, and now the Russians.
Reacting to the fear of many nations, the United Nations initiated
inspections, hoping to keep Iran's nuclear program within the limits of
peaceful energy generation. That is the broad brush stroke of the matter,
but it does boil down to one constant: Iran doesn't trust us and we don't
trust Iran. It's about that simple."

"Thank you, that does seem to sum it up," replied Clinton.

And with that the briefing ended.

3:4 ▶▶▶ 1997 – A Position of Trust

It was a most unsettling moment.
Soung Jun-Sun had been called by the secretary of the Minister of
Foreign Affairs. He was greeted and directed through a nondescript
office door by a serious-looking young woman who said, "Take a seat
Mr. Soung." Jun-Sun sat as directed, waiting patiently, but nervously.

Soung Jun-Sun had been singled out at an early age to work in the
party bureaucracy. His talent and skills quickly propelled him up the
ladder of success. His duties had varied and after a time he found himself working as an analyst in the Ministry of Foreign Affairs. The work
had been interesting, but never eventful until he was asked to report to
the Minister's office.

As Jun-Sun waited in the office, one with no name on the door, he
looked around the austere space. It was sterile and plain. One very ordi-
nary lamp sat on an aged and scratched metal desk. A single bare light
bulb hung in the middle of the ceiling. Jun-Sun wondered why a department as important as the Ministry of Foreign Affairs couldn't afford a
shade for the lonely bulb. A bookshelf, nearly empty, stood against the
wall behind the desk. He noted the same party posters that hung on the
wall of every cubicle and office anywhere he had ever served.

As he surveyed the familiar posters, Jun-Sun wondered why he had
been called into this particular office. For just a moment, his mind
flashed to the days of his youth and the training he had received from

his father. *Could they know?* It has been just one month since his last report to his American handler.

Jun-Sun dutifully waited in a cheap wooden chair situated in front of the desk. There was but one file on the desk. It had no label, at least not one he could see. Knowing that someone could be watching, he looked cautiously, but covertly toward the file. It was moderately thick. Since only he and the file were in the room, he wondered if the contents documented his life. A bead of perspiration appeared on his forehead. It was less from the heat than from concerned thoughts erupting in his mind. He felt a drop of sweat roll down the middle of his back and began to fear that he was losing control over his emotions. Jun-Sun closed his eyes and breathed deeply.

Why am I here?

Jun-Sun had no answer but knew he had to prepare himself for the worst. He began to take control of the fears that were seeking to ravage his mind. He was, in effect, a man who could be accused of treason. He thought about the self-serving party members who were more than willing to report anyone who appeared to be disloyal. A nice reward might be earned for revealing the activities of a traitor. Jun-Sun thought back to the secret communications he had been sending to his contact in the United States. Every precaution had been taken but there was always a chance of detection.

He subconsciously pulled at his collar. In addition to his personal concerns, the heat in the room was taking its toll. Once more, Jun-Sun worked to settle himself with deep breathing and clearing his mind of all thought when he was jolted by the sudden and jarring opening of the door.

A man quickly walked around the desk and seated himself, his eyes piercing Jun-Sun from the moment his body hit the chair. The man wore the uniform of the North Korean State Security Department. Sternly he began without introduction or pleasantries. He asked pointed and sometimes caustic questions for nearly thirty minutes. Finally, he stopped, stood, and left without a word.

Moments later, a second man entered the room with a demeanor and questions that duplicated those of the first man, but this man was dressed in a suit rather than a uniform. At last the second man finished his questioning. He actually thanked Jun-Sun for his candor and, without fanfare, left the room.

In total the interviews had lasted an hour. Neither man had given his name. They had asked about Jun-Sun's family, his education, his former duties, and his private life. Both interviews were probing. They were an unabashed look into Jun-Sun's life in an effort to determine if he was a faithful party member; or to discover any potential security risk. Questions had begun pricking his mind as the interviews progressed. *Are they suspicious? Is my secret safe?*

Jun-Sun waited once again. Sweat continued to trickle down his back. Although his jacket was stifling, he hoped it was hiding the streak of sweat that must now be showing through his shirt. At last the door opened and the same young woman from before told him to follow her. Jun-Sun arose and followed the her into cool, fresh air and down a hallway to a more formal part of the office complex. To his surprise, he was escorted to a door that read: Minister of Foreign Affairs. The young woman knocked, waited for a reply, and opened the door. She gestured, now showing just a hint of a smile, for him to go in.

Jun-Sun peered in to the office before entering. It was very different from the one he'd just left. It was comfortable, but spoke of authoritarian power at the same time. The walls were covered with pictures of important party members and, of course, a large photo of their beloved Supreme Leader. Most surprising, however, was a name plate that announced the name and position of the man who was perusing the same file that he had seen on the other desk. It was in fact, the Minister of Foreign Affairs. The flowing sweat doubled in production. After several minutes, the Minister closed the file, placed it on his desk and looked up at Jun-Sun, who was still standing.

"Please be seated," the Minister said.

Jun-Sun sat in a plush leather chair and began, once more, to answer questions as proffered by the Minister. His questions were probing but without accusation. He asked Jun-Sun to talk about his family, particularly his father. He wanted details of his father's defection from South Korea. He asked about his education and his personal activities. After thirty minutes, the Minister leaned back in his chair and studied Soung Jun-Sun. His eyes were penetrating; his insight seemed infallible.

It was difficult for Jun-Sun to remain stoic. He was hiding a story that would certainly mean his death if exposed. At the same time, Jun-Sun had a record of achievement and success as a faithful party member and worker in North Korean political circles. He wondered which face would win out: the Communist or the American spy.

At last the Minister spoke, "Soung Jun-Sun, you must be wondering why you are here. I've been reading reports about you and your activities. You have proven to be a valuable asset in the duties of your office. You have been in a position of trust and have proven to be deserving of that trust. You have also shown great talent and skill."

Jun Sun's inward sigh of relief was almost audible, and suddenly the room felt much cooler.

"I have interviewed you because I need a new Under Minister to serve me. You are a highly recommended candidate. Your background has been checked and you are clean of any accusations. As I've spoken to you, I've come to believe that you are the ideal person to serve as my Under Minister."

Jun-Sun was not easily flustered, but was nearly swept away as the words of the Minster echoed in his mind, shadowed by his own thoughts: *I've worked hard. I've sacrificed much and my talent has been noticed.*

Soung Jun-Sun was quickly installed as the new Under Minister in the Ministry of Foreign Affairs. Those close to Jun-Sun knew he had the talent to succeed in his new duties, but many wondered why such a young man had been appointed to such an important position. It was unusual for someone so young to be given this great status.

3:5 ▶▶▶ 1997 – How Have I Come To This?

How have I come to this? How can I do this thing? How can I have this woman stoned to death? Allah will surely choose to spare her life. Aadil dared not speak the words aloud.

It was a question Aadil Rouhani had asked himself more frequently in recent months. He had felt joy in the Islamic Revolution of 1979. The reign of the Shah had been brought to an end, and the Shah's demise should have given the Iranian people an opportunity to experience the freedom of democracy, but Iran had fallen short of that ideal. A new leader had been installed. He had been a Mullah and a Cleric, and now the new Ayatollah. Aadil had come to feel that the battle for democracy and the proper application of the Law had been lost. His disappointment had become deep-seated.

As with so many dreams, Aadil's hope of freedom had fallen into a heap, lying crushed under the wheels of reality. It had been nineteen years since the Shah had been ousted. One oppressor had been removed only to be replaced by another, equal in power but stricter in his tenets. Freedoms once known were taken away. Strict adherence to the Islamic Law of Shari'a became the daily ritual, but not just a ritual; it had become an imperative. Clerics, Mullahs, and Imams ruled society. Those found guilty of breaking the Law of Shari'a could receive up to one hundred lashes or worse. Long prison sentences became common. Serious breaches could result in stoning.

I became a cleric to serve Allah, Allahu Akbar, not to be His executioner.

As a member of the Public Court system, it was Aadil's duty to carry out sentences. As he approached that duty he felt great turmoil in his heart.

A complaint had been lodged by a husband claiming he had found his wife having sexual intercourse with another man. The Law required the testimony of a firsthand witness to justify the full sentence of death by stoning. A second male witness had given his testimony which meant there was no escape for the woman, innocent or guilty.

The woman, bound in handcuffs, was pulled from her cell, her wrists stained with blood from oozing abrasions. She stumbled into a waiting area visible to Aadil and was thrown onto a bench, appearing weary and disoriented as she slumped to her side, hanging on to the last moments of her life.

"Don't be so rough with her," he commanded, as kindness welled in his heart.

Though a rare occurrence, the stoning of a man required that he be buried up to his waist. A woman was to be buried up to her chest. The act of stoning was strictly specified and must be followed to the letter. Rocks had been brought into the courtyard and heaped in a jumbled pile. But it was no common collection of stones. This assortment was special—each rock had been specifically chosen. In the search for the most perfect tools of death, many were cast aside. Each rock was to have enough mass to break the bonds of cloth and skin. The stones must have sharp edges, sharp enough to cut and tear through human tissue. But no single rock could be large enough to singularly exact killing vengeance. The criminal must die in pain and humiliation. It was Aadil's ghastly duty to carry out the sentence for this woman convicted of adultery.

"Is the pit properly prepared?"

Aadil wanted to stall forever but knew he could not.

"Yes, it has been dug to depth and is prepared."

"Please see to her attire."

The criminal had been clothed in a level of decency though the motives were in question. Her body was covered with material that would not completely rip away, yet it offered no protection from the slashing impact of sharp-edged stones.

"She is properly attired."

"Are the witnesses present?"

"They are waiting."

Aadil could stall no longer.

"Call the witnesses in."

Two men walked into the dusty, barren courtyard. Their demeanor troubled Aadil. Rather than mournful, their faces appeared awash in blood lust. They have not come to witness the application of the Law; they came to satisfy their coarse and base desires. They came to see a killing.

"Let us proceed," Aadil quietly commanded. "Bring her before me."

The woman was pulled from the bench, dragged more than walking, until she faced Aadil. Barely able to hold the tears, Aadil looked into the woman's eyes, finding a pleading in them that he could scarcely resist. He reviewed the case in his mind, seriously doubting the authenticity of the husband and his witness, but the weight of their testimony, under Shari'a, was unmovable.

Aadil thought of the three daughters who would be left motherless. He wondered what would become of them. *Will a father, prone to treat his wife in this manner, treat his daughters with patience and kindness? I think not.*

The courtyard was within the walls of the prison. There are but a few prisons in Iran, and Aadil had been given a great and honorable responsibility in fulfilling the sentences of those who were convicted of breaking the Law of Shari'a. The stoning was to take place away from public view. Even though the Law demanded such justice, it was best for people to hear rumors of a stoning, but be saved from the horror of seeing one. Public attitudes were still important despite the great hold of the Imams. The woman was brought into this courtyard, hidden from the eyes of the world, but within the earshot of rancor and rumor. She came to receive justice. She came to receive death.

Though she was to be humiliated, Aadil could barely watch as she was shoved and dragged toward the pit, her lolling head and open mouth evidenced her daze. Aadil blocked his mind from the treatment hinted by her torn and soiled clothing. A criminal guilty of these great crimes had no rights.

A rope was coiled under her arms and she was unceremoniously dumped into the pit. She fell to her knees under the weight of her penalty and the weakness of her flesh. The rope was used to pull her to a standing position. Several men with shovels began heaping dirt about her. Aadil watched the earth as it filled the pit. He saw dust swirl and float, creeping into every fold of her clothing, into each cut, scrape, and scratch. Her handcuffs had been removed, but her hands had been tied to her side, preventing her from wiping the dust from her nose and eyes.

He watched the dust attack her nose and eyes. At first she licked her lips, trying to keep them moist. That effort lasted but a few moments. Aadil imagined that her parched mouth could no longer wet the drying dust. Layer fell upon layer. It pressed upon her legs, her groin, and then her stomach. As the dirt piled about, its press constricted her breathing. She choked and wheezed; even the smallest breath appeared to be a labor.

Under a veil of dust, the shoveling stopped. The hole was now level with the surrounding courtyard. She was buried to her chest. Some required the head to be left bare, a stinging insult to a Muslim woman who had lived a lifetime with her hair covered while in the public view. The bare head stated her value—worthless.

"Cover her head," Aadil ordered. He had the power to do that much at least and intended to keep her humiliation to a minimum.

By Aadil's command, the woman's head was covered in a hijab, which offered little protection. Her face was still an open target for the stones.

"Bring the accuser forward."

The husband stepped forward. His humility before the judge was countered by his hatred toward his wife. He was to throw the first stone. Others were selected to participate, including his witness. They would follow his lead in the stoning.

On the ground lay the pile of carefully selected stones. Some had been used before, bearing the signature stain of blood stolen from a previously assaulted body.

How can we treat this woman in this barbarous manner? She is a child of Allah and deserves more than this, even in her supposed sins.

The condemned woman was once again presented with the facts of her crime and the sentence was repeated. Through the Law, Allah would be avenged, and she was to know of his anger.

"Let the stoning begin."

The first stone found its mark, revealing the bone of her forehead and drawing blood.

Aadil looked away from the woman, to her husband, his face in twisted revelry. Aadil recoiled in horror at the visage of that evil face. *How can one human being treat another with such unbridled malice?*

One by one, the hurtled stones found their mark. Each carried its own destructive force as skin and muscle were torn and bone made bare. As her head slumped to her breast, Aadil could see that the last of her strength was released in a barely audible but rasping moan. Her few remaining tears burned shortened trails down her dusty cheeks. Aadil felt that she must have had a desire to speak out or a need to cry, but neither passed her lips—whether by failing strength or the pride of innocence, none knew but Allah.

"Blessed be Allah, Allahu Akbar," whispered Aadil. Anguish burned within his disturbed mind while watching the bestial treatment and, at the same time, he struggled to appear stoic.

Gratefully, Aadil noted that the woman had lost consciousness. He could see her face turn from twisted agony to calm and blessed peace.

"Allahu Akbar."

Seeing the complete and lasting slump of the torn and blood-soaked woman, he demanded the stoning cease.

"Remove her quickly and take her to the grave." *Surely this is not how things should be. Something must be done to stop such torture, such atrocities, and such gross disrespect for human life. Even the infidels do not impugn the human form with such barbarity. There may be those who deserve such an end but was she one of them?*

Aadil walked sadly to his humble quarters. He could do no more this day. His thoughts drifted back and forth in a tumult he could barely contain.

Yes, Qanon-e Qesas, the Retribution Law demands punishment for crimes against God and against others. A life for a life, as the Law states, but where is the grace? Where is the loving forgiveness and protection that surely emanates from the Greatest of all?

Aadil had serious doubts about the woman's guilt. Yet, the interpretation of the Law left him no choice but to carry out the sentence. The witness of two men, seeing her in a state of adultery, had sealed her fate.

"Two men, two liars," he muttered to himself.

After kicking a stone on the dusty earth, painfully bruising his toe, he thought, *Should a sin against a husband, real or contrived, demand her life?*

3:6 ⫸ 2000 – The Plan

The Kahn sat with the two men who had been part of the plan from the very beginning. Seated in yet another office in a new location, feeling some heat from the Russians in Chechnya, and the Ukrainians, he had set up operations in Bulgaria, near his two nuclear bombs.

"Neg, have we completed the construction of the dirty bombs?"

In a very matter of fact tone, Neg assured him, "Yes, they are now complete. We have sixteen dirty bombs. We were able to make two bombs from each of the artillery shells. Since completing them, they have been moved to another secure location. As our clients make their payments, they will be available. Of course we will need some lead time."

"Khoyer, give me a report of the terror cells."

"There are well-developed cells in both Western and Eastern Europe. Our support has been important to their development. We are working with activists in many other countries, including Yemen, Syria, and Lebanon. We also have very secret operations in the United States and Russia."

"The plan in the United States, tell me how it is progressing?"

Khoyer began again, "There appears to be no detection. The planners are making good progress. Our funds and training have benefited them. They will be ready in 2001."

The Kahn wanted details, "Has a date been chosen?"

"It appears that the trained pilots will be ready sometime in September. This attack will be unprecedented. The Americans will be shocked and hurt by the loss of the financial operations in the World Trade Center. The result will likely create a catastrophic change in American life. The Americans will be sure to react, fomenting even more radical anger among fanatic jihadists."

"Will we be suspected participants in the terror plan?"

"I do not think so. Our efforts of support are well-concealed. No one factually knows that considerable support came from our network. Our contribution has been disguised through people who are not known as members of the network."

It was important to The Kahn that his organization was not suspected as an accomplice in this major act of terror.

The Kahn made no fidgeting movement in his inexpensive office chair. "What of the other nations whose citizens are in the building?"

"There will be extensive collateral losses. Those allied with the Americans will react, but I believe world-wide participation in reprisal will be limited."

The Kahn's pensive eyes maintained their character. He had been laying the groundwork for serious and deadly terrorist actions. Some were direct actions and others were indirect. He considered Iraq, Afghanistan, and Pakistan to have been important fostering nations. They had played vital roles. Fanatic elements in other countries like Saudi Arabia had also been critical. Two more key players were being courted and molded for future use—North Korea and Iran. His long term plan called for the destruction of Israel, and Iran would happily be the destroyer.

As for North Korea, the leadership is so arrogant that given the right prodding, they would likely launch nuclear missiles just to punish the Americans for their presence in South Korea. Their leadership simply wants a recognized place on the world's nuclear stage.

3:7 ▶▶▶ 2000 – Haleema Gains a Friend

Haleema was struggling with her shopping at the market. She was just fifteen and had two children with her; one was walking and the other was in a stroller crying uncontrollably. She was also beginning to show a third pregnancy. She was tired, frustrated, and at her wits end. In her moment of despair, a slightly older woman walked up to her.

"You look like you could use some help," the woman said.

"Oh, thank you! Yes, you may help me."

"My name is Faiza."

"I am Haleema."

So began a fast friendship in the open air of an old, urban section of Tehran, home of the anciently-rooted Bazaar. Faiza was four years older and became a mentor to young Haleema. They came from very different circumstances. Haleema had been poor. Faiza was from a middle-class family. For all but the very wealthy, the market was the great melting pot of Tehran's economic classes.

As fast friends, they often spoke of things that were forbidden in public discourse. Most of their moments together were in the market so they exercised care in their discussions. Nonetheless, Haleema and Faiza often talked with disgust about Reza Shah in their private moments. He was the destroyer. Though his reign of destruction was so many years ago, they were still affected by his callous infamy. They played a little game as they walked through the market. They would pick up a particularly deformed produce item. Faiza would say, "The destroyer did this." It was a safe way to deride the author of their diminished rights. Haleema would retort with a scowl and agree, "Yes, it was the destroyer. May Allah's fury be upon him."

Both young women would laugh and continue through the market.

Haleema and Faiza lived in an old part of south central Tehran, near the Grand Bazaar. Haleema's husband worked in the Bazaar. He was not a merchant but worked for wages.

Haleema knew Iranian history. Though young, she had worked to educate herself. Iranian women living before her had experienced a roller coaster of changes in women's rights. She came to understand that Iran had taken a positive step forward after the Persian Constitutional Revolution of 1905. Persian women began to work in education, journalism, even as authors.

Haleema had learned of a time when women enjoyed some level of freedom through the golden period of the Constitutionalists. She had learned that in 1921, Reza Shah overthrew the Constitutionalists. That rebellion signaled the loss of women's previously protected rights to publish journals. Existing journals were destroyed and women were banned from working groups. She felt contempt for Reza Shah.

But not all of their discussions were about "The Destroyer." The Shah of Iran, though despotic in so many ways, had given some rights to mothers and families. In their private moments, they wistfully looked back to 1962. It had been a good year for the women of Iran.

3:8 ⫸⫸ January 2, 2000 – The Passing

Soung Jun-Sun opened the door to the hospital room. His father, Soung Dae-Ho, looked up and, seeing Jun-Sun, smiled brightly.

"Come to my side, Jun-Sun."

Always the obedient son, Jun-Sun complied. He was grateful to have received notice of the decline in his father's condition. He was now in death's cold and clenching grip. He was thankful to remove himself from the rigors of his work to honor the most noble of all men—his beloved father. At times, Jun-Sun's duties were so consuming that breaking away would have been impossible, but gratefully, not on this day. *Our ancestors look over us,* he thought. *This is the man, of all the men in the world, that I most want to be with.*

"I am always at your side, if not in your presence, then in my mind."

Looking at Jun-Sun, his eyes filled with great love, Soung Dae-Ho said, "You are solace to my departing soul. You validate the reason for my life. You have always been faithful to me and to my ideals. I am honored by your place as the leader of my posterity."

"You give great honor to me, my father. I will strive to be worthy of your high regard."

"I will soon leave this Earth," Dae-Ho said. "With my dying lips I express my confidence in you and ask you to keep the truth of our union. We worked hard to form and nurture that union. Our cause has always been before us."

"I hold sacred our cause. It shall not fail."

"I am at peace, my son. I have done all that a humble worker could have done. I go to my fathers knowing I have been true to them and to myself."

As life passed from Soung Dae-Ho, Soung Jun-Sun thought of the purpose his father had instilled in him. He had listened to the lessons. He had internalized the concepts. With honor and respect, he had sought to follow the life path his father had shown him. He had reached a position of power and prestige where he might affect significant changes. *But what should those changes be? How can it be done? How should it be done?*

He took a moment to contemplate his successful path and the comforts of his position. His personal choices, looming before him, raised questions that required answers, and would, at a future time, demand them. What changes would Soung Jun-Sun, Communist, and Son of Soung Dae-Ho, author? What changes could he inspire?

3:9 ⟫⟫ 2001 – The Storyteller

Less than a year after their first meeting, Haleema and Faiza sat in a quiet spot, chatting, trying to entertain Haleema's young toddler, struggling to control an older toddler, and comforting a babe in arms. They were in a quiet spot, discounting the commotion of the three small children. It was difficult, but they talked about matters important to them.

Faiza opened a new subject in their discussion. "I read that the old Family Protection Law, now banned, gave our mothers some level of legal protection. Family matters could be tried in special family courts."

Haleema looked at Faiza and asked, "What kind of family matters?"

"They dealt with issues such as deeming wives as property, instant divorce, and child marriage."

Haleema's face winced in emotional pain.

"Take you for instance. Your father could not have married you off at thirteen."

Haleema's scowl changed from pain to sadness. She lowered her eyes and said, "I was too young."

Tears began seeping from the corners of her eyes. She dried them on the wrap of her baby. It wasn't hard to love these beautiful little ones, but she had been wrenched from her own childhood and missed the carefree days that most young teens enjoy.

As the daughter of a poor man, Haleema was an early candidate for marriage. Her father felt it necessary to cast her off, by marriage, at thirteen. If she matured and became more womanly, the required dowry would increase. A man would accept a smaller dowry for a girl of thirteen, happily seizing upon an opportunity to raise and train her in his own ways.

Haleema should have benefited from the dowry, which consisted of funds paid to her husband at the time of marriage. But the dowry, deemed to be the bride's in case of widowhood, was taken by her husband, as it often is, for his own purposes.

Ali Aslani married Haleema in 1998. The ways of Ali Aslani included a quick pregnancy. Haleema's first child was a son, born that same year, before she even turned fourteen, and welcomed by Ali. The second child was a daughter and a disappointment to Ali. Haleema had given birth to yet another daughter, all before she was sixteen.

"Haleema, had we lived in 1963, you would still be single. We both could learn, and earn, and write."

Haleema interrupted, "And you do love to write, don't you?"

"Yes, I do," replied Faiza. "My love for writing came from my great grandmother, Bah Amin Shalah. She was at the center of women's rights causes in 1907. It was a time when the Danesh magazine was published.

Protected by the constitution, it was published for women, addressing women's and family issues, excluding political topics, of course."

Faiza looked at Haleema and winked.

Haleema was fascinated by the thought.

Faiza continued, "My great-grandmother was a strong proponent of women's rights. That heritage flowed to her daughter, Shahrzad. Shahrzad made good use of her time in fighting against Reza Shah. In the battle of words, protests, and civic disorder, Iranian women felt a great hope for increased freedom. She passed her passion and skill to my mother Azadeh. Azadeh was an important woman in the overthrow of the Shah of Iran. She blessed me with two of her passions—a love of words and women's rights."

Haleema mentally salivated over the ideas in Faiza's words and responded, "Your family was involved in very great events?"

"Yes, those and more. My mother lived to see the fall of the Shah of Iran. She believed that life might improve; that people might have greater freedoms. She frequently told me about the great hope they felt in those days. In that day of hope, she gave me life. I was born just after the revolution."

Haleema suddenly jumped up, babe in arms, and scrambled away. Her two-year-old boy had escaped, and she had to quickly retrieve him. The recovered boy was forcefully seated by Haleema's side.

Reaching out, Faiza took hold of Haleema's baby and asked, "Shall I tell you more?"

"Yes," replied Haleema, as she gave up her youngest treasure to Faiza.

"Our hopes have been too often dashed. When the Shah of Iran was deposed, clerics became the governing controllers. Islamic women lost many hard won rights. The Family Protection Act of 1979 was repealed. Clerics became the adjudicators of Shari'a Law. Women once again became the repressed commodity of men."

Haleema looked mournfully at Faiza. She felt as one sentenced to a prison term. While tightly holding the toddler and grappling with her oldest, FarZan, she said, "I have no rights." Another tear seeped from her eyes. "The repealing of that law was my warrant to servitude. I cannot attend school. I cannot go to the center of the Mosque. I must wear this clothing or suffer the wrath of my husband."

Again there was a moment of silence while Haleema dried her tears, struggling to keep FarZan from running off again.

Faiza juggled Haleema's baby, freeing up one arm, and placing it around Haleema's shoulder, a pure act of kindness, which Haleema appreciated.

This time the silence was broken by Haleema. In a wistful tone she said, "I would like to write."

Faiza nearly exploded in her surprise, "You would? What would you write?"

Turning her head away with a twinge of inferiority, Haleema softly said, "I would like to write stories."

In an air of excitement, Faiza asked, "What kind of stories?"

Her head slowly turned back to Faiza. "Children's stories. I've been telling children's stories to FarZan at bedtime. They are very simple, but he likes them, and I enjoy making them up."

"Why, Haleema, that's marvelous! I never knew."

Feeling inferior to Faiza, Haleema added, "I don't come from a journalistic family like you do. I felt it hardly worth mentioning."

Faiza juggled the baby once more and placed an encouraging hand on Haleema's arm, "But you must, you must write down your stories."

Glancing downward, Haleema said, "I barely have time to finish my duties, let alone write down my stories."

Haleema was well aware of Faiza's work as a young journalist, and she had secretly read some of her articles in the Zanan. Like its predecessor from eighty years ago, it was a magazine dedicated to women, their opportunities, and matters of health. Above all, it was dedicated to their families. Faiza's next statement was no surprise.

"Then do something about it. Come and join me at the women's rights rally. Help me make a change in our system."

"Oh, there are too many accusing eyes following people to and from such activities," Haleema said. Girding herself in strength from deep within she added, "Besides, I am content. My husband is good to me, and I love my children."

Faiza knew her statement was false and hoped to entice Haleema into involvement. "Can't you imagine a day when we can walk about without restriction?"

"I have little hope for such a day."

Faiza juggled the baby once more, reaching around Haleema with both arms, the baby in the middle. "Come with me, help us, and maybe that day will come more quickly."

Wanting to change the subject and avoid her discomfort, Haleema feigned a sudden realization of the time. "I've got to go. I have to finish my shopping."

"You and your shopping," Faiza said in a smile which Haleema interpreted as taunting.

As Haleema placed her baby in the stroller, she simply said, "Faiza, you have a great desire for your brand of independence. I find mine in the market. I can browse and shop with little fear, and I have joy in these small moments of independence."

Faiza did not give in. "Do you ever read our magazine?" She suspected Haleema's secret reading sessions.

"On no, my husband, as kind as he is, would never understand my interest in the magazine."

Standing, Faiza tried one more time. "So you really are content with your life?"

Haleema did her best to appear stoic. "Yes, I am content."

Haleema also knew there was falsehood in her statement. She had felt the diminishing warmth of her husband. His attitude toward Haleema had become strident, approaching resentment. She was not sure what it meant, but she would give him no reason to promote disdain. She worried that he might look for an excuse to divorce her. No, she could not take the Zanan home to read.

They each said goodbye and went their separate ways. After parting, Haleema guided her children to the market. She had much to do and the day was getting short.

I shall be content for now with telling my stories to my children.

CHAPTER 4
THE EARTH SHUDDERS

4:0 ⟫⟫⟫ September 11, 2011 – Terror

Haleema had finished her morning duties when she heard an urgent knock on her door. Faiza loudly called her name and burst through the door before Haleema could open it.

"Have you heard? A mighty blow has struck the Americans!"

"No . . ."

Faiza could not contain herself as she told Haleema of airplanes crashing into tall buildings; buildings that had burned and fallen to the ground.

As Faiza spoke of the destruction in America, Haleema's thoughts turned in on themselves. Though her ears collected the sound of Faiza's voice, Haleema's sentient being could not process Faiza's euphoric tone.

Without speaking a word she mulled her thoughts. *I take no joy in death and destruction. I take no comfort in destroying a culture that has done more on this Earth for women's rights than any other. I feel no pride in malicious attacks on those who treat women as equals.*

Haleema tried to hide the surprise she felt in her friend's revelry, which seemed to be at odds with Faiza's personal crusade. At length Haleema's thoughts focused on the very purpose for which she praised Allah: we are to be at peace. We are to love those who seek peace. In contempt, she mused over one last thought: *the fanatics of jihad have committed a sin before Allah. They lack an understanding of the true concept of jihad, the holy struggle. One day they will answer to Allah. Insha' Allahu.*

To Haleema, Allah was the greater. Allah was the only God. All others were but prophets and good men. She would practice jihad in her own way, striving to follow Allah and His peaceful path. She would strive to be a woman of peace. No, she found no joy in the pain of the Americans, even if they weren't believers.

Sensing Haleema's lack of enthusiasm, Faiza's visible celebration began to wane. Soon she stopped and Haleema saw that Faiza's focus was now entirely on her. Her demeanor began to change. After a few moments, Faiza sat down. Haleema hoped that her thoughts had been somehow transferred to Faiza.

"Haleema, you take no joy in this event."

Sitting down she said, "No I do not."

Suddenly, a pall of quiet settled into Haleema's home. She watched Faiza sit back in her chair, descending deep into thought. While the quiet reigned, Haleema's mind turned to her son, FarZan. The stories Haleema had been telling him, though simple, were replete with the experiential events of her own life. She wanted desperately to mold her son into goodness, kindness, and with a love for all men. Today's event suggested that FarZan would live through the repercussions of a destructive event that would undoubtedly become part of her future stories.

Then suddenly it hit her like a ton of bricks. Her mind involuntarily exploded with the details of her dreams. Arcing lights and stone towers! *Could this be the fulfillment of my dreams?* Haleema rushed to turn on the TV. The programming on her favorite channel had been interrupted by a breaking news story. She saw airplanes flying into buildings, watched the smoke billow into the sky, and eventually saw the twin towers plunge to the Earth. She looked at Faiza, who seemed to be caught in her own dilemma and watching without a word.

As the video images spun around in her mind and reportage filled her ears, she tried to make sense of it all. There were common elements, it was true, but the images in her dreams were different from the destruction of the World Trade Center.

4:1 ►►►► September 13, 2001 – Trial

Michael arrived in Manhattan on the 13th of September, 2001. He and a companion volunteered to travel to New York to help with the disaster. They left Boulder, Colorado within hours of seeing the second building collapse. They had driven the nearly 1800 miles in just under 28 hours of driving time. Taking turns at the wheel, they stopped only when gas, food, and other essentials required it. Their truck was packed to maximum capacity with all kinds of supplies. Their rate of travel was just over the speed limit, and they hoped that empathetic Highway Patrolmen along Interstate 80 would give them a break. They were trained to drive at higher speeds, but it bothered Michael to drive so fast for so many long hours. As the miles clicked by, needs blunted caution; the most important and immediate goal was to help those suffering in New York.

The scene was a shocking horror to any sensitive human. It was just before midnight when they entered Manhattan, and it looked like a city under siege. The siege was not of artillery and mortars but of large trucks and cranes working to clear broken vehicles and debris. Smashed and torn car hulks were piled one upon another. The crushed carcasses of ladder trucks, ambulance, and police vehicles had been dragged away from Ground Zero and left to collect layers of dust. Firefighters, with their hoses and water, had turned some of the dust into mud. At every point people could be seen working in caked-on mud or dust saturated clothing.

Michael had worked at other disaster sites, but this one was far beyond his experience and imagination. Manhattan looked alive and dead, all in the same moment. Emergency vehicles and rescue workers clogged the streets instead of commuters and tourists. The only businesses open were those that were assets to the recovery. The bustling activities of Manhattan had changed from commerce to survival. National Guard troops carrying M16s guarded locations considered potential terrorist targets. On every wall, on every window, on every pole was a flier with a photo and the words: "Have you seen…?"

The devastation was beyond the scope of what news reports could communicate. Photographs and the all too vivid video broadcasts could not convey the immensity of the disaster. It affected the city in a radius far greater than the debris field.

There was no time to stand in wonder. Michael quickly attacked a mass of twisted and tortured steel buried in pummeled and pulverized concrete. He dug past broken office furniture, smashed machines, and shattered cubicles. Each inch of debris was peppered with shards of broken glass and plastic. There were burnt and blackened materials reeking of incinerated chemicals, including some that looked inhumanly familiar. The sheer volume was astonishing, incomprehensible, and overwhelmingly shocking.

And then there was the dust. It was everywhere and it was stifling. For every pound of solid material there were two pounds of dust: one pound on the ground and one pound in the air.

"I wonder what's in this stuff," was a common question among first responders.

Volunteers had been assured that the air was safe, that it contained no dangerous toxins. In time, investigators realized that 1,776 feet of skyscraper, including 104 stories of fluorescent lights filled with mercury vapor, and tens of thousands of computers made with various heavy metals, along with tons of asbestos, had been pulverized into massive volumes of fine white powder. That powder entered lung after human lung with every breath of air. Each breath contained an elemental fuel necessary to sustain muscle, but poisons piggy-backed the life-giving oxygen, becoming harbingers of ill health and the possibility of future disability.

Michael had brought his own respirator and all the charitably discounted carbon filters they could beg or buy at Boulder hardware stores, but the thick dust soon overwhelmed the very fine filters. New filters were impossible to obtain in the beginning. Simple fiber masks kept the worst of the dust out, but left them vulnerable to the unknown and lurking dangers of microscopic contaminants. Some found it easier to work without filters of any kind. Their efforts required great focus, and most, including Michael, didn't dwell on the dangers.

There wasn't much idle discussion among the rescuers, but when it took place it was inevitably about home, family, and jobs. When asked, Michael said he was a theoretical physicist.

In responsive shock, the burly volunteer looked at him and exclaimed, "You're a physicist?"

"Yes, don't I look like one?"

Remembering a nerdy, frail-looking kid with glasses in his required science class, all the man could say was, "No!"

After a moment of reflection, the man asked, "Do you teach?"

"I teach and I do research."

"Hey Jonesy, we've got us a school teacher here, but not just any teacher, he's a college professor and he teaches physics."

Michael smiled; he knew there was no disrespect. He had been told many times that his profession seemed out of character for a 6 foot 2, well-muscled man.

"He's a whaaaat?"

"Some kind of theorist," chimed a nearby worker.

"He sure doesn't work like a college professor."

Despite Michael's desk job, he worked with the same strength and pace as the burly firefighters. He didn't fit the traditional template of a slight bookworm with a professor's glasses, long hair, and beard. He gained the respect of the rough and tough as he capably worked in the debris field of shattered dreams.

"Give 'em a shovel," another shout resounded. "He can handle it."

As Michael continued to work in the wreckage of Ground Zero, he noted the size and strength of those around him. Most of them were big men. Inside he smiled at them and their awe-filled thoughts of a professor who could work with the same power and stamina as their best.

"Hey professor, how'd you get so big?"

"I wrestled bulls when I was a kid. There wasn't a bull fast enough to run me down or big enough to knock me down."

The retort brought a roar of laughter. It was good to laugh. It spread a healing balm over their emotions.

After the laughter subsided, he added, "Besides, I had the best food and water money could buy: our own. We grew it, we ate it. We drilled for it and we drank it. It was ours and it was healthy.

His statement brought plenty of ribbing about his healthy lifestyle and clean living. And when his new friends offered to buy him a beer, he shocked them by saying he was a non-drinker. It was almost too much for them to assimilate.

"Hey professor, are you religious? I hear all you science people are atheists."

It was a fair question. Many of the men were from Irish Catholic suburbs. Raised in a religious home, Michael had been taught Christianity. He was taught of a Heavenly Father and of His Son, Jesus Christ. Michael willingly accepted those ideas in his early life. He was, however, in his core a seeker of facts which guided him to the sciences. His studies in science complicated his early perceptions and gave basis to his question about God. If there is a God in Heaven, where is Heaven and where is He? His cosmologist friends pointed to the absence of a supernal being in the known Universe.

"Well, I haven't seen God yet so I can't prove that He exists, but I can't prove that He doesn't exist either. The truth: I just don't know for sure."

"That's fair enough but one day we'll have to talk about faith. That's where you'll find your proof."

"How's that?"

The burly fireman continued, "Well, you have to have faith first. You have to believe in something that is unseen but true. If you believe in something that is unseen yet true, it's called faith. If it's true, yet unseen, it can bless you. That's what faith does; it blesses you even though you can't see it or prove it."

"Okay Mr. Fireman, did you say you have a degree in philosophy?"

"No, I just go to church."

"Touché."

The fireman added to the conversation, "So you don't go to church on Sunday, is that right?"

"No, I don't."

"Why not?"

"I guess I'm just too busy."

Michael rested on his shovel for just a moment. The man who asked about church attendance was still working, unaware of Michael's gaze. Michael wondered if his personal rescue efforts were as suitable as going to church. His brand of service, which had been as a volunteer fireman and EMT in his small boyhood town, had put him on a path leading to New York City, to the disaster that had become known simply as 9/11. He mused: I might have been safer if I had gone to church.

The volunteers were doing the hard work of rescue, but the rewards of success were almost non-existent. Michael had learned of that disappointment from their faces and from their discussions. With so few found alive, the job had become one of restoration. It became an undying determination to fight back, to rekindle the life that had been stolen from a great city. Activity was everywhere, but it wasn't the activity New Yorkers were accustomed to. Their activity became the work of rebirth, as the rise of the phoenix. From the carnage, a new city would arise, one that had been smitten but not beaten.

"Hey, you loafer, get back to work. You must not be as tough as you look."

Michael took his weight off his shovel, bending once more into community service, but he had to admit he was a little tired. After a day and a half in the car, his arrival was accompanied with fatigue and mild dehydration. Large amounts of fluids required too many stops. Sleep and water had been sacrificed to arrive in New York quickly. Any rest taken had been on a foam mattress roughly laid over the supplies and under the camper shell in the bed of the truck. The lumpy respites were brief. Michael's powerful body was taxed to a limit that most people could not have endured even before he started his work in the city.

4:2 ⟫⟫ September 14, 2001 – Rejuvenation

As Michael worked into the daylight of the 14th, having arrived just after midnight, he became aware of a commotion off to his right. The ruckus grew in intensity until it was hard to ignore. As he scanned the scene of growing tumult he saw President George W. Bush walking around the corner of a nearby building. The President was being carefully led through the wreckage of Ground Zero by those directing the efforts. While Secret Service agents scanned the area for threats to the President, his escort helped pick the safest paths to navigate the rubble, amid firemen in FDNY coats and other volunteers in their coats of dust. President Bush raised his hand in the air in a thumbs-up salute to the men and women working in the midst of the carnage.

As President Bush confidently walked through the debris field, work stopped and surprise appeared on the faces of the workers. The sight of the President of the United States was thrilling and invigorating. As minutes ticked by, workers began to gather around him. He looked toward a fifty-foot high pile of rubble. His eyes scanned the area with solemn regard and at length returned to the tower of debris. He then changed his focus to those who surrounded him. As the eyes of the crowd were met by the eyes of the President, they sensed his empathetic pride in the body of determined heroes.

The crowd around President Bush grew into a throng. With a fireman's assistance, he stood on a small but stable stage of wreckage. He looked over the gathering heroes as spontaneous cheers broke out. The Commander-in-Chief was in their midst. Surely this diabolical attack would not go unpunished. Gaining a level of quiet, President Bush was compelled to speak the words now immortalized in print and video.

"I want you all to know—that America today—America today—is on bended knees—in prayer for the people—and lives that were lost here—for the workers who work here—for the families who mourn."

"Go get 'em George," someone shouted from the crowd.

With determined sobriety, the President continued, "This nation stands with the good people of New York City and New Jersey—and Connecticut as we mourn the loss of thousands of our citizens."

"We can't hear you!" another voice shouted out. Taking but a second to stop and evaluate the crowd, the tenacity of his resolve increased, showing in his face and in his voice, "I can hear you!"

The volume and energy in the response of cheers and whistles was overwhelming. "I can hear you; the rest of the world hears you . . . "

President Bush looked upon the visible emotions that had been held back through the stressful, maddening, and sometimes depressing work. Grown men, strong and burley, tough and macho-minded, broke into tears. Those tears tracked down dusty faces like rain on glass, giving needed relief in a desert of despair.

The President also saw that the tears were quickly wiped away as spirits appeared to rise up in the strength of unity. He absorbed the determined cheers coming from a crowd of heavily toiling and weary heroes who felt acknowledged and appreciated for their sacrifice. The vocal outcry spoke volumes. These men and women were there to serve and protect. The President knew that the towers had not been protected; the economy and industry of the United States had not been protected. He committed to a new level of service, conceived in that moment, and in subsequent years, to rebuild both buildings and spirits. The President hoped that men and women across the United States would concurrently feel a new resolve to rebuild and protect the great land that they loved and honored.

President Bush wanted to shake hands with these heroes, so after his impromptu speech, he began to walk among them. He felt their commitment as he shook their hands and expressed his love for the devotion that both surrounded and humbled him. Workers once again wiped tears from their eyes. He saw men, normally bold and fearless, reveal tugs upon their exhausted and softened hearts. It was a moment never to be forgotten. The world would experience it vicariously, but for those at Ground Zero, it was a moment when the reality of life struck chords of heartfelt and eternal resonance.

Michael had been watching and cheering and was caught up in the emotion of the moment. As the President Bush began walking through the crowd of responders, Michael realized that he was in the path of the President's travel. Michael was thrilled at the opportunity to be in the presence of the President of the United States. He could see in the eyes and demeanor of this great man the same determination he had felt in past hours. His heart swelled with pride for the great country that he called his own; a country where freedom reigned, where presidents were elected, and where men and women could move freely in the chosen courses of their lives.

Caught up in his own thoughts, Michael was surprised when the President of the United States put forth his hand and expressed his love to Michael. The handshake was brief but powerful. With it came the mighty leverage of three hundred million people who would work together to restore their stolen peace. In that handshake, Michael felt a new resolve to maintain the place of the United States as the most powerful yet benevolent nation in the world. It was an experience that Michael would treasure and from which he would gain great strength as his life coursed into the future.

4:3 ⟫ September 16, 2001 – Another Disaster

The strengthening moment of the President's visit was now history, and time gave way to the demands of the mighty task at hand. After days of arduous labor, both physical and emotional, and while working next to wreckage that towered above the rescuers, a black shadow shot past Michael, heralding an inescapable menace. Thousands of pounds of carnage had shed its restraints, falling around him in thunder and mayhem. A crushing mass of steel and concrete pummeled the wreckage on three sides, missing him but knocking him to the ground with a concussive force. For a moment, his senses were dazed and confused, grasping and reaching for understanding, but the moment quickly passed as his mind made sense of the incident. Lifting his head and peering at the newly fallen wreckage, he thanked God that he had not been crushed. As the dust began to settle, Michael felt unusual warmth on his thigh.

Even a small projectile can seriously damage the soft tissue of the human body. The crushing force of material spewed a shower of debris into the air. One shard of twisted metal had rocketed toward Michael. The splinter of steel hit its mark, the inner part of his upper thigh, with devastating force. His heavy clothing was rent, both garment and flesh vulnerable to the kinetic energy of the destructive fragment. It was over in an instant, and Michael felt no pain, thus no awareness. But jagged metal had sliced through skin, muscle, and tissue, severing a major life-giving artery, disrupting the flow of blood to his leg. His first clue had been the warm flow down his leg. At that moment, Michael knew he was in trouble.

4:4 ⟫ September 16, 2001– Triage

Elizabeth Mitchell began her service in Bellevue Hospital Center, about four Manhattan-miles from

Ground Zero. Arriving one day prior to Michael's appearance, she had endured twenty-six hours of driving marked with limited food and rest stops. She traveled with a team of doctors and nurses in a rented van. Leaving from Houston, they traveled through Little Rock, Memphis, Nashville, Harrisville, and Philadelphia, then into Manhattan.

Liz wished she could have stopped in Nashville. She was an avid country music fan and wistfully considered the excitement of the Grand Ole Opry. But it was not to be. She knew that death and devastation awaited her. She hoped to increase the probability of life and survival.

Her hope pushed thoughts of personal recreation out of her mind. *"And miles to go before I sleep, and miles to go before I sleep."* The immortal words of Robert Frost kept tracking through her mind. There were no woods at the site of the former World Trade Center, only deep darkness, and she had her personal promise to keep, the promise to ease pain and suffering wherever they might exist.

As injured victims, mostly first responders, came through the door of the triage, Liz separated those with acute injuries from those with minor wounds. The seriously injured were treated first. Minor injuries had to wait. The hours were long and the pace had been frantic.

There was so much initial carnage; it was hard to fathom the extent of human slaughter. Liz struggled to process the stories of the first day. Injured people streamed through the door in a seemingly never-ending flow. Days later there were still a number of family members hoping to learn the condition of their loved ones, some gratefully discovering that they were present. Desperate families hoped to find their dearest tucked into a hospital bed. Some were never found. A serious injury became a relief when compared to other possibilities.

The determination of the extent of injuries was not dependent upon nationality, citizenry, age, or creed. The humanity of many cultures had worked in the Twin Towers. Altogether, as one, they had been taken by a great leveler. There was no color or sex, just an injury in need of care. In this pronounced assault, the victim was humanity.

By September 15th the pace had slowed. The most common injuries of the first responders were bruises, cuts, broken bones, dust inhalation, dehydration, and other maladies. Liz felt her heart would burst as the heroes passed through her doors. Some walked but too many entered on gurneys. They were all exhausted, completely worn out. The fatigue had taken its toll and the dog-tired bodies were susceptible to tears, anger, depression, colds, and flu. Liz found that if an injury could be visualized, it would soon pass through the door.

On the 16th, there was a break in the procession of the mangled and maimed. Liz managed to take a break to eat a sandwich and drink a soda. She had taken only a few bites when, as part of an obvious commotion, the doors to the triage unit burst open. "We've got a man with a severed artery here!" shouted the EMT.

Liz noted the bottle of saline hanging above the gurney, the blood soaked gauze and tourniquet around the victim's thigh. She knew the flow of blood must be completely stopped, the artery repaired, and the lost blood replaced. Like so many others meals, the sandwich was left to go stale and the soda to go flat.

He was dirty, his pants soaked in dust-laden blood. Thankfully the tourniquet had slowed the worst of the blood loss. If there anything good about Michael's injury, it was the place where it had occurred, a place among people who knew how to handle trauma. His fellow workers had quickly staunched the flow of blood and, even though the wound was very serious, Michael's life was secure.

The EMTs had focused on Michael's injuries, so dust and grime still covered his face. As Liz waited for Michael to be taken into the ER, she used a sterile wipe to clean him up. He was a mess. His hard hat had been violently swept away in the falling debris, leaving the hair that hung below it totally saturated with dust. Beads of sweat had created rivulets tracking down his cheeks, something akin to the Texan cow trails of her youth.

While Liz gently cleaned his soiled face, she became aware of two beautiful blue eyes looking up at her. Michael's unabashed stare made her blush. Still in a state of shock, he blurted out, "You are the face of an angel."

Liz was caught off guard and hesitated in her response. She was caught in the words of his statement like a deer in a car's headlights. She couldn't speak. *He didn't say that I look like an angel; he said I am the face of an angel.* Liz could barely hold back the tears as she considered this heart-felt compliment and expression of gratitude. She had spoken so much to so many broken bodies that the words had begun to feel trite. She wanted to say the right thing to this wounded warrior, but the words evaded her.

"Am I going to be okay?" he asked.

Liz was relieved to hear a question to which she could sensibly respond.

"You've got a nasty gash there, but you've been well attended. We have everything we need to make you good as new. You're going to have a little pain for a few days, but the stitches will be out before you know it."

"I don't suppose I'll be able to go back to the site."

"No, I think not," she said with a smile. "You've lost a lot of blood; you're dehydrated and overly fatigued. The saline has been running and you're receiving universal blood products. We'll soon have your blood typed and cross-matched. That will put the color back into your cheeks, you handsome young man."

Liz noticed Michael's pale skin began to blush as the compliment grappled with his senses. Liz wondered if she may have crossed the line with the "handsome young man" statement.

Not one to be bashful, and taking advantage of the moment, Michael asked, "Will I be lucky enough to have you join me in the OR?"

"Well, Mr. Fireman, I just might have a little time to keep you safe and sound in this not so heavily burning building."

Michael laughed at the spark of humor, "You know, I've never been rescued before, but at this moment, I kinda like it."

With an unexpected catch in her throat, Liz's heart skipped as she fought back a tear. In that moment a bond formed, and Michael became a favored patient. Liz was drawn to this attractive, well-muscled man. She was bold enough to ask to join the team in the OR and for a change in duties so she could see him on a regular basis. Liz soon realized that Michael looked forward to every visit. In her heart, each visit was too long in coming and passed all too quickly.

4:5 »»» September 17, 2001 – Observations

The Kahn had learned much from the 9/11 attack and the myriad of unfolding events after the infliction of jihadist terror. Al-Qaida had achieved a very successful tactical assault on the Great Satan, and The Kahn was happy to have been an important, though, unknown contributor.

The Kahn watched closely as the world reacted. There was plenty of anger, enough to rouse the ire of most people in the western countries. There were also celebrations by some Muslim factions, particularly in Iran, Iraq, and Afghanistan, which was as he had hoped.

The Kahn watched ongoing, global news reports. The Americans had reacted quickly. Security changed within hours, and he heard stories of a rapidly changing world. Many travelers had been stranded for days. Some interruptions were highly disruptive while others were minor inconveniences. One news report spoke of a couple waiting in the Honolulu Airport, which was being guarded by National Guardsmen with M16s, a sight never before seen. The report said they had ordered a personal size pizza. The pizza was presented as a whole pie.

"We asked them to cut our pizza into slices," they said. "And we were told they that they had nothing to cut it with. All of their sharp tools had been taken away. Even the plastic knives were gone. We tore the pizza apart as best we could." The story made The Kahn smile.

'As best they could;' that will be the mantra of the new America.

The Kahn's influence had twisted the face of a nation from smiles into a grimace, and he reveled in this success. He saw that transportation was hard hit and business suffered greatly. He heard of investors who walked away from many unsigned deals. He heard numerous reports of disappointed small businessmen who were vowing to do the best they could.

What opportunities will arise out of this?

The Kahn salivated over the potential increase of his markets. There would be newly motivated buyers of weapons among yearning, maddened terrorists. The Americans and others might blunt their noses, but he knew they would not go away. The Kahn believed that the more the West fought against the responsible terrorist groups, the deeper and more motivated the pockets of terror would become. He believed cycles of attack and counter-attack would soon develop.

Yes, new avenues of profits are before me and with those profits come power.

Closing his eyes, The Kahn took his mind off the television reports and directed it to the future. He would travel his expanded path as a provider of tools to those who desired to fight against the West. The Middle East was awash in oil money. It was just a matter of determining who was willing to spend it and, more importantly, who would spend it on his goods and services?

4:6 »»» 2001 – Assets of the Mossad

The disaster in America also prompted changes in Israel. Raphael was given a new assignment and was quick to plunge head first into his new duties as director of the Mossad Merkazi Le-modiin U-letafkidim Meyuhadim, or Institute for Intelligence and Special Operations. Most people referred to this Israeli intelligence operation as simply the Mossad. Raphael was a no-nonsense man of action. The Mossad, with an already distinct record of effectiveness, needed to be even more vigilant. One of their prime enemies, Iran, had regularly called for their destruction. Raphael was the man chosen to make sure Israel knew every move that Iran was making and, even more importantly, every move they were about to make. The world had been caught off guard by the destruction of the World Trade Center. Israel could not afford such a disaster.

Seated in a rather plain chair in an office of glass and metal, Raphael shuffled through a handful of files arranged on his metal desk. One file contained data on one of Israel's most promising covert operations in Iran. He wanted to learn more about the covert assets in his newly assigned stewardship. One asset in particular stood out.

"Leib, tell me about Pearl, one of our covert agents in Iran," Raphael said as he continued to scan the file while his subordinate began the recap.

"Pearl has been in deep cover for many years. It is well that you understand him. He has been in place but has never been activated."

"Tell me the entire history."

Leib began, but started farther back in history than Raphael had expected.

"You remember, I'm sure, when the 1917 League of Nations gave Great Britain authority to act as administrator of the British Mandate for Palestine over lands taken from the Ottomans during World War I. The Ottomans had held that land since the 16th century. Of course, we know them today as the Turks and they still hold a grudge toward us."

"Wait, Raphael said, "Pearl's placement has ramifications that go back to the very beginning of our state?"

"Yes, sir."

"Your account sounds like a good history lesson. Assemble the Iranian section. I want them to hear this. I want to increase their desire to be the best section in the Institute. Our very existence depends upon it."

Once Raphael's entire staff were seated in the cramped conference room, with no opportunity for interruptions, he began. Raphael wanted his first day with them to be memorable. He wanted to command their respect, and he wanted *them* to be worthy of *his* respect. He wanted this team to be the best unit in their section. In accordance, he wanted them to review the history of events that contributed to the placement of a covert asset known as "Pearl."

Raphael nodded at Leib and said, "Now that we are all together, you may continue."

Raphael began observing Leib earlier in the day. They had just met, and Raphael had a second reason in asking for the report. He wanted to learn about Leib. *What are his qualities? What are his capabilities? Does he have weaknesses?*

Leib began, "For thirty years, from 1917 to 1947, Israel and its Arab neighbors lived under the British Mandate for Palestine. During those years the land was divided into two groups. There were the Arab Nationalists, also called Palestinians. Our fathers and mothers were called Jewish Nationalists. Some named them Zionists. Many attempts were made to solve differences between the two groups, to no avail.

"In 1947, the United Nations passed a resolution known as The United Nations Partition Plan for Palestine. The U.N. resolution called for the termination of the British Mandate for Palestine, partitioning Palestine into two states: one for our Israel and another for the Arabs. Our beloved Jerusalem was to become a Special International Regime for the City of Jerusalem. The plan was not well received."

Leib continued, "On May 14, 1948 our glorious nation declared its independence. We announced ourselves as the State of Israel."

The conference room spontaneously broke into a state of applause. Back slaps and high fives were exchanged throughout the room. *Good,* thought Raphael. *These are the people I want around me.*

"Immediately after our declaration of independence, the armies of Egypt, Lebanon, Syria, Jordan, and Iraq, making up the Arab League, invaded our homeland. They would not accept the U.N. designed division, and they would not accept our independence. In their lust, they looked upon our land as their land.

"As we know, the Arabs were unsuccessful. We showed them the wrath of the one true God."

Again there were cheers. Raphael began to wonder if this group was too zealous. *No, I think not.*

With another nod from Raphael, Leib resumed, "In that short battle we gained the regions known as the West Bank, the Gaza Strip, and the Sinai Peninsula. After the war, the wealthy Palestinians left, and the poor stayed with us. The Arab states developed a tenet known as the Three No's: 'No recognition,' 'No peace,' and 'No negotiations with the State of Israel.'"

"And nothing has changed," came a growl from another part of the conference room.

Without hesitating, Leib continued. "The oil fields of Iran are a key element in the history of our nation. They were controlled by the British during World War II. Late in the war, oil flowed from Iran through the British to the Soviets. Soon after World War II ended, the Iranian Parliament voted to nationalize the Iranian oil industry. The British were unhappy about losing control of that oil source. Britain quickly developed a plan to install a government favorable to their cause. The goal was to incite a coup for the purpose of overthrowing the Iranian government. The Americans, at first surprised by the plan, soon became willing participants."

Raphael stopped Leib and faced his team, "This is old news to you, but I've asked Leib to share this because we have a number of assets in Iran. One of them is in deep cover, and we are about to activate that asset. Please listen carefully. I want you to have an understanding of what it took to install this asset and to have kept him safe until the day of our need. Continue, Leib."

"Part of the British plan was to instill unrest in the population. They took advantage of the strife sown by the Communists. They even convinced the Americans to plant some agents into the Communist organization. The Mossad used the same tactic. Two Mossad agents posed as a married couple. The coup, promoted by the British put the Shah of Iran into power.

"Under the Shah, Communism was not allowed, so the family withdrew from the Communist party. They played a new role as loyal and hardworking Iranian citizens, moving into the countryside and into a new residence. They developed trust with new friends and neighbors, erasing the label of Communists. It was in this village that the family adopted a child.

"Pearl is his code name. He was truly an orphan, smuggled into Iran in 1964 before he was one year old. The covert couple never had children. It was normal that this childless couple should, in their later years, adopt a son. It was said that the child's parents had been killed in an accident, and they were chosen to raise the boy. As Iranian citizens, Pearl's parents were given great honor through the adoption of the orphan. In Islam, Muhammad taught that parents who care for orphaned children receive a blessed place beside him in Paradise. Muhammad was said to be an orphan and had created an environment friendly to orphans. That environment gave Pearl a strong start in life.

"Pearl grew up as a respected young man in the family's home. The 1979 Islamic Revolution swept Iran and the Shah was deposed; Islam now ruled. The family became loyal to Islam and its code of belief. They taught Pearl the principles of Islam, while supplanting those principles with an abiding love for Israel. He went to prayers five times each day with his Shia friends and recited Jewish prayers in his bed at night. He became a Shia Muslim in every way—every way except one: he was an Israeli, and his loyalties were firmly bound to Israel. His purpose was to help thwart any aggression against Israel by Iran."

Leib nodded to Raphael indicating that his review was complete.

Raphael then took control. "So my friends, now we know how Pearl came to be. It is up to us to use and protect him. He can only help Israel if he is safe. I give my thanks to each of you and look forward to successfully completing our joint goal: the protection of our homeland."

CHAPTER 5
BLOSSOMS

5:0 ⟫⟫ September 18, 2001 – Romance

It was his second day after surgery when Liz walked into Michael's room and asked, "How's my favorite patient?"

Michael give Liz a rich smile and said, "Still watching for flying shrapnel."

Liz chuckled at his joke and said, "I wanted to let you know that you're about to get your first physical therapy treatment."

"Physical therapy. Wow, that's quick."

Liz looked into his eyes and smiled, "Yes, we want you up and walking ASAP." The statement was followed with a wink.

"Your presence is the best medicine," Michael said following the statement with a Cheshire cat smile.

Liz looked behind her to see if any staff members were watching. She felt like she was being a little too flirtatious, but with a warm smile she said, "Let me check those dressings before you take your walk."

"Check all you want, I'm completely in the power of my guardian angel and . . . enjoying every moment of it."

Liz noted the broken thought in Michael's statement. It seemed that he had changed the nature of his expression in mid-sentence. She wondered what he had actually intended to say but kept to the business at hand. "I'll stay here with you to make sure the therapist gets you up without you taking a tumble."

"The best care possible, right?"

"You got it, professor."

Very soon, the physical therapist entered the room. Liz stepped back to let the therapist do his job. She was glad they sent in a good-sized man, one with the strength to manage Michael's large frame. Within minutes, he had Michael on his feet and ready to walk down the hall. Liz was never far away in case her help was needed.

She walked along side Michael and the physical therapist. Falling in love with a patient was considered bad form, but she could not help herself. There was something about this man . . . .. He had a heart and character that was appealing and engaging. She was careful not to let her eyes linger on him too long, but at the same time, wanted to hug him tightly.

Liz believed she felt a return of affection from him, but was uncertain of its nature. Patients had become infatuated with her in the past. She felt their interest usually originated from medical dependence, and the fact that she was somewhat attractive was a part of that, too. If this was to be love, she hoped to win it through the power of her character, not just her medical care or physical beauty.

After the very short walk, they both helped Michael sit down on the side of the bed and recline back into it. Liz assisted the therapist; it was completely appropriate, but there was more in the physical contact than a simple assist, and Liz knew it. Though Michael was experiencing de-conditioning, he was still strong. But that wasn't the real attraction; there was electricity in their contact, and it seemed to be growing stronger. He was so complimentary and kind, appreciating every moment of attention that she so willingly gave. *What will it all mean in the end?*

Michael soon started walking the halls under his own power. Liz tried to schedule her activities to walk at his side, making sure he did not fall and re-injure the deep trauma to his leg—or so she said. It was unusual to spend so much time with a particular patient, but the staff cut the out-of-towner and volunteer some slack. Liz suspected that they enjoyed the excitement of the budding romance; at least something good was coming out of the terror.

Liz did have one legitimate concern, and she kept a close eye on it. Michael was coughing more than usual. For that reason, among others, she pressed to keep him in the hospital. Liz purposefully watched for symptoms of pneumonia. She also compared his symptoms to those expressed by other first responders. Some were suffering from severe respiratory distress. The cause of the coughing and distress was unclear and generally chalked up to the large amounts of dust that the lungs were working to expel. Liz wasn't so sure about that diagnosis and made a silent promise to watch him closely.

On the fifth day, Michael asked, "So when do you think I'll be released?"

"You're getting stronger every day. The doctor's notes indicate 'great progress.' Our time together is limited."

5:1 ⫸ September 20, 2001 – Malingering

Liz had been the first to say it, "Our time together is limited."

That comment, made just hours earlier, struck Michael's heart like a thousand shards of steel. *I do not want to be released. Am I a malingerer?*

His thoughts of malingering were cut short when Liz walked into his room. He had been disconnected from his electronic monitors long ago and suspected Liz was taking advantage of the situation, pulling out the cuff to check his blood pressure. Michael loved the attention, but the idea of leaving was troubling.

Liz noticed he was not quite himself and asked, "What will you do when you are released?"

Michael wasn't sure, and it was easy to admit it. "That's hard to say. The University told me to take all the time I need to return to good health. It seems they've been making the local headlines, having sent one of their best and brightest to become a 'wounded warrior,' who also shook hands with the President. It's brought a little extra prestige to the University. The follow-up call from the President to my hospital room increased their publicity opportunities. Someone in the PR department is working hard to cash in on my injuries."

Michael looked up at Liz with a budding smile. She responded in kind and said, "That was exciting."

"It was a big surprise to me," said Michael.

"And the hospital, too," said Liz. "It created quite a commotion. Such a thing has not happened here before, at least not in anyone's memory."

"I appreciate all the attention, but I also miss the routine of my life at the University." Then Michael hesitated, his eyes resting on Liz. "By the same token, I am not anxious to leave. I could stay in New York, but I don't know what I'd do. The city is still in mourning, and it seems inappropriate to do the tourist thing. But, even though I miss it, I really don't feel like returning to work. I just can't seem to shake this cough."

Michael knew there was a certain amount of smoke and mirrors to his statements, trying to hid his true intent. *I simply don't want to leave you.*

Fiddling with some equipment, Liz upped the ante. "I think you should stay in New York for a while. Most of the hotels are empty. Tourists have left or canceled their plans to come here. The hotels are giving huge discounts to any remaining volunteers who came to help in this senseless disaster. I have a rental car, and I could be your guide, although a guide without any real knowledge of the city."

With barely a second's hesitation, she stopped attending to the medical equipment, turned toward Michael and added, "It would be fun to explore the area with you."

Michael hadn't stopped looking at Liz and, with his eyes lighting up, said, "I'd really like that." Before she could respond, he added, "So there are probably rooms in your hotel. Where are you staying?"

Their relationship began to change in that moment. A threshold had been crossed, but there wasn't a euphoric rush to embrace.

Liz' smile became very broad. "The Marriott Marquis, and they even gave me free parking."

Michael took control, "It's settled then. I'll get a room in your hotel. Let's see if there's some town left to see."

Stepping a little closer, Liz added, "We might have to drive out of the city to get away from all the abnormal activity. I'm told the commute is far easier now; there are no traffic jams."

Michael asked, "Haven't you left the city yet?"

"No, I've had more important matters to attend to." Liz squinted slightly and let a hint of mischievousness light her face.

Still caught up in her eyes, Michael responded, "And what was so important?"

The grin on Liz face deepened but remained slightly coy.

Smiling even more brightly, Michael added, "Well, now that those important matters have been taken care of, it seems a bit of recreation is in order. Let's explore the world around us and see what it holds."

After lingering for quite a while, Michael watched Liz leave his room. He felt excitement well up in him as he considered spending time with this exquisite new woman. Suddenly, he felt a twinge of guilt. *How can I be so blessed when around me there so much pain and suffering? It seems incongruous that the two worlds can live so closely together.*

5:2 ⟫⟫ September 23, 2001 – Released

On the day of Michael's release, Liz had made arrangements to take the day off in order to drive him to the hotel. Pulling her rental car into a spot dedicated for patient pick up, she was exhilarated beyond her expectations. Michael could have walked out of the hospital, but it was policy to bring patients out in a wheelchair. She hurried out of the driver's seat and noticed another nurse watching through the window. She had developed a kinship with this particular nurse and felt a tug in her heart as she thought of the woman's support. But the tug could only last a moment as the hospital door opened, and she saw Michael in the wheelchair. She could tell that he hated being wheeled out of the hospital to the car. She was sure, however, that he now looked forward to being under her care and her care alone. Liz felt the same way.

Michael slid easily into the car without any help. Walking around the front of the car, Liz felt an unsettling anticipation in her stomach. She pulled out and into the minimal Manhattan traffic, easily negotiating the fifteen minute drive to one of the more elegant hotels near Fifth Avenue. Liz loved the hotel. It was beautiful and near the center of New York City where Time Square, the Rockefeller Center, and the theater district were located, although she had seen nothing of them. The hotel staff had been wonderfully kind to her. She had been treated like royalty. She knew they would be just as kind to Michael.

Their arrival was just as she had hoped. They were greeted by the doorman who whisked away Michael's luggage to the room which she had already arranged. Michael insisted on walking through the elegant lobby. It was large and stunning in its decor. For the first time, Liz actually felt like she was in New York. The excitement of fun days in the city filled her heart and lightened her mind, but the most exciting part was that Michael was standing at the elevator with her.

When the elevator doors opened, Michael motioned her to enter first, took his place beside her and, with a quirky smile, asked, "What floor, my dear?"

"The highest one, silly."

Michael raised his eyebrows and pressed 49.

Liz reached out, slipping her hand into Michael's, her eyes searching his. Michael responded with a squeeze and turned to face her. Despite their closeness, they had not kissed.

She allowed him into her personal space, hoping he would understand the invitation. She was not disappointed as he stepped closer. He raised his arms, wrapped them around her, drawing her in tightly; she felt the excitement of his great strength. Slowly, like the drift of a snowflake, their lips met. It was serene, it was sensual, it was gentle, and even arousing. It was a kiss unlike any kiss she had ever before experienced. It was deep-rooted, confident, and almost regal. It didn't overreach and demand. But it said with all its strength, "I love you."

The elevator quickly whisked them away. Suddenly it slowed and the stop was announced by a tone that ended the long and haunting kiss. The embrace broke just as the door opened. Another guest looked in, hesitated, and suspecting an intrusion, the woman said with a wink, "I'll catch the next one."

Liz' face turned beet red, but she mustered a "Thank you."

When the door closed, Liz looked at Michael and started to laugh. Michael joined in, and within moments a duet of laughter filled the elevator. It continued until another tone sounded the last stop: the 49th floor.

Liz and Michael stepped out of the elevator. The walk was just long enough to be away from the noisy elevators. At the door to Michael's room, Liz opened her purse. She withdrew the key card and handed it to Michael. With a smile he accepted it and opened the door. It was a beautiful room, far beyond his expectations.

"I splurged," she said.

"Yes, you did," Michael said. "The room is elegant."

"They gave me a really good deal."

"Who are you really?" he asked in the pretense of an inquiry. "First you save my life, then nurse me back to health, and then bring me to the Presidential Palace, or Suite, or whatever this may be called."

"Oh, I'm just a girl who may have found what she's been looking for."

They crossed the threshold and went into the room. With a nudge from Michael, the door swung closed, and the kiss began all over again. Liz nearly melted during the intimate embrace and the exquisite sensuality. This time, there was no tone, nor interruption to bring it to an early end.

After a moment, Michael broke away and asked, "And what is that?"

Liz arched her brow in question.

"What have you been looking for?" he said.

Finally understanding, she flatly stated, "Tell me who you are, and you will have described it."

Michael looked intently at Liz as the corners of her mouth turned up into a smile. He shook his head back and forth in astonishment, "I . . . I don't know what to say. I've never felt this way before, and I've never been with someone who has said anything like you just said. I'm in awe. How did this happen?"

Before Liz could answer, Michael looked around the room and stepped away from her. "This is an incredible room!"

Liz felt some level of disappointment as Michael's attention was diverted to the room.

"They offered it as a special gift to us."

Michael looked back to Liz. "To us?"

"Yes, to us," her smile deepening once more.

"I thought we had adjoining rooms."

"Well, sort of. It's a suite with two bedrooms." Nodding to the right, she said, "Mine's here." With another nod, she indicated, "And yours is over there."

The room became very silent. Liz stood still as Michael looked around the suite and at both bedroom doors.

"I'll be a perfect gentleman," he said. "What you've arranged here is beyond description. You are amazing!"

Not sure how to feel, Liz asked a "How about the weather question?" and "I'm starved. What shall we do for dinner?" one followed.

Turning to her, Michael said, "Let's hit the hotel restaurant. It's close and it's my treat."

Liz held Michael with her eyes. She wanted to clearly state her position.

"It's really nice to be here with you, Michael."

Michael did not avert his eyes.

"Liz, I may be in love with you, but let's take it a little slow. We don't want to make mistakes that we may regret. Let's see if a few days together will prove your theorem."

Liz cocked her head to the side, "My theorem, what do you mean?"

"It's possible that I may be what you've looked for. Let's take some time to see if it's really true. You know, we scientists like to prove our theories are facts, before we publish them as facts."

Feeling slightly reproved and a little disappointed, Liz could only say, "I think I understand. I'm with you. Let's eat some dinner."

5:3 ►►► September 22, 2001 – Time Together

Their first evening together was peaceful and relaxing, to a point. Ever the attentive caregiver, Liz knew that despite his accelerating recovery, Michael still needed more rest than activity. Liz considered every detail in coordinating a space that was comfortable and well stocked with food and refreshments. One great amenity was a big screen TV with a superb sound system. They nestled together on the sofa to watch a pay-per-view movie. He noticed a mini-feature about John Nash, Nobel Prize winning mathematician. Michael, a fan of John Nash, was immediately interested in the true-to-life story of John Nash and prelude to a soon-to-be-released movie, *A Beautiful Mind.*

Reaching for her hand, he asked, "Liz, what do you know of John Nash?"

It was a simple enough question.

"I've never heard of him."

With an odd smile Michael said, "Let's check him out."

Michael kept an eye on Liz as she intently watched a documentary revealing the life of John Nash. He was a brilliant mathematician who was also plagued with paranoid schizophrenia. He pushed the bounds of common sense, overcame his illness, and in his later years received the Nobel Memorial Prize in Economic Sciences.

"Well, what do you think?" an excited Michael asked.

It took a moment for Liz to respond, "I was impressed with the genius of John Nash. I was also taken by the relationship between John and his wife."

His face a quandary, Michael asked, "What do you mean?"

Liz spoke softly, "I think Alicia was as much a hero as John. He got the Nobel Prize, but the character award should have gone to her."

After some thought, he suggested, "It must have taken great courage to divorce and then remarry a schizophrenic."

Liz drew back slightly and Michael wondered if she were sizing him up, having second thoughts. After a few moments of quiet she said, "And here I sit, with a math genius. Should I be worried?"

Michael put on a mysterious face. "You probably should be, but let's find out," and they both laughed together.

Suddenly Michael stopped, "Liz, I think this is actually an important matter for us to consider. Mr. Nash said his illness was the basis for his brilliance. I've thought of his statement on many occasions. So many brilliant men have serious limitations. I keep wondering what my limitations are, or what they will become."

A moment of silence followed, neither knowing quite how to fill the space. Liz broke the spell.

"Michael, I don't know what our future is to be. It appears that we are two people both drawn into the unknown worlds of the other. I guess it's for us to explore those new worlds to discover how alien or how familiar they are."

Raising the corner of his mouth, Michael said, "Wow, that's right out of a cosmology book. But you know, scientists are a weird bunch. Are you sure you want to take the risk?"

With a wink she said, "Go to your room, young man, and recover.

I'll go to mine to decide if I can date a genius."

The next morning Liz went to the hospital while Michael continued in his recovery. When she checked on him at noon, she learned that the University had agreed to give Michael one more week to recover. In addition, the hospital told Liz she could leave any time she wanted. Liz elected to stay until Michael went back to Colorado.

After work, Liz drove back to the hotel. She stood still for just a moment before inserting her key into the door. She'd had a sleepless night and an early morning call at the hospital. All night and throughout a hectic day, she continued to think of Michael. The story of John Nash continued to haunt her. She'd only known Michael for a few days, and really, there had been so little time to interact. *Have I fallen in love, or have I become a hostage? What might life be like with a math genius?*

Liz unlocked the door and stepped into the room. It was clean and orderly, despite the fact that Michael was on the sofa, watching a movie. *There's a plus, he's not a slob.*

Michael looked up just as a Jap Zero dropped a bomb on the Arizona in his pay-per-view movie. He couldn't pause the movie so he simply turned down the sound.

"Hi Liz! This really is a great room, and oh, I'll pay for all the movies I've watched. It's been a little boring."

Eying the TV, she said, "So it's Pearl Harbor all over again?"

"Yup, I guess our changing world gave them a chance to add it to the reruns."

Liz kicked off her shoes, went to the sofa, and plopped down beside Michael.

"Long day?"

"Yes, long and difficult," she said. "And how are you?"

"I was bored but no longer," following with a wink.

Smiling she responded, "What a nice thing to say."

Michael flashed an even brighter smile.

"Seriously, how was your first day out of the hospital?"

"Fine, I'm doing fine."

Liz raised her eyebrow, "And the cough?"

It's still there, but it's okay."

"I want to listen."

"Go for it," Michael beamed. "I'll do anything to get your angelic attention."

Liz removed the stethoscope that still hung from her neck, knowing it would be cold from the air conditioning. She quickly pressed the cold device onto his warm skin.

"Hey!" he howled. "That's cold!"

Liz quickly pulled back the scope, a look of whimsy on her face, and began warming it with her breath. The sensual character of her lips was all it took. Michael reached for her, drawing her into his arms, revealing the joy he felt at her return.

"Wait, wait, wait. While you've been lounging, I've been working. I need a shower and food, and in that order."

"Gotcha covered," Michael beamed. "I have a reservation for dinner and tickets for Dreamgirls. I understand that proceeds from ticket sales are going to the Actor's Fund of America, and Giuliana said we should all go to a play. So, we are going out, and it's on me."

Liz moved closer to Michael, blew an erotic breath into his ear and said, "I'll be right back," and quickly walked away.

5:4 ⟫⟫ September 28, 2001 – Revelation

Michael kept them busy each afternoon with well-planned forays of adventure and sightseeing trips that would have made most tourists jealous. Liz stopped working at the hospital to spend more time with Michael.

Their intimate moments were limited to the sofa, where their bodies often pressed tightly together, but never moving to the bedroom; Michael never made a move to undress Liz. They would lay together for long periods, fully clothed, and wrapped in sensuous desire. During one of these moments, Michael looked deeply into her eyes and asked, "What are you thinking?"

He continued to look into the most striking green eyes he had ever seen. They seemed to reveal the depth of the eternities; not the abyss of black holes, but the breathtaking splendor of the cosmos. He thought they possessed the mysterious beauty of infinity, a state as enigmatic as it is wondrous. He knew at that moment that he didn't want this woman to leave him. Knowing she might not understand his personal cosmological metaphor, he simply said, "I just enjoy looking into your gorgeous eyes."

But Liz didn't respond quite as Michael had expected.

"Michael, you aren't gay are you?"

The question caught him off guard. With a shallow laugh and an innocent smile he asked, "Why, do you think I am, or that I might be? I think my kisses and long embraces are quite telling."

He could see that Liz was embarrassed, guessed why she might have asked the question, and didn't want to prolong an uneasy moment.

"Liz, I'm probably not like most men that you've met. I believe very strongly that a man and woman's intimate relationship is, well, simply put, very special. I believe there is no stronger tie than one that has grown out of honest and deep-seated emotional intimacy, and that certain things should wait."

He hesitated, seeing the confusion in her eyes, but she was the first to speak, even though it was cautiously.

"Does that mean . . . you've never . . . had sex before?"

His look was telling.

"Never?"

He shook his head, no.

Michael noted her look of amazement.

"But Michael, sex is such a bonding experience, what are you waiting for?"

"I'll tell you why, using my theory on sex, since I *am* a theorist. Here it is: sex is too often the beginning, and too often the ending of a relationship. It is not necessarily the most important bonding element in a relationship. I want our love to survive. I don't want our connection to feverishly start with sex, and then wane as we face separation, which is soon to come. I want to make sure we have the glue, the real glue, the epoxy glue that holds people together forever. We are going to face a long distance separation, and we won't see each other as often as we'd both like. Will sex hold us together, or will it require something deeper?"

Liz' eyes were wide open in amazement. No words came, so he filled the void.

"I'll explain. For so many people, sex is a very early and physically intimate experience. I know very few men who aren't looking for sex at the first meeting. Gratification seems to be the initial motivator. Does that make sense?"

"Yes, I get that, all too well," Liz admitted.

"In these cases, sexual intimacy develops long before emotional intimacy. In some relationships, emotional intimacy never develops."

He wanted that idea to sink in, so he paused briefly, and then continued.

"When two people base their connection on sex, and not on emotional ties, all too often, when their erotic tie is broken or becomes a mundane trifle, an unraveling may take place. The relationship often begins to shrink, and eventually two people can emerge who are bored and out of love."

Furrowing her brow ever so slightly, Liz said, "Okay, so you are also telling me that you've never developed a deep emotional connection with a woman."

Michael's face turned red and he was caught, but quickly admitted it. "No Liz, frankly, I haven't . . . at least until now. You have touched me in my deepest parts, affecting me far more intimately than the feeling of physical gratification. I don't want to destroy the grand opportunity that I think we may have, and I want to wait until I am sure that we are symbiotic."

"Symbiotic?" She faced him full on with furrowed brows, wanting to understand. "Okay, man of science, what does that mean, and when will you know?"

Michael smiled, realizing he had gone too far. "I'm sorry. I know most men would have already tried to take you to bed. Believe me, I've had the desire, and sometimes I've felt like I could no longer resist, but I believe we have something beyond physical attraction. I want to know if that is really true. My hands-off attitude is a testament of a love that grows every day. I'd like to experience interdependence, a life of mutual giving and mutual respect. I want an equally-footed, foundationally strong structure of love that will withstand the worst that nature can throw at us. I don't want our relationship to start with sex, because I don't want it to end with sex, whether in a few months, or in a few years, or worse at an older age when sex is less important. I want to start our relationship with the deep seated love of Romeo and Juliet, a couple willing to give their lives for each other, not the selfish folly of Samson and Delilah."

Michael had thrown out a lot of verbiage and feared he was trying to dazzle her with words. He decided to shut up, hoping to gauge her reaction.

Liz didn't speak but continued to examine his eyes with her mouth agape. After a moment, her countenance softened.

At last and very softly, she asked, "Where have you been all my life?"

Looking for just the right words, Michael answered, "I've simply been waiting for the right moment to introduce myself."

That bit of wit brought a wide smile to both of them. Their eyes sparkled and welled with tears as they each gave the wholeness of their hearts. The glue had begun to form.

5:5 ⟫⟫ September 30, 2001 – Leaving

The sofa had become their place of repose. It was where they sat together, talked together, laughed and planned together. One evening Liz broached the subject they had both been avoiding, "Can we talk about the future?"

"So this is it, the infamous, 'we need to talk moment'."

Liz looked surprised. "What do you mean? I . . . I thought we could talk about anything. This doesn't have to be something difficult."

Michael looked at her and knew he'd made a mistake, but his logical, analytical brain had overruled his heart. *Where can this relationship possibly go? How can two lives so impossibly apart in their careers fold themselves into one?*

"I'm sorry, Liz, that was very callous, but I know what's coming, and it's difficult for me to face."

"What's coming, Michael?"

That question made him uncomfortable all over again. *Surely she understands. She is a smart woman.*

Unwillingly Michael responded, "The big question—what do we do now? You as much as suggested it in your query."

"My query?"

Michael knew he was in trouble.

Liz pulled away slightly, folding her arms and stating flatly, "Well, we have to address it. We can't run from it. I've feared our separation too, but we have to talk about it."

Looking straight ahead, rather than at Liz, Michael responded, "You're right; we are in a difficult position. The problem is I just don't have a solution."

Liz asked the over-arching question, keeping her eyes on Michael. "Is there any chance we can be together?"

Michael didn't respond, not because he refused to respond, he just didn't know what to say.

After a moment of silence, Liz posed a dismal supposition. "So you don't see any way that we can be together?"

Michael at last looked back at Liz. "Our careers are so disparate and so entrenched." It was all he could muster.

Michael then stood quickly, his nervous energy demanding action, but there was no action to be taken. He paced away from Liz, turned and blurted his thoughts. "I'm in Colorado, you're in Houston. Who's gonna move?"

Crossing her legs and re-folding her arms, Liz said, "It is a problem. I guess we both believe that the other one should move. In the end it may be that neither of us is willing to give up our careers and our established work places."

Michael spoke very softly, "You may be right, but I hope that isn't our final reality. I know I don't want to give up my station. I'm too intricately woven into the fabric of the University, but I could never ask you to give up your position."

"There has to be a way for this to work out," she said solemnly.

Michael felt like he knew what was on her mind. She had dropped a few hints, probably with the hope that he would bring it up, but he couldn't. It was too soon to talk about marriage. After all, they'd only known each other for two weeks.

Breaking the silence, Michael spoke up, "I know that the feelings of this moment are not the desires of our hearts, but I don't think we can resolve this right now. I think we need some time to sort out our feelings. We may have to ask ourselves really tough questions. What I do know is that the last two weeks have been the best of my life. I don't want that happiness to end."

They both fell silent. Michael moved toward Liz, as though to implore her to make a statement. Liz turned away, her eyes moist with hidden tears.

Michael sat down, wrapped her in his arms, and pulled her tightly to his chest. She didn't resist.

"Liz, I want to make this work. I don't know how, but I want it to work."

Liz at last turned and looked into his eyes, "I do, too."

There were lots of tears but no decision as the night wore on. They were both leaving in the morning, one for Houston and one for Colorado. There was too much disappointment to find harmony. In exhaustion, they fell asleep in each other's arms, despite their differing perspectives. As the dawn broke, it was the first time they had actually awakened in each other's arms, still cuddled together on the couch.

5:6 ⟫⟫ September 30, 2001 – Separation

The flight to Houston was without incident as was the drive to her condo. Liz twisted the key to unlock her door. She stepped through, stopped, turned, and said to Michael, "Thanks for coming to my home."

"I'm glad I did. Thanks for inviting me. I really didn't want to part from the 'Mistress of my rehab'."

Liz only half smiled; her feelings too solemn for much more. After all, there had been no compromise, no long term plan; all they had done was put off the loneliness for one more day.

Still smiling, Michael tried again. "Truth is, I did malinger in New York until it was time for you to return home. We both understood that reality."

In a matter-of-fact tone she admitted, "You're one of the few malingerers whose guise I actually supported," joining in his attempt at humor, then offering a thin smile.

"It was a wonderful rehab," he said.

Her smile broadened, but just slightly.

Happy for a slight improvement in Liz' mood, Michael moved closer to her, stooping down to look into her still saddened eyes. He lifted her chin and straightened, drawing her in. He loved her eyes. His life hadn't been the same since they pierced his being in the emergency room. Though it was true, he still hadn't told her that they are the same eyes he had imagined so many times. *Why haven't I told her that?*

He pulled her in even more closely, feeling her smooth skin on his cheek. He gently caressed her blonde hair, feeling its softness against his face, inhaling its sweet subtle aroma. This would be a forever moment in his mind and senses. As before, when he found himself in her arms, the trauma of death and injury fled as though they feared to be caught in the light of her presence. Such moments were difficult to let pass and in hanging onto this particular moment, he realized there was one more absolute truth in the universe: he could not let this woman get away. That truth, however, was matched by two more truths: he could not stay in Houston, and she would not leave Houston, unless her conditions were met.

Michael breathed in her scent once more. He buried his face in her golden hair and pressed his five o'clock shadow onto her cheek. She responded with a yearning that he clearly understood and felt all too strongly himself. He steeled himself for his next move.

Michael drew back, immediately recaptured by her eyes, "Our last day will end all too quickly."

"All too soon," she repeated.

There were more kisses of tenderness and yearning desires.

Liz's eyes filled with tears, "I don't want you to go."

Michael responded with honesty, "I don't want to leave."

Liz decided to ask Michael a tough question. "Will you commit to a short departure as an *absolute truth*?"

There was hesitation in Michael's response. "Liz, I'll do the best I can, and I'll do all I can to make it work. I truly hope and believe it will work, but I can't absolutely promise without reserve. I'm sorry. I just can't do that."

The evening passed somberly. Michael wondered if it had been a good idea to travel to Houston. It seemed only to lengthen the misery. Once again they held each other until sleep overcame them.

5:7 ⟫⟫ October 1, 2001 – Security

Just as morning follows the night, so came the hour of departure. Michael paused, looking back at Liz after passing through security, which had been a nightmare. People were being searched, bags were searched, and in general chaos reigned. It had been a tongue-biting experience for people who had experienced a previous freedom in travel that would never be possible again. The whole process only served to stiffen his mood. His gaze lingered as he watched her trying to hide her tears. His heart fell to its lowest ebb in years. *How can happiness bring such pain?*

Turning his back on her and walking to his gate felt like abandoning the most important thing in his life. It was far more difficult that rescuing victims from fiery buildings or removing fatalities from mangled cars. Still, it had to be done. The logical analytical side had spoken and won.

Seeing Michael pass through security filled Liz with an awful emptiness. She turned, covering her face, as she wept uncontrollably. Never had she felt so conflicted. Michael was the man of her dreams. *How can he walk away? How can I let him?* She noticed people look her way. She wiped her tears and assumed a face of stoicism, controverted by her reddened eyes.

5:8 ⟫⟫ 2002 – The Kernel of an Idea

Nearly a year after leaving Liz at the airport, while ensconced in his office in Boulder, Colorado, Michael closed his eyes and thought about their separation. He realized that in this moment he was being torn between two forces: his work and his desire for Liz. Two PhD certificates hung on his wall, one in mathematics from Harvard, the second in physics from the California Institute of Technology. Michael had already built a solid reputation in the scientific community. His research had been brilliant. He was chin deep in the principles and protocols of science and wondered if he could still be effective if his time was split between work and a marriage, and the possibility of children. Would he still have the time and peace necessary to allow his free-ranging thoughts to explore the mysteries of life?

His questioning thoughts had driven him to his most recent mental ruminations. Though trained as a young man in religion, he had not actively participated. The idea of God was still an enigma. He was well indoctrinated in the laws of physics and the pure language of mathematics. Though appearing to be a creature of proofs, as required by science, he was also fascinated with creation. He knew every scrap of known fact related to the Big Bang and its competing theories but held competing thoughts of creation in recesses unknown to his peers.

Michael got up and walked to the white-board, and began to write.

Big Bang = Everything from nothing / everything from a singularity / everything from a previous existence.

Matter: Always existed / or explodes into existence at the Big Bang?

Time: Existed before the Big Bang or starts at the Big Bang?

Beginnings and endings: If there is an assumptive beginning, then is there an ending?

Conversely: If there is an ending there surely must be a beginning

The Universe: A single phenomenon / multiverses / parallel universes

Creation vs. Big Bang: Which is the more astounding, amazing, unlikely?

God / Intelligent Design / Happenstance

As a theoretical physicist, Michael's job was to ask questions, to wonder about possibilities. He thought back to his childhood—How and Why?

He paced back and forth, then moved to a second white-board and began writing again.

Atheist / Agnostic / Faith-based

He wrote the words . . .

What am I?

Mumbling to himself, "I don't know." He walked back to his desk, stopped, turned, and asked the question more loudly, "What am I?"

Below his question he added more words:

Higgs Boson (God Particle), Higgs fields, Dark Energy, and Dark Matter, String Theory.

On still a third white-board he wrote:

Is there a God?

1) If there is a God, by what law does He accomplish His work?

2) If there is a God, how does He operate; how does He make things happen?

Hypothesis 1: God moves or pushes/propels matter by applying some kind of material force to that matter. If so, what is that force? . . . . I don't know.

Hypothesis 2: Matter reacts to the will of God and moves by its own choice or will/. If so . . . how?

Hypothesis 3: Matter has some form of intelligence and through its own independent will it behaves according to the will of God.

Hypotheses 4: Matter can control its movement.

Michael walked away from the white-boards and around his desk. Resting his hand on the back of his chair, he stared at the expression of his thought. His mind raced. He considered thoughts beyond the grasp of the greatest share of sentient beings. He pushed back his chair and sat down. At last he spoke out loud. "Hypothesis 3 is the most intriguing;

it infers that matter has probably always existed, it possesses some level of intelligence, it has the ability to choose, and the power to move on its own."

His door was locked but he was interrupted by a knock.

Startled and slightly disgruntled, he called out, "Just a minute, please."

Michael had several mobile white-boards arranged in his office. Giving in to the interruption, he got up and re-arranged them to cover his notes. *I am not anxious to have people see my work.*

Michael went to the door, unlocked it and welcomed a student who was stuck on a difficult physics theory. Michael kindly took the student to yet another white-board and taught once more the subjects that he loved—physics and the perfect language of mathematics.

5:9 ⟫⟫ 2002 – Baylor University

Liz was pressed for time. She looked from one monitor to the next. She had two patients in Intensive Care and was concerned about each one of them. Checking the monitors again and again, she reset her evaluation of each patient. Liz insisted on personally managing at least two patients when she was on duty, a heavy load since she was also the managing nurse in the Intensive Care Department at Baylor University Medical Center.

Satisfied that both patients were stable for the moment, her mind created a "what if?"

What if I had left my position here at Baylor? Would I have to give up my career?

It was a question she had asked herself many times, but as before, it would remain unanswered. She had to hurry to an appointment.

Liz liked being at Baylor. The hospital tackled some of the most difficult cases in the Houston area. They were second to none and were highly ranked in their number of specialties. More importantly, Baylor was highly ranked among the esteemed Highly-Performing institutions. Such hospitals were known to be most successful in providing safe and effective care, and that was the reason she was in the office of the Director of Patient Care. She sat down, an expansive oak desk separating her from the Director.

"Liz, we love having you work with us on our boards and panels."

The office was not large, but it was well appointed and the Director was well-regarded.

Liz smiled. "Thank you. I'm grateful to serve, both with our patients and on your hospital boards."

Liz expected the reason for her invitation into the Director's office but waited for him to state his case.

"I'd like to offer you a permanent, full-time administrative position. You've shown tremendous skill; not only in patient care but also in your management of the Intensive Care Department. I believe you could enlarge your sphere of influence in training and management, and by doing that, even more patients would be served."

Liz' heart and soul was fully immersed in patient care. She was willing to do all within her power to raise the level of care for patients across the board, but she could not leave the acute needs of Intensive Care. Her great desire was to personally see that each patient was treated with the greatest of dignity and attention while receiving the very best in medical treatment.

Liz purposely folded her hands together, understanding the variable messages of body language. She wanted to send no false signals.

"I'm sorry; I truly love my current position. I love our patients, and I don't want to give up those duties. I'll help on some of your boards, but I don't want to give up patient care."

The Director rose and disappointedly said, "I am sorry too, Liz. If I offered more money, would it make a difference?"

"I don't want to seem ungrateful, but it isn't about the money. I just love my patients.

Liz was relieved to leave the Director's office. Even though she loved her patients, there was something else on her mind. Michael was flying in later today. His speaking engagements were in high demand, and he was coming to speak in Houston. His plane landed in an hour. She was excited to see him and hurried to get ready to pick him up from the airport.

Michael was as handsome as ever as he cleared security. Their embrace was warm and satisfying. Liz held onto Michael longer than usual. It had been many months since she had seen him.

"So you did miss me," he quipped.

Liz pulled back and scowled, "Yes."

"I missed you, too."

Liz had made reservations at her favorite Italian restaurant. As they dined, she nearly burst with the thoughts she'd been considering. It was all she could do to keep quiet so she contrived a decoy.

"Michael, are you sure you can't leave Colorado and move to Houston? Baylor has a great science department. Wouldn't it be wonderful to work on the same campus? Just think, lunch every day with your long-term significant other."

Before answering Michael took a long look at Liz. At last he responded, "Liz, you are wonderful and tenacious at the same time. I am about to reach tenure and that is a big deal. If I left CU, I'd have to start all over again."

Liz knew that his response put an end to the *why don't you move* discussion. She'd been thinking again about a move to the Denver area. She wasn't willing to settle. She had to find the perfect position to go along with her perfect but absent love. She realized it would take time, maybe a long time, but she would keep searching, and he must never suspect.

Having failed to generate the "move' discussion, Liz asked, "Do you have a good doctor in Boulder?"

Michael put down his fork and asked, "Why, are you applying for the job?"

Liz laughed, "If only I could."

"You'd make a good doctor."

Liz tilted her head. "I'm content."

"You are an amazing woman, Liz. I honor your earnest desire to care for others. Are you sure that's not why you're hanging onto me?"

She looked Michael straight in the eyes. "Come to think of it, how's the cough?"

"See, there you are, forever the caregiver." Smiling even more broadly, he said, "It's fine."

With a wink, Liz warned, "I'm going to listen to your lungs tonight."

Pretending to be tempted Michael retorted, "Careful there lady, don't get fresh."

She responded, "I'll get as fresh as you'll allow, okay?"

"Okay," said Michael, knowing he would stick to his guns despite the flirting.

The visit came and ended like so many others. Nothing seemed to change, just the dates on the calendar. They did all they could to visit each other as often as they could manage, but the visits were becoming more infrequent. The sporadic trips were over long weekends or as part of Michael's speaking engagements. Occasionally they worked out a real vacation. Liz was most often the driving force. Michael was highly preoccupied with some great, but secret, breakthrough he'd been developing. But the fact was, they loved each other, and that love just continued to endure.

CHAPTER 6
CONTINUUM

6:0 ⫸ 2003 – North Korea

The death of the Minister of Foreign Affairs had created a vacancy in North Korean Leadership. The Premier of North Korea had called his ministers together to discuss candidates for the position of Minister of Foreign Affairs. The Minister of the Armed Forces had developed a close friendship with Soung Jun-Sun, the Under Minister of Foreign Affairs, and he hoped to persuade his peers, while at the same time influencing the Premier into appointing Under Minister Soung to the open post. In the course of the meeting he offered Soung Jun-Sun as the replacement and worked toward that end.

One response came quickly, "He is so young, only 48."

"Yes and very successful, said the Minister of Foreign Security," who had worked with Under Minister Soung Jun-Sun and was pleased with his work.

The Minister of Commerce added his affirmation saying, "The road traveled by Soung Jun-Sun has been trodden with skill and success. We have rarely chosen young men to be our leaders. However, I would consider Soung Jun-Sun as the new Minister of Foreign Affairs.

The Minister of Finance spoke next, "As first a staff member and now Under Secretary of Foreign Affairs there is simply no one that knows more about our Foreign Relations. He seems with ease to grasp the nuances of political relationships. I've never known anyone who can work with others while leading them to see matters from his own perspective, feeling good about it in the process."

"He has been impressive," said the Premier of the Democratic People's Republic of Korea (DPRK).

The Minister of the Armed Forces wanted to speak enthusiastically about Jun-Sun, yet his words were measured. He dared not press the leader of the Republic. Like Jun-Sun, he had the ability to bring others to his viewpoint. He wanted to carefully lead the Premier to the notion that the final decision was his own. That was usually not too difficult. The leader was a true narcissist and the center of his own world.

"Tell us your vision of the future of North Korea," the Minister of Armed Forces asked the Premier.

The Minister of Armed Forces listened closely as the Premier streamed a discourse on the importance of North Korea and its place in the world. He needed the very best minds and the most loyal of men to promote their great cause. It was critical to secure the continued support of China, while keeping North Korea free of Chinese interference. By the time he ended the dissertation, he had delineated the needs of the Republic, the qualities of Sun-Jun, and why the two matched. Soung Sun-Jun would make the perfect Minister of Foreign Affairs.

Supporting the Premier, the Minister of the Armed Forces said, "You are most astute as only our Supreme Leader can be."

The Cabinet could not have been more pleased, and so it came to be that 48 year-old Soung Jun-Sun, the dichotomous son of a peasant, was chosen to join the highest ranks of elite party leadership as trusted Minister of Foreign Affairs of the Democratic People's Republic of North Korea.

6:1 ≫≫ 2004 – Space-time

Dr. Michael Benson was one of several presenters in an open forum for high school students designed as a guide to their future disciplines of study. The forum was conducted on the University of Colorado campus. Taking his turn, Michael stood at a podium that faced a typically large lecture room filled with students in stadium seating. After an introduction from a university administrator he began.

"Thank you for attending today. I'm Dr. Michael Benson. I am a theoretical physicist and my job is to consider the fringes of science. I think about possibilities. I question the mysteries and look beyond known solutions for potential answers.

"I'm going to talk about space and time, or what we refer to as space-time, also known as the space-time continuum. When you leave today, I hope you have a better understanding of how we perceptually and actually move through the space-time continuum. And please note that I am suggesting that there is a difference between our perception of space and time, and the reality of time and space.

"In the classic model of Euclidean Space, there are three dimensions, X, Y and Z. In academics, we use the Cartesian coordinate system to make graphs. We use this same system to define space, using three axes and coordinate points along those axes."

Dr. Benson turned to the board and drew the X and Y axes on the white-board, at a right angle to each other.

"X and Y represent the two dimensions we recognize as being flat, as on a piece of paper. And remember at one point, these two axes defined our world as flat.

"Today we know our world is not flat, and we use the Z axis to define the space we exist in as being three dimensional."

Dr. Benson added a representation of the third axis, Z, to the white-board.

"We define space as being three-dimensional, and the X, Y, and Z axes help us define points in three-dimensional space. But, there is another dimension that we regularly speak about, one that we continually experience, yet that we actually know very little about. That dimension is time. Time, the fourth dimension, is something in which we are continually immersed but of which have very little understanding.

"Our immersion in time is dominated by repeating cycles. Some cultures use the moon as their timekeeper. Ancient astrologers used the movement of the sun not only to chart the time of day, but also the days, months, and years. An interim timekeeper was the ticking clock. Today we use atomic clocks to keep time. Atomic clocks use the vibrations of a cesium atom to mark time. Cesium atoms vibrate at a frequency of exactly nine billion, one hundred and ninety million, six hundred and thirty-one thousand, seven hundred and seventy Hertz."

Michael turned to the white-board and in large characters wrote: *9,192,631,770 Hz, or cycles per second.*

"Over nine billion pulses a second, that's how quickly cesium vibrates. In our world of technology, we count the vibrations, or ticks if you will, of the cesium atom to mark time. At the beginning of each second we start counting the vibrations. When the atom has vibrated nine billion, one hundred and ninety million, six hundred and thirty-one thousand, seven hundred and seventy times, we know one second has elapsed. We used that same number of vibrations to mark the end of the next, and the next, and the next second. Cesium is the world's official timekeeper. And, in fact, the National Institute of Standards and Technology (NIST), right here in Boulder, Colorado is responsible for setting and maintaining time standards for the critical financial, navigational, and military systems of the United States. It is the official timekeeper for our nation.

"Atomic clocks are very accurate. NIST's atomic clock will only lose or gain a second in a hundred million years. The nearly absolute accuracy of our atomic clocks is an important part of the security of the United States and upon which NIST depends upon to maintain time accuracy and synchronization. At some point in the future, we may be able to measure time even more accurately. Think of a pocket watch that could maintain accuracy for more than three billion years without resetting it. That's astounding!

"Nearly everyone understands how we use time to plan our days, to schedule our events, or to record experiences. Despite our great immersion and dependence in our use of the cycles of time, we still cannot say, with absolute surety, what time is. There are some who say that time only exists when someone is marking the events in the passing of time. Others have suggested that if you have a clock, you have time. That could mean that time is mere perception and not a thing, and that concept becomes a fascinating discussion

"Isaac Newton proposed that time is an absolute dimension, like the measure of a meter, or the vibrational cycle of a cesium atom. Newton believed that time moves at the same rate for everyone, no matter where they are located. That means that time would pass at the same rate for

Earthlings as it would for aliens on some faraway and unknown planet. The concept of time, as a constant for everyone, is our experiential reality. My minutes seem to be just as long as your minutes, just as they seem to be the same as our neighbor's minutes. But in this case, our experiential perspective is incorrect.

"People believed in the universality of time for many years until a pesky patent clerk developed a radical new theory. Albert Einstein's special theory of relativity was a huge step in man's quest to understand his surroundings. Unlike Newton, who considered time to be an independent and fixed dimension, Einstein theorized that the dimension of time is inextricably melded with space. That idea sparked what we now call space-time. As dizzying as that revelation was, it is accompanied by one that still makes our heads spin even more perilously. Einstein said, and we've proven it over and over again, that time is variable; time is not constant."

Michael stopped his presentation to gauge the reaction of the students. There was very little talk, and he wondered if it was because they were not surprised by that statement, or that they simply did not understand the substance of the idea.

"Let's clarify that statement."

Michael then pointed to a student sitting in the front row of the lecture hall. "Would you kindly stand and walk to the back of the lecture hall and stop?"

The student agreed, rose, and began to climb the stairs to the back of the room.

"For me, and those of you who are seated, the rate of time is exactly the same. The minutes on our clocks are all ticking by at the same rate. However, the minutes on the clock of our volunteer are ticking off more slowly."

Michael paused, and then asked, "Does anyone know why?"

He expected no response, but a timid hand was raised.

"Please, go ahead," said Michael.

"It is because he is moving," was the reply.

Michael was pleased that someone in the room had some understanding of the concept.

"Thank you, you are right. When compared to bodies at rest, the time for bodies in motion flows at a lesser rate."

The student had reached the top of the stairs, at the back of the room and had stopped.

"Please notice that our volunteer has stopped. Now that he is stationary, his clock and all of our clocks are ticking at the same rate. But as soon as he starts to walk back down the stairs, his clock will slow down again and remain at a slower rate until he stops."

Michael gave a nod for the student to return to his seat.

"Let me say right here and now, that the rate difference is extremely small, but the Hafele–Keating experiment of 1971 proved that those small differences do exist. They compared the time of stationary atomic clocks on the Earth to the time of atomic clocks on jet airplanes flying around the Earth. In that experiment, the time difference was about forty billionths of a second. These experiments have been repeated over and over again with consistent results. In every case, it has been proven that time is variable based on the relative speed of the clocks.

"In the reality of our slow moving world, a time shift of forty billionths of a second, or forty nanoseconds, means nothing to us. None of us felt or recognized the slowed clock of the student walking to the back of the lecture hall. However, if we could compare our time passage with another who was traveling near the speed of light, we would easily recognize the far slower ticking of that other person's clock. The bottom line is that time is relative. It is a relative measurement that differs from one to another based on the relative speeds of the two.

"The next time you are on an airplane flight and the time on board seems interminable, remember that, in fact, your clock is actually running forty nanoseconds slower than stationary clocks on the ground. In such a case, time is more perception than reality. You'll feel like time is moving far more slowly than its accurately measured rate, which is literally more slowly than time experienced by a stationary companion on the surface of the Earth."

Michael saw signs of interest in some of the students. They became his target audience.

"So what does this mean to us? It may mean very little on a practical basis, but as we delve into the mysteries of the cosmos, it means that we have to think differently about space and time. I'm going to make a big jump in logic here, but the relativistic properties of time suggest that all time exists all at once. In short, relativistic time screams out the idea that all current, future, and past events exist all at once. I can't take the time to discuss that concept, but it is an integral aspect of space-time. I invite you to join us as scientists of the future to delve into that mystery and lay bare its reality.

"Should you embark on the study of the sciences, you will begin to understand that mass curves or warps space-time, and that space-time/ mass interaction may be intimately connected to gravity. This means that if you could get into a spaceship and travel around a body with immense mass, like a black hole with its monstrous field of gravity, your time would slow down. It also means that as you study light from distant stars and galaxies, you would learn that light is often bent by warps in space-time. If you are asking, 'What does that mean?' It means that light actually bends around large bodies of mass in the universe, as it travels through the universe.

"In the study of the sciences, you will learn a very important concept. When you travel in a northeasterly direction, you cannot separate the northern component of your travel from the eastern component of your travel. It is very similar with space-time. When you travel through space and time, you cannot separate the components of space and time. We are always moving through time even though we may be stationary in space. When we move physically, we move through both space and time. The laws of physics, or the equations that we write to describe the operations of the universe, tell us that space and time cannot be separated.

"As a part of my presentation today, in the hope of interesting you in the sciences, I want to point out that our beautiful mathematical equations say that time is not only variable, but that it can also flow both forward and backward. That concept has given rise to the hope of time travel, either into the future or back into the past. Our experiential data suggests that time is only forward-moving. This is one of the reasons that I get up every day with a smile on my face. Each and every day I face this great enigma, this confusing conundrum: the experiential fact that time only moves forward for us is *contradicted* by mathematics that says it can flow *both forward and backward*. If you like puzzles, this may be one of the greatest puzzles of all time."

Michael stopped and smiled just for a moment, hoping they would get his pun. While waiting, he noted a loving couple among the students. Pointing to them, he asked them to stand up. They clearly didn't want to do so, but complied.

"What are your names?" Michael asked.

Mitch and Yoshi was their response.

"Wow, Mitch and Yoshi, there's almost as much similarity in your names as there is between space and time."

Tepid laughter filled the room.

"Mitch, please ask Yoshi for a date."

Even more embarrassed, Mitch turned to Yoshi, his female friend, and said, "Will you go on a date with me?"

Before she could answer, Michael quickly stopped the exchange. Appealing to the group of students, he asked, "Now, Mitch just asked Yoshi for a date. Is that the end of the story?"

Heads shook back and forth negatively.

Next he directed Yoshi, "Tell Mitch yes."

Yoshi looked at Mitch and said, "Yes."

"Great! You have both agreed to a date. Subject closed." Michael stopped and acted as though he would proceed to a new topic, but just as quickly, spoke again.

"But wait, where will you meet?"

Both students shrugged their shoulders, almost in unison, and the rest of the class joined in with a laugh.

"I'll tell you what. I'll settle that. Meet at the student center."

Looking down at his notes, Michael almost absentmindedly said, "Good that's settled." He pretended to fumble with his papers for a moment and then suddenly looked up. He noted a strange commotion in the room. "What's wrong?" he asked.

Yoshi spoke up, "What time shall we meet?"

Hearty laughter now spread throughout the room.

Michael made a faux slap to his forehead. "I almost forgot! You need to know when to meet. Mitch, what time should you meet?"

Mitch looked at Yoshi and said, "Six?"

Yoshi shook her head in agreement.

Michael interjected, "Do you mean 6 a.m. or 6 p.m.?"

Mitch smiled and quickly said, "6 p.m."

"Good, that's settled," said Michael, and then he stopped cold, his face taking on a more serious look. "But it was important to know which it was, correct? Imagine if Yoshi had arrived at 6 a.m. looking for Mitch. What would she have found?"

"Her anger!" came a shout from the room, and laughter filled the room again.

Looking to the rest of the students, Michael asked with a devious smile, "How could they have ever met up for this date if I hadn't forced them to set a time to go along with their chosen place? And all this for a simple date!"

There was a considerable amount of laughter and discussion in the room. Waiting until the discussions quieted, Michael said at last, "Can you see how your lives are inextricably tied to both space and time. First, there was the question of the date. That's almost like the question of our existence, right? But then, we had to learn the place of the date. Then there was the time of the date. But that was not all. We also had to know the standard of the time chosen to set the moment of the date. a.m. and p.m. are a big deal when discussing time between two people."

Once more Michael paused while the students considered his demonstration.

"Let me also assure you that if Mitch were traveling at or near the speed of light, he would have to consider very seriously the relative passage of time when asking Yoshi for a date. And since his clock would be ticking at a far slower rate, the words he spoke would be heard by Yoshi as if he had spoken in slow motion. Yoshi might have had to wait for minutes or even hours to hear a trail of words spoken in seconds. Do you understand now, in some small respect, how space and time are tied together?"

Once more Michael paused, then added, "Believe me, the connections between space and time are even more profound than the elements of that little demonstration. Once again I say, come and join us. Let's search those connections together.

"Now, I have one more matter that I'd like to present and it has to do with the expression 'space-time continuum.' Our first-hand perspective says that time will simply keep moving forward into an infinity that is beyond our grasp. The number line, which so many learned about so long ago, moves both forward and backward to infinity. We have labeled space-time as a continuum. Why have we done that? There is a very simple reason. Space-time is a four-dimensional existence and all of its points in space are inseparably formed into one existence with all the instants of time.

Holding up a single sheet of paper, Michael spoke out. "I've prepared a handout for you. It is two sentences long and written by Dr. Sten Odenwald. I'll read the contents of the handout which is entitled *The Space-time Continuum.*

"'It is believed to be a 'continuum' because, so far as we know, there are no missing points in space or instants in time, and both can be subdivided without any apparent limit in size or duration. So physicists now routinely consider our world to be embedded in this four-dimensional space-time continuum, and all events, places, moments in history, actions, and so on, are described in terms of their location in space-time.'"

After reading the quotation from Dr. Odenwald, Michael looked into the faces of the rows of students. He maintained quiet in the room by the power of his searching eyes as he tried to peer into their minds. After a very long minute, he continued, "What is reality? What is the truth? Our experiences say that the space-time continuum is linear, that time only flows forward moment by moment, one after another, and in a very linear fashion. One could say that the space-time continuum expresses space as a linear form, in slices of life, like one frame of a movie film following another.

"Our mathematicians describe a very different form of space and time. Our mathematic formulas tell us that space and time are malleable, shapeable, compressible, expandable, and not the constants that you and I experience. The one thing that we feel quite certain about is that we are located in space-time. The point of our location may be questionable and may depend on perspective. It could even be an illusion. Having said that, some suspect that time, something we live our lives by, is an illusion. If you want to consider the philosophy of that statement, stick around for our next presenter.

"Let me sum up my viewpoint. The research and study of such topics is, to me, fascinating, almost to the level of compulsion. It has become the bread and water of my life. I'm here today, extending an open invitation to every one of you, to join us. Join us as we search for answers to the questions that we know enough to ask, and in a search for the *questions* that are, for now, unknown."

6:2 ≫ 2005 – Restification

Michael was excited to call Liz. She answered almost immediately.

"Hi, Michael!"

Michael stood in his excitement, "Hi Liz! Guess what?"

"You've decided to move to Houston."

There was a hesitation on the other end of the phone that transitioned into an attempt at laughter, followed by, "No, I'm afraid that's not my news."

Over time, Liz had skirmished with Michael regarding her condition for moving: marriage. Having sent one salvo she resigned to defeat and said, "Well, let's hear it anyway."

Michael detected a subtle hint of annoyance. It had been six months since they had been with each other, though there had been numerous phone calls. Despite her slight undertone, Michael proceeded.

"They've finished my Cuda."

Liz chuckled as she said, "Oh, your 426 Hemi Cuda, right?"

"Yes, and don't forget that it's a convertible."

Adopting a slight smile, she responded, "Wouldn't dream of it."

Michael braced himself and asked, "Liz, please come to Boulder. I'd like you to see the car and take it for a spin."

After a pause, she asked, "When?'

"As soon as possible, or anytime you can get away."

"Let me look at my schedule and I'll call you back tonight."

The call had been short, and as Michael hung up the phone, he felt disappointed in the conversation. He thought about the many years that had passed. He'd seen Liz too little, spent too little time with her. He loved her but couldn't find a way to commit to marriage. There were several reasons. He still volunteered in times and places where his life was endangered. Could he marry, only to leave her in a deathly accident? But his biggest reason revolved around his work. Would marriage affect its quality? Could he dedicate himself to science and a marriage? It was a worry. And how could he factually know that marriage was his best course?

But how long will she wait?

6:3 ▷▷▷ 2005 – A Hemi in Boulder

Liz planned her visit to Boulder. Michael had been talking about the car for several years. She knew very little about cars and could not comprehend Michael's excitement at the completion of the car, but it was clearly something of great importance to him. Liz went online to research Michael's car. If she were going to see the car, she'd better know something about it.

A 1970 Hemi Cuda was considered by some to be the ultimate of classic muscle cars. Only 652 of these cars had been built in 1970. She also learned why Michael reminded her that is was a convertible; only fourteen of the 652 were convertibles. Liz thought about the numerous times Michael had excitedly talked about this particular muscle car. He said he loved the way the words sounded as they rolled off his lips: 70 Hemi Cuda.

Liz also saw that wanting a 70 Hemi Cuda and owning one are two completely different matters as these old collectibles sold for an exorbitant two million dollars, and more for an original, un-restored but well-preserved car. Michael had money, but not that much. His best-selling book, *Science in the Minds of Everyday People*, was in its third edition and very successful. The first edition had been limited but sold out quickly. New versions of the book adopted cutting edge technology. A whole new generation of students bought the book and enjoyed its video game-like qualities. Michael earned a good living from it, and the success of his book had given him plenty of discretionary capital, but not enough for a two million dollar car. So he had decided to do the next best thing. He would have a less expensive clone built.

Liz learned of the process from Michael. Buy a '70 Cuda, a car that wasn't rusted out, put a massive Hemi engine in it, have it updated with current technology, and make it look just like the classic. It was called *restification.*

Liz had often questioned why Michael would want such a powerful car. As a volunteer EMT and First Responder, he had rescued many shattered bodies. He simply said, "It's not power that destroys, it's the reckless management of power. Power is for the disciplined, not thrill seekers or aggressors."

The flight to Denver was without incident. During landing, she felt the stirring of excitement, but she thought *her* excitement to see Michael might be greater than *his* excitement to show her the Cuda. Liz could not bring herself to look at other men. He was the one she wanted. It became a test of endurance which included loneliness and frequent heartache.

How long can I wait?

Their embrace was as warm as ever. Liz felt a renewed hope that Michael might even be more interested in her than the car.

The car is at least a good excuse to get together.

The Cuda was at Michael's house. A walk around the car revealed it to be a thing of beauty. The top was soon down, and Michael looked like he was going to explode with excitement.

"So what's the deal with this Hemi engine," Liz asked.

"You remembered!"

With a smile and a wink, Liz quipped, "Yes, I remembered."

Michael opened the hood.

Liz knew very little about what she saw, other than she knew the spark plugs sat in the middle of the valve covers. She did find a way to express all the appropriate words of adoration. In truth, though, she had to admit that it really looked cool, especially with the top down.

"Are you ready?" Michael asked, beaming.

"Yes."

"Well jump in."

Liz slid into the passenger seat. The door closed solidly. She watched like a parent watches a child open their first electric train set at Christmas. The engine truly did roar to life. She could feel a tremor in her body and was surprised by the deep-throated rumble of the powerful engine. The car coasted down the driveway.

"Are you really ready?" Michael shouted.

Liz nodded, yes.

The car smelled and felt new. The paint glistened and the chrome work gleamed. The dash and the instrument panel looked new and vibrant. Michael eased through the gutter and into to the street. Liz noticed a look that, in the past, seemed only to appear when he talked about physics theories. She had seen little else that caused this much excitement in Michael. Without warning, the powerful engine roared to life, Michael released the clutch, and the engine caused the rear tires to spin, belching smoke and the smell of burned rubber in the air!

The car shot forward like a rocket. Liz squealed and reached for something to hang onto. There was nothing. She was pressed back into her seat by the extreme acceleration, the bottoms of her feet tight against the firewall. The pressure let up for just an instant as Michael shifted into second gear. Again, Liz' body was forced back into the seat, and she strained to keep her head up. Chancing a glance at Michael, clearly in his own world, she noticed that in mere seconds they were already exceeding eighty miles an hour—in less than a hundred feet! After reaching eighty, Michael slowed to a more sensible speed.

Liz called out, "Which was that, aggression or thrill-seeking?"

As his smile turned cheeky, Michael shouted back, "Oh, that was discipline!"

Liz shook her head in disbelief. After years of knowing him, Michael could still surprise her. She was even more surprised when he slowed down, turned the car around, and pulled over to the curb.

"It's your turn," he said.

"Oh no, no, no! I'm not going to take the risk of crashing your new baby. It's obviously fast and, as you know, I'm not a fast woman."

Michael looked at her more intently.

"But you could be today," he said with a broad smile.

A hint of a blush warmed her face, and they both burst into belly laughs.

Knowing the reality behind the statement she said, "I'm going to leave this moment as yours and yours alone. Maybe I'll go fast on another day."

Michael quickly raised his eyebrows a couple of times, teasing her.

Liz realized it was all bluster. Despite the banter, she knew Michael was not yet ready. She also knew he was in love with her, and she had already decided to continue to wait. She had renewed her search for a position in Denver, to no avail.

Maybe I should work harder at it.

6:4 ≫≫ 2005 – Facing the Fear of Dreams

Once more in the protection of their market sanctuary, Haleema and Faiza sat, talking as the dear friends they had become. All three of Haleema's children were in school. Her husband feared too much for the birth of a third daughter, so there had not been another pregnancy. Haleema chatted with Faiza without interruption. Quips about the destroyer had lost their humor but the truths of life for women in Iran were still a passionate subject. Haleema also enjoyed reliving some of the more joyful moments of motherhood. With some prodding, she agreed to tell Faiza some of her stories. The stories were filled with characters of intrigue. There were heroes and villains, and good always overcame evil.

"Your stories are delightful! Tell me more," asked Faiza.

Haleema hesitated. She looked Faiza in the eyes, but then her gaze darted away.

I want to tell her, but should I? I've been in misery for so long; perhaps I will tell her today. Maybe it will ease my fears.

After years of holding and hiding a frightening companion, she decided to open up. For Haleema, this day became a day of fortitude and honesty. She related the imagery of her dreams.

"Haleema, you say they came out of the ground?"

"Yes, they rise up like giant pillars."

She was pleased to have captured Faiza's attention as she pressed for more information. "What do they look like?"

Haleema's face screwed up and a look of quandary crossed it. "I don't know how to explain them. They are black at the base and transition to a top that appears as a brilliant light, almost like a crystal. The pillars seem to shimmer in some way that I don't understand."

"What do they do?"

Haleema's face took on the look of fear. "They thrust from the ground, destroying everything in their path. The Earth is broken and life is lost . . .."

"And you've been having theses dreams on a regular basis?"

"Yes, in the middle of too many nights."

"What happens after they rise? They surely do something."

Haleema looked away from Faiza. The dream-scape was strange and she hesitated, out of habit, to continue. Finally, after a breath and a long sigh, she turned back to Faiza and told the rest of the story. "I also see small, but countless points of light rise from the ground. I can't define their origin but they rise and seem to have a predetermined path. They fly toward the pillars."

Faiza's face took on a look of amazement, and Haleema could see that she was enthralled with the dreams. Amazed at Faiza's intense focus, she faltered and stopped.

"Come on," begged Faiza, "there must be more."

"Yes, the lights fly toward the pillars but when they get close, the pillars shoot out some kind of energy, like a death ray. When the rays hit the arcing lights, there are brilliant flashes. The heavens are lit in a way that I could never have imagined. The brilliance of the flash always wakes me, and the dream ends there."

Faiza sat back in her seat, but her eyes fixated on Haleema.

Haleema wondered if Faiza knew she had left out an important detail.

"You must write this down; it would make a great story."

Haleema was relieved that she had not been pressed for more. Then she looked at Faiza in a very firm way, "Faiza, the dreams frighten me. I don't think I could write them down. It would be too hard."

"Why are you frightened? They are just dreams!"

"I have no real reason, but somehow . . . somehow they feel real . . . and they frighten me. My heart recoils at their nightly presence. I awake, almost in terror."

"You are serious about this, aren't you?"

"Yes, they terrify me so. I've never been able to talk about them even though I've been having the dreams for years."

"And this is the real reason for your exhaustion, not just your children."

Haleema shook her head once more, "Yes."

In a determined tone Faiza said, "You must face your fears. Let me help you write it down. What is the central theme, the pillars?"

"Yes."

"Are they small, large, short, or tall?"

"They are very tall and somewhat slender."

"And you call them pillars?"

"Yes, and sometimes I think of them as pinnacles of rock."

"You must name them. If you are going to face them, you must name them."

Haleema looked down to the ground and scraped her shoe over the surface. I don't know, a pillar just doesn't seem right, neither does pinnacle."

Faiza sat back in a thoughtful pose. After a moment, she asked, "Does anyone live in them?"

"No, not that I've seen."

After another pause Faiza said, "Why don't you call them towers?"

Haleema looked up from the ground. She suddenly felt some kind of kinship with the structure that had previously frightened her. It was a dramatic turn around, and oddly, the fear seemed to abate. "Towers," she said. "Yes, towers. Somehow that seems right. I feel good about that."

"Okay, it's settled. You'll call them towers. Now let's get these dreams written down. You've faced the main character; now let's take on the arcing lights."

Haleema shook her head. With a courage she had not felt before, she said, "Yes, it's time."

In a cathartic exercise, Haleema wrote down the dreams with their many facets. As she wrote, she forgot about interpretation and let her mind wander, creating a story of peril and delivery. *What will FarZan think of this story*, she wondered. *I bet he'll like it. It's got monsters of another sort.*

6:5 ⟫⟫ 2006 – Inducement

Dean, as he was known to the sales branch, and the negotiators of his network, was the architect of the sale of his weapons and other assets. Only Neg and Khoyer knew he was none other than The Kahn. Dean's negotiators consisted of three men and their proxies. One negotiator dealt with the Pacific Rim nations, another with Eastern European customers, including Russia, and the third worked with the jihadists.

Dean had worked hard to orchestrate the relationships that would facilitate his plans. It had taken years to develop back-door relationships with entities in each of these world regions. The President of Iran, his associates, and subordinates had been ideal candidates. They were dedicated to the elimination of Israel and the Americans.

Dean made it very easy to export terror. The terror sponsor simply needed to place the order with Dean's negotiators, which was then processed by The Kahn's network. The network acquired the weapons and passed them to the fulfillment section of Dean's network. To the outside world, the organization became a tangled and bewildering mass of shoots and branches that was hard to untangle; that tangled mess suited The Kahn's purposes.

Dean knew that Iran wasn't a wealthy nation, but there was always money for technology, arms, the export of terror, and the destruction of Israel. He met their needs, skillfully facilitating a flow of weapons and ammunition to the terrorist groups that the nation supported. Iran had developed a deep level of trust and confidence in their supplier, and the Iranian President found the idea of dirty bombs, as presented by Dean's negotiators, especially appealing. Dean had been one of many catalysts in Iran's export of terror and the development of the nuclear program.

North Korea proved to be more difficult for Dean, but he had eventually achieved his goal; the difficulties were challenges to be faced and overcome. The North Koreans contracted with Dean to buy western technology. They grew to appreciate a supplier that would work outside the purview of their Chinese friends. Money earned by Dean from the sale of western technology was reinvested into bribing high level contacts in North Korea. Dean often laughed quietly to himself at the thought of using cash received from the North Korean government to bribe North Korean power centers. He had developed the perfect double-edged sword in North Korea. By purchasing Dean's goods and services, the North Korean government provided the money that paid the bribes to influence North Korean policies in a way that was favorable to The Kahn's purposes.

It had been more difficult to develop influence in China, but there were two groups that were ripe for The Kahn's enticements. The greedy, selfish Communists and the Muslims. His research indicated over twenty-three million Muslims were living in China, stemming from the introduction of Islam in the early sixth century. He also learned that some members of this two percent of the population felt persecuted. The Kahn found that persecuted Chinese Muslims were willing to use jihad as a means of revenge against their persecutors just as their Middle Eastern brothers were doing.

Dean's sales in China included secrets that his network had acquired through NATO embedded spies. Once more, the money paid to Dean was poured back into the country through The Kahn, buying more favors, information, and influence. The flow of goods, services, secrets, and money appeared as disjointed events when, in reality, they were simply part of one big circle—the circle of influence of The Kahn.

CHAPTER 7
THEORIES

7:0 »»» 2006 – Truth

Michael had been an ardent seeker of truth and, as such, he had to ask, *"What is truth?"* He had read all the great debates. Philosophers argued the definition; historians contested realities; courts struggled to determine who was telling the truth; religionists had a variety of seemingly interlinking but disparate truths; and science was an entity unto itself, constantly discovering new truths that invalidated old truths.

Thinking on the very edge, Michael came to believe that there was more to the principle of truth than people understood. He had been working on an advanced and sophisticated theory supported with an embryonic mathematical equation which might shed some light on the matter.

He had noted two statements about truth. They pushed and pulled at his intellect. One came from his father's beliefs. It suggested that if one has the truth, he has knowledge of things as they are in the moment, as they were in all previous moments, and as they will actually be in the future.

When considering the words he had learned from his father, Michael realized the possibility of another meaning. Although it is important to have a knowledge of the truth it was even more important to be truthful, to become a being of truth, a being without falsehoods. Such a being could aptly be defined as truth, and thus truth can be classified as an entity.

There was another similar statement that expressed the concept of truth in a different way. The change was in the truth of the future, suggesting that future truth is what 'it may become.' Though similar with regard to the present and past, both concepts considered future truth in very different ways. One suggested that the future could be changed, the other suggested the possibility that truth, both behind us and in front of us, already exists. That last idea was congruent with theories on time, based on quantum mechanics. That difference was the motivator of today's phone call.

Michael called from his office at the University, hoping his father would be at home. Upon hearing his father's voice, he announced himself. "Hi Dad, it's your wayward son. You know, the one that doesn't go to church."

"And the son I love," replied Big Al.

His father's love transcended the phone's ear piece and Michael's throat constricted. It took him a minute to speak in a natural voice.

"I appreciate that and you know how I feel about you."

This time it was Big Al who experienced a crack in his voice.

"Yes, I know that."

Ignoring emotions, Michael began quickly, "I want to talk to you about truth."

Clearing his throat, Big Al asked, "What about it? It either is or it isn't."

Michael chuckled. His dad had a way of working around the bull, both literally and figuratively, being a prize bull breeder.

"That's a good one Dad, and in fact you're absolutely correct. But I'm thinking of something you taught me. You know that phrase about truth, that it is a knowledge of things in the past, in the present, and in the future?"

"Yes, I remember," Big Al said with a groan as he plopped into his easy chair, accompanied by the telltale and familiar squeak of his most comfortable place of repose.

"Dad, you also talked about truth being independent in its sphere of existence and that without that independence there could be no existence."

"It sounds like you've taken up philosophy, surely not religion."

"Some of my associates would say the same thing."

Big Al leaned back, "I'm glad we're having a talk."

Michael continued, "You see, we all talk about the truth of today or yesterday, and into the future, but your concept of the independent property of truth suggests a much deeper meaning. First of all, the phrase suggests one can know the truth of the future, but seems to imply that it is fixed. But secondly, the idea of truth having independence is too fascinating to ignore, and if that is true, how can the truth of the future be fixed?"

"So are you thinking about God knowing the future?"

"Yes."

"Do you believe He can?"

Michael felt a little pressure on a topic that had always been difficult. "I'm still struggling with His existence; let alone what He can do."

"Okay, where exactly is this leading?"

Michael figuratively pulled at his collar, "There is a reason for that, but I don't want to say just now."

"I can't help you much if you don't come clean. What do you want from me?"

Knowing he had stepped into a trap of his own making, he continued. "It has to do with my world, and you may not be able to help, but I do need a sounding board."

"Hit me, and let's see what bounces off."

Michael made a decision, and took a big breath, "Thanks, Dad. So let me blather on. You can stop me when you feel the need."

After one more nervous breath Michael began.

"I believe there is a factual description to every truth. It has to be factual and accurate or it isn't truth. We know many empirical facts, but sometimes the truth is hidden, and sometimes we are simply wrong, learning that the truth we knew is actually false."

Michael cleared his throat. He felt a little nervous expressing his deep, almost philosophical thoughts to his father. "A knowledge of things of the past is an elusive search, and as long as humans are telling the story, that truth is often misunderstood and misrepresented; whether by mistake, or design, it makes no difference. It is still not the truth."

Big Al responded, "I have no quarrel with your thoughts."

Michael was standing and began to pace.

"Thanks, the truth of the moment is just as difficult. The moment a word is spoken, it becomes the past. It may have been misspoken carelessly, ignorantly or willingly. It can easily be misunderstood for any of the same reasons."

"The thorn of communication," Al inserted.

"You're saying the truth in communication is the rose and misunderstandings are the thorns."

"Sounds about right."

Michael walked to his white-board and picked up a marker. He began tossing it in the air and added, "And looking into the future is infinitely daunting."

"Granted, but don't you do that?" Big Al questioned.

"I do, in fact I try to look at the now, the past, and the future in my work."

Big All did not respond, waiting for more information. Michael continued, "I use mathematic models in an effort to peer backward into the cosmos. I can do that because large heavenly bodies, such as planets and stars, all affected by gravity, have very constant and predictable actions and reactions. Similar models can also be used to suggest the future of the cosmos."

"That is if your models are correct," suggested Big Al.

"That's true. Now before I say more, I want you to know that I am going to use the word 'truth' as an identity, not just knowledge."

Big Al smiled. "An identity? Do you mean an entity or are you afraid to use that word?"

Michael stopped in this tracks, running a thought through his mind. *He is so perceptive!* After a moment of hesitation and thought, Michael resumed his pacing and chalk-tossing. "Okay, I concede. In my context, truth actually becomes an entity described by its primary property, which is truth."

Still smiling, Big Al said, "The fringes of science, huh?"

Stopping his pacing, Michael said, "Yes, and this is really fringe work. I'm beginning to believe that every combination of molecules, atoms, including fundamental particles like electrons and protons, are described by absolute truths that pronounce their makeup and their potential interactions. There are also absolute facts explaining how and why all elemental combinations have formed in the past, are forming today, and will form in the future. I am developing a theory that there is an absolute descriptor of everything. That descriptor can only be truth, and the thing that is being described by truth is an entity."

Al added his affirmation. "A theory? What I see on TV science episodes are often represented as fact, when in actuality they are a collection of theories."

"You're good, Dad, always the analytical observer."

"That's quite a compliment, coming from a genius son."

Michael chuckled and went on, "I have something on my mind that's very bizarre and I have to be sure I'm taking the right approach. You are a finely-tuned analytical observer and what you said about TV programing is," and he laughed, "the truth."

Big Al joined in the laugh, adding, "People too often—sometimes by mistake and sometimes with purpose—promote falsehoods."

"True, and Dad, I'm focusing on the role of truth, or the identity of fundamental particles."

Michael held his peace for several minutes. He wanted a response, but wasn't getting one. He continued in his silence.

At last Big Al said, "You're making an incredible statement. It sounds like you're implying that these particle entities have the ability to reason, and that those reasoning properties make up their identity. Am I grasping your point?"

"Yes, you are."

"Whew! You weren't going to tell me this, were you?"

Feeling relieved, Michael admitted, "I hadn't planned on it, no."

"I'm glad you did. You know, you're going to raise some eyebrows."

"Yes."

Big Al sat forward in his chair and asked, "Is there more to it?"

Michael gave the marker an extra high toss, almost like it was a Hail Mary.

"Yes, I'm certain that these elemental particles do what they do, not by chance, but by a response to a higher order, a higher order that exists as truth, and operates only as truth."

"Now you are on the fringe. You just said that elemental particles have intelligence. That's a step from reasoning and implies sentience. So basically, you're suggesting that all things have sentience."

"It may not be sentience in the way we think about it, but to a degree, yes."

"And these sentient particles, etc. respond to a higher order? It sounds like you are approaching a belief in God."

Michael rubbed his temples. "Not yet, but I'm just having a harder time believing in coincidence. The being I envision will likely be different from the one that most believers revere. If there is a God, I believe that He acts by science and not by some mystic, magical, unfathomable basis. This may be shocking to you, but I'm beginning to believe that if there is a God, he uses mathematics in his work."

Big Al whistled.

"And where did this all come from?"

"It started with my analysis of all the operations of the universe, including those in the microscopic world. I've considered the inner-complexities of the Earth and the even more staggering complexity of man. It's been weighing on me. I don't think any of this is an accident, but I also don't accept the view of most religionists. Too many believe that miracles are unexplainable. If the events that we call miracles really occurred, I want to explain them."

"Your peers will disparage you and religionists will call you a blasphemer."

"I think it depends on how I approach it. If I lead them to the conclusion, maybe they will accept it. There's a little more. I'm also developing a theory on how this higher order of intelligence can know the hearts and intent of people."

"I'm listening," said Big Al.

"I've developed a number of postulates and two are especially intriguing. First, I'm thinking that each being is a product of their own history woven together in a tapestry that includes interaction with all other people and all other things, their inclusive history, plus all surrounding environmental factors. Their fundamental, elemental, and cellular foundations are complex, and they work together to form patterns of choices and consequences."

Michael stopped again, waiting for a response. What he got was,

"Go on."

"At the elemental level, I have the feeling that their truth may be the limiting basis of their operations and functionality. It may also be that the sum of all the truths of the simple add up to and describe more complex combinations and operations, up to and including humans."

Big Al rubbed his temples, working to grasp his son's ideas and said, "It's getting deep. I'll try to follow along."

"I also have the thought that all truth, including fundamental and elemental truths, has the ability to choose how it acts. The choices of elemental particles are very simple. Higher orders of truth, more complex orders, like humans, are also influenced by their truths, but there is more complexity in their choices, and it becomes more difficult to make the best choices. However, it seems that the very simple entities consistently make proper choices, while very complex entities struggle to make the best choice. Some choices are just dumb and wrong."

Big Al interjected a question. "So you think complex truths, for instance humans, are less capable of responding in truth, to the truths around themselves."

"Yes, and hang onto your hat, Dad. My second line of thought is a possible definition of God."

Again, Michael purposefully stopped to illicit a reaction from his father. There was none. His father knew of his struggles with the concept of God and did not typically interfere. Realizing the wait would likely be fruitless, Michael went on, stating the real kernel of his burgeoning theory. "If there is a God, if He is infinite and eternal, and is the creator or organizer of the known universe, and possibly beyond that, He has to know all truth. You taught me that God knows the hearts of all mankind."

"Yes, and I truly believe that," said Big Al.

"For that to be true, it seems to me that God would have to know everything about the entirety of that person, from the beginning of his or her existence, to the present, including every interaction with everything around them; only then could the truth of the heart and soul of each being be known. And all that knowledge would be included in the database of God's mind. In those known truths, there must be a description, a factual way to completely and accurately describe every single human and their distinct existence and every factor that made it up."

Michael wished he could have seen his dad as he responded. "So God would have to know and comprehend all things."

Michael then asserted, "God has to know the history of everything, including each and every man and woman from the beginning of their existence, along with the operation of every subsystem in their body and mind, down to their very most elementary particles, and the sum of their interactions."

Big Al asked, "And what brought you to this concept?"

Michael responded, "It is a line upon line principle. Just as lines of computer code describe characters in video game or the CGI of a movie, I can see, in an extreme way, how some kind of line upon line experiential description of a human could be brought together into an expression that describes their life, including their individual variables and potentially their future. I have the thought that humans are made of myriad fundamental truths that combine with other truths to prop-agate the most complex truth of all: humanity. An incredibly brilliant man, or being, could write a mathematical sequence that describes each, and every operation, and every living entity in the universe, from the simple to the complex."

Al's head was swimming so he asked, "Want to stop and take a breath?"

"Not really. Do you want to respond?"

Considering Michael's ideas, he pondered, "Are you saying that everything has an absolute destiny?"

Michael reacted quickly and forcefully, "No. I believe there are vari-ables, somehow understood by the higher order, that allow men to take different paths, promoting different consequences, but this higher order of intelligence, or God if you will, has the data and intellect to predict those consequences, based upon the infinite database stored in the mind of that being. That's one way that knowledge of the future exists in truth. Or it could be like some scientists theorize, all time already exists and so do our future events."

"Both views are very extreme, Michael."

"Yes, they both are. And somewhere in all of these ruminations is the truth."

Baiting his son, Big Al asked, "Are you the man to write the code?"

"Thanks, Dad. But I think you're making fun of me."

"Maybe, but I am speaking with a level of seriousness. Who knows? Someday you might be able to do it."

Michael sat on the corner of his desk, pondering the possibility.

"There's not a chance. It's simply too complex for mankind, at least the way we are today. Today an equation describing the billions of working elements in just one human being is impossible, but given another ten thousand years, even the seemingly impossible may become child's play."

"You never were a small thinker, son. You have some truly amazing ideas."

"I've said it before, you're very perceptive Dad. You actually seem to understand the subject."

"Where do you think you got your brains from?"

"Mmm—I thought it was from Mom." Michael smiled to himself.

Big Al laughed and followed it up with his own personal hope. "It sounds to me like you've discovered God."

"That's still under review, but that statement about truth that you quote, as of now, requires a very high order of intelligence. One might call that order 'God.' I'm still not sure. However, if mankind knew the equations for all operations, whether they are fundamental or complex, they would be as this order of intelligence. Wouldn't that make mankind God-like?"

"That seems like a distinct possibility."

"But without empirical evidence, it is still theoretical and many scientists would prefer to call it philosophy."

"Well, get crackin' then."

"Okay, I will. Thanks for the discussion. You were very helpful."

After hanging up the phone, Michael continued his thoughts. He saw a problem with his theory. It was questionable since any flaws in the theory might be hidden by his personal perspective, his own desires, and his personal status. It was an enigma inside a conundrum. It was a quantum leap from the ideas of the day, but was it truth?

7:1 ⫸⫸⫸ 2006 – Perspective and Ideas

                    Liz had watched from afar as Michael worked through all his mental machinations. Despite the absence of the consummation of their love, she had become a great confidant and sounding board. She was often confused by his somewhat outlandish ideas, but that was a good thing. Her questions helped him sort out and simplify the veins of his investigations.

Spending time with Michael was always a relief from the loneliness of separation. Long distance phone calls, online video chats, email, and texting became their communication conduits, but they fell miserably short of the joy of warm embraces.

Liz was excited to learn that Michael would be coming to Houston. Once more she wanted to talk marriage. It would be easy to be confrontational and nagging, but she determined once again to restrain her natural tendencies. Reaching deeply into her character, Liz decided it would be better to be patient, and in the end, win Michael's commitment rather than engage his anger and possibly losing him forever. She believed that Michael truly loved her. She simply didn't understand why he wouldn't act upon it.

Liz watched excitedly as Michael cleared security in the Houston Hobby Airport, her heart already racing. Their embrace was warm and deeply affectionate and her questions about their relationship vanished when she found herself in his arms.

On the drive to her apartment, it was Michael who began the conversation, but it was not what she had anticipated.

"Liz, do you believe in God?"

"Whoa! That came out of nowhere," Liz said. "We've talked about God a bit, but you've never point-blank asked this question."

"I've been thinking about something for some time, and I want to bounce it off of you. You are science-minded with a spiritual background. I trust your thoughtfulness, and I'm very interested in your reaction."

Michael had turned his head, smiling at her. "I believe you will respond openly but not critically."

"You mean you won't have to put on your emotional armor?"

"Precisely," Michael said.

Liz kept her eyes on the road.

"Sounds like it's a big deal to you."

"It is. I'm not sure I have the courage to share it with my peers."

Her eyes still on the road, Liz disguised her disappointment in his previous lack of candor.

"You've been working on it for years, and you've never shared it with me?"

"I'm sorry, Liz. I had to work through it for myself, but I'm going to share it with you now."

"Well, I guess there's something to be said for that."

Turning toward her, he added, "The only other person I've shared this with is my dad, but not in the same way. You have different qualifications and perspectives and that's important."

"Have you applied your legendary math skills to the matter?"

He chuckled. "To a degree, yes, but it's embryonic. I've made some attempts, but I'm not sure that, at this point at least, it is even possible to derive the math."

She stole a glance from the traffic to Michael.

"What, the legendary Math-Master, promoter of the 'perfect language of math' is at a loss to communicate in his base language?"

The sparkle in Liz's eyes revealed her mischievous jab of humor. But Liz quickly added before he could respond, "Okay, spill your guts, my friend. Let's see what that magnificent brain has cooked up."

He began, "If there is a God, and I think the likelihood is high— well, I've wondered, how does He do His work?"

"What?"

"How does God perform what we call miracles?"

Liz turned her head once more from the road.

"I'm afraid I'm going to have to ask the *what do you mean* question."

"Too funny, Liz."

"Maybe, but I don't know where you're going with this."

"Well, if God created the Earth, the universe, plus everything that's in it, how did He do it?"

"I've just never seriously thought about it."

Michael sat in silence, staring straight ahead. Liz wondered what had taken him. After an uncomfortable moment, he continued.

"Let me approach it another way, one that you'll be familiar with."

"Okay," said Liz in a tone of hesitation.

"From our past discussions, I know you've seen what some would call miraculous medical outcomes. Sometimes people are healed when it is unexpected, even considered impossible. Sometimes they die when they should live. I know you've seen those things, but have you never wondered how they came to be?"

"Yes, I have wondered how they happened."

"It would certainly give me a reason to wonder."

Liz exited the freeway.

Michael continued, "Medical personnel, although trained in science, are made up of religious people, agnostics, and atheists. Their perspectives are varied, right?"

"Correct."

"And there is no consensus?"

Liz thought of her past experiences. "No, not really"

"Let me get to a specific scenario. A patient has acute cancer, with advanced and inoperable tumors scattered throughout major organs. The patient is too weak for any treatment and not expected to live beyond a few days, maybe even a few hours."

The traffic was becoming heavy, but Liz focused on the discussion.

"I've seen that too many times. Most of those patients die, but there are some who've experienced a remarkable recovery. In one case the tumors just seemed to disappear. It made me wonder if the diagnosis was right in the first place."

"Did the family attribute it to a miracle?"

"Yes."

"Liz, we often express God as a being of miracles, but that implies that He doesn't work in methods that we can understand, or by what I would call science. I think He does."

"Well, if there is a God, I assume He can do anything." Then, after a moment of hesitation, Liz added, "Maybe we don't understand what miracles really are."

"Exactly, and they might be a Standard Operational Procedure for God—SOP."

"Okay."

Michael went on, "Let's theorize for a moment that those tumors factually existed. They were physical, made up of matter. They lived in that body, propagating and destroying. Let's also suppose the tumors just disappeared, and that it was God's doing. This suggests that the matter making up the tumors had to be physically removed or changed in some way. They may have become benign forms or simply de-constructed."

"Yes, I can see your point; the tissue making up the tumors must change in some way."

"So did God exert some power that pushes or forces the matter in the tumor, particle by particle, in a direction of His choosing? Did He de-construct the cells, and if so, what was that causal force?"

"The causal force?"

Liz' face took on the look of intrigue.

Michael continued, "Yes, what made the atoms move? If you simply say that God is the causal force, then you leave out the possibility of knowing how God operates, and it doesn't resolve the 'how' of the question. Do you see my quandary?"

"I do, and I am sure you know that I can't resolve your quandary. To me, God has always been a mystery, beyond understanding."

Michael became animated, "But why should God be beyond understanding? He is supposed to be our supporter, our benefactor, our mentor. Wouldn't He want us to understand Him?"

"That makes some sense." Using Michael's own tack, she added, "Theorizing that this is all true, I'd have to say that He changed the tissue. Somehow the cancer tissue broke down, losing its destructive properties, combing with other tissues or sloughing into the excretory systems."

Michael looked at Liz, holding her in his gaze.

"We teach that matter maintains its current state until acted upon by some force. It is a basic law of physics. Or in this case, the matter of a tumor maintains its character, whatever that character may be, until it is acted upon in some way."

"Okay."

Michael continued his focus on Liz.

"So does God emit some magic ray or force field that moves or changes the matter?"

Liz didn't answer.

"Have you ever seen some kind of force field moving around a miraculously healed patient?"

"No."

"I can tell you that no scientist has ever detected, measured, or reported such a force."

Once again, Liz made no response.

"I have a controversial thought. Is it possible that matter, or let's say atoms and molecules, somehow recognize God as their Master and willingly obeying His desire. But in doing so, they act according to their own agency, to move, or change, or to even disassociate themselves from other elements and the form they had defined?"

Liz' eyebrows furrowed, and she practically yelled, "Are you crazy?"

Quickly rebounding from her uncensored statement, Liz turned to Michael, resetting her face into a smile, realizing she may have insulted him.

Michael smiled back.

"Yes, it may be a crazy idea. But can you see why this fascinates me so much?"

"I can see that it excites you, Michael, but it's bewildering to me."

Michael added more thoughts. "We say that God can move mountains, make it rain, heal the sick, and protect people. And moving a mountain is simple compared with the complexities of a human. In addition, consider the complexities and symbiotic relationships of the universe. I simply cannot compute a scenario where a completely self-supporting, self-sustaining, symbiotic, and progressive system of life could accidentally and, supposedly by happenstance, burst into existence and maintain itself. I think the elements of the universe chose to do so by His direction, knowing it was the will of God and choosing to obey His will."

Liz was once again speechless as she considered not just the question and the ramifications, but also Michael's passion about the subject. She pulled over to the curb, stopping on a residential street. Silence reigned while Liz sorted through his ideas. She finally said, "I understand your logic, but even religious people may not believe in the idea."

Michael held his peace.

At last, Liz added, "Your ideas imply that matter has some way of sensing, or understanding and/or analyzing and obeying. That implies intelligence."

"Precisely and it's been driving me crazy with excitement!" exclaimed Michael.

Liz backhanded Michael's chest, "Well, you're the scientist. You have the qualifications to consider such a question. You can do the math. So go for it!"

Michael sighed, deflating his lungs.

"There are so many things we don't know. We don't even know what we don't know. This is not something I can do, at least not today."

"Has any scientist ever broached these ideas?"

"Ha!" Half laughing and half scoffing, he said, "No one in their right mind has, at least not publicly. In past times, scientists went to jail for such thoughts. Remember Galileo?"

"No, but I remember the controversy about a flat world."

Liz squinted as she looked at Michael, "So what does that say about you? Are you about to spiral out of your 'right mind'?"

Michael flashed a cheesy grin.

"I've always maintained I'm nutty as a fruitcake. I think that a nutty mental process is actually what makes my thoughts possible. At least that's what John Nash believed, and I think I agree. A sane man may be incapable of such conjecture."

"So this exercise is right up your alley, Mr. Math Man."

Michael remained silent, so Liz filled the void.

"Of course you're assuming that there is a God, and that He can move matter."

"That is the assumption or premise under which I am approaching the problem. That is the basis and will be the cause for refutation, even ostracism—by my colleagues—if I make the proposal."

"I can see your concerns."

"I'm not going to announce that I have scientific evidence that there is a God. There may be a God, but I still don't know for sure."

"So God is a theory to you."

It was Michael who squinted this time. "Yes, because I am a theorist. Theorists see or imagine possibilities and theorize a way to answer difficult questions. I take that job seriously. I am not beneath theorizing about God."

And so the weekend passed. There were lots of physics discussions, although some may have called them philosophy. There was also some romance, but there were no concrete commitments made. Once more Liz kissed Michael goodbye and went home to a place that she wished were filled by two people.

7:2 ⟫⟫ 2007 – Arrival

It had been a year since Michael had shared his thoughts with Liz in Houston, but Liz had been keeping track of Michael's progress. She knew he had worked hard to formulate an acceptable presentation for his peers. He was to make his presentation to the scientific community in San Antonio, and Liz was going to join him.

The flight from Houston to San Antonio was just under an hour. The final double-chime cued the flight crew to prepare for landing. Liz was not afraid of a flying incident but always made a point to identify the closest exit. It was just good policy. The touchdown was perfect. There were no crosswinds to challenge the cockpit crew of the Canyon Blue 737.

The airport was familiar, the luggage carousel turning, and she soon spotted her luggage sliding onto the belt. She was pleasantly surprised. Her suitcase seemed always to be the last one delivered. Today it was first. Was it a portent? She caught the shuttle which whisked her off to the hotel where Michael would be staying. It felt like a good day.

The conference was being held at a prominent hotel right on the San Antonio Riverwalk. The hotel was also near a popular restaurant nestled into the hillside between the hotel and an outdoor amphitheater with a stage that had been built on the other side of the small river, across from the audience. It was a most unique setting and Liz always enjoyed her visits. She walked up to the front desk.

"Reservation for Mitchell please," she said as she was greeted at the check-in counter.

"Yes, I have it right here."

"Arrangements were made for two adjoining rooms. Are they in order?"

After a quick perusal of the computer monitor, the clerk replied, "Yes, everything is as requested."

After a moment of flying fingers over dark keys she was given two room keys and directions to her room. After entering, Liz was happy to see that it was clean and fresh, and more importantly, with a view of the Riverwalk. Liz had made the reservations and was pleased. Michael had been extremely busy preparing for the conference, so she'd been happy to help plan a weekend getaway.

Liz had made plans for them to spend time together after Michael's presentation. She allowed her mind to conjure her own hopes. She dearly wished he would ask the unspoken question. Her response would be immediate and filled with great joy. *Could this be the weekend?*

Liz plopped into a chair.

Probably not.

She buried the hope and reminded herself that the trip was to be all about Michael, and that would make her happy.

7:3 ⟫⟫⟫ 2007 – Hoping for the Best

Liz arrived early to ensure her desired seat in the last row of a large meeting room. She wanted anonymity. It wasn't that she feared being connected to Michael, but she didn't want to diminish his moment in the spotlight. The I.D. Michael had arranged gave her access to the hall, and she'd entered just after the previous session had ended.

As the room filled, Liz thought of the excitement she knew Michael was experiencing. His topic certainly came from the completely open realm of theory. She knew that Michael expected the presentation to irritate some, while acceptance might be found with others. He was going to propose a theory beyond the fringes of science. Some would suggest that his thoughts were not rational and didn't even qualify as science, being more philosophical in nature. But Liz hoped, as Michael did, that some open-minded scientists might appreciate his ideas. Though a respected man in his area of expertise, the ideas he was to present could change the way his peers might view him. He had little empirical evidence and only fragments of mathematical equations to support his theory.

There were also the reactions of people of faith to consider. Liz had talked with Big Al, and he agreed with most of Michael's theory. Would other believers be accepting? She feared that some faithful people might consider it to be heresy or even disrespectful to God.

Liz had learned from Michael that theories were to be the result of cogent, well-thought out ideas. Michael believed his theory qualified, but had admitted that his own built in prejudices might be affecting his conclusions. She saw Michael as embarking on one of the greatest gambles of his life. It could be a career turner. Will this be a turn for the worst or for the best? Only the passage of time would tell.

7:4 ⟫⟫⟫ 2007 – PART I: The Theory of the Operation of Truth and Intelligence

In the last few moments before his presentation, Michael sat calmly in his chair, closed his eyes, and thought of nothing at all. Life-giving and calming oxygen entered his nose and escaped his mouth. His arms hung limp. He felt totally relaxed. After meditating in a quiet mind of pure peace, he thought through the points of his theory in the sweet zone of mental focus and clarity—an essential facet of the perfect presentation.

In his brilliant, far-thinking, and cataloging mind, Michael brought the entire presentation into play. His opening words and premise, the body of the work, and the conclusions flowed from beginning to end. In this small way he could see into the future by framing his thoughts in a future time and place. In his mind, he found a personal place where there was no fear. He feared neither his peers nor their potential criticisms. The only thing in his mind was the presentation of his theory. After his meditative rehearsal, he stirred himself to action.

Arriving at the rostrum and stepping up to the podium, Michael received a grand applause, even before he was introduced. He was pleased with the response. The National Science Foundation (NSF), responsible for awarding government grants for research, had sponsored the conference. He had been told that the NSF Deputy Director, appointed by the President of the United States, would be in attendance. Michael looked for the Deputy Director and noted his presence in the front row, along with all twenty-four of the board members who served as technical advisers to the President of the United States.

The introduction presented Michael in glowing terms of the highest praise, as his reputation demanded. He was thought to be one of the most forward-thinking physicists in the world, and his mathematical models were beyond the grasp of many scientific minds. The members of the NSF loved him, and the audience was enthusiastic in their reception. There was, of course, jealousy but even the strongest jealousies were tempered by a level of respect.

The solitary podium and waiting microphone were accompanied by cold water in a sweating glass. Cloth napkins were in place should the Texas heat become overbearing. As the applause continued, Michael surveyed the audience, looking into the eyes of fast friends and noted protagonists and antagonists alike. He had debated with so many of them and had agreed with many of them as they all attempted to understand the universe through the science of physics. He knew almost everyone in the auditorium, but at length, his eyes focused on one very special member of the crowd seated in the back. Her presence increased his strength, purpose, and determination. The applause settled, and the hall at last became quiet. Without arrogance or guile, and without clearing his throat, he began.

"Ladies and gentlemen, colleagues and friends, it is an honor to stand here. You honor me with your attendance and the expenditure of your precious time. I thank the NSF board and the selection committee for giving me this opportunity to address you.

"I have been, for some time, developing a theory that might explain much of both our witnessed and theorized world. There is much we can prove by observations and measurements. There is much we can infer with models and simulations. But even with a variety of powerful tools, there are reasonable postulates that remain unproven. As scientists, we work tirelessly to find answers that evaded the brilliance of Einstein and many after him. We search daily to discover the unifying theory of everything and have instead found more questions, forcing us to consider new hypotheses."

Michael showed no nervous tics, just a calm and confident demeanor.

"Today a considerable portion of science is theoretical. In many cases we rely on influences we can observe or measure as a basis of proof for our theories. Many of our advanced theories relate to unseen particles, forces, and interactions, most of which are impossible to see, even with our very cutting-edge technology. It is, of course, our hope that the theories of the unseen can be proven as fact or relegated to the cobwebs of a flat world, when proven false."

There was a smattering of laughter in the hall.

"The title of my presentation is the Theoretical Operation of Truth and Intelligence. I kept the title out of published documents until the program was printed this morning. Some or perhaps all of you will struggle with this theory, and that is to be expected. You've asked me to be free-ranging and far-thinking, and you'll quickly realize that I have done just that."

Michael took a sip of water.

"I will be presenting a theory that addresses the foundational interactions of our world at elemental levels, primarily the sub-atomic, atomic, and molecular levels.

"First, I want to speak about truth. Truth describes things as they have been in the past, things as they are today, and things as they will be in the future. Everything and every process can be defined by words and numbers that correctly describe their makeup, character, or operation. This concept includes all energy and all matter from the most elemental particles, to the greatest complexities of matter. Everything that exists has an accurate description of its truth. We believe that we have accurately described much of what we see in our known universe, but we also know there is much that remains unknown, unproven, and possibly inaccurately characterized. The list of what we don't know surely exceeds what we do know."

Many of his peers nodded in eager agreement.

"The first part of my presentation will be more in layman's terms rather than in the language of the advanced disciplines with which you work. The words I speak today will at some point be reported in public forums. I will start with words, terms, and ideas that people with a high school education should understand.

"I will begin to describe my theorem by making a statement that some will find outlandish. First of all, I am going to talk about truth as an entity."

Michael held his presentation for just a moment to gauge the effect of his statement. What he saw surprised him. There was very little reaction.

He continued, "I am going to suggest that truth as an entity acts through its own independent will, in its own sphere of existence."

He stopped again, expecting to hear hushed murmurs of astonishment and revulsion. To his surprise, he heard very little commotion. *Maybe they are in shock and can't react.*

"I need to explain what I mean by truth. For our purposes today, I'm suggesting that truth is a thing, as it factually or empirically exists—a thing, a creature, a being, a particle, or energy. Today I am calling any one of those things 'Truth'."

There was one white-board on the rostrum. In large letters, Michael wrote one word: Truth. That one word would be his sole visual aid.

"I am talking about matter and energy as described by their truthful properties. In my presentation, truth will take on a different aspect; one you may not have considered before, because in the form I will be describing, truth cannot harbor even the slightest error, misrepresentation, falsehood, or, even worse, a lie."

Michael heard a slightly audible murmur echoed through the audience. That woke them up.

Michael wore a smile on his face as he said, "I've given you one blast from a double-barrel shotgun. Now here is another. All truth acts according to its innate, unique, and independent will, in its particular sphere of existence."

Deep inside, with no visual evidence, Michael smiled. They were shocked once more. Realizations had taken hold and their minds began to race. He observed an audience alive with animated discussion. He waited a few minutes for the room to become quiet and then called it to order.

"Yes, ladies and gentlemen, that statement is, in and of itself, a startling idea. It has taken me many years to develop this thought, but I postulate that independence is a property of truth and implies, as one of its properties, that truth, or in other words all matter, has intelligence. Independence combined with intelligence gives all things in our universe of matter and energy the ability to act, and to do so independently. That independent intelligence is the basis for their interaction."

Michael paused again to assess his audience. He certainly had their attention. Most were wide-eyed with astonishment. Many were talking to the person next to them. The hall was filled with an air of excitement.

As the discussion settled once more, he added, "No, your ears didn't deceive you, and yes, I just said that truth is independent to act in its own sphere of existence. I am suggesting that truth, and therefore matter and energy, with their unique measures of intelligence, can discern their environment and act according to other truths within that environment. There can be no falsehood in the world of truth, and that is why elemental particles act as they do. And that is the basis of actions by sub-atomic, atomic, and molecular entities."

Michael looked directly into the faces of the NSF board. Their reputation was at stake. What he saw was disquieting, but he continued, "Since truth can only respond in truthful manner, we live in a world of consistency. In our world, when we drop a shoe, it always falls.

"Truth is what was, what is, and what will be. Truth is a fact and can never be anything more than that or anything less. Any addition or subtraction from that truth creates a falsehood. But, and think carefully about this, falsehoods have no existence, other than in our minds."

The audience became very quiet. Michael could see looks of astonishment, frustration, and even anger. He also knew that scientists despise falsehoods, and the concept would be appreciated, and possibly applied as a label to his presentation.

"Please think of an electron. Think of what it is now, what it was, and what it will be, or what it may become. Its existence both past, present and future is precisely defined. We've worked very hard to define the properties of sub-atomic and atomic particles, and I am not suggesting a change in our definitions as long as they are correct. If we are incorrect in our conclusions, we have created falsehoods. In reality, nothing but truth can exist. It is the truth that we seek.

"Now, let's stop for a moment. I am talking about truth in the physical world. I am not talking about the things that we say or portray. Our words frequently contain or convey both truths and falsehoods. The truth of the physical world conveys only truth.

"Let's go on. We all know and accept that the operations in our world are limited by situational parameters. Matter and energy, and under my theory, both are defined as truth and as possessors of intelligence, can only interact within certain situational parameters.

"Five oxygen atoms do not combine to form a molecule of five oxygen atoms or O^5. Is it because of the instability of such a combination? If so, how is that potential state of instability recognized by oxygen elements? In this case, I'm suggesting that oxygen atoms recognize the truth of the failing properties of five atoms of oxygen. Those failing properties are a falsehood and can't exist. Through their intelligence and by their own will, they ignore the falsehood of O^5. We know that one oxygen atom and two hydrogen atoms can combine in their states of truth to form H^2O; there is no other way to make water. H^2O is new truth unto itself. Three oxygen atoms may combine together to form O^3 or ozone: another truth.

"I'm going to build on my previously provocative statement. Truth cannot combine in a way that creates a falsehood. If truth could, in some way, combine in the creation of a falsehood, it would cease to be truth and would cease to exist. Please remember that I am speaking about truth as things, as entities in the physical world.

"I will now add another layer to this idea. I am suggesting that although truth is independent to act, that independent action can only be achieved through the light of truth, or let me call it the enlightenment of truth, or an intelligent understanding of truth. In this case, it is an intelligent understanding of their truth, and the truth of other matter or energy. Without that understanding, matter and energy could not recognize and interact in a predicable manner.

"I hope that this presentation opens minds. Rather than the accidental or random existence of our universe, in the next hour I will proceed to provide a logical, structural reason for its existence.

"Thank you for your time. We'll go to our scheduled break. I'll resume in twenty minutes."

7:5 ⏵⏵⏵ 2007 – Reactions

Liz had watched in awe and wonder as the presentation had progressed. During the twenty minute intermission she closely surveyed responses in the audience. The applause at the completion of the presentation was typical of those between competing scholars, each looking to build their own prestige while planning the source of their next grant. A new idea, not of one's own divining, could be difficult to accept. There was respect in the applause, but she sensed a level of discomfort. There were a few who rushed to shake Michael's hand, to ask questions, and even challenge him. Some stood back and pondered. Others formed small groups, talking and discussing in demonstrative tones and gestures. Some appeared to be positive and some decidedly negative.

His theory was mind-expanding. To suggest that all matter has intelligence and through that intelligence may choose to join in resulting actions was an idea, believed by Liz, to have never been proposed by a scientist in front of his scientific peers. It had taken great courage for Michael to make this quantum leap.

The concept might also be a hard sell to religious groups, some of which had very inflexible beliefs regarding the spiritual side of life and the grand creator. Oddly enough, if the theory could be proven, science might be far more willing than religion to accept the concept of an infinitely intelligent God, working through scientific principles that God understands, but that we cannot comprehend. And why should God give us an explanation if we are not advanced enough to understand? It was a question of great consequence, and Liz had considered it carefully. Of course, Michael hadn't presented that idea yet.

As she watched the activity in the hall, she noticed a flurry of motion and discussion among the board members of the NSF. Eyes darted here and there and especially toward Michael. She got the impression that they didn't want Michael to get a glimpse of their debate. Liz watched as the board members finally made their way out of the auditorium as a group.

7:6 »»» 2007 – During the Break

Mostly in pairs, the board members of the NSF entered a small meeting room. Deputy Director Becker entered and immediately took his place at the front of a u-shaped formation of tables and began the discussion.

"Gentlemen, we only have a few minutes. I know some of you are upset with what we just witnessed. Please, quickly express your thoughts."

The chairman nodded to the board member who seemed the most agitated, and who immediately expressed his frustration.

"We are supposed to be at a science symposium, not a philosophy clinic. Our job is to promote science, and Dr. Benson is not promoting good science."

Several board members started speaking at once. Deputy Director Becker raised his hands, "Please gentlemen, we have less than ten minutes. Each of you can express your concerns, but it must be orderly and quickly."

The DD pointed at the first member to his right and said, "Let's begin with you. You have one minute, then we'll go around the table, one at a time."

As the DD listened, there was a variety of perspectives, some negative and some neutral. Only one was positive. As the extemporaneous meeting ended, the DD knew he had a problem on his hands.

7:7 »»» 2007 – PART II: The Theory of the Operation of Truth and Intelligence

Standing once more at the podium, Michael began the second half of his presentation.

"Thanks for joining us again. I hope that the last hour was stimulating, and that this following hour will be just as moving. I would now like to talk about some similarities and contrasts. I work on the edge; I work on the edge and ask: Why does this happen and how does it happen?

"Included in our scientific protocols are some very bizarre traditions. The exacting and inviolate values in our mathematical equations often embrace the inexact and indefinable value of infinity. Infinity is a serious problem for a physicist. Infinity is not a real number but an abstract concept used in our calculations. Infinity is used in an effort to describe black holes.

It is remarkable, don't you think, that we use indefinable theoretical concepts to define objects and/or operations that we cannot see but that we believe do exist, like black holes? The math-illiterate have no hope of understanding how we use infinity in our calculations.

"Among religious people, faith is defined as the "substance of things hoped for, the evidence of things unseen." That also expresses our approach. We first believe and then hope that our predicted actions of an unseen object are true, based upon some hinted substance, or evidence, even though we cannot directly see that object or system.

"We know so much and yet so little. As a community we fail to agree on a single theory of how the universe was created. We talk of black holes and the idea of a singularity. We speak of dark matter and dark energy. We consider vibrating strings to be the smallest bit of matter in the universe, and we speak of the God Particle. All of these ideas are theories. Even the Big Bang is still theory. Is the universe finite or infinite? Our suppositions are changing. Do multi-universes exist? If they do exist, did they play a role in the creation of our universe and possibly many other universes? These questions have yet to be empirically proven.

"We have mathematical calculations that express the possibilities within our theories, but too few have the skills to understand the math. The rest of the world must depend on what we represent to them. In the world of faith, many people rely on the testimony of what others have seen, like those who claim to have seen God. In the world of science, we generally regard those assertions as folk lore, and they may be just that. However we have no empirical data to prove that religious claims are, indeed, folk lore.

"My dear colleagues, I bring these things to the front of your minds because what I am presenting falls into the same category. We have accepted so much that we cannot see and prove. I hope our minds are open to new concepts and ideas that cannot be proven at this time. In a way I am comparing theories to the concept of faith because there are many people working in science who are faith-based. Eighty-four percent of the world population is faith-based. Non-religious scientists are the minority in the world of humanity.

"As you listen during the next hour, and this statement is more for the public than you, please consider that much of what we know today was never dreamed of one hundred years ago. One hundred years is barely an instant when compared to the passing of time in the cosmos, and yet in less than fifty years into the future, our successors may look back and consider us to be stupid, even ignorant in our approaches.

"In the next hundred years, we will think in terms that are unknown to us today. Those discoveries will become facts to our descendants. Our protégé's will prove truths that we have not even dared to dream. Today we see darkly, but with hope that enlightenment will illuminate our gaze.

"I hope that old views, traditions, and, in some cases, prejudice will be set aside. I hope open minds can address . . . new possibilities. I am offering a theory and not facts. I want never to hear a science channel stating this theory as a fact, until it is proven as fact.

"Now, I want to address one last issue before getting very technical. Religious people have a view about how things happen in the universe. We in science also have a view. Seldom do our views coincide. I hope that all people will consider the possibility—that what appears as a mysterious or miraculous event may be explained in the principles of science.

If there is a God, I suspect that He works according to principles that we call science. I hope that believers don't feel I am taking something away from their God. If anything, I think it makes the concept of God more credible. If this is all truth, it suggests that God is the greatest genius of all time, or maybe in all eternity, or all existence, or whatever term you may want to use. I believe that if God does exist, He works by principles of truth and intelligence and in no other way, or He cannot exist.

"What I have given you is a verbal introduction. I will now provide more in-depth ideas. There won't be a tremendous amount of empirical meat on the bone. Instead it will be marbled with assumptions, mixed with logic and theory. And it is, just has I've said, a theory. I will provide some science and some mathematical models to express my ideas. The math will be very challenging, even to this group."

Michael continued for another hour, expressing his ideas in the deeply-rooted foundation of mathematics. As he looked at the audience, he found he was correct. Most struggled with the math. He knew there were only a handful of people in the world who could truly understand the mathematic substance of his presentation.

7:8 »»» 2007 – Contentment

Once more Liz watched closely at the conclusion of Michael's presentation. There had been much discussion, but at last the auditorium had nearly emptied, and Michael was saying goodbye to the last of his colleagues. It wasn't until this moment that Liz approached him. She so loved Michael and savored his moment in the limelight. She knew there would be some supporters and many detractors in the days to follow. Journals, newsletters, bulletins, and blogs would buzz with myriad discussions of this very fringe proposal from one of the premier theoretical physicists in the world. Michael's reputation demanded consideration of the idea. The reaction to Michael's ideas, however, could also kill his career, if the most prominent and powerful groups of scientists took offense.

At last Michael turned to Liz. He looked happy. She did not rush to embrace him but stepped forward as he approached her. The ensuing, but short, embrace included great relief and was more of an encirclement of support than a romantic moment.

"It is over," Liz whispered in his ear.

"Yes, at least, until the release of this evening's blogs and tomorrow's headlines."

The embrace broke, and Liz pulled back feeling like the path of Michael's new journey would soon be revealed.

"Let's go home," Michael said.

"If only that could be true," she said with a twinkle in her eye.

They both let the unspoken message recede, as with the fading of a sound. Liz knew that after so many grueling hours of thought and preparation, Michael would want to rest and freshen up. Liz was happy at the thought of few quiet moments together. They could, at last, say hello in a more intimate way.

The walk through the hotel corridors was silent. Liz wanted to talk but knew that Michael was absorbed with a rush of thoughts. She had attended some of his presentations in the past and knew that self-examination always followed.

"Yours or mine," Liz asked.

"Mine. I have some cold water in the fridge," said Michael.

They entered their set of adjoining suites through Michael's door.

Just inside the door, Liz turned to face Michael. She took him by both hands and said, "You did a great job."

"Thank you. I'm so glad you were there. Your presence was strengthening."

Liz smiled, kissed him on the cheek, and then embraced him.

"I loved watching you. You are a master."

Liz felt Michael relax his embrace. He pushed her back slightly, his eyes seeking hers. In their conjoining gaze she remembered once more how much she loved his eyes. She loved everything about him, even his stubbornness. She waited for a kiss and was not disappointed.

"In your arms I am not the master," Michael said, pulling her close again.

"What are you?"

"At best an equal, at worst your slave."

Liz puzzled over the statement during a short silence.

Michael added, "And this slave wants to you to have a drink, that way he can have one, too."

Disappointed, but shifting with the change, she added, "This Texas heat is parching."

"What would you like, Liz?"

"Just water, please."

"Hmmm, I think I'll have some juice. I need the energy."

Michael broke out a bottle of water and juice from the refrigerator, and they settled into the comfort of the couch. Liz felt a degree of satisfaction while nestling into the arms of her loved one. She was content to be held, and she sensed that same attitude from Michael. Soon sleep crept over her with sweet dreams of contentment, and Michael joined her in repose.

7:9 ⟫⟫ 2007 – Whispers

The Deputy Director and twenty-four board members of the National Science Foundation had called an emergency board meeting. It would not be on public record. The meeting place was held in a small conference room in the convention center with the same garish carpet but with slightly upgraded chairs that didn't hook together, were on swivels, and allowed a slight recline. There was no pitcher of water, no glasses, no mic, and no podium. Hastily thrown together, it was soon filled with NSF board members. Their faces wore expressions of incredulity and amazement. Some were reserved, but others were demonstrative. The Deputy Director entered, and they all took their places around the rectangular table.

The Deputy Director started the discussion, "Well, ladies and gentlemen, we certainly had a bombshell fall in our laps today. I am not sure what to say about Dr. Benson's presentation. It was not what I expected. Your comments, please."

Even though there were no official differences in title, the board was traditionally organized into a hierarchy based on seniority. The most senior member was the first to speak.

"I am appalled at what we heard today. To suggest that an electron or a quark has intelligence: it's preposterous."

Another member spoke up. "But remember, Dr. Benson is a theoretical physicist. It's his job to think on the fringe."

An additional member added, "My problem is comparing our hypothesis to the faith of religious people."

Still another stated, "But his thoughts are intriguing. We certainly have no explanation as to why certain actions take place. He has given us something interesting to consider."

"I disagree," said another. "He gave us very little fact and some mathematics that were understood by probably three other people in the auditorium. He is asking us to take him seriously when he gave nothing but ideas without any provable basis."

From still another, "But he was upfront when he said it is theory, and that most of us wouldn't understand the math. I know I didn't understand it."

The ping pong discussion continued.

A heretofore silent voice spoke up, "But some will understand the math and over time, they'll be able to give educated responses to his basis."

Still another offered, "He's provided some wonderful ideas in the past, and they were based on very solid calculations."

After all had spoken in one way or another, the Deputy Director asked the obvious question, "So what do we do?"

Silence reigned for a few moments. One very brave member spoke up.

"I, for one, would like to hear more."

This was followed by more silence, as though no one dared speak. Eyes focused on the Deputy Director. He had direct influence on their membership and few wanted to cross him.

"Is he religious?" the DD asked.

A member said, "I've never heard him speak of religion. That was out of the blue to me. He often works on Sundays, so I doubt that he goes to church."

Another asked, "What does that have to do with our decision?"

The room hushed to perfect stillness. The question was a challenge to the apparent attitude of the DD.

The Deputy Director fixed his eyes on the bold board member and said, "You are right to probe my question."

A collective but inaudible sigh was released; the momentary tension abated.

The DD continued, "The NSF is a federally-funded program. We are to work without prejudice toward politics, race, and religion. The question of religion and the answer should have no bearing on our decision today. Given the parameters of our operating standards, I believe that even though some of you are upset, as the board of the National Science

Foundation, we should not promulgate the suggestion that Dr. Benson has no right to his ideas, opinions, and theories. Such a position would be contrary to a number of constitutional principles, to our scientific quest for answers, and to the unfettered freedom we all have to consider far-ranging ideas. After all, some dispute string theory as philosophy rather than science, and we haven't censured them."

The Deputy Director looked around the room.

"Does anyone have a dramatically differing position?"

There was no response.

"Okay, let's leave things as they are. We'll support Dr. Benson as we would support any other scientist who has offered a bold new idea. We'll accept it as his theory, and we'll question it, or we'll work to disprove it. But we will do nothing to demean Dr. Benson."

A lone hand went up and a voice asked, "You're making a statement as the Deputy Director of the National Science Foundation. What about personal opinions?"

The DD sighed and gave an answer, "It would be a big mistake to censure personal opinions. There will be those who will try to discredit him. And there will be scientific militants who will want to crucify him. Pardon me for using that phrase. As a board, I don't think we should do either of those two things. As individuals, we all have the right to investigate and to question."

7:10 ⏵⏵⏵ 2007 – Disappointment

Liz awoke, lazily opening her eyes. Michael seemed in a deep sleep. She slipped away and went into her suite. She thought of the pressure he'd been under and hoped he would rest a little more. There was still plenty of time to walk along the river before dinner, and the delay would put the hottest hours behind them. Barely a few minutes later she heard Michael stir.

"Hey beautiful, where'd you go?" he called.

"Just wanted to freshen up," she called back.

"Are you decent?"

Liz brushed at her hair with her fingers, "Sure, come on in."

Michael entered her suite with a fresh bottle of water and a yawn and said, "I'm looking forward to dinner."

"That sounds great, but we have time to walk along the river first, right?"

"Sure."

Liz turned to him, "I'm assuming we have reservations?"

"Yes, for 7:30. I'd like a relaxing walk myself. We have plenty of time."

Liz was stirred in the depths of her soul as Michael moved up behind her and placed his arms around her waist. He drew her in as close as he could. She had been standing in front of the vanity, adding fresh makeup. She reached for his hands, bringing them to her lips and gently kissed them.

She noticed that Michael was watching her eyes in the mirror as her lips brushed his hands. She felt a desire and longing and was sure he felt the same way. Liz turned around and looked into his eyes. There was a depth of character and profound quality that she could not describe, merely feel. Breast to breast, they held each other for a long, lingering moment. Michael nibbled on Liz' ear, then drew back. His longing eyes were hard to miss and their lips met.

It wasn't a kiss of pure passion, yet it wasn't a kiss without a sexual edge. Passion yet to be experienced held them in a world of entrancement. A deep emotional intimacy had become the core of their interwoven, yet sometimes distant lives. The sensual world had been subjugated to principles and values, but at such moments, the ease of shredding commitments and falling into carnal paths was ominously alluring. The embrace tightened, hearts quickened, and blood flowed hot. It was Michael who eased back first.

Liz felt her passion rise as she noted Michael's gaze into her eyes once more. She gave him a "formal invitation" with softened eyes, mysteriously veiled behind slightly closed lids, pursing her lips just enough to be tempting. She searched the depths of his eyes. They flickered back and forth and then closed until she was pulled once more into his tight embrace. Their relationship was now in its sixth year. She held him even closer as if to force him to move forward by the power of her will. Still entwined she began to sense a change. His passion seemed to abate, and she felt him relax. They had been over it many times. He wanted no compromises. His vision of their love was well-defined, and she knew once more that he would never give up on that vision.

It was difficult, but it was Liz who broke the embrace. Still holding Michael in her gaze, she said, "You know I love you."

"Yes, I do."

Without averting her eyes, she continued, "And you know I'd do anything for you."

"Yes."

Michael dropped his hands to his sides.

"I've never pressured you, Michael, but will the day ever . . . "

She wasn't sure how to finish the sentence and hesitated.

After some hesitation, Michael reached out, grasping both of Liz hands, "What day?"

"Our day . . . our time. The time when all else is second to us."

Michael continued to hold her hands.

"That will be a momentous day, Liz."

She nodded her head, "Yes, it will."

Stepping back into an embrace, Michael said, "Can you give up your life as it is? Can I?"

Liz gave no answer. She knew that a union would mean great, mutual changes. Passion for work had, in its own way, overtaken and exceeded the passion she felt for Michael. She had even stopped looking for a position in Denver, wondering if it would really make a difference.

Michael tightened his grip on Liz hands.

"Let's go for that walk now," he said.

Without speaking, Liz increased the distance between them.

Once more she heard the words, "The day will come, Liz."

Will it, she wondered, then added, "I've waited a long time for that day, but waiting has become very dreary. The only way I can push the dullness away is to convince myself that I'd rather wait for the perfect day than to walk through a day that is hollow, but I'm telling you it is becoming harder and harder."

"It's hard for me, too, and I hope it isn't an infinity away. But you know we scientists consider infinity to be an achievable impossibility."

The look on her face said the joke hadn't gone over well. At first she made no attempt to moderate the look, but then felt a need to lighten the discussion and, after all, this had been his moment. She saw his attempt to hold onto a waning smile, but knew it wouldn't last. Digging deeply into character seldom known in men or women, she decided once more to continue her wait and, in doing so, she would make the wait the most pleasant it could be. A smile began to spread across her face.

"Infinity, a remarkable impossibility that certainly defines your truth."

Michael's smile broadened, "Touché."

Seeking some levity, Liz smiled and said, "Let's hit the trail, cowboy. I'm ready for that walk."

Liz had made a grand bowing gesture that belied her feelings. Her emotions felt crushed once more, but her logic and sense of humor took over. She went to her closet and pulled out a prop. Slipping the cheap, straw cowboy hat onto her head, she smiled and asked, "Are you ready pardner?"

It was all for fun and contradicted their professional lives, but Michael couldn't resist, "Yee-haw, let's go!"

7:11 »»» 2007 – The Riverwalk

Liz loved teasing Michael by calling him "The Cowboy." His Idaho roots and his Colorado hideout were nothing like the city life of her everyday haunt. She tossed the straw hat onto the couch and took his arm as they stepped into the hallway. She put away her disappointment and veiled her heart in happiness as they moved into the humid San Antonio heat, down the steps of the hotel, and onto the Riverwalk.

"Left or right?" asked Michael.

"I like left, it's quiet and peaceful."

"Yeah, the restaurant area can be noisy."

A native of Texas, Liz had been to the Riverwalk many times. It was a wonderful piece of the San Antonio cityscape. She recited an old observation, "Isn't it amazing that although less famous than the Alamo, the Riverwalk has become a favored reason for visitors to return to San Antonio?"

"I've never thought about it. It is a beautiful spot."

Looking at the river, the trees, and shaded gardens, she added, "I love this place."

Michael stopped as though struck with terror. He spun around and focused on her eyes, "So that is the real reason you came this weekend. You just wanted to spend time on the Riverwalk!"

Not moving an inch she stated, "Exactly!"

They both broke into laughter.

"Well, lead me on," he said.

Liz started walking down the walkway along the river. The river was slow-moving and lined with a broad walkway on each side. She took on the mantra of guide.

"Did you know, Mr. Colorado cowboy, that the San Antonio River starts from a system of springs just four miles out of town?"

"Nope," he said in cowboy slang.

"Yes, it flows through the city, but they created a channel that loops into this part of San Antonio before merging back into the main river."

As though to confirm her tour-guide role, he replied, "Fascinating."

"Note the well-kept walkway, the arching bridges, and the lush and fragrant greenery that surrounds the river flowing with pedestrians, water, and slow-moving boats."

Michael stopped, raising his hands in recognition of the sights and sounds around him and said, "Amazing," and added, "What are those?"

"Why, those are wooden shape-shifters, which only move when not looked upon."

Michael turned his head in amazement. "You've been studying your quantum mechanics!"

"True. I've been told that the shape shifters—AKA tree roots— only take their form when observed. When unobserved, they move in patterns of probabilities."

Squeezing her hand just a little more intensely, he said, "I am impressed."

Liz played the knowledgeable, charming hostess, with warmth and refreshing cordiality, mixed with love and quietude. She applied the same tools used in her medical practice, hoping to enrich the life and vitality of the one she had chosen, for whom she had waited and even mourned.

Liz led Michael around both forks of the river. She even convinced him to take a ride on one of the small river boats. The guides spoke with an accent which often escaped their understanding, but added charm and warmth to their memories.

After the boat tour, Michael led Liz to their dinner destination. Its rustic architecture opened onto a shaded and flowered terrace filled with outdoor tables and chairs. Michael's reservation was confirmed, and they were ushered to a table overlooking the river they had just navigated. Today Liz would enjoy Michael's choice in culinary delights.

"You may love your Riverwalk, but I love this restaurant and the setting—and the people that I've brought here," said Michael.

Liz turned her head, and bowed it, affirming her understanding that she was the one he loved.

With a broadened smile, he continued, "The location is hard to beat and the rib-eye steak is the best I've ever eaten."

"So I am in for a royal cowboy feast?"

Michael puffed out his chest.

"Darn right. Tain't nut'n too good fer my fav-o-rite city slicker."

They laughed and Michael added, "Seriously, this restaurant has, what is to me, a very unusual nature and is probably one of the reasons I love it so much. First of all, it uses a name similar to the famous Rhine River. Second, despite its European name, it's nestled in San Antonio, Texas on a smaller, quieter river than the Rhine. And they serve Colorado beef . . . ."

"Yippee kai yay," she said loudly, causing the couple in the next table to turn their heads.

Michael forced a grimace, "Smart alek!

Liz gave him a mischievous look and then a go ahead wave of her hand.

Michael continued, "Anyway, the beef is grown in Colorado, but not just anywhere in Colorado. It's grown in the mountains within the limits of a certain elevation."

"On a grass-eating, Rocky Mountain high," she said with the straightest of faces.

Michael put on a spurious pout, and Liz laughed.

"Okay, back to your story, cowboy."

Michael feigned hurt, but continued, "Well not only is the altitude controlled, and the grass that they eat," Liz made a face at him, "they are also fed corn, but not just any corn. Their corn comes from a specific area of Nebraska."

Liz couldn't contain herself. She had to break into his speech again.

"So let me get this straight, we are eating at a European restaurant, on a small river in Texas, chewing the bones of Colorado high beef, stuffed with Nebraska corn."

There was a twinkle in her eyes, and she puckered up her face as if to say, *Could it ever be as good as you say it is?*

Michael smiled, raised his nose in the air, and said with the best back country accent he could muster, "I know t'won't be as good as yur big city viddles, but it'll sure stop the hankerin' in a cowboy's belly."

"What's that, a Gunsmokeism? Who are you talking to, Marshal Dillon or Miss Kitty?"

"Could be, could be, and could be."

"Then bring it on cowboy."

"Your wish is my command."

"If only that were true."

After dinner they walked quietly back toward the hotel. Liz internally mused over their Riverwalk experience. The glib humor had been a mask for deep emotions. It was so different from their normal activities; both those together and apart. It was almost comic relief, a relief from loneliness, hard work, pressure from peers, and the quiet, but roiling currents in the river of their relationship. Most of all she knew the weekend would be over far too soon, decisions would be dragged out far too long, and their passions would be deeply buried. The years continued to pass without change. Liz watched as Michael became embroiled in the consequences of his theory and the negative reactions from his scientific peers. Liz lost herself in her work. It was her way to burying the disappointment and heartache of love that seemed to be in remission.

CHAPTER 8
STAGING

8:0 ▶▶▶ Management

In many ways it had been a trying time for The Kahn. He had worked tirelessly for many years to develop his plan and his network. The reach of the network had to be permeate a very complex world in order to fulfill the entirety of a very aggressive plan. From time to time he had to carry out unpleasant duties, but duties that ensured rigid adherence to the purposes of the network.

The Kahn had carefully orchestrated the tribunal and the arrangement of the room. It contained one table and four chairs, not well-lit, but well enough to fulfill his purpose. He had placed himself in the most noble of chairs. His dress included a great cloak, reminiscent of his noble ancestor. He had covered his face in a mask of armor.

Pivoting his head from right to left, The Kahn looked at the two individuals who had regular and known interaction with him. They were in their places and appeared prepared.

The Kahn looked at a fourth chair being warmed by a dirty, sweaty, and manacled morsel of a man, broken by hours of punishment and torture. His face was masked in a way that protected his identity but revealed his punishments.

An ominous set of fixtures belied the simplicity of bare walls: a video camera, studio lights, several monitors, and communications gear facilitating an encrypted Internet connection. Five generals, in separate locations received the transmission. Their likenesses filled the screens of the five monitors in the presence of The Kahn, his number one and two prime ministers: Neg and Khoyer.

As The Kahn looked into the monitors, he saw the faces of his generals who functioned similarly to a board of directors. However, they were paid sums that far exceeded those from even the most lucrative corporations in return for their dedicated and highly developed skills. The group shamed most Harvard graduates in training and skill. There was, however, at least one critical difference, they served at the complete discretion of The Kahn and implicitly followed his orders. Anything more or less than The Kahn's will was a grievous breach of their sworn duty. He did not maintain his authoritative power by their will; rather, they existed at his pleasure.

As directed, and by his nod, the single camera in the court of The Kahn panned from the visage of the facial armor of The Kahn to the accused and convicted. The Kahn addressed his generals, speaking of the hooded convict, his identity conspicuously hidden.

"Generals, this man was once one of your peers, but no longer. We learned that he kept certain goods for himself and then sold them to his private and personal customers for his own purposes, not the purpose of the network. He has been charged and found guilty, and you will witness his punishment. You should also know that those who bought from him are no longer in business. They have been eliminated."

Choreographed in the planning stages of the court, the proceedings paused while remote camera lenses zoomed more closely into the faces of the faraway generals. The pause served to amplify any deviations in their behavior. The Kahn looked carefully into their eyes and their expressions, assiduously studying each general.

At last The Kahn continued, "As each of you know, you are in my view. I can see your faces. I can see the temperature deviations in your skin, the color in your faces, the changes in your pulse rates."

This moment, known by the network as the court of The Kahn, provided an opportunity for The Kahn to look into the eyes of his generals in a moment of duress, in an effort to read their faces, minds, and hearts.

"It is wise for you to understand my ability to know the details of your work. Should you ever consider following the actions of this pitiful pile of pus, you may know that I will see your shame."

He let that statement hang for many long minutes. Though the generals were powerful in their positions and highly skilled in their responsibilities, he could, and did intimidate them.

Each general willingly focused on the monitor in front of them, displaying the "pitiful pile of pus" that was slumped in his chair. The Kahn played a dangerous balancing act. His generals had to be ambitious and far-ranging in their methods, while keeping their desires within the scope of The Kahn's template of duties and loyalties. They had to be willing to do all that was necessary to achieve those duties. Their success ensured their position of power and wealth. But that wasn't enough for The Kahn. They also had to be principled and satisfied with their rewards of power, wealth, and void of an ambition to take his place. There are always those who will, at any cost, attempt to climb to positions of greater prestige and power. The Kahn could never tolerate a personality that lusted for the seat of his own power and destiny, or that looked beyond the scope of The Kahn's vision. When identified, such disturbances were eliminated.

The pitiful man had been known as General M to The Kahn and his two prime ministers. He was an unknown entity to the other generals, as were they to him. It was understood that there were other generals, but no one had a detailed knowledge of the entire network, unless it was by rumor, and rumor was deathly frowned upon.

M simply stood for money, which had been his domain. He was responsible for laundering the vast sums of cash that flowed into the network. His task was critical to the cause of The Kahn and an important surreptitious influence in the realm of international banking, both in its known activities as well as the activities hidden from the sight of the world's population.

Each of the generals had his own domain and tag. General A managed the Small Arms branch of the network and the complex logistics of acquisition and distribution. General W was responsible for Heavy Weapons and their stealthy movement to strategic settings. General D controlled both the supply and distributors of drugs, including the management of the cartels of South America, Asia, and the Middle East. General C managed chaos throughout the length and breadth of the world. He breathed life into the jihadists, political factions, proponents of social change, and any extremist group that was worth exploiting. General X supervised a two-channeled branch, the mercenaries and slaves. Certain types of slaves were delicious distractions to the more inscrutable principals, both in politics and in crime. Mercenaries were contracted to handle actions separate from the network's scope. They were his spies, his investigators, and his enforcers. More feared than the vaunted former German SS, they were the big stick that The Kahn fearlessly wielded.

"Neg, please proceed."

"Yes, master."

The image seen by the generals switched to a split screen. The condemned man was still in their view, but the disguised visage of Neg had been added.

He began, "Though none of you know the identity of this man, he had certain duties. He is guilty of breaking the laws regulating those duties. He has been found guilty of breaking his oath to The Kahn, to each of you, and to the network. The penalty for that is death."

The tribunal was not held to obtain opinion or consensus. The sole purpose of the agenda was the administration of punishment. It was a graphic display of the quick and complete administration of justice according to the oaths taken in the service of The Kahn, an oath each general had also taken, as well as all network members.

Neg continued, "Each of you and each of your subordinates must know that our laws are inviolable and aggressively enforced. There are no second chances. You will confirm this fact to the members of your branches. You are directed to make today's action well-known and to apply these same principles, as required."

Unseen by the five generals, Neg looked toward The Kahn. The Kahn nodded his head. An instant later, a single gunshot split the silence. The head of General M was shocked into an involuntary jerk and a final slump onto his chest.

The Kahn looked across the scene in satisfaction. A testimony of his iron-clad will had been shared. Life and power were both given and taken at his will. He was not fickle. All things were done according to his law and never outside it. The Kahn was determined to have a kingdom where each member knew his place. If their place was well-maintained, the promise of rich rewards was kept without fail. It was important that his network made that principle the directing compass of their personal character. They must know and completely understand that any action outside the law would not be tolerated. In a very pure and simple way, a breach of the law meant death. The Kahn believed that such methods ensured continued, although slowly developing, progress toward his long-planned goals.

8:1 ≫≫ Top-Secret Fabrication

The brainstorm had been many years in development and was now in its final phase. So much had transpired but seemingly all in his favor. Most importantly, he had kept his possession of two nuclear warheads secret and the deadly armaments safe.

This new mission had become the most secretive of all his efforts. The Kahn trusted only his two prime ministers with the full details. In addition, it was the only mission he had personally participated in for many years. He had commissioned the building of a yacht that would transport the necessary components of a nuclear bomb into the United States. The Kahn wanted to sail on the yacht as it made its way from the Caribbean to Florida. He would join the crew for that one short leg of the voyage.

A trusted high-level network member, Captain Marko Ivanova, would sail the yacht from Varga, Bulgaria to St. Thomas, in the Caribbean. It was one of only a few times that The Kahn had put his personal work into the category of recreation. He wanted to experience the leisure of sailing with the wind, enjoying both the dangers and the peacefulness. Though he would be available to his prime ministers for emergencies, it would, in some small way, be a vacation—the only vacation he had ever taken.

A sixty-five foot sailing yacht with a medium displacement hull had literally been built around the elements of a nuclear bomb. The fiberglass hull was laid up with a special compartment at the bilge where the keel is formed into the hull. The special compartment was lined with

woven lead shielding. A search of the boat would yield nothing physically revealing, especially a nuclear device. Embedded behind the cockpit instruments and attached to the bomb, was a receiver that would
pick up a remotely controlled command from a distant firing trigger.
The antenna simply appeared as a gauge on the control panel.

It had taken considerable time and expense to design and build a
yacht that would conceal a nuclear device. The keel, projecting into the
water from the hull, offered the best chance for such a hiding place. To
interested builders, the boat was described as the custom development
of a new style of keel.

The manufacturing operation was situated on the Black Sea. The
business had been purchased by The Kahn through his expansive network. In the guise of an oft-visiting investor, he would verify the layup
according to the specifications in the plan. Khoyer was on site as project
manager to closely watch the build. Neg often appeared in the role of an
inspector as the fiberglass compartment at the top of the keel was laid
in. The compartment, with its bracing and mounts, was unusual and
had to be perfect.

Only one workman was trusted with the fiberglass layup of the special compartment. He was told the yacht was a cutting-edge design with
an innovative ballast system that would make the boat more stable in
the high seas. He would have loved to have seen the ballast system, but
he had been around many eccentric boat builders and knew of their
secretive natures. When the compartment was finished, the workman
was dismissed for a day. Neg and Khoyer carefully placed the nuclear
components in the keel. The nuclear warhead was now resting safely
in the unseen compartment, mating point of the hull and keel of the
yacht. It was encased in lead to avoid radiation detection.

Once the installation had been completed, the worker was called
back to lay in fiberglass over the ballast. Naturally curious, he was told
that the builder wanted to keep the ballast system out of the view of
prying eyes. Khoyer watched to make sure curiosity didn't overpower
the skilled craftsman. The worker was willing to agree since the eccentric investor was paying him in cash plus lavish bonuses for meeting his
deadline. The details made no difference to him.

After completion and according to a precise schedule, the yacht displaying the Ukrainian name: **море скарбів**—Sea Treasure in English—was launched, passed its sea trials, and was ready to carry a crew for a sailing vacation around the world, or so they told the authorities.

The yacht left Varga, Bulgaria on a route that would take them through the Bosphorus Strait, across the Mediterranean Sea, and into the Atlantic. The Sea Treasure's course would take it south from the Mediterranean and west across the southern part of the Atlantic Ocean.

A very dangerous part of the voyage was the initial leg through the Bosphorus Strait. The strait was full of many kinds of vessels: large freighters, passenger liners, small cargo boats, power boats of all sizes, and sailing boats. Sailing boats were at a big disadvantage. Using their sails to tack through the strait was simply unfeasible. Instead they spent several leisurely days motoring, at a slow speed, through the strait.

Surreptitious arrangements had been made to license the Sea Treasure as a Ukrainian vessel from the port of Odessa. The Sea Treasure would carry three passengers: Marko Ivanova, Jon, and Lavina. The names were fictitious, Ukrainian, and common. They purported to be a wealthy couple and a friend sailing across the Atlantic Ocean, then back to their home port of Odessa. The voyage was not unusual. Marko Ivanova was the captain, and Lavina played the role of girlfriend. He manned the wheel while Lavina and Jon functioned as the crew and, currently, as lookouts.

"Powerboat to port, coming hard," cried out Lavina.

The boat was coming closer than Captain Marko Ivanova wished. At the last moment, it cut a deep curving trough into the surface, casting spray upon the Sea Treasure, leaving an annoying wake.

Captain Ivanova wiped spray from his cheek. "What an idiot!" He refrained from using the Russian slang that burst into his mind.

His emotions still in check, he gestured towards Lavina and said, "Thanks, that was close. Keep watching."

"Aye," she said with a flirtatious smile.

Captain Ivanova was glad to have Lavina on board. She was cast as his mistress on the voyage. It was perfect typecasting since she was factually his mistress. He had been secretly seeing her for some time and looked forward to the long sea voyage.

Captain Ivanova stole a glance at Jon. Jon knew nothing of their prior relationship, which was against the rules. The Kahn would never have allowed two lovers to work on the same boat in such a critical mission; but a lie to everyone else was actually the truth between Captain Ivanova and Lavina.

I must be careful. Jon must never know.

Captain Ivanova looked back to Lavina. She was beautiful and his heart's desire—and she felt the same way about him. He had decided in the days prior to the mission that it was worth the risk.

Captain Ivanova spent time with Jon and Lavina while on the Bosphorus, going over their route. Captain Ivanova explained the phenomenon that formed the currents of the Atlantic Ocean, making the edges of the huge body of water flow clockwise between the two continents. Their voyage would take advantage of this circular flow which was generated by hot air forming at the equator, flowing to the North and South Poles, then falling as cold air.

The seasonal formation of hurricanes had been an important consideration in their plans. They would plan to reach St. Thomas before the hurricane season in August and September. The Sea Treasure was scheduled to lie up in Hurricane Bay off St. John's Island during the hurricane season. It was a safe place to anchor with easy access to larger ports in the U.S. Virgin Islands and the British Virgin Islands.

8:2 »»» Open Water Surprise

Jon felt like he had taken more than his fair share of night watches. Captain Ivanova and Lavina wanted the cabin to themselves at night. He believed they had taken advantage of their role-playing, developing a relationship that could prove dangerous. On a particularly dark night, in the middle of the ocean, between the Cape Verde Islands and the Caribbean, he sat at the helm with the yacht on autopilot. They were nearing the mid-point of the Atlantic. It was a long voyage, punctuated only by two equipment failures. In some ways, John appreciated the failures; they had broken up the monotony of his personal solitude.

Jon's eyes searched the darkness ahead. It was black below the assumed horizon, crowned with a field of stars above it. The sea was light with only two-foot swells. The rhythmic undulation of the ocean made his eyelids heavy. He'd already downed a mug of very black coffee but it had only taken off the edge. He wore his safety vest, which was tied by a life-line to a hand-hold, near the pilot wheel. His eyes drooped until they were mere slits. His conscious mind lost track of the horizon and the stars above it.

In reviewing the incident, Jon wasn't sure how long he had slumped against the wheel. What he remembered was a dream replete with a great herd of black and white horses galloping toward him, their hooves booming like a summer tempest with the rumbling portent of an approaching thunder storm. In the short span of his dream the tumult became all encompassing. The hooves were nearly upon him: his body jerked to avoid the cascade of thunder and darkness. In the moment of his jerk, his eyes opened to see a thirty-foot wave crashing into the boat. The boat was never in danger, but caught unaware, he was swept off the boat while frantically, but futilely, grabbing every possible hand-hold.

Captain Ivanova and Lavina were shaken from their sleep as the boat listed ten degrees to port, before being pummeled on the starboard side with a thirty-foot breaker. Captain Ivanova ran up the ladder to the deck. He couldn't see Jon. He was not at the helm, but his life-line was still tied to the hand-hold. Captain Ivanova followed the line to the railing. Out in the black he heard a faint voice crying for help. He grabbed a life preserver and thought to throw it into the churning sea. But where should I throw it? In the muted moonlight he couldn't see Jon.

Captain Ivanova grabbed Jon's life-line and started pulling it towards the yacht. Lavina, now at his side, grasped the line as well. Soon they saw Jon thrashing in the open sea.

"Throw him the life preserver," Captain Ivanova yelled to Lavina.

Within seconds, Jon had the preserver in hand. He blessed the life-line that had kept him close to the boat and the life preserver that now kept him afloat.

The rogue wave was now a distant threat, the water had calmed and the boat regained its course, as directed by the autopilot. Jon scrambled aboard with the help of Lavina and Captain Ivanova. He flopped to the deck and coughed up ocean water. It had been a close call.

Jon was too embarrassed to admit to falling asleep. In his defense, had he been awake, it is likely that he could have done nothing to protect the yacht. He might have avoided a dunking, but could not have avoided the sudden wave.

8:3 ⫸⫸ A Near Disaster

The voyage continued to a point about 475 miles east of the Caribbean islands. The yacht was fitted with the best in equipment. One critical piece was a weather radar system. Captain Ivanova was at the helm. Jon was inside the cabin resting after another night watch. Lavina was sunning on the deck, swathed with sunblock and little else.

Captain Ivanova first saw a change on the radar screen forecasting a change in the weather pattern behind them. A storm was brewing. It was still far behind but moving their way and would likely catch them based on their current course and speed. He called to Lavina. The radar return predicted something more menacing than a mere thirty-foot wave.

"Lavina, there's a storm approaching," he said, motioning toward the horizon. "Go below and get Jon."

As Captain Ivanova looked to the stern, behind them to the east, he could see the tops of some very dark clouds just over the dimming horizon. He was looking at the tops of the clouds lofting to nearly 30,000 feet.

Jon emerged from the cabin with Lavina following behind.

Captain Ivanova, pointing to the east said, "We'd better run for it."

After looking at the distant darkness, Jon shook his head in concurrence.

Captain Ivanova began shouting out commands to Jon and Lavina, "Get the sails down. Then make sure everything is tied down, Lavina. Jon, get the parachute sea anchor up on deck. Lavina will tie it down. Bring up the speed limiting drogue, too. I don't know what is behind us, but I want to be prepared."

Captain Ivanova was the only highly experienced sailor on board, but Jon and Lavina had been well-coached. They jumped to their duties with only minor delays. Before long, everything was ready for a storm of unknown power and punishment.

It took nearly four hours for the edge of the storm to hit with force. The ocean had become dark, the wind was gusting heavily, and the swells climbed to between six and ten feet. Rain was pelting them, rolling down their recently donned yellow sea slickers. The boat was becoming hard to handle. Captain Ivanova's skill was no match for a heavy storm.

"Throw out the speed limiting drogue."

It took ten minutes to get the speed limiting drogue unwrapped and into the water with its tether secured to the stern around heavy-duty cleats. Jon took precautions and tied the drogue off on two different cleats. The drogue played out behind the boat. As it drifted out to its entire length, it began to fulfill its purpose. Acting like a brake the drogue parachute caught the water, thus limiting the speed of the yacht. The boat slowed down to six knots, and Captain Ivanova regained control. Some waves, blown by the wind, crashed up, and over the stern, but the medium-sized sail boat handled them well.

Captain Ivanova wiped the salty surf from his brow. Water dripped from the brim of his hood, blowing into his face. The salty water filled his eyes and mouth, even with his back turned to the storm. The waves began to exceed fifteen feet in height at their crest. Their position was becoming alarmingly precarious. Fearing for her safety, Captain Ivanova sent Lavina below deck. Jon stayed with him. Captain Marko Ivanova had felt like he was in control, but that was changing. The ferocity of the storm continued to increase, the waves became mountainous, and the wind more violent.

"Jon, get Lavina. We need to change out the drogue for the sea anchor."

Jon went partially down the ladder into the cabin and called for Lavina. She was sitting upright, clenching a hand-hold. Jon called to her; she turned her head to him but did not move. Jon read stark terror in her face.

"Come above, we need to make some changes."

Lavina shook her head, no.

"Come on, Lavina, I need your help."

Again, she shook her head but more dramatically, No!

Jon was frustrated; he hadn't wanted her on board in the first place. All the fury of his long night watches and his jealousy over their intimacy burned in his gut and enraged his mind. He scrambled down the stairs and grabbed her by both arms, pulling her terror-filled eyes close to his. Mustering a modicum of control he screamed above the storm.

"We're gonna die if you don't come and help."

It didn't seem to faze her. He wanted to throw her to the floor and beat her into submission, but that was beyond his character and his immediate need. He adopted gentler approach.

"Lavina," he said in a kinder voice, "we will get out of danger and into safety if you come and help me. We've got to get the bow into the wind. Once we've done that, you can come back down into the cabin. We'll close the hatch and weather the storm. If we don't make the change, we will die. Do you understand?"

Jon saw what he believed was recognition in her face. Her eyes seemed to focus more precisely on him. She gingerly shook her head, yes.

"Then come now."

Jon held Lavina's hand as he guided her toward the ladder. Realizing she wasn't wearing her slicker, he helped her get it on which wasn't easy given their pitching surroundings. Precious seconds had been wasted.

After emerging from the cabin and moving to the bow, Jon began removing the parachute sea anchor from its storage bag while Lavina watched. Every effort was hampered by the rolling of the deck. Jon remembered his last dunk in the drink and wondered why he wasn't wearing a life-line. *What a fool I am.*

He secured the sea anchor line to a cleat on the fore deck but wasn't sure what to do next. Should he throw the parachute into the ocean now, or haul in the drogue first. He looked up at Captain Ivanova, giving a quizzing gesture. Captain Ivanova jabbed a thumb toward the stern. Jon got the message. He rushed back to the stern, which was above him in one moment and below him in the next as the boat was tossed and pitched by the whims of the storm. He had to haul in the drogue. He was also pulling a struggling Lavina behind him, using the railing to help them keep their feet.

Jon spread his feet wide hoping to gain stability and started pulling on the speed limiting drogue line with Lavina beside him. The two pulled with all their might, but the pitching deck and howling wind thwarted the best of their efforts. It was a merciless impossibility. They were, in affect, pulling against the entire boat as it was pushed by the wind, while struggling to maintain their footing. Wrestling with all their strength, their progress was nil. Jon had secured the drogue to two cleats. Now he wished he had secured it to a block that was nearby. From the stern they were facing the gale head on. He knew they must finish the job to avoid certain death. He could not look to Captain Ivanova for help. Captain Ivanova had to keep the boat properly vectored using the slight control that the speed limiting drogue provided. It was up to Jon. Jon had to solve the problem.

Using one hand, he unwrapped the drogue line from the second cleat. Almost everything he did was one-handed since the pitching of the boat compelled him to hold on with the other. Despite the difficulty, he succeeded, and his efforts freed up the end of the line.

He sent Lavina to retrieve another rope which was stowed in a deck locker and watched as she was slammed to the deck by a monster wave. Clumsily standing, she stumbled to the locker, grabbed the rope and returned. She wound the rope around a block, a nautical pulley that they would use to reel in the drogue. The free end was secured to the drogue line. Jon was forced to ignore his own safety and used two hands. He felt destined for another swim and assured death in the furious, foam-capped, black water. He cranked the handle of the block to take up the slack. The next step was critical. They had to unwrap the drogue line from the cleat. This could only be done by pulling the drogue chute closer, taking the pressure off the cleat.

Jon had Lavina man the block, making sure it was locked and secure. As she held onto the block, he considered her to be safe. He pulled on the line attached to the speed limiting drogue with all his might, the muscles in his back and arms bulging from exertion. But his effort was fruitless. He chanced a look forward to Captain Ivanova who was intently watching him. Captain Ivanova gave him a nod and a look that implied their lives were in his hands. Jon began to feel certain that they would die if he should fail. He put his might into another pull. It felt as though his arms would be pulled from his shoulder sockets; but he refused to give up. In an effort that summoned strength well past his normal ability, he managed to get just enough slack to release the rope from the cleat, but on the pitching deck he couldn't hold the drogue and release the rope from the cleat at the same time. Letting the drogue slip back and losing the slack, he beckoned to Lavina. She would have to leave her place of safety and help.

Lavina had seen the problem and knew what to do. She scuttled across the rolling deck to help Jon. Jon summoned all the power of his mind and heart and pulled once more on the drogue line. The rope cut into his hands, and his muscles burned hot in revolt. It was no use, he could not free up the slack. He removed his hands from the rope, worked out the knots in his muscles, rubbed the abraded flesh, and made ready to try one more time. With his feet up against the short rim of the deck, he put his very life into the pull. Suddenly an unusual wave welled up from under the bow of the boat. The bow was tossed into the air. Time seemed suspended, almost coming to a halt. Jon was pitched into the rail, and Lavina was nearly thrown overboard. It seemed as though the last of their luck had just run out, but at the apogee of the lift of the bow, the forward progress of the yacht stopped just long enough to release a few inches of slack. Sensing more than seeing the advantage, Lavina fought for stability while reaching out to free the line from the cleat with both hands.

Just as suddenly as the bow had been lifted, it crashed back into the sea. In a sudden snap, the rope was torn from both of their hands and pulled tight. Jon shot a look at the knot he had made. It was holding and so was the block. He reflected on Lavina's heroic move: *There might be more to this woman than I thought. Was that the same woman who wouldn't leave the cabin?*

In the middle of those thoughts, Jon looked at Lavina and saw that she had collapsed, clenching the cleat in a white knuckled grip. He read terror in her face, and it was justified. She had placed herself in extreme danger.

Jon didn't have time to give any more consideration to Lavina's bravery. He clumsily sprang to the block and started cranking on the block. The block was designed to help sailors control the sails. Since the sails were stowed, it became their saving boon. Slowly, very slowly he was pulling the drogue toward the stern of the boat. It was still hard work and required all that he had to give. He wished that Lavina could have helped, but she seemed frozen in the clenching of the cleat. After many minutes the drogue was within ten yards of the stern of the yacht. This was a dangerous time since the drogue performed the function of positioning of the boat in the wind and at this distance, it was less effective.

Captain Ivanova had been watching Jon and Lavina. When the drogue was within ten yards of the stern, he called to Jon, "Tie it off!"

Jon could not hear him, the roaring wind and crashing waves had carried the captain's voice far away. Captain Ivanova waved at Jon and finally got his attention. He made a motion of wrapping the rope around a cleat.

"Tie it off!" he mouthed.

Captain Ivanova hoped that Jon understood the rationale. He did not want Jon to bring the drogue onto the deck, at least not yet. It was still needed for stability. He had never trained Jon in this matter. If Jon did not understand, he was showing great faith in his captain. Captain Ivanova took a moment to appreciate the vote of confidence. Jon locked the block, securing the drogue, and looked back to Captain Ivanova.

Captain Ivanova motioned Jon to come to the bow of the boat, but he saw that Lavina was frozen in her grasp of the cleat. He saw Jon, despite the pitching deck, reach for her. She was staring at the deck and ignored his hand. Captain Ivanova suspected that she must have felt some safety in her focus upon the deck. Though he could not hear, he saw Jon shout at Lavina. Slowly, her focus turned up to Jon, but she still refused his hand. Captain Ivanova helplessly watched as Jon seemed to be pleading with her. She began to focus more intently on Jon. Lavina then turned her gaze to Captain Ivanova. He was grateful that her eyes were now upon him. He gave her a look of encouragement. She remained unmoved.

Captain Ivanova became more demonstrative in his pleading posture, but Lavina still did not move. Captain Ivanova felt frustration welling up inside. She couldn't remain in her frozen state. They were all doomed unless she rose to their need.

Captain Ivanova reached inside, putting away frustration, resorting to love. His face changed from one of anger to one of kindness. He spread a smile across his face and held out his hands imploringly. The change in his approach was having an effect on Lavina. It appeared to have reassured her and given her strength. Captain Ivanova saw her break her hold on the cleat. She placed her hand in Jon's. He helped her to her feet and led her from the stern toward the bow, using the railing to steady their travel.

As they passed, Captain Ivanova shouted, "I'll bring the bow to starboard. Throw the parachute out as far as you can. Once the current catches the parachute, I'll bring the boat end for end. The current will pull it out and away from the boat. But during the middle of the turn, you must pull the drogue up close to the hull. Don't cut it, tie it off!"

Captain Ivanova saw Jon turn to Lavina, who was hanging onto the railing for life, looking like she might collapse again. He heard Jon shout and surmised rather than heard the words, "Please, help me one more time."

Lavina weakly looked up into Jon's face and then up into Captain Ivanova's.

Captain Ivanova could see that she was spent, but hoped she had a little more strength to give.

Jon, seeing Lavina look to Captain Ivanova, who gave her another look of encouragement, hoped that she could once again rise to their needs. Her eyes drifted back to Jon. After a moment she shook her head, yes.

Jon grabbed Lavina's hand and led her to the bow, which was rising and falling more than thirty feet along with the rise and fall of the ocean waves. It was nearly impossible to maintain their footing, let alone do any work.

The parachute sea anchor was wet with water and very heavy. It was all they could do to get it near the railing. Jon looked at Captain Ivanova as if to ask what to do. The task seemed impossible in the roiling storm. He saw Captain Ivanova throw his hands in the air. *What does he mean?*

Jon watched Captain Ivanova throw his hands into the air two more times. *I don't get it,* thought Jon.

Jon felt Lavina grab his arm.

"He wants us to throw the parachute into the water when the bow is at its peak height."

With that knowledge, Jon's mind snapped into understanding. He realized that they could use the momentum of the upward thrust of the bow to help them get the parachute into the water. Jon gave Captain Ivanova a thumbs up and got one back from him.

Jon watched Captain Ivanova turn the wheel, and the bow moved to starboard. *I hope we are on the same page.*

Captain Ivanova turned the wheel slightly, and the bow moved starboard, just a little more. All of them were watching for the next wave, which would thrust the bow high into the air. In sync with the rhythm of the storm, the bow climbed to the crest of the next wave. Just at the top, and in a clumsy off-balance effort, Jon and Lavina mostly dropped, but managed to give the sea anchor a little pitch into the water. Jon wasn't sure which hit the bottom of the trough first, the boat or the parachute. What he did know is that he was once more hanging on for his life, and the rope had slipped from the block. His eyes watched Lavina as she recognized both this danger, and the danger they all faced. She grabbed for the rope and caught it, once more without regard to her own safety. In the most efficient move he'd ever seen her make, she had instantly wrapped the rope around the block and was reaching for him.

Jon was hanging onto the railing with one leg and part of his body hanging over the side. The surety of her grasp and her hold made all the difference in the world. He pulled himself back upon the deck, despite the boat's continuous break-neck motion.

Once on the deck, Jon and Lavina both grabbed onto the block, using the nautical pulley, to hold the parachute until the current began to pull it out from the boat.

Jon noticed that Captain Ivanova was waving at him and yelling. This time he understood.

"Go get the drogue!" he shouted while jerking his thumb in that direction.

Jon yelled to Lavina, "Let the line out slowly as the parachute gets farther away from the boat. Don't hold it back, but don't give it any slack or it will tangle."

Jon once more moved toward the stern. As he went by the Captain, he was told not to cut the drogue loose. Jon realized they needed to get it on board so it couldn't foul the parachute. It would be disaster if it were to tangle with the parachute. Their lives and their future hopes depended on the proper deployment of the parachute sea anchor. Now at the stern, Jon started reeling in the line with the block. It was a much easier task as the turning boat had taken the pressure off the drogue. The drogue willingly responded.

Lavina was still at the block at the bow that held the parachute sea anchor. While Jon pulled in the drogue, he saw Marko give her a nod, a signal to let the line out. As the wind pushed on the boat, he watched Marko fight to keep it away from the parachute sea anchor. Little by little, Lavina let out more rope. Jon was pleased that they were all working together.

Captain Ivanova wanted the parachute to be deployed beyond the stern of the boat before he turned the boat end for end, but things weren't working the way he had hoped. The sea anchor was simply floating alongside the yacht. He brought the bow a little more to starboard, hoping some monster wave didn't crash over the port side. The parachute still wasn't cooperating. It was still listlessly floating along the side of the yacht. Captain Ivanova realized he would have to make his maneuver without the full deployment of the parachute.

Captain Ivanova had been keeping an eye on Jon, waiting until the drogue was secure against the stern. The next step would be the most dangerous part of the task. Captain Ivanova watched the pattern of the swells. He was watching for a moment with the least likelihood of being hit broadside and capsized by a massive wave. He had already started the diesel motor, which was at idle. Using his best guess, he quickly brought the bow more to starboard. He pushed the throttle to full power. Within seconds they were broadside of the storm, the most dangerous position possible. It seemed in Captain Ivanova's mind that the wind blew more furiously at that exact moment. He felt the boat list to starboard as the wind blew over the boat from the port side. The swells washed up against the yacht. It listed to almost thirty degrees, seemed to hang there forever, and finally settled back. *What will the next swell bring?*

The diesel motor strained to push the boat around and into the wind. The ocean battering became less from the side of the boat and more from the bow, and that was what Captain Ivanova needed. Now he needed the parachute to fill, putting resistance onto the bow of the yacht.

Just before the bow was windward, he cut the power to the motor. Without propulsion, the boat was suddenly blown back by the wind. This served his purpose. The boat was pushed backward by the winds more quickly than the parachute. The parachute began to fill. As it filled it became resistant to movement through the water and pulled on the bow of the boat.

Within seconds, the line slammed taught. In that moment, the sea anchor became completely filled with water and fully effective. The great mass of water resistance was now pulling on the bow of the boat. The wind was blowing into the bow of the yacht, forcing it backwards. That backwards course was being limited by the sea anchor parachute. Best of all, the waves were now attacking the boat at the bow, which was exactly what Captain Ivanova wanted.

Luck had been with them. The yacht had turned 180 degrees and they were spared the crushing broadside energy of a large wave. The bow was now facing into the wind and waves. As the waves broke upon the boat, they would strike the bow which was designed to manage such waves. The parachute was slowing their progress and keeping the boat oriented in an "into the wind" position. It was a saving tactic that would keep them safe until the storm was over.

Captain Ivanova had everyone stay on the deck for a moment. He wanted to make certain that he had played out enough rope. He wasn't completely sure what was required to make the sea anchor the most effective, but felt like more would be better than less. When one hundred feet of rope had been played out, he asked Lavina to lock the block. She gave him a smile, and a, "Yes sir!" and snapped the latch. Captain Ivanova took a moment to look at his crew. Despite the continued pitching and rolling of the yacht, there came a sense of satisfaction and peace to his mind. It wasn't over yet, but they may have beaten the storm.

As quickly as possible, Jon and Lavina moved carefully to the cabin opening and down the ladder into the galley, all without being thrown to the deck, or worse, into the ocean. Captain Ivanova fell in behind. They quickly closed the hatch to lock out the wind and the water. The Sea Treasure was bucking in the heavy winds, but they felt some level of safety. All pretexts aside, Lavina threw herself around Captain Ivanova. Her force and a sudden swell nearly knocked him to the floor. His eyes went to Jon. There was no sense pretending, all pretext and inhibitions were thrown aside.

After a seeming eternity, the storm blew past them, and the sea began to calm. Captain Ivanova knew that the parachute sea anchor was no longer necessary and was turning into a liability. He asked Jon to join him and went up on the deck leaving Lavina to sleep. From the bow, he could see blue sky and calming water. Beyond the stern, the saw the storm as it continued in its rage. Not prone to a belief in religion, Captain Ivanova looked at Jon who returned the gaze. In typical Russian tradition, they hugged each other, showering faux kisses upon their cheeks. They had beaten the storm. Captain Ivanova took his place at the wheel and sent Jon to haul in the sea anchor.

8:4 ⟫⟫⟫ Mastermind

It was daring, unimaginable and so far-fetched that most would never have seriously considered the plan. It had taken years to formulate the rationale and even more years to converge the elements. The principal figure in the plan had been careful to keep his centrality unrealized. The fanatic Iranians thought it was their plan. Al Qaeda, ISIS, ISIL, the Muslim Brotherhood, the Caliphate, the Taliban, Hamas, and a variety of independent terrorist cells all believed their needs were being served.

In Syria, he had played one side against the other, both the revolutionaries and the King. The arrogant North Koreans were anxious to flex their muscle. The Russians were dreaming of a new era of world-wide power. The Chinese wanted a bigger role on the global stage and loved seeing the Americans squirm. The overconfident Americans became one of two major but unwitting focal points. In every instance, The Kahn had inserted his insidious influence through network members sworn to his allegiance and to either money or ideology.

The biggest single motivation had been Israel. There were so many in the world who still hated the Jews. Nearly every bordering country, wanted Israel destroyed. The stage was being set for international change. A number of nations, including many subcultures, were playing a vital role. The chaos that many desired was about to be loosed in a way that no one but The Kahn had foreseen.

As The Kahn reviewed the plan, he became puffed up in his ego.

It is my plan. I am the mastermind, the prime mover, the indomitable, the unconquered and unconquerable spirit, and the one well-chosen for this path. I burn with the fire of the dragon, and I am driven by the tenacity of the ram. I am the author.

He took a moment to concentrate on two others. They were loyal, brilliant and efficient in their assistance, and they were the only men who knew the entirely of the plan: Neg (**один**), his Number One Prime Minister, and Khoyer (**два**), his Number Two Prime Minister. He saw their names in his mind in Mongolian text. He liked using Mongolian names and text. It helped him feel a connection to his great ancestor, and it was only appropriate that his two prime ministers be thought of in the same royal context. In the mind of The Kahn, they had all become connected to his heritage, keeping him sharply focused. His life was solitary, but that was a small price to pay for the power and soaring accolades of the future.

8:5 ⟫⟫⟫ The Ayatollah's Review

The Ayatollah had taken a path in life that some thought to be disrespectful, but he had successfully pulled it off. His name, Ahura Mazda, was the name of the ancient Zoroastrian deity, coming from an aged Iranian religion predating Islam. Zoroaster, the founder of this ancient religion, used the name, Ahura Mazda, to describe the most-high spirit in Zoroastrianism. The Imam, now Ayatollah, had changed his name early in life. He liked the idea of being the most-high. Prior to his appointment as Ayatollah, he had dreamed of the day when he would become nigh unto the most-high. His name had somehow grown to suit him; he had become the Ayatollah Ahura Mazda, the supporter and protector of Islamic justice.

Ayatollah Mazda stood gazing through the window within the Niavaran Palace Complex in Tehran. The palace was ringed with a large grove of deciduous trees, most of them slightly taller than the palace. There were times when he wished for an unobstructed view of his beautiful Tehran. From the proper vantage point, the city was beautiful with rolling hills, aspiring towers, colorful mosques, and many tall and beautiful buildings.

Tehran was a remarkable city. He'd often thought that it could have been one of the great tourist attractions of the world, were the world a different place. Their differences with the world made it impossible to open up the city to a large influx of tourists from the world of infidels. Those differences distinctly centered on two irreconcilable problems: one was cultural and the other was a matter of nuclear weapons development. Both affected the place of Islam in the world. Islam had yet to fulfill its purpose. His mind shifted to the crux of their great plan, to promote the return of the Twelfth Imam.

The Ayatollah laughed in his heart at the foolishness of American leadership. They had foolishly made it possible for Iran to develop the very weapons they sought to delay. It had not been easy for Iran to develop nuclear weapons, while keeping them secret, but they had done it. He had been forced to take drastic measures when loose lips had babbled. At each occasion those lips were permanently silenced under the justice of jihad. It did not take long before peers and associates became painfully aware of the consequence of speaking of hidden nuclear development facilities, of high tech centrifuges, and growing stores of enriched uranium.

In another irony, he also ruminated over the idea that he had originally needed the man named "Dean" to provide the dirty bombs. Although it had been more convenient to use him, Iran had progressed and they no longer depended upon Dean for nuclear materials.

Only three Iranians knew the Iranian part of the plan in totality: the Ayatollah Mazda (The Supreme Leader), the President of Iran, and Cleric Gholam-Hossien, head of the Council of Guardians. Many subordinates knew parts and pieces of the plan but none of them knew the whole. It was at lower levels where the danger of detection was highest and the prime reason for his heavy handed punishment for anyone too foolish to talk about their activities.

At a future point the Council of Guardians would be informed and a day or two before the attack, the Assembly of Experts would be notified. Parliament would not be informed until the action became public. This was a bold move, but held little danger for the three most powerful men in Iran. Even though their power was tied together with the Guardian Council of the Iranian Constitution, and the Assembly of Experts, they had the hubris to bring everyone together.

The Ayatollah Mazda wondered if every detail had been appropriately considered. Was there anything they had not anticipated? Believing they had considered nearly every possibility, he thought of the six masterfully chosen locations in the United States for their dirty bombs. Three of the locations were for the operational dirty bombs which the Iranians had obtained through Dean. Three more locations were destined to receive fake dirty bombs. The fakes were added to confuse the snooping authorities. The cost of six completely operational dirty bombs was just too much when added to the sum of all the other costs. Each location was selected with great care. The Ayatollah went over the sites in his mind.

New York City—an obviously beautiful bomb site.

He couldn't help but finish the thought out loud, "It will be a great insult to once again terrorize the rebuilt complex with its renewed prestige at the old Ground Zero."

Back into the silence of his mind he thought, *San Francisco is an unsecured target with a big payoff in terror.*

Though the Ayatollah had never been to the City by the Bay, he imagined the bomb nestled in the hold of an expensively purchased yacht. He imagined the yelping seals and swarming tourists. He didn't have to imagine the store fronts filled with decadent western goods; he'd seen photos of them. He closed his eyes to conjure up the feel of humidity, the cool air of the spring, the street performers, and the smell of fish from nearby open air markets. *It's odd,* he thought, *that such a highly progressive city would have open air fish markets.*

Aurora, Colorado: It was the third city on his list to receive a real bomb. The site was a hospital, and it held little interest for the Ayatollah, after all they are just sick people. Who cares about sick Americans? But the Iranian President had nearly demanded the hospital as a target. He sought to clearly demonstrate that no city in America was safe, even those tucked into the heartlands.

The operation was expensive, but a flood of new funds had been used to finance his new export of terror. The Ayatollah picked up a sheet of paper with a recap of the coded budget from his fastidiously organized desk. Despite his new money supply, The Ayatollah's eyes scanned down line after line of exorbitant expenses, his mind recoiled. So many of my people could have been helped with this money, but if jihad is to succeed, money has to be spent. As he lingered over the list he thought of the sanctions that had nearly crippled their economy. Most of the money had come from their meager government budget. Some had also come from interested and supportive private parties. Not enough money has come from private sources.

One line item expense that was particularly large was money paid to the man named Dean. Their acquisition was expensive. It has been very costly, but it was worth it. He closed his eyes to envision columns of smoke and radiation drifting into the skies of the Americans. *My gift to Allah, horror in America.*

Money had been spent on services in Libya. Several ports in Libya had been chosen for the collection, and distribution of the dirty bombs. Money had spent to bribe six ship's captains and their crews. Gratefully the Muslim Brotherhood provided most of the manpower. They are bustling ports, so he was told, and part of a constant flow of ships through well-navigated shipping lanes to the major ports of the world. The Ayatollah breathed a sigh of relief knowing that each device would leave separately, on different ships, arriving at their final destination within weeks of each other.

Another expensive part of the operation was the transport and placement of the bombs in the land of the Great Satan. *I honor the brave men who will sacrifice their lives to place and detonate the bombs.*

He considered once again the containers for the roller bags filled with bombs. Would they be water tight? Would the transmitters work? There are so many details, none of them small, and all would have to work together without failure.

The route was long, and filled with many dangerous bottlenecks. The dirty bombs began their journey in Ukraine, part of the former Soviet Union. The man called Dean received a very large fee from the Iranians in exchange for the Cesium-137. He agreed to transport the Cesium out of Ukraine to a safe place on the shore of the Black Sea where he had assembled the dirty bombs. Dean had also agreed to transport them over the Black Sea and into the Bosphorus Strait, where they would be transferred to Muslim Jihadists.

The Ayatollah Ahura Mazda sat down in the chair behind his desk. He pulled at his beard and smoothed it out. It is a very good plan, yes, a very good plan.

8:6 ⟫⟫⟫ Covert Transport

Viktor pulled the large roller bag across the dock, toward the powerboat. The wheels played a melodic rattle on the wooden planks, as they passed over the edges. Viktor was not a Russian. He had taken a Russian identity to escape attention on his journey across the Black Sea. Wealthy Russians were common and the perfect cover for Viktor. A long-time favorite vacation destination for Soviet and KGB political and military leaders, seaside dachas were numerous and well-positioned around the shore line and his place of departure.

Viktor was actually Chechen. A Chechen in a powerboat on the Black Sea could be construed as suspicious. A Russian captain was far more common. The engine roared to life and he settled into his chair. With a pull on the throttle lever, the boat surged forward. His dock was in a medium-sized cove. He obeyed the wake-less boat rule as he slowly exited. After leaving the quiet inlet, he found himself in the immensity of the Black Sea.

Viktor pushed forward on the throttle. The deep sound of the powerful twin engines was music to his ears. He adjusted his weight in the seat as the boat surged forward. The bow, plowing through the waves of the sea, lifted out of the water. He accelerated to speed, the bow still high, adjusted his trim controls, and the stern began to rise, allowing the bow to settle, skimming effortlessly across the surface.

He loved the slightly salty spray from the sea. It was cold and refreshing, but he was happy to be wearing a wind and waterproof coat. He removed his cap and let the wind blow through his hair. It was a joyous moment.

Viktor looked out over the sea and considered its mass: 165,000 square miles. He looked to the west, knowing it was on the same longitude as Venice. He had enjoyed the mild climate many times. He thought of sunny days and warm western breezes, and then a spray of water caught him and reminded him how cold the water could be. He wiped his cheek and tasted the salinity. Istanbul and the Bosphorus was his destiny, and he reveled in it all. *How could any journey be more glorious?*

After hours of motoring, Viktor slowed the powerboat to enter the Bosphorus, also known as the Istanbul Strait, and the narrowest international shipping strait in the world. The Bosphorus, along with the Sea of Marmara and the Dardanelles, is the boundary between Europe and Asia, the meeting place of two very different continents.

The boat navigated the straight at the speed of a typical pleasure craft. Viktor's crew of one seemed to have little to do so he put him to work.

"Dimitri, the traffic is heavy. Come stand by me and watch. We must avoid those who pay little attention to the courtesies of the water. We cannot afford an incident."

Dimitri took up his position as a lookout. Each craft was considered a dangerous threat, and Viktor's seamanship was defensive in nature. As he motored west, he thought of the concurrent reverse flow of deep river water moving from the Mediterranean to the Bosphorus. *How can a river flow two ways?* He shook his head in wonder and continued to watch for danger, even though he felt little. He traveled with an air of confidence. A large body of water with a high volume of water traffic from industrial goods, retail products, and tourists seemed a custom built route to move illicit freight.

Three watercraft had launched into the Black Sea, each crewed by network members. Viktor was one of three captains, each with one crew member, and all specifically chosen for their loyalty and dedication to The Kahn. The law for such a mission: succeed or die. Should he be caught, he would willingly give his life before divulging information about his employer.

Not one of the six people in the three watercrafts knew they were carrying nuclear explosive devices. None of them knew of their partner boats. The bombs were contained in six large black roller-bags. Fanatic loyalty made locks unnecessary, but the bags were locked nonetheless.

The journey was a time of some anxiety. Each knew the mission was vitally important. Viktor knew the stress would increase when they made their first stop. Each powerboat was directed to pick up two unknown passengers along with their new cargo. The new passengers would become the interface between agents in the network of The Kahn and the soldiers of Jihad.

8:7 >>> Clandestine Transfer

The two Chechens, with Russian I.D.s, had navigated the strait without incident. Viktor powered down the boat and pulled into an available dock. This was to be their port for the night. Normally they would have stayed on the boat to sleep. On this occasion, only Dimitri would sleep on the boat, with an AK-47 at his side.

Viktor stepped lively across the planks of the dock carrying his small bag. He walked a block to a small inn with a restaurant. Dimitri would have to fend for himself, eating the rations on the boat, but Viktor could enjoy a quiet, but tense dinner. He checked into his room, tossed his bag on the floor, and flopped onto the bed. It was a cheap bed but better than the cushions on the boat. He was to meet a party of two in the restaurant, but having time to take a nap, he spread out on the worn mattress.

After his nap, Viktor went down to the restaurant. During his meal, two men entered the inn. They looked Moroccan, as they were supposed to. They were to become two new passengers with additional cargo. The two Moroccans sat at the table next to him. They began a conversation in broken English in a ploy of practicing the language. That was their identification code. Viktor started up a conversation about the waterway. They explained that their boat had broken down, and they were in need of passage to the Mediterranean. Viktor said he had extra cargo space, a deal was struck, and money exchanged hands. It was all set and, of course, all pre-planned. After an evening of food and drink, they all retired.

When morning came, Dimitri was greeted by Viktor and the two Moroccans, Simo and IsMaiL. They had two large wooden containers piled onto one unwieldy dolly. Introductions were made, and the four men lifted the two containers onto the powerboat. Within minutes they were on their way.

One important task given to the crews transporting the roller-bags over the Bosphorus was inserting them into larger water-tight containers. The wooden crates were opened when the boat reached the middle of the strait. Viktor kept his distance from other watercraft while his crew worked with the containers. The wooden crates contained dark, heavy, plastic containers, including heavy duty plastic bags, large enough for the roller-bags to be placed inside. The bags were sealed with heat guns, making them waterproof. The sealed bags were then placed into the larger plastic containers, being padded with great care. Every precaution was taken. The plastic containers were enveloped in another set of heavy plastic bags which were again sealed with heat guns; then the entire carton was encased in a wooden crate. The last detail was the inclusion of an electronic transmitter that could be remotely initiated.

When finished, the cargo looked like typical ocean freight. The entire process took several hours and was finished before they made their next stop.

Viktor negotiated the waterway up to the docks of their next stop. Dimitri and Simo tied up the watercraft. All four men left the boat, walking to an outdoor bar, next to, and within sight, of the docks. The boat would remain in their view as they gave the appearance of stopping for drinks. It is uncommon to see Russians and Moroccans drinking together, but also unsuspicious in a melting pot of port cities. The Bosphorus had become a melding of cultures and little attention was paid to the four drinking men. The Russians and Moroccans enjoyed their alcohol and appeared to be typical travelers at the bar.

After a few rounds, considerable talk, and laughter, the four men departed. IsMaiL and Simi returned to the powerboat. Viktor and Dimitri left the wharf for an unknown destination. The Moroccans took over as captain and crew of a boat carrying cargo to Libya. Their task was to make sure the sea-going crates were loaded onto cargo ships moored in Libya.

8:8 ⟫⟫ Ocean Cargo

The port of Tripoli is of medium size. The other two ports were Abu Kammash and the Benghazi port. The newly packaged dirty bombs arrived at the three different ports at three different times. Each arrival was scheduled to coincide with the arrival and departure of other specific ocean-going freighters. Hand-picked members of the Muslim Brotherhood handled the crates and specially chosen jihadist clerics watched over them. The cargo of three powerboats were split up and loaded onto six freighters. The crates were said to be important to jihad. There were no other explanations given and none were sought.

Six freighters had made port in Libya, each from varying manufacturing and shipping hubs. Each captain had received a down payment in the form of an electronic money transfer for personally ensuring that a particular crate was loaded in Libya and transported across the high seas. Though not participants of the exchange, agents of The Kahn watched over the operation; some were on the docks and others worked as crewmen on the freighters. There was little that The Kahn did not monitor. At a certain point, the captains were each to have the cartons thrown overboard. After nearby ships retrieved the cartons, signals were sent, confirming that the crates had been delivered successfully to yet another jihadist soldier. After the confirmation, a second series of electronic deposits were made. The captains could, and did, monitor their deposits with online access.

In the end, six containers, three with functional dirty bombs and three with fake dirty bombs, were loaded and effectively hidden on six cargo ships. The voyages were to be long and circuitous, being held on the ships until early in the following year when they would be delivered into the hands of jihadist soldiers who would transport and place them in six locations within the United States of America.

8:9 ⫸ Taking a Chance

The Sea Treasure had been anchored in Hurricane Bay for several months. Captain Ivanova, Jon, and Lavina stayed on the yacht waiting for The Kahn to join them. Their ventures to the small, nearby port were aboard an inflatable dingy powered with an outboard motor. The waters were calm and the journeys a little long, but all were without incident. Jon's duty was to stay on board. He kept an AK-47 nearby just in case there was trouble, but then he would ask himself: *what am I guarding? There is nothing on board this yacht.* All he knew was that the boat was to be delivered to Boston Harbor before winter set in. That meant that they needed to clear the Leonard P. Zakim Bunker Hill Bridge before Thanksgiving.

In late September, they received word over the UHF radio that a network VIP had arrived in St. Thomas. They sailed the Sea Treasure to the port to pick up the passenger. This was indeed a first. Prior to that day, only two people knew what The Kahn looked like: Neg and Khoyer. Captain Ivanova, Jon and Lavina would soon know what the man looked like but would not know that he was The Kahn. The Kahn considered disguising himself, keeping his likeness from them, but it was unfeasible to maintain a disguise on a small boat in wet and humid circumstances.

He decided to risk the journey undisguised, but still unknown. These three people would never have expected The Kahn to make the voyage, in keeping with his ever pervasive mystique. He would observe firsthand how the presence of a network VIP would affect them. It was the first time in many years that he had openly associated with network members. In addition, he wanted to enjoy the journey. For once he wanted the freedom to be himself without facade and the normal barriers of protection.

CHAPTER 9
INTO THE HEART

9:0 »»» The Canary's Song

Mack Adams entered a small, nondescript conference room in the Department of Justice building in Washington, D.C. He sat down in a chair at the conference table and waited, as he had been instructed to do. He was accompanied by his boss, who was a high-level supervisor in the Drug Enforcement Agency. Within a few minutes, two advisors joined him. One was an advisor to the Attorney General of the Department of Justice. The second advisor worked with the Secretary of State. Adams was not a fan of these meetings, which were called every three months. Each meeting was purposed as a time to report to his superiors and to justify his position. It was when he reported to the dual-headed bureaucrats that ran his life, including a high level supervisor in the DEA.

After all the greetings, Mack was told to begin his report. He was five minutes into the report when his cell phone rang. He checked the CID. "Please, excuse me," he said. "This is one of my informants."

Both the DOJ and State advisors nodded their heads, showing their willingness to sit through the call.

Adams began the conversation, "Hello Juan, what's up?"

"I need more of your gringo dollars, and I have information that I think will be helpful. Can I meet with you?" asked the confidential informant, or CI.

"Yes, I can be in Miami tomorrow morning. I'll pick you up in the alley where we last met."

"Agreed."

It was a short conversation. Juan hung up immediately.

Wanting to show off and to justify his value, Mack's supervisor asked, "Was that Juan?"

"Yes, and I'll have to be in Miami tomorrow to meet with him."

The DOJ looked at both Mack and his superior and said, "You've been given a lot of latitude, Agent Adams. Your work has been exemplary, but your costs are high. Make sure you continue to bring the results."

Mack was slightly offended by the statement. His results had been instrumental in both the interdiction of drugs flowing into the United States and the discovery of previously unknown terrorist cells. Despite his hidden annoyance, he answered, "You can count on my continued efficiency. My post in the DEA with ties to State gives me unusual access to cross-connecting information. I think your idea to have a man from Counter-terrorism work in the DEA is a good one. As long as we can keep my secret identity quiet, I believe I can promise continued results."

Mack's superior in the DEA followed up, "Mack has a superior work ethic and an unusual interest in Counter-terrorism and drug enforcement. We've worked hard to maintain his cover and will continue to do so. No one in the DEA knows that he is actually an employee of the Counter-terrorism Department."

The statement from his boss was heartening, and Mack finished up with his report. As they left the conference room, everyone seemed satisfied with his results and committed to keeping his dual role active and secret. There were only two other men who knew of Mack's role in both departments. They felt his efforts would ensure a simplified cross sharing of information between the DEA and the Counter-terrorism department.

The following morning, Mack requisitioned a car from the DEA office in Miami. He drove the heavy Miami traffic to his meeting place with his CI, or his canary, as he privately called him. Mack pulled his gray sedan into one of many alleys common to Miami. His man was standing in a darkened doorway halfway down the alley. When Mack stopped, an ill-dressed, rotund Cuban opened the door and sat on the vinyl seat. Mack was not fond of men that sold information for money because he was never sure who had just offered the highest bid for sensitive information. He'd bought information from Juan before, however, and it had always been proven to be reliable. Mack drove on down the alley, stopping before entering traffic. Barely looking at the man, Mack asked, "Okay, Juan, what's up?"

Not above humiliation, Juan turned to Mack.

"As I said, I need some more of your gringo dollars."

Mack pulled out of the alley and made a right hand turn into traffic.

"So do I, but I have to work for it."

Juan produced an artificial chuckle.

"You make jokes, my friend, but I work very hard for you, and for you I live in grave danger."

"Yeah, yeah, I can see by your size that you work very hard. What have you got?"

Juan had been looking over his shoulder, watching the traffic patterns of following cars. He watched for many minutes before answering. At last he spoke up, "It is said that important cargo is sailing north from South America. It began its journey in Afghanistan, made a transfer in Columbia, and will soon dock in Florida."

This time Mack looked at Juan.

"What's the important cargo?"

"They say it's a shipment of heroin."

Mack grimaced but said nothing. He'd served in Afghanistan, and the memory made him sick. Like a man overcome with a hallucinogenic, his mind careened into the past. He drove through traffic as though on autopilot, his psyche mired in old nightmares.

In a long-ago experience, a Taliban-fired RPG hit their helicopter with little more than a second's warning. The wounded UH-60 Black Hawk bucked and pitched, wrestling control away from the pilot. Lieutenant Mack Adams knew they were in trouble and felt grateful that the helicopter hadn't exploded, but that could change in a heartbeat, and Mack wanted out of the wounded bird. It might only be seconds before an inferno engulfed them.

The captain, knowing the chopper was too crippled to fly, headed for the ground. Two Apache gun ships were close by; he requested support. Acrid smoke began to fill the cabin. It burned Mack's eyes and made him cough. The ground was coming up fast, and Mack began to worry about a crash. In the distance, he saw muzzle flashes from small arms fire as Taliban fighters took aim at their wounded bird.

The ground erupted into fire and dust as the Apaches discharged their rein of death onto the ground troops. In his headphones, he heard the Captain's call for evacuation. It would be seconds before they were out of a sure coffin, and onto terrain that offered very little cover. He braced himself as the ground rushed to meet them.

The assault of gravity and metal upon his body was beyond all experience. He was slammed into the cabin floor, and then thrown into every protrusion of the Black Hawk's interior. The helicopter tumbled, but it didn't break apart or burst into flames. With blood erupting from his nose and ears, he finally came to rest, in a heap, on the ground.

For a moment there was complete silence. He took inventory of his limbs; everything seemed to be working. After shaking his head to clear his senses, he raised it to look around and found that the Black Hawk was engulfed in flames. He dropped his head back to the ground. *It's awful quiet,* he thought.

Lieutenant Mack Adams was not aware of his expulsion from the helicopter or the ensuing explosion; all had been stripped from his mind. As he shook his head, he finally realized that he could hear nothing but ringing. He rubbed at his ears and discovered a trickle of blood. He wiped at the blood, not daring to wonder if he would ever hear again. He sensed the too familiar coppery taste of blood that poured from his nose and onto his lips. He lifted his head once more to reconnoiter the area. Letting his training take over, he tried to make sense of his condition, and position.

Nearby there was a thicket of brush. He crawled toward it. The ringing began to diminish and transition into more normal sounds. He could hear gunfire but could see no soldiers. Hiding in the brush, he took a more complete inventory of his condition. His left leg was visible through the torn material of his uniform; a gaping flesh wound was oozing blood.

Good, no cut arteries.

Mack realized that his helmet was gone as the torment of a thundering headache attacked his senses. He had no weapon. In short, he was alone, defenseless, and wounded.

He laid back down flat on the ground and looked up into the sky. As his ears labored towards equilibrium, he began to hear the thud of helicopter blades. The whump, whump, whump seemed to help clear his foggy mind. Casting his senses about, he strained to locate the safe haven of another helicopter.

There it was—another Black Hawk traversing the countryside. It was winged by two Apache gunships. He realized they were scanning the earth near him, around the wreckage of his Black Hawk. He stood and waved his arms, not considering the danger of such a move. A single slug tore through the meat of his left bicep. The shock spun him around. He fell to the ground.

Suddenly the world around him erupted in gunfire and flames. Lieutenant Adams heard the screams of people nearby. For the first time in many years, he felt tears well up in his eyes. He had believed that he was beyond such emotions. The tears, and a realization of the horror around him, ignited a tenacity that forced him once again to his feet. He waved with one arm, the other of little use. The friendly Black Hawk turned for him. The delay was excruciating. Mack felt like a target on a gun range. At last the Black Hawk settled between him and a hail of small arms fire. The rattle of Apache cannons and missile explosions continued to pummel his damaged ears. Lieutenant Adams stumbled toward the open door as Special Forces troops covered his staggering sprint to the chopper. Gunfire was all around him. Pushed on by adrenalin, he flopped through the door of the Apache where strong and supporting hands helped him aboard.

Mack collapsed on the floor and felt the power of the blades lift the chopper into the air. They were still not safe, not yet. The Black Hawk tilted its nose down in an aggressive move to gain speed. The two Apaches loitered to cover the retreat of the rescuing Apache. In shock and completely exhausted, Lieutenant Adams let the sweet serenity of unconsciousness overtake him, relieving his sentience from the harshly inflicted trauma of war.

His relief was short-lived. Mack had relived that day over and over again, when as the lone survivor he was plucked from certain death, amid the fire and carnage of battle in the hills of Afghanistan, one of the world centers of the heroin trade. He hated that country and hated their poisons.

Biting his tongue, snapping back to the moment, and narrowly missing a pedestrian, Mack finally replied to Juan, "Okay, let's hear it all. How big will the shipment be?"

Mack knew right then that he wanted to stop the shipment. It represented all that was wrong in the world. He had shed his own blood to protect people who had now spurned his sacrifice by attacking his country with deadly drugs. It was an insult too large to ignore. He had to stop the shipment.

Juan responded, "I don't know much. All I know is from rumors, but very dependable rumors say that it will be on a pleasure yacht."

"Does it have a name?"

"The rumors do not say for sure, but it is a foreign name, Russian or Ukrainian, which implies some kind of ocean treasure."

In the middle of a different alley and $100 richer, Juan left the car.

I've got to stop it, was the thought that kept spinning in Mack's mind.

9:1 ⟫⟫ A Pleasant Delay

The weather had been marvelous from the day Captain Ivanova and the Sea Treasure left St. Thomas to the day it docked at Key West, Florida. Key West was an unplanned stop which added considerable time and distance to the voyage, but the boarding VIP had insisted on the change of course. Working outside the usual chain of command and using the appropriate general, Neg had personally arranged the yacht ride for The Kahn. Captain Ivanova had been singled out as the best man for the job. Neg had also made it very clear to Captain Ivanova that it was the job of his crew to take care of the VIP, and to comply with his every request, no matter how silly it might seem. The stop was not a distasteful addition to their adventure. Captain Ivanova felt good about stopping one more time before sailing to the U.S. mainland. *Yes, the stop was fine, but the VIP was another matter.*

Captain Ivanova had kept a close watch on the VIP, not knowing his identity. He was satisfied that the VIP seemed to have enjoyed the leisurely pace of the voyage, and giving him credit, he had not been demanding. Sailing with the ocean currents and tempered breezes had been pleasant and without incident. The VIP listened intently to the story told by Captain Ivanova, accounting the terrors of the storm. Jon added his experience, first as a man swept overboard, and secondly as a man forced to the pitching boat railing, with the drogue and the sea anchor in hand. Lavina had little to say. Captain Ivanova explained that she was still a little shook up from the trauma of the experience. The VIP had said that he was grateful that his part of the voyage was uneventful, peaceful, and enjoyable. It was just what he needed to cast off the stress of his busy life. The story behind the clichéd words was far more than Captain Ivanova realized.

The island of Key West became a delightful refuge from The Kahn's harried world. Though he was still fully invested in his destiny and the elements of his plan, the reprieve had been invigorating. It was the first time in his life that he had taken advantage of the perks of his station.

In what he felt was one of the larger risks of his lifetime, he discovered an out of the way recess in an outdoor restaurant, where he sat sipping margaritas and watching the parade of tourists in all their varieties and lifestyles.

Occasionally he would explore the sidewalks of Key West. He found the shops to be charming and the shrimp pleasing. He felt a lifetime away from a stressful life that had begun an eternity ago. Relaxation was something he had not known for many years. He had always felt driven, but for once he had taken himself out of gear. He could not remember being more relaxed and felt a world apart from the one he had always known. Key West seemed the perfect place to unwind, but two days was all he felt he could spare. There was much to be done and so little time for a plan as ambitious as his.

9:2 ⟫ Another Canary

Nelsis was another DEA canary, and his roost was Key West. He would watch boats sail in and out of the harbor. He had an eye for drug smugglers. He could smell the caution in their body language and sense from their speech that something was being hidden. He supplemented his income as a dive instructor by selling information to the DEA. As he walked the pier, he happened across Captain Ivanova and Lavina while they lounged on the deck of the yacht. It was unusual for a crew to stay on a moored yacht without ever leaving, unable or unwilling to enjoy the atmosphere of Key West. And there was the name: **море скарбів**. *What an odd name,* he thought.

The boat and its crew captured his interest. He noted that Captain Ivanova and Lavina spent most of their time together, and that Jon merely hung around as required. The crew rarely left the boat, and it was never left alone. There was a fourth man who stayed in a hotel. He was obviously an important man. He spent his nights in a cool and dry hotel room while the other three sweated in the heat and humidity of the boat. Nelsis' sense of investigation told him something was very different about this boat and crew. They could be worth some money. The DEA would pay well for the name of a boat carrying drugs to the mainland.

Nelsis watched the crew of the boat with the strange name for a day and a half, up until the moment they sailed from the quay. He decided to report the boat and made contact with a local DEA agent, reporting the suspicious activities of the yacht and its crew.

9:3 »»» Detection

Miami was to be the point of departure for their VIP guest. They were to meet two powerboats. The boats would resupply them, and their VIP would board one of them and leave. Captain Ivanova was looking forward to the disembarkation of the VIP. There was something about him that was unsettling. The man was obviously important, and he carried himself with a confidence that was just short of chilling. He spoke like he was in control and undaunted by the world around him. *Yes,* Captain Ivanova thought, *it will be well to see him leave my boat.*

The ocean winds began to pick up as they sailed away from Key West and toward Miami. They were forced to sail east into the wind, which required tacking back and forth against stiff breezes. Captain Ivanova had an opportunity to hone the skills of his crew. Eventually they sailed past Key Largo, where they plotted a course in a northerly direction, taking advantage of the gently blowing southern breezes.

The senior DEA agent, Mark Adams, had taken the report from Nelsis which had been forwarded by a Key West DEA agent. Nelsis had been dependable in the past and, despite a lack of detail, the DEA agent believed the reconnaissance was worth the effort. Mack asked Lieutenant Alvarez, commander of the reconnaissance center, to watch for the reported oddity. A command was passed to a desk-bound pilot who controlled an Un-Manned Aerial Vehicle, or UAV. The grounded pilot soon discovered **море скарбів**. Long range cameras transmitted video to the command center and the discovery was shown to Alvarez.

"Get me a translation of that name," agent Alvarez said to an aid.

The room was alive with video feeds from a number of drones in the air, participating in various missions. They were also receiving reports from a variety of Coast Guard vessels and one E2C Hawkeye reconnaissance airplane owned by the DEA. They were vigilant in their efforts to interdict drugs from the south. Staff members scurried about the control center, each with a purpose—to keep drugs out of the United States, an effort that was persistently overwhelmed by the seemingly unstoppable flow of drugs from the south.

The DEA lieutenant's request for a translation had sent several subordinates bustling away in haste. It only took a few minutes for the translation to return.

"Sir, it's actually Ukrainian and it means Sea Treasure."

Alvarez thought for a moment, then said aloud, "This matches the Intel on a possible drug shipment on some kind of boat named something similar to Sea Treasure."

A subordinate reviewed the report, "The Intel was unclear, sir. The reporting agent wasn't sure if the Intel was even accurate. The snitch wasn't sure of the boat, its course, or even its name. All he really could say was that it was coming from Columbia with Afghani heroin on board. As for the name, he could only report that it was something like an ocean treasure."

Agent Alvarez stared vacantly into the monitor screen, at last muttering, "What are you, my little sailing dilemma?"

Speaking to the subordinate he said, "Let's assign a watch to them. I want to know every tack they make and every action on deck. Let's see if we can identify who's on board and what they are up to."

It was the middle of the night after the first day of watching the Sea Treasure. Mack Adams was startled from his most recent nightmare by his ringing but secure cell phone.

"Adams," he said in irritation.

"Mack, I've got some news that you ought to be aware of. There's not too much to it but I've picked up some noise of some terrorist activities being launched from Libya. There is absolutely no detail but word is that some supplies important to jihad have left in a variety of ships. I know it's not much, but I thought you'd like to know."

Mack hung up the phone and laid back down in bed. This is the reason for my existence.

Mack's new tip came from a counter terrorism source outside the normal world of covert Intel. Mack had carefully groomed a variety of people around the world to feed him bits and tips of information. It didn't matter if it was drug-related or from the realm of the terrorists, he took all calls.

Sleep would not return to Mack. He tossed and turned, his mind animated by recent events. He had news from two canaries and now a tip from a third that could be inter-related. His thoughts fixed upon the **море скарбів**. Was the boat and crew part of something big or innocent bystanders? His guts churned, and he decided to act. He had to call Alvarez and build a bigger fire under him. Mack's guts told him that **море скарбів** was important in the mix of world trouble, and he wanted to know more about it. Of course he couldn't tell Alvarez about the connection to possible terrorist activities, but he'd have to convince him to watch the yacht even more carefully.

Alvarez didn't appreciate the call that came in the middle of the night from Adams, but it was his duty, as commander of the reconnaissance center, to protect his country, and he was serious about his job. He also knew that Adams was just as serious about his job, and if Adams wanted more eyes on the yacht, then he would get them. Alvarez picked up the phone and called the officer on duty.

"Seth, we've been surveilling a sailing yacht named **море скарбів**. I just received some information that makes me even more suspicious than I've been about that boat. I want more eyes on it and on it at all times. I don't want that captain to blink without a report making its way to my desk. Get on it right now."

The might of the United States Drug Enforcement Agency, as well as the U.S. Coast Guard, was now trained on the **море скарбів**, or Sea Treasure. Cameras detailed four people on board: three men and a woman. One man appeared to be a passenger, and the others all worked as crew members. The group did not seem typical of a drug smuggling operation nor any other clandestine activity. Their investigation told them the yacht was licensed in Ukraine and had sailed from Odessa, not Afghanistan. The route had been established with detailed records of its moorings. It hadn't been to Columbia but rather had spent time in St. Thomas. It didn't quite fit the tip but there was too much similarity to ignore it. After watching the yacht for a day, Alvarez had an odd tickling feeling on the back of his neck that warned him of some devious action.

They don't act like drug smugglers, but why the similarity? What are they and why the coincidence in the name?

Once more Alvarez gave his subordinate a command, "Keep a watch on them. Let's learn all we can about them."

9:4 ⟫⟫ Comprehension

Captain Ivanova was the first to notice the Coast Guard vessel in the distance. It seemed to be shadowing them, nearly out of sight. Their course would bring them north past Biscayne National Park, near Miami. Their destination had been the coastal waters off shore from Biscayne Bay. Captain Ivanova did not want to enter Biscayne Bay and was glad he had not been ordered to do so. Although he didn't know the details of the mission, he had always felt its importance and didn't want to attract the attention of the many prying eyes of Miami. There were simply too many of them looking and watching, or so he had been told.

"Sir," that was the only name by which he knew the VIP.

The Kahn raised his head and nodded to Captain Ivanova.

"I've just noticed that we are being shadowed by a Coast Guard cutter."

With that statement, the countenance of the VIP changed dramatically. He was no longer a passenger, he took charge.

"How long has it been there?"

"I noticed it a couple of hours ago, and I've been watching it to see if it had any interest in us. I can only conclude that it may be watching us."

"Why was I not told sooner?"

"I wasn't sure."

"Next time report sooner, and be sure later."

It was clearly a command, and Captain Ivanova's opinion of the VIP continued to evolve as he noted the changes. The VIP had undoubtedly become concerned with their shadow. *What is on his mind?*

"Captain, if they are watching us, they may board us. They may think we are drug smugglers. Since we have no drugs on board, we are in no danger of being arrested, or detained. Do you understand me?"

The VIP locked onto Captain Ivanova's eyes and held them with the strength of his gaze. Captain Ivanova wanted to ask if they were carrying something illegal but could not utter the question. All he could do was shake his head, "Yes."

The flurry of conversation attracted the attention of Jon, who had been working the sails. He moved closer to the captain. Lavina had been helping Jon and followed in behind him. Captain Ivanova, turned to Jon and simply said, "It appears we have caught the attention of the American Coast Guard or possibly the DEA. We've all been on this boat for months, and we can all say, with confidence, that there are no drugs on this vessel."

"Why would they suspect us?" asked Jon.

"I don't know," replied Captain Ivanova.

Lavina looked at The Kahn and asked in a slightly offensive tone, "Do you know anything about this?"

Captain Ivanova recoiled inside after hearing Lavina's question.

The Kahn fixed his eyes upon Lavina, implying his superiority and said, "What I know and what I don't know is of no concern to you. Be content with the fact that we have no drugs and nothing the Americans should be interested in."

After a second of silence, he turned the tables, "Unless you've brought something on board that could endanger us. Have you?"

At first flustered, Lavina replied in a submissive, "No, sir."

The VIP turned to Captain Ivanova, "We continue as we have planned. We'll make no changes. All will be as we have previously determined. We have nothing to hide and nothing to fear. Captain Ivanova, you are the captain, and you will deal with whatever interference the Americans may decide to inflict upon us."

He turned to look at the crew, "I have not told you my name. I am Yuriy Gurka. Just as you, I am traveling on a Ukrainian passport. Should we be boarded, Captain Ivanova will do the talking. If you are asked to provide your passport, do so promptly. Do not kowtow to the Americans, but do not show any defiance. We are simply Ukrainian citizens sailing to America and back. We have money and pride, but we will be neither antagonistic nor subservient. Is that clear?"

The Kahn moved to the stern of the boat and sat on a bench. He looked at each crew member hoping to surmise their ability to handle a potentially difficult situation. Captain Ivanova's eyes stayed fixed and courageous. *As a network member ought to be*, thought The Kahn. Lavina's eyes did not show the same courage seen in the captain, but he sensed strength in her. Something that told him she was a survivor. Even though he had scolded her, she had not completely cowered at his piercing scrutiny. He had thought that Lavina might be the weak one, based on the fear she had shown after the storm, but he began to reverse his opinion. *She'll be fine.* Jon was the last to be analyzed. To his surprise, he saw something of a concern. It was the way he looked back, the way he blinked, the way his chin rose ever so slightly. He sensed an attitude of rebellion. Jon was unhappy about something. *What is it?*

The Kahn quickly reviewed the on-board events since they'd begun the last leg of the voyage. He realized he had missed something. He had been too willing to let his attitude dwell on pleasure and relaxation. Never again. His eyes shifted from Jon to the Captain. He noted that Lavina's position often shifted in Ivanova's direction, almost as though she favored him. Captain Ivanova had glanced her way more than once. So this relationship is more than I suspected. It has become a barrier between Jon and his captain. I shall have to watch the situation closely.

Captain Ivanova was pleased that the VIP had identified himself. The name didn't mean anything to him, but it was at least good to know it. Ivanova was aware of Yuriy's inquisitive gaze. It had been uncomfortable. But now it appeared to be diminishing. As the former object of Gurka's attention, he felt as though he had moved from the bright sun into sheltering shade, finding relief from the heat of Yuriy's searching eyes. It was that sense of relief that marked the beginning of Captain Ivanova's personal inquiry. *Who is this man? He cows us with his eyes and his words. I've never met a man so in charge. Who is he? It's almost as though he is The Kahn.* The thought burst upon him in a flood of realization.

Could this be true? The possibility was both wondrous and terrifying. *Am I in his presence?*

Captain Ivanova called up the best of his bluffing card game persona, hoping to hide his questioning recognition. If this man was The Kahn, Ivanova did not want him to know that he had suspected his true identity. Such a suspicion could mean death! Deep in contemplation, he realized that he had once again become the focus of Yuriy's scrutiny. *Has he read my mind?* No one knew the identity of The Kahn and Captain Ivanova did not want to know the identity of The Kahn. It was simply to terrifyingly dangerous.

The Captain and his crew had remained near the wheel. No one had spoken, nor had they gone back to work. The Kahn noted the quandary in the group and called out a command, "Okay, everyone back to your posts. Life goes on as normal. Remember Captain Ivanova, you are the captain. This is your crew, and I'm your wealthy friend and passenger."

This time there was a slight bow of Captain Ivanova's head, as he replied, "Yes, sir."

Ivanova was glad for the spoken orders; it took away the burden of trying to figure out what to do. He let the identity of Yuriy lapse from his mind and gave directions to his crew.

"We are nearing our rendezvous point. Jon, I'll need you to drop the sails; Lavina you must assist him. If we are boarded, we'll have to come to a full stop, and you'll need to cast out the anchor."

He turned to look at Yuriy Gurka and said simply, "Yuriy, my friend, we shall continue to take good care of you."

There is a telling in his eyes, thought Captain Ivanova. He may suspect. If he is The Kahn, I am now working to save not only his life but my own.

9:5 »»» Interdiction

Captain Bassett, of the United States Coast Guard, had been given the task of shadowing the yacht, which they now freely called the Sea Treasure. Based upon the two reports from paid snitches, and the coincidence in the name, the DEA wanted the vessel boarded. The Coast Guard had two teams of six seamen at the ready to board the Sea Treasure. The only question left was when to execute the interdiction.

The Sea Treasure had dropped anchor near Biscayne Bay, just off Miami Beach. Along with the other teams, Captain Bassett had been ordered to hold and observe. For thirty minutes, there was no activity, but then two powerboats approached the yacht from out of the bay. *If there is to be a drug exchange, this will be the moment*, thought the Captain. He waited until the three boats joined.

Captain Bassett ordered his Coast Guard cutter closer to the Sea

Treasure. As soon as the two powerboats tied up to the yacht, he sent a RB-M. The Response Boat-Medium was often tasked with port security. The RB-Ms were fast, maneuverable, and easily up to the task of deploying boarding parties. Today the craft was occupied by a team of six men. They would close the gap quickly. If the powerboats decided to run, he had plenty of resources to track and detain them.

An MH-65E Coast Guard helicopter loitered nearby. It could be called into action at any moment in either a search or a rescue effort. Captain Bassett had also been apprised of several DEA watercraft which were nearby, along with a supporting DEA helicopter. Bassett didn't know what the medium-sized yacht had done, but the full force of the United States was upon it.

Captain Bassett had been instructed to board and secure the three watercraft, along with their occupants. He was then to hold for the DEA, who wanted in on the search. He was also told that someone from the DEA had a strong desire to board the yacht. That someone was Mack Adams. Captain Bassett watched as his personnel approached the Sea Treasure in the RB-M. He monitored the team's communication through his headset.

Through his binoculars, Captain Bassett could see that the crew of the Sea Treasure made no change in their behavior, other than to watch the approaching RB-M. There were no attempts to hide anything. The apparent supplies had been loaded onto the Sea Treasure from the powerboats. A few boxes were being placed aboard them. It might be contraband, but could also be garbage.

Hoping the crew understood the English language and the English translation of **море скарбів**, the team leader called out with the loud speaker, "Sea Treasure, this is the USS Coast Guard. Stand by to be boarded."

The boarding was accomplished quickly. The Coast Guardsmen were quick and efficient. The four person crew of the yacht willingly responded to their directions. Missing the action, Captain Bassett decided he wanted to be on board. The determined will of the DEA signaled an unusual situation, and he wanted to witness the mission up close.

"Get me to that yacht," he commanded.

While Captain Bassett boarded a RB-S, a smaller version of the

RB-M, he noted that two more vessels were making for the yacht; they contained DEA agents. It was not a matter of protecting his territory, or even his pride, that drove the captain's desire to be at the scene. He simply wanted to learn why this particular yacht was so special.

Captain Bassett was the last to arrive. He climbed aboard the Sea Treasure and gave a hand gesture to the Guardsmen who stepped back, shifting their automatic weapons to point up into the air. Two DEA agents were talking to the captain, while four other agents were talking to the powerboat crews. In all, noted Bassett, there were six DEA agents actively involved along with six Coast Guard members. He smiled inside; there are twelve military and drug enforcement personnel, plus me and my sergeant. That's fourteen people all interested in a crew of four on a luxury sailing yacht. They must be wondering who they pissed off to get so much attention.

The lead DEA officer, Mack Adams, approached Captain Bassett.

"Welcome aboard sir, it's unusual to have you here with us."

"I couldn't stand the boredom," answered Bassett. "What have you found?"

"Well, they aren't from Columbia or South America, as we already knew. The captain confirmed that they sailed from Odessa, Ukraine last spring which matches up with the paperwork that we've examined. He said he picked up his friend, the guy on the right, when they were at St. Thomas. They sailed to Key West and are on their way to Boston."

"Could they be the drug boat from Afghanistan?"

"It doesn't seem likely."

"Do you intend to search the boat?"

"I'm debating that with my team. Some say it's a waste of time, but I figure since we have them here, we might as well look the boat over."

"I agree," said Bassett.

"Let's do it then," replied Adams as he turned to the captain of the Sea Treasure and said, "We are going to search your boat. You are in U.S. waters and we have Intel that suggests you may be smuggling contraband from the Middle East. The Guardsman will assist us in the search. I want you and your crew, along with your friend, to sit in the stern of the yacht. I also want each of the powerboat crews to move back to their boats. Of course, you must certainly understand that we are highly motivated and any resistance will be quickly subdued."

Adams hesitated for a moment and pointed to the Guardsmen. "We have very nasty assault weapons trained on you. I trust there'll be no incidents."

Adams gazed into the eyes of Captain Marko Ivanova, "Right, captain?"

Captain Ivanova nodded his head, "There'll be no trouble. Search until your heart is content."

Bassett watched as the above deck lockers were opened and searched. At the same time the powerboats were being searched. The resupply boxes were opened and inspected. They found the normal equipment for boats of this nature and all the items of a typical resupply. At length their attention turned to the cabin. Captain Bassett went below to observe. He asked Captain Ivanova to accompany him. Bassett wanted to continue to watch Ivanova's reaction as his boat was searched.

The yacht was nicely equipped and well-maintained. Everything was first class and looked new. He thought that this might even be its maiden voyage. And it didn't have the feel of a drug running boat. They were usually used, cheap, and poorly maintained.

Ivanova actually seemed to be enjoying the routine. He was obviously proud of his boat, as shown by his perpetual smile. But the smile troubled Basset. He felt like Ivanova was smiling too much. Basset wondered: *is he hiding something with his smile?* It was a possibility.

After a search of the cabin, Adams asked some of his agents to check the engine compartment, bilge, and other potential hiding places. Bassett continued to watch Ivanova's face as the command was given. He didn't even flinch; he simply maintained his effusive smile.

In less than thirty minutes the search of the bilge and engine compartment was completed. They had come up with nothing. There wasn't the slightest thing out of place. The boat was clean.

In an attempt to move things along, Captain Bassett spoke up, "Okay, let's get topside."

As the group began to climb the ladder up to the deck, Captain Ivanova looked at Bassett and said with a thick Russian accent, "So what do you think of my boat, Mr. Captain?"

Bassett mused inside; this guy is either innocent or has more bravado than anyone I've ever met.

"A very nice boat," Bassett replied.

"I tell you what, I take you for ride on my little boat, and you take me for ride on your big boat."

Bassett stopped his egress and smiled, "That's not a bad offer, Ivanova, but I've got work to do. There is, however, one last thing I want to do. I want to interview your friend. What's his name, Yuriy?"

"Yes, sir. That is his name."

"Agent Adams, please send Yuriy down here. I want to talk to him."

"Okay," Adams called out.

In moments, Yuriy Gurka climbed down the stairs followed by Agent Adams.

Captain Bassett turned to Yuriy.

"So you are a friend of Captain Ivanova?"

"Yes, that is correct."

"And you are Ukrainian?"

"Yes, that is correct, too."

It was a study of character. Bassett was very good at looking into the eyes of another human to discover either deceit or innocence. He felt like this man might break before Captain Ivanova would.

"Why are you here, Yuriy?"

"I just wanted to sail with my friend from St. Thomas to Boston. It was something I had never done, and he was kind enough to invite me."

"You're going all the way to Boston with Captain Ivanova?"

"Yes, that was my intent," hoping that his change in plans would not be detected.

The cat and mouse game went on for several minutes. Captain Bassett saw no flinching in the eyes or demeanor of Yuriy, as he continued to query him. He was calm, poised, and appeared to be more than comfortable. He acted like a man who was usually in control. He had the aura of money, and power, yet he showed no arrogance. Bassett began to feel like he might be the kind of guy he'd want to sit down with and have a few drinks. He was educated, experienced, firm, but not imposing. The man could very likely tell some remarkable stories.

If they could have truly known each other's minds, Bassett would have been utterly amazed at the stories Yuriy could have told, not as

Yuriy, but as The Kahn. As good as Bassett was, he lacked the skill to break the facade that Aayan Nikita Mstislav, AKA, The Kahn had contrived.

Bassett dismissed Yuriy and sent him up the ladder to the deck. When Yuriy was out of range, Bassett said, "Okay, Adams, I'm satisfied, are you?"

Agent Adams responded, "We've turned this boat upside down. I can find no reason to detain them."

Waving his hands to indicate the entirety of the galley, Basset asked, "There are no hidden compartments?"

Looking around as though to make sure, Adams replied, "No, we've checked every conceivable possibility and found nothing."

Adams keyed the mic on his radio speaking to an officer back at the base, "Alvarez, I think we are clean here. It looks like our canaries got it wrong."

Bassett watched as Adams listened to the response in his headset.

"I'm sorry, there's just nothing here. We've been all over and through this yacht from bow to stern. There's simply nothing here."

The conversation went on and Bassett continued to listen.

After a few minutes of silence, Adams added, "I'm sorry, but we've got nothin' here. It will be in my report."

After signing off with Alvarez, Adams turned to Bassett, "I'm sorry sir, our entire team felt like this boat was dirty. It looks like we were all wrong."

Captain Basset shrugged his shoulders, "That happens."

"Okay," said Adams, "Let's get out of here and send them on their way."

Basset motioned to Adams to climb up the ladder. Captain Basset followed him.

Once on the deck, Bassett turned to Ivanova, "Okay, Captain, we're going to let you proceed."

It was the only mistake that Captain Ivanova made. He shot a look to The Kahn that was too telling to miss. Bassett clearly read the look. *We got away with it.*

Neither the DEA nor Bassett had any reason to hold the Sea Treasure, but with that last look, Captain Ivanova gave away a hint of some tightly held secret. Bassett was sure there was something they had missed.

"Adams, I'd like to talk to you for a moment."

Bassett led Adams to the bow of the yacht.

"Something isn't quite right here. Did you see the look that the captain gave his friend?"

Shaking his head, Adams said, "Yes."

"What do you think?"

Looking away from the bright sun Adams spoke his mind, "I'm the one who got the tip from our first canary. I also spoke to the second one in Key West. I was certain this was the boat. Everything on this boat was perfect as can be, but that last look was suspicious. I've got a very uneasy feeling."

"I agree," said Bassett. "Let's make sure the people upstairs understand our concern."

Adams caught Bassett with his eyes and said, "You can count on it."

The DEA agents motored back to the shore. Captain Basset returned to his Coast Guard cutter along with his six Coast Guardsmen. Once aboard, he made a call.

"Alvarez, this is Bassett. Listen, I have no hard evidence, but I think you should keep an eye on this yacht as it proceeds to Boston or to wherever it is going. There's something that isn't quite right."

Alvarez who at one time had also been firm in his suspicion about the boat asked, "Are you sure about this, Bassett? You're asking me to commit a lot of assets on a hunch? We spent a lot of money today on what most will see as a failure."

"Am I sure? No. Would I make the call to tail her if it were mine to make? Yes. And I think Adams agrees with me. Follow up with him to get his take on it."

"Sure thing," said Alvarez from his desk at Miami DEA headquarters.

Bassett was standing near a window on the bridge watching the Sea Treasure finalize its resupply operation. "One more thing, where is Adams from? I've never met him and have never heard of him."

"He came in special just for this mission. He has a stooge that's supposedly highly placed in the Mexican Cartel. Adams will have to eat crow over this one, unless we find something else. He had us all convinced that this boat was dirty."

Bassett shifted his gaze from the Sea Treasure to the DEA boat that Adams was aboard, which was nearly out of sight. "Make sure you talk to him again, compare notes. He saw the same thing I did. I think he's a sharp guy. Maybe we missed something."

"I'll do that. Thanks for the tip, Bassett. You take care."

"Say hi to the missus for me."

"Will do."

9:6 ⟫⟫ Coastal Sailing

Captain Ivanova piloted the Sea Treasure north from Miami. Two of his eyes concentrated on the sails and the winds; his third eye kept track of Yuriy Gurka. Yuriy had been seated at the stern of the yacht for more than an hour, talking on his satellite phone and studying a laptop. A continuing question filled his mind: *am I in the presence of The Kahn?* Captain Ivanova tried to pull his mind away from the mysterious man. *No, it can't be him.* Doubts flooded his mind. *The great Kahn on my boat? No, it is not possible.*

As a network member, Captain Ivanova held the same awe for The Kahn as any other. It was clearly known that no one but his two prime ministers had ever seen his face. Captain Ivanova considered once more the gravity of identifying the face of The Kahn. It could be a death sentence.

With great effort, Ivanova concentrated on his sailing, relegating Yuriy to an unconscious corner of his mind, until he noticed a shadow beside him. He turned, surprised to see Yuriy standing close to him.

"Yes, sir?"

"I need to get off this boat."

Captain Ivanova was taken aback. He sought for a proper answer but none came.

"As you know, I was to disembark in Miami. That became impossible."

Captain Ivanova nodded with an air of understanding, too troubled to speak.

Yuriy continued, "I know, as do you, that we are still being shadowed."

The man misses nothing.

"There is small port city on the Georgian coast named Brunswick. There are docks that are close to an executive airport. I want to get off there."

Captain Ivanova responded, "And what of our shadow?"

"I've called ahead to arrange for an aircraft. We'll tie up at some docks that are very near the airport, in fact it is less than a mile. A cab will be waiting for me. I'll quickly leave the boat, and the cab will take me to the airport. I'll be at altitude within fifteen minutes of your docking. They will not have time to react to my departure. Besides, I am merely your friend, and a friend's plans can always change."

Captain Ivanova noted the slightest form of a smile that crossed Yuriy's face. It wasn't a friendly smile. It was a smile with a message. Ivanova did his best to read the smile to determine the translation: *I will be your friend as long as you take care of me. And since I suspect that you suspect who I am, you may consider your life to be at risk if you do not properly care for me: succeed and you live, fail and you die.*

Captain Ivanova wasn't completely sure of the translation, but he felt certain that it was very close to what his "friend" meant. Captain Ivanova was going to take no risk. He would act as though the translation was accurate. *Is it prudent to divine such a meaning from the smile? Yes, it is!*

He smiled internally at Yuriy's method of communication; it was very safe. If Captain Ivanova had not noticed the smile, it would have meant nothing. But since he already suspected Yuriy's identity, the message was loud and clear. Cautiously Ivanova asked, "What would you have us do while we are docked?"

"Surely you have some needs you must attend to. If there are no needs at this moment, then you must safely create them."

It is uncommon for the hull of a sailboat to experience failures but the numerous pieces of equipment are susceptible to many kinds of failure. Captain Ivanova contrived the idea that one of his blocks was about to experience such a failure. It was surely the block that was abused during the storm and it was something that could easily be repaired with a visit to a maintenance shop. The repair would be deemed a necessity.

"Yes, sir, I've been noticing a problem with one of our winches. I think it needs to be repaired or replaced."

"You are very astute, Captain. Let's take care of it."

With that last statement, a plan was in place, and it was the captain's job to execute it. The sailing time from Miami to Brunswick would have been approximately sixteen hours, but Yuriy had complicated matters by wanting to arrive at Brunswick at night, so Ivanova had to increase their sailing time, stalling to make a late arrival. The complications, in some small way, were pleasant. Captain Ivanova tacked the yacht through the southerly winds and out into the Atlantic.

While Captain Ivanova skillfully worked with his crew, he maintained an awareness of Yuriy. Yuriy's eyes seemed never to rest. They were always watching, always weighing, and always analyzing the situation. Ivanova felt like he was under a microscope. He was very conscious that one of the network's prime purposes was to protect the identity of The Kahn. He became concerned about their safety. *What is he learning about me, and my crew? Are we now in danger?* Captain Ivanova had heard rumors of the courts of justice held by The Kahn. Captain Ivanova considered that the realization of Yuriy's identity might force him into one of those courts.

The wind blew much harder as the Sea Treasure sailed into the evening hours. Despite the rising winds, the yacht sailed into the St. Simmons Sound on time, passing between Jekyll Island and St. Simmons Island.

Having made his final tack, Captain Ivanova had Jon and Lavina drop the sails. He would use yacht's motor to sail the last few miles to the pier. He kept the boat to the north side of the sound, where his maps had indicated a small set of docks were built into a sheltered passage between Lanier Island and St. Simmons Island.

Captain Ivanova watched Yuriy look to the shoreline on the starboard side of the yacht. It appeared that he was looking for the airport. Captain Ivanova had called ahead and found that there was an open dock. That news had been a relief. They docked just after 10:00 p.m. and, as promised, the taxi was waiting.

Ivanova didn't need to tell Jon and Lavina to tie up the Sea Treasure. They had taken care of the task like experts. Nearly all that they knew about sailing, they had learned from him. He felt that he'd been a good teacher.

The timing was perfect, just as the last line was being tied to a dock cleat, Yuriy turned to Captain Ivanova and said, "Thank you for a pleasant voyage, Captain. I hope the rest of your journey is under fair skies and mild breezes."

Yuriy nodded to Jon and Lavina, then stepped onto the dock. Within a minute, he had traversed the 150-foot walkway and disappeared into the waiting yellow taxi. In seconds the taxi was out of sight.

Captain Ivanova wondered if the farewell was either a true wish or a stark warning. It was probably both since the boat had to be in Boston before the weather turned. Ivanova knew that the mission had some unnamed importance attached to it, but now he felt it had an even greater level of magnitude, something beyond what he might have ever suspected. Sailing a network yacht into Boston had been a great honor, but to know that the network Master might have been on board distilled a realization that he had been given an honor much greater than he had previously considered. Ivanova tried to put those thoughts aside. They had many more miles of sailing and much could transpire in this last week. He suddenly felt an even greater necessity to get the job done and was even surer of Yuriy's message: get the boat to Boston, on time, and undamaged.

Jon turned to Captain Ivanova, "Who was that guy?"

"I think it is best that we do not ask and do not speculate. It is never a good idea to question network business or personalities."

"He gave me the creeps," said Lavina. "He watched everyone and everything."

He turned to Lavina, "I think you have nothing to fear. You both did your jobs well. Let's get some sleep. I'm exhausted."

As Ivanova made ready go below deck, he heard the sound of a small jet aircraft taking off. He looked eastward into the night sky and saw the lights of an executive jet climbing into the air. "Probably a Gulfstream," he muttered to himself. He shook his head in amazement and climbed down the ladder into the cabin.

In the last few moments before slumber, Captain Ivanova recounted the recent weeks. The tenor of the boat had surely changed when Yuriy boarded. *He rarely commanded us but he was in command at all times. He was neither arrogant nor humble. He felt intimidating but not aggressive. Did I play my part well? Will I be well-remembered or scorned as an incompetent captain?* Questions swirled through Ivanova's mind as it wandered off into solitary sleep. *Was he really The Kahn? Yes, I believe he was.*

9:7 ⫸ A Decision

As The Kahn relaxed into the luxury of the Gulf Stream, he appreciated the comfortable accommodations. The cabin temperature was perfect. It was dry and without incessant sea breezes. However, he was troubled by the events on the Sea Treasure. He could have been arrested and worse. Unaware that a similar boat transporting Afghani heroin had been boarded by Somali pirates, The Kahn wondered why they had been stopped. *Is there an informer?* Neg must certainly look into that possibility.

The Kahn's mind turned to Captain Ivanova. He was a very competent sailor. He was smart, skilled, and managed the crew well. He was not harsh, but he maintained his position as captain, a man not to be questioned.

What should I do with this captain? Can I use this man, who may now know too much, or must I protect my own identity with his death? The questions were clearly important, but for now he was forced to put his trust in Captain Ivanova, after all it was Ivanova who must surely, but unknowingly, deliver his hidden treasure to the harbor of Boston. *Whatever I decide to do with Captain Ivanova, it cannot be done today.*

The Kahn, during his time on the boat and in the guise of Yuriy, had learned much while on his satellite phone. Neg had identified the small port city of Brunswick as a convenient place to disembark. In the discussion, The Kahn also learned that Brunswick was only a few miles north of Kings Bay, Georgia. An educated man, The Kahn knew that Kings Bay was home to the American Naval Submarine Base and the Navy's ballistic missile nuclear submarines that sailed the Atlantic and Indian Oceans.

Fascinating, I was so close to some of the most powerful weapons of the American arsenal with a nuclear bomb of my own. What a wonderful absurdity.

9:8 ⟫⟫ The Last Leg

After a night of sleep, followed by morning repairs, Captain Ivanova sailed the Sea Treasure out of St. Simmons Sound and toward their final destination: Boston Harbor. He enjoyed their sail up the eastern seaboard. They had stumbled into a period of good weather, calm seas, and perfect breezes, which moved them pleasantly along their course. Ocean traffic was less than he expected, which made the sail even more pleasurable. There was, of course, another persistent matter, their ever present shadow. Captain Ivanova had kept a careful watch on both the water and the sky. There was always something in a loitering position, either above them or in the sea around them. Their presence was inescapable. He was simply grateful they had not been boarded again. He was also glad that Yuriy had made it off the boat without the intervention of their tail.

Ivanova piloted the yacht around Cape Cod and westward into the very busy Boston Harbor. It took all of his focus to tack the Sea Treasure through the sea lanes, in between the dozen islands that dotted the entrance. It would have been so much easier to have pulled down the sails and to have used the motor for propulsion, but Captain Marko Ivanova wanted to show off his skills. A real captain didn't motor his yacht into a major port city like Boston.

He had successfully navigated the outer waters and entered the mouth of the inner seafront. For a moment, he once again considered dropping the sails, but his Chechen pride reared its head once more, and he tacked through the narrower port corridor. At last, as he neared the fork in the interior waterfront, Captain Ivanova commanded his crew to drop the sails. They had performed as well as any crew he'd ever captained. Pleased with himself, he motored the Sea Treasure to its prearranged birth in the Constitution Marina.

He and his crew stepped onto the dock. They carried their few bags with them. Just a few feet away from the Sea Treasure, Captain Ivanova stopped, turned his head, and looked back to the yacht. His heart longed to stay with the boat that had so faithfully served him and his crew. He thought again about the yacht and wondered about its purpose; he only knew that it was for the purposes of the network. With dread, he decided that he already knew too much. Pushing that thought away, he turned his back to his surrendered friend and set his thoughts upon their next mode of transportation: a taxi.

Captain Ivanova had taken but a few more steps when he heard a stern voice, "Stop! Don't move. You are under arrest."

Captain Ivanova wasn't surprised to be stopped, but he was surprised to be arrested. They willingly complied with all the requests made by the arresting officers. They were ushered to a marina building and placed in a small, vacant office. They were each personally searched along with their luggage. While they waited, Captain Ivanova imagined that the Sea Treasure was also being searched.

Eventually, they were loaded into a van and transported to a location that he believed was part of a local DEA office. They were each questioned, multiple times, but the truth bore out. The boat had not been loaded with drugs. The crew knew absolutely nothing of anything illegal or unlawful about the boat. Every detail of their individual stories matched. Each crew member seemed to honestly believe there was nothing criminal about the boat.

Agent Mack Adams had been observing the interrogations. The one thing he did note was the crew's seeming nervousness about the mystery passenger, Yuriy Gurka. Gurka had managed to get away from them. They had scrambled to get personnel to the dock at Brunswick but had been too late. Gurka was already gone. Adams also learned that a business jet had landed, picked up one passenger and quickly departed. The jet had filed flight plans that put it in the Cayman Islands. If Gurka was on the plane, he was long gone. In some way, Yuriy was the key. Mack needed to learn the real identity of Gurky.

After the interrogations were completed, the DEA and undercover NCTC agent, Mack Adams, were still left with an unsettling story that the crew obviously believed to be true. The DEA had to consider that the two canaries must have been wrong. There was no choice but to allow the crew of the Sea Treasure crew to go free. But Mack was not the DEA, and he remained troubled. He knew nothing of the events in Somalia, nor would he ever learn of them. In the dark of unknown truths, he had not wholeheartedly accepted that his canaries had been wrong.

9:9 ⟫⟫ Results

Allyson had been carrying the burden alone. She had said nothing to Jim about her medical difficulties. She entered the doctor's office nearly ten minutes before her appointment. She couldn't bear to put off the news of the test results. The waiting room was quiet. She was the only patient there.

Her name was called right at the appointed time. She followed the medical assistant down the hallway and was invited to step through a door into a well-appointed office replete with a massive oak desk. Behind the desk was a very comfortable-looking executive chair. The room was filled with plaques and photos. Suddenly she felt overwhelmed. This was the kind of thing you saw on television but never experienced in real life. Allyson had never anticipated that a doctor would actually invite a patient into his office, especially one as lavish as this. She took a seat in one of two chairs in front the doctor's desk and waited for him to arrive.

Within moments the doctor nearly burst through the door, but upon seeing Allyson, his demeanor changed to one that seemed to have all the time in the world.

"Hello, Mrs. Anderson."

"Hi," was all her dry mouth could muster.

She noted a kind and simple, but restrained smile on the face of the doctor. The dread began building more quickly in her stomach.

"Please come and sit over here."

The doctor guided her into a sitting area. The experience became surreal. She fell, more than sat in the chair. As she settled herself, the expression of the doctor became very solemn. She could feel her heart begin to race, blood rushed to her face, and her palms turned sweaty. The doctor looked at her as if he couldn't find the words.

"Allyson." There was a stifling pause. "There is no good way to say this. Of all the duties I have as a doctor, this is the worst."

Allyson's heart leapt to her throat. She realized she was about to field a bombshell. The trauma was numbing.

"As you know we did some routine tests at your last physical. Based upon your statements during your physical and the results of the first test, I asked you to come back in for more lab work. I lacked enough real evidence to make a conclusion, but I couldn't shake the thought that something was amiss. The second round of tests has given me an answer."

The doctor took the next five minutes to describe the type of cancer that was ravaging Allyson's body. The news was horrifying. It was rare: a type of cancer that affected only 1 in 250,000,000 people. It was so rare that little effort had been made to find a cure. She was going to die. The only question was how long would it take? How much longer would she have on this Earth among the people that she loved?

Christmas and New Year's had passed, and she hadn't told Jim, who was home on shore leave. He had spent most of his time holed up in his den. He would be going back to sea in a few days. *Should I tell him?* After much thought, she decided to wait until he returned from his cruise. He had been facing retirement, and this was to be his last tour of duty. She had been watching Jim struggle with some kind of personal crisis. She had asked him about it, but he admitted to nothing. She had realized that facing retirement itself may have been his personal crisis. Allyson doubted herself. Maybe she should tell him now so his planning could include this new twist. She elected to wait until her returned from his last voyage.

9:10 ⟫⟫ Shore Leave

ISIS (Islamic State of Iraq and Syria)—ISIL (Islamic State of Iraq and the Levant)—Caliphate—The Twelfth Imam—Imam Al-Mahdi—The Shia—the Twelvers—Muslim Brotherhood—riots—disbanding of constitutions—the Ahadith—world turmoil—unrest.

These and many more topics had plied the recesses of Captain James

Anderson's mind. Jim had read many books in his lifetime, but in recent years, he'd been studying about world religions and had developed a great interest in a comparison of Christianity, Islam, and the Jewish faith. He was an avid reader of the Bible and the occasionally debated Apocrypha. He had read both the Jewish Torah and the Talmud. He had also immersed himself in Quran, said to be the verbatim words of Allah to the Prophet Mohamed. He'd also read the Islamic Ahadith, which had become a book of guidance for most Muslims.

Jim had previously believed Islam to be a peaceful faith, but a gnawing apprehension had begun to develop in him since 2001. He feared that fanatic Islamic activists were contaminating the peaceful tenets of Islam. Surprisingly, Iranian activists had actually disturbed the sacred feasts at Mecca, a previously unimagined act of heresy. As he studied, listened, and investigated Muslim and Islamic tenets, he was approaching a troubling conclusion. Though most Muslims were peaceful, the balance of power in the Earth could be tipped by fanatic Islamists.

Fundamentalists made up the ranks of the fanatic jihadists, a faction that was growing and seemingly supported by Iran. ISIS had become synonymous with terror and bloodshed. The Muslim Brotherhood had become more aggressive in the Middle East and in western nations. There were many who actively sought the return of the Twelfth Imam; the Iman who is to come in the midst of chaos. Worse yet, the most malicious of anti-Christian incidents were becoming more frequent.

Though far away from each other, but on simultaneous shore leave, Captain Anderson and Captain Jameson were both in port. Jameson was in Hawaii, home base of the Pacific fleet of nuclear missile submarines. Andrew Jameson had been promoted to command the USS Lexington. They had both accomplished the goals they had set so many years ago. They were both the commanders of nuclear missile submarines.

Captain Anderson was at his residence near the American submarine base in Brunswick, Georgia. Unlike the months during their deployments, the two captains were a simple phone call away from each other. Both were highly-educated, well beyond their naval requirements.

Anderson was a student of religion and philosophy when he wasn't studying naval battles and the strategies of great military commanders. Jameson had studiously researched the confrontations and similarities of science and religion. His beliefs suggested a more complimentary relationship rather than common refutation.

The interrelated interests of the two captains added another facet to their friendship. Both were highly intelligent, learned in science, human relations, leadership, and psychology. They were resolute and relentless in using their knowledge to achieve their goals and would execute their concluded actions without question or hesitation.

Jim had waited to call Andy until 3 p.m. in Brunswick, Georgia, believing that Andy would be having his morning coffee in his land-based home in Honolulu. Andy's phone rang and the CID indicated it was his friend, Jim.

"Hey Andy, good morning to you, but I heard about your bad news. They said you had to scuttle that rat trap of yours."

"Ha, not a chance, Jim, but I did hear that I'm way behind your record of ships lost at sea."

"Lost at sea, my eye! The only reported loss at sea is that sorry bunch of melon heads you call a crew."

"Melon heads? That's better than a bunch of sponge heads, full of soggy sea water."

Despite their intelligence, they still loved a little useless friendly banter. It belied their heady intellect and experience, but was often the source of relief from their stressful careers. Between the two of them, there were no pretenses. After the last jab, Jameson laughed.

"So what's new, Jim?"

"Andy," Jim said, "I'm in turmoil."

"What's unusual about that?"

"Humph. This is serious. I've been studying the Twelfth Imam. Have you ever heard of him?"

"I've heard about him, but haven't read up on him."

"It's really interesting stuff, and I think I'm beginning to understand the motives of the Supreme Leader and the President of Iran."

"What? Power, wealth and women on the side?"

"Well, there is that, but really, I've learned some troubling stuff. Do you know what the difference is between a Shia and a Sunni Muslim?"

"No, you know I stick with science and religion, but I understand that they've had a few differences over time."

"Yes, true—Andy, my attitude about the more fanatic elements of Islam is changing. The focal point of my concern is the Shia in Iran."

"In Iran? That's a big surprise."

"Well, let me tell you, first of all, it's important to know that Shia Islam is Iran's official religion as dictated in their constitution. The Shia faction includes the 'Twelver' school of thought in their ideology."

Andy put his feet up on his desk, coffee in hand, realizing this might be a long discussion.

"Okay . . . next?"

Jim was upright in his chair, leaning in toward the phone on his desk.

"I'll try to keep this short, but that won't be easy. The Shia believe that after the death of Muhammad, only his descendants should have leadership in Islam. They contend that only members of Muhammad's family can head up the Islamic faith."

"Hmm, all in the family."

"The Sunnis believe that leadership should be called of God; that God himself would determine who his leaders would be, and no mortal should ever have a say."

"I like that idea."

"The President of Iran is a Shia. He's a 'Twelver,' or a believer in the Twelfth Imam. Are you ready for an interesting story?"

Andy looked at his watch, "Yeah, I've got time."

Jim took a breath and began, "The story goes that the Eleventh Imam had a son. He's got a long name, but they call him Imam al-Mahdi or just Mahdi."

"Muslims and their long names, it's a sign of insecurity."

Andy's legs began to fall asleep, so he moved them into another position.

Jim continued, "The names have meanings and people try to fashion their lives after those meanings. Remember the American Indians? They did the same thing but the names were simple like Running Bear or Singing Bird."

"Maybe they had the same insecurities."

"Maybe."

His legs still asleep, Andy removed his feet from the desk and leaned forward in his chair saying, "I may change my name to The Hammer of Death."

Jim leaned back, "That suites you—I could be the Anvil of Death. Between the two of us, the hammer and the anvil, we'll conquer all."

"Ha, Insha' Allah: If Allah wills."

"You're a sarcastic bum, ya know?"

"Yeah, yeah, yeah. So what's new?"

Jim cleared his throat and continued, "Well, this Mahdi guy was to be the Twelfth Imam after his father, Hasan al-Askari. I'll read a quote from the Ahadith that justifies the Shia position regarding the Twelfth Imam. Most Muslims consider the writing to be holy."

Jim took a sip from his own coffee mug, "Sit back and hang on to your views of God. Here's what it says. 'I and `Ali are the fathers of this nation; whoever knows us very well also knows Allah, and whoever denies us also denies Allah, the Unique, the Mighty. And from `Ali's descendants are my grandsons, al-Hasan and al-Husayn, who are the masters of the youths of Paradise, and from al-Husayn's descendants shall be nine: whoever obeys them obeys me, and whoever disobeys them also disobeys me; the ninth among them is their Qa'im and Mahdi.'"

Setting his mug on the table, Andy had to speak up, "Whoa, that's worse than a science journal and, come to think of it, I'd rather read a scientific journal. This sounds like Old Testament stuff."

Anderson laughed, "Yes, it's complex. Can I continue?"

Andy checked his watch once more, "Sure, go ahead."

"Well, Hujjat ibn al-hasan al-Mahdi, now al-Mahdi, was born in 869 A.D. The story says that when he was five years old, his father died and he attended the funeral. His uncle, Jafar ibn Ali, was to give the funeral prayer, but before the uncle could start, get this, this five-year-old stepped in and said, 'Move aside, uncle; only an Imam can lead the funeral prayer of an Imam.' So, amazingly, his uncle Jafar moved aside and al-Mahdi, the five-year-old boy child led the prayer at his father's funeral. Then they say that the boy suddenly disappeared in an occultation."

Andy jumped in, "So, he just vanished? Sounds like he was lifted up by God."

Jim responded, "That's precisely what the Twelvers believe. The rest of the story is that the Twelfth Imam, namely al-Mahdi, will return to save Islam, like the return of the Messiah. In fact, some Muslims tie the return of Jesus to the return of al-Mahdi. Some actually believe that Jesus is a prophet, and that al-Mahdi is to come first to prepare Islam, and he will turn Islam over to Jesus."

Andy interrupted, "They are preparing Islam to meet Jesus?"

"Yes, but not as a god or the Son of God. It's their job to prepare the world for the judgment of God, according to most Muslims."

"I'll be damned."

"Probably right, Andy."

"I'll see you there, Jim."

"Ha! But here's the real kicker, and this has me worried. The Shia believe that Imam al-Mahdi can only come if there is unrest and chaos in the world. The world has to be full of war."

Andy interjected, "And this has something to do with us, doesn't it?"

"Yeah, but I'll get to that. There's something else, the ex-President of Iran is a Shiite."

Andy stood up, "Yea, it seems like I heard that, but what does it mean?"

"As a Shiite, he believes his life's purpose is to hasten the return of the Twelfth Imam, or al-Mahdi. His solitary purpose, reason for existence, and motivation is to prepare for al-Mahdi. As Mayor of Tehran, he made certain the roads around the city were built so al-Mahdi could get around easily to and from the mosque that he disappeared from— and that same mosque is where he will return. So get this, the President built a railway that Mahdi can use to enter into the city."

Barely containing himself, Andy laughed, "Amazing, al-Mahdi will take a train to the mosque?"

Jim continued, "And by the way, the new and current president is also a Shiite."

"Makes sense, so what's he gonna do at the mosque?"

This time, Jim stood up. He was getting excited.

"Wait, I'll get to that. In his speeches, the ex-President always prayed for the hastened return and good health of al-Mahdi. Remember I said that al-Mahdi would only come if the world is in chaos? Our dear friend, the ex-President of Iran, worked very hard, as President, to bring about that chaos, and that is why he and the new President are still exporting terrorism. That's why they are behind ISIS. That is why they want to attack Israel; it's why he wants a nuclear arsenal. The new President has been less blatantly outspoken, but his more silent attitude is overshadowed by his outward actions, which have followed those of his predecessor."

Jameson also rose to his feet and began staring out of the window of his high rise condo toward Diamondhead.

Anderson continued, "There's more, the President is vetted by the Guardian Council as are all presidential candidates. Iranian leadership is self-propagating. The whole system is set up to make sure everything operates according to Islamic Law as defined by the Shiites."

Jim now began pacing around his den, which was a tribute to naval history. Both men were on their feet.

"I'll read you a quote from their constitution: 'The compatibility of the legislation passed by the Islamic Consultative Assembly—with the criteria of Islam and the Constitution.'"

"It's collusion," Andy said, watching the surfers in Waikiki Bay.

"Yup, they're all in it together, at every level of the government. Based on all my study, I think the West should be expecting an eventual launch of nuclear missiles on Israel."

Jameson finally caught the horrifying sum of Anderson's anxious rant.

"So you really think that Iran will launch on Israel?"

"Yes, once they have the capacity, I think they will," replied Anderson.

"You really have had your nose in the books."

With a big smile Anderson retorted, "I've kept this beautiful brain engaged haven't I?"

"And I thought beauty was only skin deep. So what's al-Mahdi gonna do, save the whole world?"

Jim answered, "It gets a little muddy there, and it depends on which groups of Muslims you talk to. The bottom line is that the infidels will be converted or destroyed, and the Earth will be prepared for the judgment of God. I think it pretty much assumes that they'll either convert or wipe out all the unbelievers."

Shifting from a view of the surfers back to Diamondhead, Andy added, "I thought we already had enough crazies in the world. Rather than the Prince of Peace he sounds like the Master of Disaster."

"You've been watching wrestling re-runs again?"

"Actually, I think I saw an old video tape of yours with that title. It just sort of stuck in my mind."

Smiling but pushing for less levity, Jim countered, "Seriously, it will be a disaster as far as I'm concerned. It appears that the fanatic Shia in Iran are stirring up the more peaceful Muslims in the world in the hope of hastening the return of the Twelfth Iman."

Andy said, "It's a little unlike you to get so riled up. There must be more."

"Yes, there is and guess what? The former President of Iran spent millions of dollars on that mosque. It has been renovated and dolled up to welcome the Imam of all Imams. It's looking like the day of the Romans, all roads lead to the mosque where the Twelfth Imam will return and they've spent a lot of money to make that dream a reality."

"I can't wait," said Jameson.

After Andy's comment, Jim sat still, not saying a word.

"Is there still more?" asked Andy.

"Andy, this might be the scariest part of all. Do you know what the difference between ISIS and ISIL is?"

"Not really. I just thought it was a presidential distinction."

Jim's face, already serious, took on the look of deep concern.

"ISIS stands for the Islamic State of Iraq and Syria. ISIL stands for the Islamic State of Iraq and the Levant."

"What's the Levant?" asked Andy.

"Here's where it becomes a harbinger of real danger. The Levant includes Syria, Lebanon, Jordan and Egypt, and guess what else?"

"Iran?"

"No, it's worse. It includes Israel."

The air went cold and silent and the revelation settled into Jim's heart and mind. At last Jim spoke up. "So ISIL is claiming Israel. That means the revolution in Syria is intended to spread far beyond establishing a Caliphate that would include the entire region. Maybe even Iran."

In a deeply concerned voice, Jim responded, "That's what I'm afraid of, Andy."

The men, each captains of America's greatest single destructive platforms, sat in silence. The wheels of experience turned. Two men, as near to being blood brothers as they could be, without sharing the same blood, grappled with the serious events of the day.

"Andy, I'm going out on what will probably be my last tour of duty. For several months, the hair on the back of my neck has been twitching, and now that I'm about to leave again, I've got a gnawing in my gut that I can't shake."

"That's why you've been hitting the books, and that's why you've discovered all this information."

"That's right, Andy. Something's going on, and it's big. I can feel it. I don't know what it is, but I am sure there's a storm approaching. I don't think this will be just any storm. It will make an F5 hurricane look like a tempest in a tea kettle. To be honest, I hope it hits during my last duty tour. If it's gonna hit, I wann'a be there to do my part."

"You're not thinking a nuclear release, are you?"

"I am."

"Nuclear? So you really do believe that the jihadists are going to launch nuclear weapons."

"I don't know what to expect, but I have a feeling, a feeling like I've never had before: it's that feeling in the gut like Patton used to talk about. What I really want to tell you is that I'm ready. I'm ready to do whatever it takes. Remember our Brass Lamp discussions? I can't help but feel that our nightmares may quickly become realities. I want to know if you are still with me."

Captain Andrew Jameson drew up straight and tall, as though exhibiting a personal commitment, "Wherever you go, I go, too. Whatever you do, I am right beside you. I'll be with you through it all, no matter what it is. It's you and me, Jim. You and me."

9:11 ⟫⟫ Captain's Chair

Allyson Anderson, wife of Commander James Anderson, Captain of the USS Concord, sank deeply into her husband's leather chair. It was vacated early in the day for a round of golf. A stately oak desk spread out in her view, much like the deck of an aircraft carrier. She looked around the den that displayed some of the history of her husband's work. The room was full of photos taken of him with important people from so many services in the military. It included names from the political landscape as well, including presidents. There was a section for golf trophies, of which there were many.

She looked at a wooden model of the USS Constitution or Old Iron Sides, which sat on a presentation table. The USS Enterprise proudly displayed its large, flat-top, carrier deck on a second table. A third table bore a model of the USS Iowa, a venerable World War II American battleship. Oddly enough, the prime presentation was a table with a model of the first submersible that had been documented to have made an attack from under water: the Turtle, also dubbed the American Turtle. Jim had made the model himself. It had taken him years to research the Turtle and even longer to build it.

Allyson smiled as she thought of Jim's grumbling when he couldn't find a really great model of an American nuclear missile submarine to build. In a fit of rebellion, he decided to build the American Turtle. He had succeeded, and he proudly displayed it, in all its nobility, in his land-bound den which would soon be the command center of his retirement.

Allyson leaned back into the strong, supportive, and comfortable depth of the chair, her eyes closing. It reminded her of Jim, his strength, his fortitude, and his, too often, far away love. She wanted that comfort. She needed his strength. Almost subconsciously she drew a single piece of paper up to her face and held it before her eyes. She opened her eyes slowly, focusing on the words of the report, reading them once again. The horror of those words could only be defeated by surrounding herself in the State Room of her Captain and husband. She desperately wanted to overcome this enemy, but it was vicious and tenacious in its onslaught. She felt like the resting battleships of Pearl Harbor on the morning of December 7, 1941.

Allyson decided to hold fast to her decision not to tell Jim about the cancer. She wanted his last voyage as the captain of a United States Navy nuclear missile submarine to be a memorable success, and she didn't want to detract from his final days of glory. Instead she would fight the battle alone, as she had so many times before.

9:12 »»» Ruminations

Mack Adams was obsessive in his desire to keep the cancers of both terrorism and drugs from infecting his beloved Republic. It was so much easier to thwart their entry than to suffer from their horrific purpose. He had kept in touch with his DEA supervisor and his advisor in the State Department. They were more than willing to allow him to track the Sea Treasure.

Wearing his two-sided hat, Mack thought back to the events surrounding the Sea Treasure. In fact he had been dreaming about the yacht. They'd become nightmares heaped upon nightmares. The only benefit was that they had pushed his Afghani dreams aside. He wondered if he would ever again experience a good night's sleep. He could not shake the worst of the dreams. In his dream, the Sea Treasure was sailing under clear skies and a peaceful ocean, but over and over again, a nondescript monster would rise from the sea floor, erupting tons of water and foam. The violent interaction tore the Sea Treasure into pieces, reducing it to flotsam riding the surface of the sea. The dream made him even more suspicious.

He had no hard evidence, but he knew in his gut that the incident with the Sea Treasure was bad news. The counter-terrorist side of him had worked overtime in its suspicious ruminations. That strange yacht from the Black Sea and the single passenger had become even more suspicious. The more he thought about it, the more he believed that the yacht hid some dangerous secret. It was still docked at Boston Harbor as though it had been moored and forgotten by its captain.

Mack had surreptitiously planted a motion-activated wireless camera on the yacht and found that it was boarded occasionally. There were always two men, one who looked like some kind of maintenance technician and the other, singularly different in his appearance and attitude. It was the second man who caught Mack's attention, making the hairs on the back of his neck stand up, feeding his vein of suspicion. It was the way the man stood at the side of the boat and simply watched it. He would stand still for minute upon minute as though struggling through some deep contemplation.

Mack had broken the law a number of times by returning to the yacht, boarding it, and snooping around the cabin. He knew he was taking a risk, but on more than one occasion he quietly sat, out of sight, in the cabin, as he was doing on this day. *What are you and why are you here?* No matter how much he applied his mind to the question, nothing stood out. The ship wasn't giving up its secret. He wanted to ask a judge for a search warrant. He wanted to x-ray the hull and the keel, or even better, tear them apart to look inside. However, he knew it was a fruitless hope. No judge would approve a search warrant without more cause.

Mack stood up and rummaged once more around the lockers and closets; he banged on the hull, trying to identify secret compartments. It was as though his senses were trying to tell him something that his mind could not grasp. The yacht had become an obsession.

9:13 ⫸ The Satisfaction of Success

The Kahn had safely returned to his most recently established base. He had just wrapped up a management session that included reports from Neg and Khoyer. He was pleased with their reports and checked them off his agenda of important issues, the first of which was the bomb in Boston.

1. The Sea Treasure is safely moored in the Constitution Marina.

The Kahn took great delight in his success in planting a powerful weapon in what was considered by some to be the birth place of America. The Boston Tea Party and the ride of Paul Revere were great moments in the history of America. The Kahn honored the determination and bravery of the rebellious Americans, but the nation had grown too powerful and so very arrogant. The Sea Treasure, and its multi-kiloton bomb, was docked just a few hundred yards from an object spawned by the American rebellion, the old sailing vessel, the USS Constitution. The

Kahn knew his world history. He knew that the USS Constitution was the oldest commissioned U.S. naval vessel still afloat. The Americans revered this old sailing ship. They would mourn its loss, considering it to be a great affront, but they would mourn more deeply the destruction of the Boston region.

2. *A devoted jihadist has been chosen, placed, and prepared to trigger the bomb with a hand-held device. He has been insulated from knowledge of every other operation of the network and works by the direction of Khoyer only.*

The Kahn envisioned the surprise sweeping of Boston with fire and death. The Islamic devotee would find himself with Allah. Many other humans would meet their gods on that day: Islamists, Christians, Jews, Buddhists, and more. The non-believers within the blast radius wouldn't have time to question their disbelief. In an instant, everything within fifteen miles of the bomb would be turned to ash, and many more beyond that would be battered and irradiated. It would be the most extreme terrorist action in the history of the United States.

3. *The dirty bombs are on their way and will be in place within a few months.*

4. *The Iranians are preparing their for their role as the destroyer of Israel.*

5. *The North Koreans continue to bluff and bluster in an effort to force themselves onto the world's list of the nuclear Who's Who.*

6. *Innumerable jihadists are finalizing their independently planned missions in a variety of countries around the world. Members of the network are a part of every single planned mission—some in small ways but others in major roles. Neither Iran nor North Korea have knowledge of the other planned missions.*

He scanned the large world map on the wall across form his desk. There were hundreds of dots denoting the places where elements of fanaticism would wreak havoc in the very near future. Each point was either directed or influenced by elements of his network. He believed that it was the most complex world-wide network in existence.

Innumerable acts of terror would explode into action on the same day as the detonation of the nuclear bomb in Boston. Many major European cities would become victims of bombings, utility interruptions, water supply poisonings, and more. Russia would suffer in a way that would both surprise them and cripple them. His Chechen rebels had planned a devastating interruption of the export of Russian oil. Power brokers in the Orient would be crippled by the shock of their devastation. While the world was focused on the launch of Iranian missiles on Israel, many other international treasures would fall like dominoes.

In the middle of what may have been the broadest smile of his lifetime, The Kahn laughed. It was a deep laugh, welling up from the depth of his guts. All these events would be concurrent, and none but The Kahn and his two Prime ministers knew of the complex cacophony of condemnation. The initiation of his long term plan was only months away. His influence was infused into the fabric of humanity in a way unimagined by the most dedicated of intelligence services. As Genghis Kahn had been the master of conquest so many years ago, The Kahn was the master of conquest today, but in a very different way than his great ancestor. Today his surreptitious work was hidden from the eyes of world leadership.

Will the plans born from my Intelligent Practice methods remain secret? Yes, they will, he thought. But the world will reel in surprise, shock, and terror when they are unfolded.

The Kahn reveled in his treachery. No one knew where the missing nuke was. It was his most closely guarded secret, which now rested securely in Boston Harbor, amid wealthy intellectuals, blue and white collar workers, and hustling businessmen. He pitied their puny efforts. He virtually spat upon them, labeling them as dross. They were fools, fools to be destroyed and cast aside. They were as fodder to his plan of suffering. All would suffer the condescension of The Kahn and the suffering was very near.

PREFACE TO BOOK TWO

In the next four months, a cast of seemingly disparate characters will find themselves as consequential threads, inextricably woven together into a pattern of events that no one could have predicted. The weave of the future, of its material existence and course, will fall largely into the hands of The Kahn and Dr. Benson in a connection that is shared by all humanity.

ABOUT LEE R. HADLEY

Lee experienced and learned the basics of life on his father's Wapello, and Emmett, Idaho farms. At that time, he hadn't even considered writing books. In fact, his English teacher would have laughed if she were still living. But in 2011, he took on the task of writing a novel. Today, it has become a complete three book series: *The Towers Series*. Book One—*Origins*—sets up one apocalyptic scenario that could transpire on this earth. Book Two is entitled *Despair*, and Book Three is called *Providence*. A fourth book underway, *Cajun Justice*, will soon be published as a back story to *The Towers Series*.

Lee has been married for 43 years. He and his wife, Sandra, have five children—four girls and a boy, along with six grandchildren who visit often and lovingly.

Lee has said throughout his adult life and working career that he wondered what he was going to do when he grew up. He must have finally grown up. At 61, he began writing *The Towers Series*. He will tell you now that he finally knows what he wants to do as a grown up. He is especially appreciative of the many and wonderful life experiences that have made a late-in-life writing career possible.